What Mogutu saw startled him. It looked like the back of a young girl, hair long and wild and tangled, the body so thin it seemed emaciated, yet there was strength in it, the toughness of weather-beaten skin. She was making clicking sounds, and getting responses from others, but he couldn't see what she was making them with.

Suddenly she froze, and he sensed at the same instant that she was now aware of him. It was difficult for him to feel threatened by such a tiny waif, but he also knew that small size meant nothing if one were an expert knife thrower or had other weapons.

He crouched there, watching tensely, waiting to see her move. Suddenly, with an animal-like agility he would have thought impossible, she whirled, turning in midair while hurling herself in his direction. The unexpected movement and the horrible sight of her face and hands surprised him. He was a split-second slow in responding and rolling right. Her left foot struck his shoulder with great force; and she hit the ground. With catlike agility, she flipped, rolled, and was back at him . . .

By Jack L. Chalker
Published by Ballantine Books:

AND THE DEVIL WILL DRAG YOU UNDER
DANCE BAND ON THE *TITANIC*
DANCERS IN THE AFTERGLOW
A JUNGLE OF STARS
THE WEB OF THE CHOZEN
PRIAM'S LENS

THE SAGA OF THE WELL WORLD
Volume 1: *Midnight at the Well of Souls*
Volume 2: *Exiles at the Well of Souls*
Volume 3: *Quest for the Well of Souls*
Volume 4: *The Return of Nathan Brazil*
Volume 5: *Twilight at the Well of Souls: The Legacy of Nathan Brazil*

THE FOUR LORDS OF THE DIAMOND
Book One: *Lilith: A Snake in the Grass*
Book Two: *Cerberus: A Wolf in the Fold*
Book Three: *Charon: A Dragon at the Gate*
Book Four: *Medusa: A Tiger by the Tail*

THE DANCING GODS
Book One: *The River of Dancing Gods*
Book Two: *Demons of the Dancing Gods*
Book Three: *Vengeance of the Dancing Gods*
Book Four: *Songs of the Dancing Gods*
Book Five: *Horrors of the Dancing Gods*

THE RINGS OF THE MASTER
Book One: *Lords of the Middle Dark*
Book Two: *Pirates of the Thunder*
Book Three: *Warriors of the Storm*
Book Four: *Masks of the Martyrs*

THE WATCHERS AT THE WELL
Book One: *Echoes of the Well of Souls*
Book Two: *Shadow of the Well of Souls*
Book Three: *Gods of the Well of Souls*

THE WONDERLAND GAMBIT
Book One: *The Cybernetic Walrus*
Book Two: *The March Hare Network*
Book Three: *The Hot-Wired Dodo*

PRIAM'S LENS

Jack L. Chalker

A Del Rey® Book
THE BALLANTINE PUBLISHING GROUP • NEW YORK

A Del Rey® Book
Published by The Ballantine Publishing Group

www.randomhouse.com/delrey/

Library of Congress Catalog Card Number: 99-90074

ISBN 0-345-40294-4

Printed in Canada

First Edition: May 1999

10 9 8 7 6 5 4

For Eva, Dave, and Steve,
as always

Visit the Jack L. Chalker Web pages
for up-to-date news, bibliography, appearances, etc., at
www.jackchalker.com

ONE

A Snake in Eden

The trouble with playing God is that the devil keeps popping up and spoiling the fun.

Humanity had grown and matured and finally spread outward to the stars as the dreamers had all hoped. Ancient Earth itself, birthplace of the race, was more a memory than a destination, and the starfields of an entire galactic arm had become the playthings of the new spacefaring race.

It had been a glorious time and, for humanity, a wondrous one, in which nationalism and tribalism had been almost vanquished; there was just "us," and occasionally "them," and when "us" met "them," well, "us" tended to win.

They called it the age of *homo in excelsis*, the Ascent of Man, master of all he surveyed, the future ever brighter . . .

And then one day, the Titans showed up, kicked everybody in the ass, and that was that.

Even now, most people didn't know what those Titans, which was what others called them after a while, really looked like. They'd come from somewhere in the direction of the Zuni Nebula, but almost certainly from far beyond that. They'd come in ships of pure energy that traveled in ways none could comprehend—ships that shone from some inner light and occasionally throbbed or rippled along their energy skins but otherwise did nothing. Ships that looked like nothing less than enormous winged moths of heaven, and they did the most awful thing, the one thing that humanity could neither comprehend nor allow.

They totally ignored everybody.

They didn't answer any hails, they paid no attention to ships sent to contact them; they simply paid no attention. And when probes were sent, they were simply vaporized, not by conscious action but simply by being in contact with those great ships.

And when, even to get attention, the great weapons had been brought to bear on the newcomers' huge shining vessels, the weapons had simply vaporized, too. The energy weapons were either absorbed or deflected or simply ignored.

The Titans did, however, like humanity's planets. They liked them a lot, only they didn't like them the way they'd been remade.

Helena had been typical of the kind of planets they liked. It had a stable population of almost three billion people when the Titans arrived, and a thriving economy; its primary job of repairing and building great spaceships and refitting the powerful interstellar drives was vital to the continuation of the whole region of planets. Still, nobody there had worked too hard unless they wanted to, there was plenty of recreation, robotics did the heavy lifting, and it was, as was typical of many mature worlds, a pretty nice place to settle down, have families, and live life.

All that life, all that energy, was connected to a vast interstellar empire that made them all proud to be a part of it. This busy hub of activity was right in the center of things and it knew it.

And then the Titans noticed it, and descended on it, and all communication with Helena ceased. In a matter of days, not a single intelligible signal went in or out. Some ships got off and out of there right at the start, but they could tell no one anything about what happened after that. The other ships never rose again, and any ships coming in or near also simply went quiet and off the tracking boards.

It wasn't that others couldn't see what was going on there. As usual, the newcomers simply didn't pay any attention as long as you didn't get too close, in which case you became part of the project.

The great shining ships simply remade the planet into some sort of personal ideal. They did it as simply as humans could remake worlds in a virtual reality chamber, only they really *did* it.

The actual method of matter to energy and energy to matter conversion couldn't be divined; nobody had any instruments that could even measure it. But when it was done a world had been remade into a pastoral ideal. All traces of cities and road systems and any artifacts of humankind simply ceased to exist; even the air tested out as if no industrial activity had ever been there.

Of the people, it was hard to say. Scans showed hundreds of thousands of human beings still down there, having survived perhaps in shelters or cracks or perhaps by design, but there was no way to get to them, no way to find out what sort of life they might be managing in this idealized garden world. They probably would not starve; much of the vegetation was not alien or unknown but rather related to or based upon what had already been there, and the fresh water was probably about as pure as one could imagine.

But now there were millions, widely spread out, where before there had been billions. And they were stuck.

The three large continents of Helena now did have one new artificial thing each, though, to replace what had vanished. On each, fairly close to the center of each land mass, one of the great moth ships had settled and, like the worlds they'd changed, each had metamorphosed into a shining multicolored structure that stretched out for a thousand kilometers, no two exactly alike, all clearly from the same sort of minds.

Minds that were not seen, but minds that had most definitely moved in and stayed. Minds that still allowed nothing out.

Wave upon wave of these new gods, these all-powerful Titans, had swarmed from the direction of the Zuni Nebula; world upon world, system upon system, met the same fate. The worlds were not uniform, but they all were quiet, pastoral, and each had every obvious trace of its former inhabitants removed, even if the Titans left some of those inhabitants there. It was impossible to guess what life down there was like, or whether the humans there now would still be recognized as human, or if they, too, had been changed.

Across the once cultivated fields of the western continent of Helena a figure ran through the incredibly tall grass that now covered the land, so tall and so strong that the winds rippled it like water; a sea, even an ocean, of grass stretched as far as any eye could see.

It was a man, naked, scarred, limping slightly but not from any recent injury, his long hair and flowing beard giving him the visage of a wild beast. He was running through the grass that was taller than he, although he was a big man, barely glancing back, knowing he could see no pursuers in this vegetable ocean and hoping that, for the same reason, no pursuer could see him, either.

He headed for a rocky outcrop that rose from the high plains like an island in the sea, a jumbled mass of boulders and weathered white and orange rock that might have been sculpted by some mad artist. He made for it now as if his life depended on it, made for that outcrop with all the last bits of energy and will he could command, a look of desperation bordering on madness in his face and eyes, his mouth actually slightly foamed.

It was the look of a man who had known for some time that he was to be sacrificed, and who now was desperate to ensure that the sacrifice would not be in vain. Nothing about him indicated any hope beyond that, any sense that he was not in a desperate race with inevitable death.

He reached the base of the outcrop but did not immediately climb up into it. Now was when he was most vulnerable; now was when he had to emerge from the grass, however briefly, and for a moment expose himself to the view of anyone watching. He paused, nervously, tensely, listening, sniffing the air, wishing he had the kind of senses those who were after him so effortlessly possessed and used.

He heard nothing, nothing but the hissing of the gentle but persistent wind rustling the tops of the two-meter-tall grasses, creating the waves and ripples all around.

Finally, he decided to take the chance, since staying there too long would be just as risky. If he had not lost them, then this was the only place he could possibly have been heading. It hadn't been clear what sort of trap that represented when he'd set out; it was one of those details that had been omitted in his instructions. One of many such, he reflected ruefully.

Quickly, now! Up and onto the rocks, and for one brief moment he chanced a look around at the tops of the grasses to see if there were any clear signs of movement. He could see nothing, but didn't dare take enough time to really see if there was something out there or not; with the steady winds and rippling grasses, whatever might be there would have to be obvious to be seen.

Now he was concealed within the rocks, and could push aside a jagged pink boulder that looked as if it had fallen there ages ago and squeeze down inside a small cavity that revealed itself. As soon as he was in, the boulder rolled back over the opening, not quite covering or blocking it, but, he hoped, enough to fool anyone looking for him.

Now, in the cool dark, he slowly maneuvered his body down a widening passage he had been told to expect. It was reassuring that things here, at least, were going by the script. Deep within, the air suddenly smelled different, the sounds ceased, and there was the deadly stillness of a tomb.

Coming to a floorlike area in the rock, he felt around, finally pulled out a small device, and, hefting it, pressed a stud on one side.

The soft glow of a flashlight illuminated the small chamber, sufficient light for him to check on his things and ensure that nothing had been disturbed. He was astonished that it worked, that it was still here at all. He must have been the first one in here in almost a hundred years, and here was the flashlight, fully charged, as if it had been left here only yesterday.

There would be very little time once he began transmission. The Titan grid would seize upon it in a matter of seconds, take hold of it, eat it, dissipate it. *Then* the fun would begin. Then they would be coming for him from all around, sensing the energy activity. It was only in those precious few seconds that he had a chance of getting a message out. Everything they'd done up to now depended on that; everything he'd pledged, even his own life, was based upon that theoretical window between action and reaction that had sometimes worked, sometimes didn't. He still didn't want to do it, but if revenge was the only thing left to him, he'd take it.

Still, he knew that if it didn't work this first time, then he would die horribly and for nothing.

If it did, he might still die horribly, but maybe, just maybe, unlike the billions who had been snuffed out in the takeover, *his* death would have real value, real meaning. If, of course, the data got out, and if, as well, the Dutchman's automated listening posts intercepted it and passed it along. It wasn't much, but it was all he had.

It would certainly be his head in the noose no matter what. There was no way to record all this, no way to input it into fancy data capsules or hand off to your Personal Agent like back in the old days here, those days that now seemed more like a dream, a fairy story from the distant past made up by people to give themselves hope when they had none. No, everything was in his head, and that would have to be the data source.

He had been born near here, in a town that no longer existed, into a civilization that no longer existed, but he'd been one of the lucky ones to get out before the Fall. Back now after all these years, he was astonished that this old butte survived. When he'd seen it, the only thing in the entire region that looked familiar, he'd begun to hope once more that perhaps not *all* had been wiped away. The Titans might have godlike, unimaginable powers, but they did have one characteristic that gave some comfort that they weren't absolute, weren't perfect: like the humans they barely noticed, they would just as soon cover something over as rebuild it. They kept a great deal of the landforms and seas the way they were because to make too radical a series of changes could unbalance the whole thing. Not that they couldn't create anew from scratch—they'd certainly done it with several planets considered dead and worthless by humans. But if it could be done by just fudging a little here, a little there, and sweeping some of the dirt under the rug so it *looked* clean, that was good enough for most.

Maybe *this* time a little laziness would cause them to stub their toe. That laziness had caused them to unknowingly leave a loaded gun buried here, one they didn't know about and certainly never dreamed could hurt them. Maybe . . .

He wasn't kidding himself that he had the key to human salvation, or even a good answer to the greatest threat in all creation, but when one side had almost "Let there be light!" kind of power and your side had spitballs and rubber bands, well, maybe something that could really hurt them would at least make them notice, and that's what he wanted to do more than anything else in the world.

He wanted to hurt them. He wanted to hurt them bad.

If this really could hurt them. *If* in fact it either existed or could be built or brought up to operational levels before it was snuffed out. *If* there was anybody left out there with enough freedom and guts and stubbornness and all the rest to find it, put it together, and use it.

He thought he heard something, something like a rock falling inside the cavern. He was still and so was the air inside, and there was no sound of interior water. Rocks didn't just fall, and he knew it. He couldn't stall any more. He wasn't up to outrunning them, and in here he could hardly hide from them. The hell with it. What the hell was he prolonging life in this place for, anyway?

The power was on; it had been building up for more than two years now, taken from a deep geothermal plant embedded well down in the mantle of the planetary crust. That was why *they* had never noticed it. Crusts moved, and mantles shifted on geologically active worlds, and they hadn't even guessed that the controlling force was right under their theoretical noses.

He slid down into a rocky seat that had once been much more elaborate, and much more comfortable, when this place was active, the remnant of a planetary defense unit left over from the days when godlike beings from the remotest regions of the galaxy hadn't been needed to make humans die. No, human beings did a lot of killing themselves, and civil wars had always been the worst.

No civil wars now. No, indeed. And all those billions and billions who'd died in those wars—what would they think now? Would they think their cause still just and true and worth the horrors of war if they saw what the result would be for their descendants?

There was another sound of something dropping and hitting against the sides of the cavern. He tensed, then found himself curiously calm, curiously detached all of a sudden. He reached down, fished out the spindly headset he'd cobbled together from bits and pieces scrounged out of a hundred buried ruins and put it on. Instantly he could *feel* the connection, feel the raw power that was there at his command. One shot.

Had both the moons been up? Of course they had. He'd worked out the lunar tables a million times. So long as they were fully in the sky this shot would find the spots on it. Find, record, relay, broadcast.

Priam's Lens. The great secret that never got finished because it ran out of time. But the math was right, the theory was correct. Full on. They could have it, and all his innermost secrets and feelings as well. He couldn't stop it. There wasn't exactly time, nor were there optimal conditions for a nice, neat package. Somebody would have to sift the wheat from the chaff.

He froze for a moment, almost *feeling* them around him. It was now or never. He shut his eyes, leaned back, and gave the mental command to fire.

There was an enormous roar, as if a great and terrible wind was contained inside the cavern, and it rushed out and past and out and was away at the speed of light. He felt as if he were falling into a great abyss, and his mind *burned*, and he couldn't help it. The animal part of him, the only part that could function, screamed in pain and terror, screamed so loud that it echoed horribly back and forth along the walls of the cave in an inhuman and terrifying wail.

Whoever else was moving in on him wasn't prepared for *that*: four lithe forms, briefly illuminated in the blast of energy, moved swiftly back out, their survival reflex overcoming any immediate plans. Besides, where was this poor creature going to go? If, of course, something that screamed like that could possibly survive.

Once outside, they looked around in the bright, clear sunlight, trying to figure out what had happened as best their minds could. Nothing seemed to have happened; it all looked the same.

The noise, the inside light, the screeching had all stopped, too. They froze, acting as one, listening, then clicked their needlelike nails and nodded in agreement, and three of them slid back in while the fourth guarded the entrance.

Infrared, which hadn't worked before, now did. Whatever had raised the temperature here and blinded that part of their abilities was gone, spent in that single blast and roar. Now, halfway down, they saw the quarry. It was still lying there, but it seemed to be coming around, groping for some kind of support. Whoever or whatever it was, it was now apparently blind. They didn't mind that, but that didn't mean they couldn't and wouldn't play with it before the kill.

Utilizing a type of telepathic connection and using their nails to time actions with a series of clicks, they made their way around and down toward the prey, who could now be heard breathing hard, sounding panicked and confused. Whatever he had done, it had hurt him.

A Wild One for sure. They didn't quite think in words like that, more in a series of holographic concepts and pictures and actions. They had been specifically bred to hunt and kill Wild Ones, particularly the sick and injured. They liked it. It was their identity, their function.

Below, enough of his senses had returned that he *knew* they were there, knew that they were there to kill him. He couldn't remember very much, not even who or what or where he was nor how he'd come to this, but he knew that those who hunted and killed had him trapped.

He pulled himself out and tried to stand, but he was horribly dizzy. As he put out a hand to steady himself on the rock wall, he heard the clicking. Behind him. In front of him. Above him.

Animal survival took over. If two predators were on either side and one was up where the exit clearly was, you went for the one. He couldn't see any of them, not in this darkness, but he got the impression that they could see him. He heard a tinkling bit of cruel laughter as he tried to lash out in the direction of a close-by set of clicks. They would do their clicking at his level, but he quickly realized that they were having their sport with him, that at no time were they where the clicks led his ears to believe they were.

There was a click, and something cold, hard, and metallic drawn softly and quickly across his back. He whirled and lunged for where he thought the attacker had gone, but all he managed to do was run into the opposite wall of the cave and draw more derisive laughter, made all the worse by its echoing within the cave. They would never let him climb out, but it was narrow and he could feel the airflow toward the exit. If he moved quickly, he might catch the one above off guard or cause the bottom two to be momentarily off balance. It was better than staying here, anyway.

With all the remaining energy in his aching body he moved as fast as he could up and along the steps and rock gradations toward that airflow. He actually made it most of the way, could almost see the entrance notch, when two small forms on either side of the path rushed out, one in front and one in back, and this time the nails drawn across his chest and back bit deeply and painfully into his flesh while spinning him around. He almost lost his balance and fell, but shock from his previous ordeal and adrenaline now kept him going, ignoring the pain, rushing for that notch and the open sky.

One of them dropped from the upper area right in front

of him, and he pushed on right to it, now visible as a small shadowy shape, pushing at it with all his might. Twenty centimeters times four fingers worth of thick, sharp needle nails penetrated his abdomen, and more went through his crotch, penetrating and ripping at his scrotum. The pain was nearly unbearable, but the attacker was small and light enough that his sheer size and bulk carried him on, screaming in pain, walking right over the one who'd so wounded him and up, out, into the sunlight, into the warmth!

Bleeding, in agony, he nonetheless managed to get himself out of the crevice and onto the side of the rocky outcrop itself. He was wounded, perhaps mortally, but if he could just get down there, just get into the tall grass and lie down, at least they might not get his body!

A small naked form suddenly popped up right in front of him, a form so amazing to his sight that he stopped dead, staring, as she clicked those needles that she had for fingernails. There was a sound on either side of him, and he turned to see absolutely identical copies of this one in front of him crouched on either side, and he heard a fourth behind.

"My god!" the last part of his sanity and humanity cried out. "You—Oh! My God! Not *you*!"

And with that the pack, who understood not a word, tore him to shreds and fought over the tastier internal organs.

TWO

A Diva among the Cockroaches

The joint's name was, appropriately, La Cucaracha, although much of the lettering was faded or worn away and the electronic enhancements more resembled an electrician's nightmare than anything coherent.

Most places this far down in the skids were shadows of places once great and legendary and respectable; this one had only the legends, and most of them were bad.

In a sense, the place was a reflection of what had once been the proud Confederacy, a federation of more than three hundred colonial worlds encompassing a multitude of races but dominated by those of Terra, also called Earth. It had been a marriage forged in blood and maintained by raw power, but it had held, and in its time it had been the lord of an entire galactic spiral arm.

Now The Confederacy was mostly a joke; worlds lay in ruins from rioting, panic, and raw fear, particularly among those too poor to book passage out in the way of the new invaders. The naval force that once could vaporize a planet or explode a star was reduced to an evacuation and surveillance service. What good was a military that could only blow up its own kind, that could neither inflict harm nor avoid being swatted like biting flies if they irritated?

There was still a government, of course, and a loose federation of worlds, but what good was it when you were retreating *outward* on a spiral arm? What happened when they ran out of worlds to evacuate to, as they pretty well already had? And who was going to put in the enormous resources and skill to create new habitable worlds when it was certain that eventually they, too, would be overrun?

Here lies The Confederacy; it wasn't as great as we thought it was, but it was all we had . . .

The joint was in a once great city, now fallen into disrepair and overrun by its lowest common denominators, those who couldn't leave and those who had already given up and lived for the moment. Only here, near the old spaceport, did any semblance of the old days exist, even if in memories.

The spaceport, now called Hacalu Naval District, was under severe martial law. The joint and the few other remnants of bygone days were inside the district, although that didn't make it more desirable. Just because it was frequented by dispirited military people and the always anarchic spacers didn't make it any more "normal," only physically secure.

Inside it was always crowded with the flotsam and jetsam of The Confederacy. Most were Terrans, but there were often representatives of the dozen or more nonhuman races that had once, willingly or unwillingly, been members of the old order. If they could exist in a Terran-friendly environment and consume the usual stuff, well, they weren't turned away.

The Terrans didn't discriminate, either. Not the spacers and the old-line Navy folks, anyway. Space took its toll on the professionals, always had. The twists and turns of time standing nearly still during journeys left them with no family or friends that didn't also move the same way, and the various forces, the radiation and warping and twisting of space-time, changed them all into different, often unique life-forms of their own.

They were a tough, violent, mutant breed, and they were the only ones left holding any part of civilization together in what seemed to be the last days of independence and freedom any would ever know.

The place was filled with noise, and body odors less than pleasant, and the remnants of puke and vile concoctions. It was staffed by real people only because the machines could no longer be trusted; still, here you could buy most anything, any pleasure, any vice, anything at all.

Nobody seemed to notice her when she walked through the entrance and into the hall. Anybody who could stand the smell had already passed the first test. Still, in a place like this, every newcomer was viewed with some curiosity and even some suspicion, particularly when they knew that no ships had come in recently that they didn't know and when the figure was unlike anyone familiar.

She was a small, slightly hunched over individual, wearing a black robe, perhaps a black dress, with a bit of tassel and lace about it. It stretched to the floor, giving little indication of what lay beneath, and it rendered the body somewhat shapeless, although it clearly was, or had started out as, Terran. She also wore a hat, one with a fancy shape and brim, from which fell a thin gauzelike film that made it impossible to see her face or tell any more about the features there. Clearly, though, she could see out of it. She moved slowly, with the aid of an ornate carved cane of what might have actually been real wood, in the kind of short shuffling steps that only the very ancient were forced into.

One huge, silver-haired man with a bushy gray beard and pointed, blackened teeth leaned over to the bartender and gestured slightly at the newcomer. "Is it me or what I've been havin', or is that one there the oldest creature in the known galaxy?"

The bartender, a rough-looking man with nasty growths on his face and arms, shook his head. "Beats me. There's some money in those clothes and that walking stick, but anybody with money wouldn't walk like *that.*"

"Not unless it was an act," the customer agreed, suspicious. He slid off the stool and casually approached the figure, who was still heading for the bar and might make it in another five minutes at the speed she was going.

She was either shriveled beyond belief or she was incredibly short; the silver-haired man literally towered over her.

"Are you sure you're in the right place, ma'am?" he asked, trying to be polite. He reflected, though, how even the small suggestion of money might mean she wouldn't get ten steps when she left the place.

"Cockroaches of a hundred varieties on the floor, roaches on the sign—I think there can not be two of these places," she responded in a high, tough, ancient voice suited to what had to lie beneath the clothes. "I need to find someone. He's a frequenter of this place, and we had an appointment to meet here today this very hour." She started creeping on toward the bar, and he followed.

"Yeah? Who? Maybe I know him."

"You probably do, but that doesn't mean much. He is called, I believe, simply the Dutchman. Is he about?"

"*The Dutchman!* I—yeah, I know him. Sort of. But he's not here, and the *Hollander*'s not in port. I'm afraid somebody just tricked you into coming into a real dangerous place, ma'am."

"I have been in worse. I know that is hard for you to believe, but you are not a woman and you weren't out here in the old days. Do you even remember the old days, sonny?"

"Yes, ma'am. Most of us do. Remember, a lot of us were born centuries ago. We age slow, and with the docs in these ports, we can keep ourselves in fairly good condition even when age does get to us. I've lived seventy years, but I was born over three hundred years ago, on Cagista."

She cackled, amused, as she finally made it to the bar itself and accepted her self-appointed reception committee's aid in easing into one of the overworn full stools with back and one arm still intact. She let out a sigh of contentment when she settled in, as if great pain had suddenly been lifted from her.

"Sonny, you want to compare old age with *me*? I was born nine hundred and seventy-one years ago next month."

His jaw dropped, and he wasn't at all sure he believed her. "Ma'am? That's before space flight! That's back in *ancient history*! Why, that would mean you'd have been born on Earth!"

"Well, they'd gone to the Moon, but not much more," she acknowledged. "Me, I was born in a small town in the west of England called Glastonbury. Nobody's heard of it these days; like England, like Earth itself, it's passed into dim legend. It was a legend then. Joseph of Arimathea brought the Holy Grail to Glastonbury. King Arthur built Camelot there and found the Grail and used it to fight evil." She paused. "None of this means anything to you, though, does it?"

"I'm afraid not, ma'am. Earth was destroyed before my time. I never even knew anybody who'd even been there before you, let alone somebody actually *born* there. I told Atair, the bartender, there, that I thought you looked the oldest person I ever did see. Maybe I'm right?"

Sharing birth years was an old sport among spacers, although not between them and the groundhogs. Space travel did all sorts of things to you when you did it all the time, some positive, some negative, but in addition to the biological effects there was always the problem of time. Like anything else, time, too, was warped and distorted by going to and fro over impossible distances using artificially created wormholes and natural phenomena to attain speeds and distances otherwise impossible. When nothing else could give, time gave as well. Spacers were literally a breed apart, not just because of the physical toll but because they were forced to sever all links to family, home, and clan. Time was linear only to them, relative to all others. How many years had she physically lived to pass through that nine hundred plus? How many had he to reach even his temporal distance from his birth?

She seemed amused by his impudence at suggesting her age. "Perhaps. Too old, certainly. Old enough to hear parents speak of world war and be schooled in the greatness of the British Empire even if they had dissolved it before I got there. Old enough to see Communism fall and a hundred isms after that. Old enough to see Earth finally bring on its own doom, and old enough to not have been there at the time. And old enough, now, not only to have seen The Confederacy at its start and height, but at its death. Let me tell you, young man, if you live long enough to reflect back on those kinds of events in a stinkhole like this, you've lived far too long and it's pretty damned depressing!"

"Well, I can see that," he admitted. "Even in my lifetime. But whoever lured you here wasn't your friend, I can tell you. You'd get mugged before you got to the street level now that you've shown up here. I'll have them call for a Navy police escort."

"That's all right. I know where I am and what I am doing," she assured him. "You are Navy, I take it?"

"Yes, ma'am. I'm a chief warrant officer on the *Hucamarea*—that's a frigate in drydock above. Been here a month and a half getting repairs and refitting. Probably be stuck here another month or more. Name's Gene Harker. Just 'sir' or 'Mister Harker' to most folks. Not much for a spacer to do when he's drydocked, I'm afraid. The kind of stuff that can be had in here makes the time pass a little quicker. Wouldn't take most of it in here, though. You give any of these hard-asses a hair and they steal the whole beard."

"I would think that they are all spacers or employees of the Navy and these support establishments," she responded. "I shouldn't think that any would stoop to the level of mugger. Smuggler, certainly, or even hired killer, but not a mere mugger of a little old lady. What the devil could I have that any of them would find useful?"

"Some of 'em were just born bad, and some are on all sorts of drugs and hackplays and just don't have the same sense of real life that they would if they weren't so fucked—sorry, ma'am—fouled up."

She gave the soft cackling laugh once again. "Sir, don't spare any language on *my* part! I've forgotten more foul language in countless tongues than you can possibly know! But every character here who is truly 'fucked up' makes himself as vulnerable as anybody is to them. No, I suspect that few allow themselves to get *that* off reality, even in this place. Enough to take away the stink, perhaps, but you come here for those things and you buy and take them away with you. If you stay, you stay for business or for the company."

"Guy was killed here not four hours ago," the bartender commented, having edged over closer to them. "Two old captains got into some kind of fight over something that happened twenty, thirty years ago. They got to screaming, and before we could stop them they shot each other. One was vaporized, the other lost a leg and a hand. Don't think they aren't dangerous, ma'am."

"I didn't say they weren't dangerous," she responded softly. "I simply meant that I am no babe in the woods, and that they are not the only ones in here who might be dangerous."

It was said so simply, so softly, so matter-of-factly in that little old lady voice of hers that both men felt an odd chill when they heard it. You just never know about anybody, not really. While it was hard to take anybody who appeared and sounded like she did as any kind of a threat, who knew what she might have under those baggy clothes?

"You say the Dutchman's ship is not in port?" she asked, changing the subject. "The message we received was that he would have gotten in this morning."

"Pardon, but if you're talking *Die Fliegende Hollander*, van Staaten's ship, then you're talking more legend than reality," the bartender told her. "Like its namesake, nobody has ever reported the ship making port. It's a ghost ship from a long-overrun world. I've heard every kind of talk and legend about him from those who come in here, but nobody's ever really seen it, let alone connected with it. It's not *real*."

The officer looked thoughtful for a moment, then sighed. "Oh, he's real enough, I'm afraid, but he still wouldn't be coming in here."

Both the bartender and the old woman stared at him. "You know of him, then?" she asked.

"Oh, yes. He's number one on the most wanted list, if you want to know. He *never* makes port. He attacks likely prey, small freighters and the like, stealing what fuel and spares he needs, sometimes taking the whole ship and cannibalizing it. He's got all he needs on that ship. You spot him, he either makes tracks at maximum speed or he attacks and destroys, depending on who and what you are. That's why they say that spotting the *Hollander* is signing your death warrant. He's totally insane, but he's damned good at what he does. But he doesn't talk, not to *anybody*, except to occasionally give an automated warning to prey to abandon ship now or be destroyed. If he has it cold, he'll sometimes do that much. We've chased him from one end of the Arm to the other at one time or another. We think he actually lurks inside the Occupied Zone, somehow keeping just beyond the interest of the Zuni Demons, as we call 'em in the Navy."

"Fascinating," she responded. "So if he were to show up here, somehow, you would be forced to arrest him or something?"

Harker smiled. "Something like that. I'm not a cop, but I've come close enough to him once on the ship to take it kind of personally that he's still at large. You know how much brass he's got? His identification signature shows up on screens and instruments as an ancient sailing ship with all sails up!"

He sensed her smiling, although he couldn't see it, and he could hear her amusement at this. "Ah, yes, the *Flying Dutchman*. I used to sing it, you know, when I was young."

"Ma'am?"

"*Die Fliegende Hollander.* It is Dutch for *The Flying Dutchman*. A captain who, consumed by jealousy, murdered his wife in a rage thinking she had betrayed him while he'd been gone on his voyages, only to discover that she had indeed been true and that only his own inner demons were the evil. Cursed by her family, condemned to sail his ship forever, making landfall only once each century for just a week or so, condemned otherwise to sail alone forever, a symbol of death and a curse even to behold, until and unless a woman of her own free will sacrifices her life to free him. It's an ancient legend, and a classical one. You've not heard of it, either?"

"I think I have, yes," the officer admitted. "One of those nautical ghost stories Navy types love, even the ones who sail in space. I wasn't puzzled by the invoking of the legend but rather by your comment that you'd 'sung' it."

"Impossible to believe now, but once I was quite beautiful," she told him. "And I had not only the looks but the voice of an angel. A soprano with a three-octave range. Grand opera, Mister Harker. Oh, it was *glorious* when it was done! An entire play that was sung, with full scenery and props and all the rest, with a full symphony orchestra, voices and instruments in perfect harmony, all musical instruments. These days the only instruments anybody knows how to play are the small portable consoles that can synthesize anything and anybody. You have to come to a place like this just to hear anybody sing anything any more, and that mostly bawdy songs and nasty little ditties off-key. Once, though, it was all done with people, the best people playing the best instruments, even if their instrument was their voice. Now you'd have to dig into some ancient archive, I suppose, to find a good VR holographic performance, but so few people do that nobody knows or cares or understands anymore. It's too bad, really. It wasn't just art, it was a total experience of a kind nobody gets these days."

"And you sung this grand whatchamacallit? That's kind of impressive," the security officer commented. "I assume you were the woman who eventually sacrificed herself?"

"Of course. Great opera usually ended in tragedy, but even that was compensated for. Why, a great soprano or great tenor with the right work might take twenty minutes to die!"

"Talk about singing your heart out," the bartender muttered.

Harker noted that even the roaches weren't having a very good time with her. While he'd just go through a decontamination chamber on the way back to get rid of creepy crawling hitchhikers, they didn't have a prayer with her. Every once in a while there would be a tiny *snap* and, if you looked hard enough at the right place on her all-encompassing dress, you'd see a tiny wisp of smoke or even a brief bright pinpoint of light. *A personal force field*, he thought. It was something you had in combat gear, but he'd never seen one on a civilian of any stripe. She definitely had money, that was for sure, and connections, too, and those type of people could buy whatever they fancied or needed. Maybe she wasn't kidding. The surprises she *was* revealing, bit by bit, indicated that any muggers might have an ugly surprise if they tried anything on her.

Harker cleared his throat. "Uh, ma'am? Why would you

have an appointment with somebody like the Dutchman?" he asked her. "And what would he want with you, if I might make the comment. I mean—"

"I know just what you mean, young man!" she came back sharply. "What he wants with me, I suspect, is money, perhaps goods he can't buy or hijack but requires for his own purposes. I don't know the price. I do know that he claims to have something that is worth almost any price if it is anything close to genuine and not a gimmick to work some scheme on my family. He doesn't want anything to do with me, I don't think. In fact, I'm not certain he knows I exist, or at least that I'm still alive and mobile, such as I am. I haven't gotten out much in the past century or so. It is why I had to be the one to meet him. I have no fear of death and I am not particularly worried about capture. I'm frail enough that almost anything coercive he can try would almost certainly kill me, and I'm tough enough not to be bothered by that. Many of the younger members of the family might well be taken in more by this, and be more vulnerable in other ways. Understand?"

Oddly, he thought he did understand her. All except what would bring her out here in the first place on the word of a murdering scoundrel.

"What does he claim to have, ma'am?"

He could almost sense a wary smile under that veil. "Some of it is best kept—private—for the moment. However, let us just say that he claims to have a method of getting into and out of occupied worlds, and that is of great interest to my family."

Both the Navy man and the bartender laughed at that. "Sure, and to everybody else, too, if it could be done, but it can't," the latter said at last. "If it had ever been done, I'd know it. They all come in here, soon or later. All of 'em. Been a bunch of 'em claimed they could do it, but they left and they never came back. Ain't nobody among these liars and braggarts claim they done it. *None* of 'em! 'Cause it can't be done! People and machines and shit—pardon, ma'am—they get squooshed there, and while you might get down to the surface, you'll never get back, and God knows what kind of hell you're in once you're stuck there. Nope, he's givin' you a line, lady. Now I *know* he's pullin' a con on you."

"If he'd shown up at all," the officer noted, looking over the half-deserted bar that nobody had entered or exited since the old lady entered. "Might be nothin' to do with the Dutchman, really, ma'am. Ever think of that? Anybody in your family or businesses who might want to get you out of the way for a while?"

She seemed taken aback for the first time since entering the place. "Goodness! I never even thought of something like that! Young man, you must have an interesting background. Still, while I can't see what good it would do anyone, it certainly provides a logical alternative to all this, doesn't it? Perhaps I should check a bit and see if anything odd might be happening back home, though. It certainly seems clear that I have gone astray by coming here."

"I wouldn't trust this fellow one bit, ma'am, particularly because it's obvious that your family has wealth and that's all that motivates him. He's a killer."

"These days, aren't we all?" she muttered, not quite loud enough to be fully heard.

"Ma'am?"

"Nothing. Nothing. Well, young man, if you will watch my back, as it were, I might as well leave. I assume you will be watching in any event, just in case this mystery man puts in some sort of clandestine appearance. I feel quite safe. It was a pleasure talking with you."

He made pleasantries in response, not bothering to deny what she had said since it was so obviously the truth. Still, the idea that the Dutchman, the *real* Dutchman, would expose himself anywhere near a full military base and conventional spaceport was almost laughable.

As she shambled across the floor, vaporizing vermin as she went, he could see eyes following her from the darkened booths and private alcoves. These were a smart lot, though; they wouldn't put their necks in a noose by so obviously following her out. Even so, he almost wished one would. While the Dutchman might not show up, somebody *claiming* to be him sure could. Who would know? The Dutchman was only a name and a colorful hologram on the radar screens. The name registered as several people from the distant past, but which, if any, of them it might have been was unknown. Those who had seen him and lived had seen only a darkened bubble on an environmental suit.

There was even a theory that the Dutchman didn't exist at all, that it was just a cover name for a whole range of pirates and scoundrels who had imitated a trademark *modus operandi* and used it as an extra mask of concealment. Certainly there was some evidence for this; the same Dutchman who had been a cruel killer at one instance had been a polite and even noble thief at another. The only way to know for sure would be to blow him to hell and then see if "the Dutchman" showed up again.

He put his hand to his jaw and pressed in a certain spot.

"Duty," came a distant, thin voice in his ear, and *only* in his ear.

"Old woman leaving the Cuca, full dress and veil, slow as molasses," he whispered in a voice so low it probably couldn't be understood a meter or two away. "Put surveillance monitors on her the moment she comes out the front door and follow her progress. Prepare to move in if anyone approaches her. She thinks she's here to meet the Dutchman."

"The Dutchman! Ha! Okay, will do. Is she out yet?"

"Just about. You should see her on the street about . . . *now.*"

"Yeah, got her," responded the duty officer. "Let me do a scan." There was a pause, then, "Wow! She's got a fortune in electronics inside that rag!"

"Well, she's got a personal force field."

"She's got a lot more than that. The readings here are *very* strong. She's got some kind of weaponry, some robotic augmentation, and she's radiating shit like a deep space probe. Infrared, UV, sonics—you name it. I wish I had a *ship* that well equipped!

The Navy intelligence man turned to the bartender. "I'll get somebody else to cover in here. I think I should take a little walk myself."

"Yeah? You really think she's gonna meet the Dutchman?"

"I dunno, but she's too smart and too well equipped to walk in here blindly and then leave so meekly."

He made the exit a lot faster than she had, but she was still gone from immediate view. "Where away?" he asked the duty officer.

"Two blocks to your left, then down one. She walked a lot faster once she turned the corner. Now she seems stopped, like she's waiting for a pickup."

"Get me an unmarked tail car," the Navy man ordered. "Have it ready in case we need to give some chase here. If she gets picked up by anybody except a limo or a service taxi I think I want to see who and what are really under that veil and dress."

"You always did lust after older women, didn't you? I've got one on the way. Looks like we won't make it for a complete intercept, but I can keep her on the trace long enough. She's got her ride. Looks like an ordinary cab but she didn't flag it or call it, at least not on any public frequency we know."

"Got it! Stay on her!" He rounded the corner to see her

suddenly and spryly entering the cab and the door sliding shut. It was off like a shot, not even waiting for her to belt in, which was another clue that this wasn't just an ordinary fare.

Almost immediately the tail car pulled up to him, door already open. He jumped in and was thrown back against the seat much as the old lady, if indeed that was what she was, must have been. The cab was out of sight, but the tail car was accelerating rapidly, making it tough for him to turn and press the controls that strapped him in for the ride.

"Okay, driver!" he said needlessly. "Follow that cab!" There wasn't any driver, and they were already in hot pursuit, but he'd always wanted to say that.

The artificial intelligence that drove and flew and guided all surface and near-surface transport on the planet, including within the Naval District, could pretty much track and, if necessary, even control or halt anything that moved. They were zipping along just a few meters above street level: high enough not to run over any pedestrians, low enough to be almost like a true surface vehicle. The screen in front of him in the dash showed their location and the location of the cab they were following. It wasn't that far ahead now; he could make it out even in the gray gloom that passed for a nice day in this hole.

"They're heading for the docks," he told the duty officer. "What's parked that looks likely?"

"Not much that's civilian, if that's a help. Aluacar Electric company shuttle, commuter shuttle to Kanlun Spaceport, Melcouri Interstellar surface shuttle, that's about it."

"What about this Melcouri?"

"Family-owned company, one of the rare private ones. Not very big now, once huge. They sold off a lot decades ago after the fall of Helena. It was almost a company planet and they may not have lost all their business, but they lost the family and the will. They still haul freight, but mostly on single contracts."

"How long has the ship been in?"

"The—let's see—*Odysseus*, of all things. Wonder what *that* means? In on—yeah, just came in late yesterday. No commercial traffic logged in or out."

"That's the one. They're Greek, or at least they're lovers of Greek, my friend," the Navy cop told the duty officer. "All out of ancient stories nobody reads or remembers anymore except maybe university professors."

"That right? *You* know it, though."

He sighed. "Yeah, I know it. I know a lot of apparently useless crap, but sometimes it rises up and justifies its existence in my mind. Everybody else lets a glorified database do their thinking for them."

"Huh? I—Hold it! You're on the nose, buddy! Melcouri it is. They've already turned on the power in the shuttle, too, and there's a request for preliminary clearance. You want me to hold them?"

"Yeah, do it. I just want to make sure this is all above board." He was beginning to doubt his instincts now, in spite of the spryness and effective getaway of the old lady. She said she was going back to check on things, and that's what she was doing. Why did he still feel that there was something wrong with the setup?

At least it explained the interest. If they had left much of their family and friends on Helena, and this Dutchman claimed to be able to get in and out, then no price would be too much for them just to see who or what might have survived down there. The trouble was, it had been tried by just about everybody. You could get in all right, but never out. It didn't seem to be the Dutchman's style, but it was clearly a con game to get a gigantic payment. Hell, if he didn't bump them off on the way, he could easily send down whoever of the Melcouri family was to go in. Why not? They'd never get back up.

Still, the Dutchman was the kind of guy who would more likely attack and ransack the whole ship up there, not somebody who'd expose himself long enough to pull a scam like this, no matter how good it sounded. "Is she inside?"

"Yeah, just entered. I'm stalling them on clearances and they know it."

The chief sighed. "Has anyone filed a departure plan for the docked vessel above?" he asked.

"Just checked. No, not a peep. They haven't even filed a preliminary flight plan for approval, so they're not in any hurry to leave. Why? You want to go up and check them out? Want me to keep the shuttle here until you can board? You can always use the routine inspection ploy."

Harker considered it. "No, let them go," he instructed the duty officer. "There's more going on here than we know yet, and I'm not sure who's playing what game. I can always go on up if they file to leave. Until then—well, have the dock workers find something that might take a few days to repair and keep it handy." He wished he had a list of who was aboard up there, but since they hadn't come down to the planet, they were still technically in transit and there was no need to provide the list. He had a sudden thought. *One* of them sure had to have gone through Immigration. "What was the name on the old lady we just chased?"

"Anna Marie Sotoropolis. Blood and prints match. It's her, for what it's worth."

Another Greek name. At least it was consistent. Nine hundred years . . .

Of course, she hadn't actually *lived* nine hundred years, at least subjectively. Still, physically she almost certainly was well over a hundred and fifty, which was plenty years enough. He wondered what kind of memories she had; what kind of life and loves and ancient lifestyle were in those experiences. Days when the mother world was still habitable, when human beings sang opera for the masses . . .

Sure as hell was a lot more romantic than the Cucaracha and this hole, that was for sure.

"I want round-the-clock monitoring of the ship with notification if anybody enters or leaves, even by the dock or in an e-suit," he instructed. "And if that shuttle comes back, I want to know immediately, no matter who, what, or where I might be. Understand?"

"It's in the console and done," the duty officer assured him.

"Good. Then log me out for now. I need a shower *bad.*"

Three days passed and nothing more was heard from the ancient diva or the ship, which simply sat up there as if parked for the duration. Gene Harker was even taking some good-natured ribbing from the local police and Naval security people over his suspicions, with tales of a romantic tryst with a nine-hundred-year-old woman finishing in a virtual dead heat with the suspicion that she was actually there picking up secret agent cockroaches.

On the fourth afternoon, though, at about the same time as the old lady had walked into that smelly bar, and with a lot more traffic passing through, another unlikely pilgrim entered the bar and asked the same crazy question.

"Yes, Father?" Max the bartender called to him. "Anything you particularly would like? The synthesizer here is still in pretty good shape in spite of the condition of this joint."

"Just a little bourbon and water will do it, my lad," the priest answered cheerfully.

At least, unlike the old lady, he was very much in the open; a ruddy-faced man with a big hawk nose and close-set deep brown eyes, physically probably pushing fifty, in a standard black clerical suit and reversed collar. Only his gold ring on his left finger gave anything else away; it was very expensive for a priest's ring, and the Maltese cross in gold against a precious polished black opal background was that of the Knights of Malta, an incredibly secretive and not exclusively religious group that was invariably composed of the best and the brightest of each generation. This guy was no dummy, and he was no itinerant missionary on his way to a new post, either. Indeed, the mere fact that he was not at least an archbishop at his age showed that he was probably even more important than he seemed. A Maltese Knight with no high position running great institutions was somebody who was maybe running things that nobody knew about.

Max turned and tapped a code into the small console just beneath the bar. This started the synthesizer working, and within seconds a whiskey glass formed and molded itself into solidity within the cavity in back of the bar; then a soft brown liquid and a clear one poured into the glass. As soon as it was done, Max grabbed it and put it on the bar in front of the priest. "Watch the roaches, Father," he warned. "They drink almost anything in the joint these days."

"They're all God's creatures, my boy," he responded and sipped the drink, obviously finding it to his liking.

"You know, there are nicer bars just outside the gates here," Max told him. "Restaurants, too, some with real fresh food, not synthetics."

"I'll take that under advisement," the priest replied, now drinking rather than sipping. The glass was soon empty.

"Another?"

"Just one more, exactly like that last one," the priest responded. As Max tapped in the code, the priest continued, "You know, I'm used to everybody telling me what company I should keep and what places I'd like. It's a misunderstanding of my whole profession, you see, although, God knows, enough hypocrites and scoundrels have browbeaten people into playing holier-than-thou for generations. Christ not only drank wine, He supplied it to others, and He spent a good deal of His time with sinners and publicans and spoke mostly about the horrid sins of religious hypocrisy. Saint Paul was betrayed by religious types but saved by a prostitute. You could almost read the Bible and find more prostitutes and thieves and the like going to heaven and more and more white-robed prayer-mongers going to hell and decide that things were all upside down." He drank down the second drink in two quick gulps, getting a wondrously rapturous smile on his face from doing so, then reached into his jacket and pulled out a fat cigar. He clipped off the end, then lit it with a lighter that looked more like a portable blowtorch.

"You know," said the priest, "I really like living in this time, for all its failings. There was a time when these things would just cause all sorts of horrible problems if you smoked them regularly. Now we can cure anything they can give you. It's always been thus. Either people have been trying to rid us of all the simple pleasures because they're bad for us, or the simple pleasures have been trying to get rid of *us*."

The bartender chuckled. "You staying long or just passing through?" he asked.

"Passing through. Truth to tell, I'm in your rather, er, colorful joint for a purpose. I'm looking for someone who is said to be here."

"I know most of the regulars. What's the name?"

"I don't know, really. He calls himself the Dutchman, I believe, after some impossibly ancient legend from old Earth."

In the Bachelor Officer's Quarters three kilometers northwest of the bar, an alarm sounded, loud enough to wake anybody but the dead.

Gene Harker stirred himself and punched the comm link. "Yeah?"

"Got a shot from Max at the Cuch," a voice told him. "Somebody else just asked for the Dutchman."

"I *knew* it!" Harker almost shouted, suddenly very wide awake.

THREE

Helena at Dawn

Littlefeet ran like the wind through the tall grass toward the day's camp. They still called themselves a family but they were really a tribe, a group of families that moved from day to day, week to week, month to month, never in one place, never allowing themselves to be discovered or captured or worse. They traveled light, almost with nothing at all, and they traveled aimlessly, lest a pattern be noticed and betray them.

They were also quite young, incredibly so. The lifestyle gave no easy out for the weak, the aged and infirm. Although Helena was a relatively recent conquest and remake for the Titans, it still had been close to fifty years. There was no one in the tribe older than mid-thirties; the average age was much younger.

The lifestyle had evolved rapidly among survivors. Those who didn't develop it, those who didn't or couldn't adapt, were all gone now. The older ones had taught the young right from the start, of course, but even after a single generation things had gotten quite muddy and confused. What counted was survival, both of the tribe and of the individual. Nothing else mattered.

Littlefeet was fifteen, although he didn't know it and had no way of counting it, let alone any interest in why anybody would think the information was important. Like the others of the Karas family, he was naked and quite comfortable with it, and he had long, shoulder-length black hair that was kept trimmed by the Mothers using the sharp tools they carried with them. It did not do to have hair so long that it would get in the way or perhaps cause you to get stuck on something. The men's beards had the same limitations, but most of them still wore facial hair that was quite prominent.

If a sociologist or cultural anthropologist had been able to study the family, and the countless others that also roamed Helena, from the time the Titans had come until now, they would have been amazed at the speed at which ultramodern civilized human beings had lapsed back not just to their primitive forebears' state but beyond, almost back to the time of the smart ape. Unlike those apes, though, they still had speech and at least a verbal tradition of what had been lost now so long ago.

Littlefeet was typical for a boy his age; he was by tribal standards an adult, and all adult males were hunter-gatherers when they were not protectors, be they warriors or guards. Modern weapons had long ago been discarded; you needed ammunition and places to get it, or power and the means to recharge, to use them for very long. As with other boys his age, he had fashioned his own spear, ax, and knife, the heads or points or blades sharpened by many patient hours of work out of rock and minerals and bound to the hand-carved wood with a cement made from various muds and then with dried and toughened vines. The ax and knife were held by loops in a thin vine belt; the spear was always carried.

Ironically, the Titan system of remaking the worlds they took over also made the survival of at least some of the populations possible, even if on this primitive a scale. The temperature was always quite warm but well within tolerable limits for humans, and there were no longer any major seasonal variations. Where once great cities had risen and networks of transportation and communication had spread, there were now grasslands and rainforests.

This was pretty much consistent no matter where the Titans settled, with necessary variations for physical reasons. This was the kind of landscape they preferred, and it was the one they strove to get.

The pattern never really varied. A Titan ship, looking strangely like a glowing egg, perhaps two kilometers long and a third as wide, would come in and orbit a planet, whose planetary defenses it would either ignore or, if they were irritating enough, simply disable with a flash of energy. After it had orbited a world so that it could map every bit of the surface, it would begin its process by bathing the entire planet in an energy plasma that simply sucked up any artificial energy sources on the world. How it did this nobody knew; scientists had been able to duplicate its behavior on a small scale but there was no way to know if it was the same method the Titans used.

Once all sources of energy other than nature were removed, civilization simply ceased. Humanity had gone too long and come too far; it was too specialized to know how to handle a preindustrial economy. Nobody was left who could plow fields and sow grain and fruit and raise animals in the old ways. That knowledge had simply been lost because it was no longer needed. Robots and quasi-organic computers did that kind of thing using vast databases of material. Without power, they could not work or even access information, nor could their masters. Riots and starvation always followed, although this appeared meaningless to the Titans. Just as they took no notice of attempts to contact or in any way interact with them, other than to flick off irritants as a man might brush off a biting fly, they proceeded to drastically alter the planetary ecosystems. The big ship would spawn smaller ships almost like an amoeba reproducing by fission; the smaller ships, which would position themselves at key areas, appeared to have sufficient power that, together, they could literally cause a change in axial tilts, reapportion air and water so that the weather was what they wished, and then sow and plant right over the surviving people, cities, artifacts of any kind.

Humans had called this "terraforming" and had done it over a few generations; many of these worlds were in that category. The difference here was limitless power; it was done in a single human generation in most cases. During that time ships that attempted to get in tended to be swatted down, and none on the planet had the power to get up and out. After between ten and thirty standard years, with an average of only twenty, populations of up to several billions numbered, at best, in the hundreds of thousands, eking out subsistence livings in the new environment. The Titans took no notice of them still. When the planet was the way they wanted it to be, they then descended. The egglike ships became glowing fixtures on the continents. Few dared go near them; those who did almost never came back.

An interstellar empire that had the power and weaponry to conquer space and some of time, whose weapons could make stars go nova and turn planets into bits of interstellar dust, was helpless against a power that just happened to regard their own rights to life and possessions in the same way that they had regarded the rights of the other races they had come into contact with, and with a power that reduced their great weapons to impotency.

And the worst part was not just being beaten, but being *ignored.* These new masters were not even genocidal in the pure sense of that word; they simply regarded the populations in their way as totally irrelevant.

The Elder of the Family Karas, called Father by everybody, and who might well have been all of thirty-five and looked half again that, watched Littlefeet come into the camp and gestured for him to approach. The lithe little hunter walked cockily over, but bowed his head in respect.

"Report," commanded the Father.

"Hunter pack roaming about one hour to the southwest," he said. They were all taught compass points based upon the sun's position and a distance system measured in the time it would take to move the entire tribe to that point, a system that only experience could prove. It was adequate.

"Did you track them? Did they see you?"

"No, they were going the other way. Five of them. They were far too relaxed to be hunting. Whatever they had been sent to get, they got. Going in to their den, most likely."

"We can assume nothing!" the Father snapped, taking a bit of the starch out of the young warrior's attitude. "They are the greatest threat to us that exist. They are bred to hunt us, and they have been born with terrible weapons that are a part of themselves. Did you get close enough to tell if they were bloodied?"

"I—I did not get that close," Littlefeet admitted. "They *seemed* to be stained, but I only saw their upper parts. They actually were very nice looking, I think, but they all looked exactly the same."

The Father nodded. "Yes, they tend to be attractive. Why not? And they are of the same source, having neither father nor mother, which is why each group is the same. It gives them great power to be exactly the same. They think the same, react the same, and know what each other would do, so they make little noise. The fact that they were not making any attempt to conceal themselves tells me that they must have been bloodied. You saw no sign of a captive or captives?"

"No, Father."

"Then they took no prisoners for fresh stock. I do not like to hear that any of them are in this area. They have stayed away in the past. We must be more on guard and double the armed watch and patrols just in case they are hunting for breeding stock and have extended their range. Still, I would like to know who they killed." The Father checked the sun's angle. "There are still a few hours until darkness. Take Big Ears and backtrack them. Be careful! They have been known to leave traps. But if you can find the remains, try and get the Family name from its tattoos and whatever else you can divine. We must know if this is a one-time thing or something new."

Littlefeet grinned, proud to have been given such a task by the Father himself. "At once, Father!" He immediately darted off, running across the encampment to the kraal of the young warriors, grabbing some dry hard meal cakes to nibble on as he did so.

The Karas Family had developed a social system that was practical but not followed by all the Families. The males and females tended to live a bit apart, although they interacted. All of the females generally lived together, to make the food, mix the tattoo inks from various minerals, and bear and tend to the young. They also enforced camp discipline and saw to its sanitation. They had the vast majority of the camp under their exclusive control and dominion, and they alone decided who could enter it.

The young males who were of age and considered adults lived in a separate group off by themselves. They played, trained, competed with one another, and did the work that was theirs to do: to scout, to guard, and to fight, and, when the women permitted, to father children with young women. The third, smallest kraal was occupied by the Elders, both males and females, who made the decisions and assigned tasks as the Father had just done to Littlefeet and his buddy, who probably wasn't going to be thrilled by the assignment. Big Ears, who was much more aptly named than Littlefeet, was not nearly as enthusiastic about long runs and sleepless days and nights as some of his brothers, and he'd just come in from a long day of scouting.

Littlefeet looked around, spotted his friend, and darted over to him. "Hey! Big Ears! Get something to eat! Father has just told us to backtrack a Hunter party!"

"*Today?*"

Littlefeet laughed. "One good rain and it'll be a lot harder to do! It shouldn't take forever. Back by sundown."

"I'm just dead tired," Big Ears complained. He was a larger boy, about the same age as Littlefeet but chunky, a wrestler type to Littlefeet's long-distance runner. Still, the bulk and weight were all muscle; Big Ears, whose ears stuck out like few others', was strong as an ox. "I figured I'd just eat and drop till sunrise."

"Aw, don't worry about it! We'll manage okay. Besides," Littlefeet added, lowering his voice to a whisper, "I spotted a newly ripened orange candybush on my way back. It's in the line they were taking; we can hit it on the way."

That was more like it. "An orange one, you say? And you didn't report it?"

"I never got the chance. Hunters are more important anyways. When we come back and report, I'll add it in, and by tomorrow they'll have stripped it. Not before we get it all to ourselves this once, though. C'mon!"

Big Ears sighed, yawned, stretched, and scratched himself. "Oh, all right. We're not goin' against no Hunter pack, though, are we?"

"Naw, they was goin' in the other direction and kinda casual, too. We don't want to find out where they are, just where they had been before that."

Big Ears grabbed his spear. "Fair 'nuff. An orange one, you say . . . ?"

The Big Knob was one of the forbidden places, places that were said to be haunted by ghosts of the Old Times, ghosts who were looking for the souls of their descendants to somehow recapture the life they'd lost. Everybody knew that you gave those places a wide berth, and, after even this short a time after the fall of everything, there was always a reason why everybody knew something.

Still, the tracks were very clear; the pack had certainly come from here, and had gone there by almost the same route a bit earlier. There was a third track, too, only one way, heading straight for the Knob, keeping low and slow by the looks of it, to avoid detection. The tall yellow grass was at least two meters high all over the plain, so it was very easy to see where somebody might have gone.

"Whoever they were chasing was a big fella," Big Ears noted. "Bigger'n me, maybe. Whoever they was they didn't know nothin' 'bout keepin' out of sight or coverin' tracks, that's for sure."

Littlefeet nodded. "Yeah, but he sure thought he did," the small boy noted. "He was just kinda *creepin'* through here. Lookit! You wonder how any grownup coulda lived long enough to, well, grow up, as clumsy as this. Where'd *this* one come from, I wonder?"

"Dunno, and I ain't gonna track that much back, not this late in the day. But he sure was goin' to the Knob, and that's one place I sure don't wanna go, even in daylight."

Littlefeet snorted. "You scared of *that*? Hey, that's just a big old twisty rock like all the rest."

"Ain't what I heard," Big Ears insisted. "I hear it's got the ghosts of a thousand of the ancestors and that it moans and *talks* and tries to sucker you in."

"Yeah? Well, I can see how the wind could play funny tricks in a thing shaped like that. Spook a lot of dumb folks. I heard a lot about devil spirits and ancestor stuff, but I ain't seen nothin' but Hunters and some powerful mean people and I been along the plains and to and from the rivers and lakes awhile. Ain't nobody else heard 'em, neither! I checked! They all heard it from somebody who heard it from somebody whose best friend got it straight. Besides, if that's the ghosts of *our* ancestors up there, why'n heck didn't they get them damn Hunters? Huh? Come on. Sun's gettin' low and I want to get this done and get back."

The trail was so plain there was nobody born who could have missed it or failed to follow it. The quarry had at least been a little devious, zigzagging back and forth and even backtracking once or twice, but he was so inept at concealing his progress that it had made no difference. For all his efforts, he might as well have gone straight in yelling and singing.

Big Ears eyed with more than a little suspicion the large rocky hill that stood out so prominent and lonely in the otherwise dead flat grasslands. Up close it didn't look so much like a monster or spook, but it did look a lot bigger and higher, too, and with no obvious way up.

"Here's where they went," Littlefeet noted, pointing. "There's some kind of ledge up there, maybe twice my height. See it?"

"Yeah, sort of. You seein' them chalky dirt spills, huh?"

Littlefeet nodded. Big Ears wasn't incompetent, only overcautious—which was possibly the reason the Father had assigned him as Littlefeet's partner.

Littlefeet tensed, went into a coiled stoop while keeping his eyes firmly on the ledge, then jumped with all his power. He was a strong runner, whose legs were quite powerful; he didn't make it to the ledge, but he did make it close enough that his hands got a grasp up there, and he was able to pull himself up the rest of the way. His hands were a little scuffed and his arms hurt, but he quickly got over that and looked down at Big Ears.

"It's a kind of trail in the rock, leading up!" he called down. "You want to try and get up here? If that guy they were chasin' made it, *you* sure can! Throw me my spear, first, and yours, too, if you're comin'."

Big Ears hesitated for what seemed like a very long

time, weighing the risks and benefits, then sighed and said, "Oh, all right. Get back. I'm a lot taller'n you!"

Being almost a head taller did help, although he, too, found the going took every muscle he had. He pulled himself up and over onto the ledge, then lay there a moment, getting back his wind. Finally, sensing his partner wasn't exactly standing over him, he turned, looked around, and got up fast. "Littlefeet?"

"Come on! I don't want it to get dark on us here!" his friend called from what seemed higher as well as farther away. Big Ears muttered a series of curses under his breath, picked up his spear where Littlefeet had left it, and started following the trail.

And it *was* a trail, too, or at least a path, clearly made long ago by somebody for some reason. It spiraled around the big rock, taking him gently upward. It was still pretty steep, and he found himself breathing hard. He was just about to sit and take a break when he came upon Littlefeet and the corpse.

It was a particularly grisly scene, even for two who had seen a lot of ugly deaths. They had hacked him open like animals, and there were blood and parts of guts all over the place. It was pretty tough even figuring out his looks; the skin on his face had been almost filleted off, and the eyes were gouged out as well. And it stunk.

"Notice anything wild about the guy?" Littlefeet asked Big Ears, just sitting to one side on a rock outcrop and staring.

"Huh? Other than the fact that they tortured and ate half of him? No."

"No tattoos. No marks on the skin we can see at all. No sign he ever wore rings or stuff, either. The hair's in a kind of fashion I never saw, and, well, what you can make out just don't look right. Don't look like nobody I ever heard of, but he looks somehow familiar, like. I can't figure out how, though."

Big Ears studied the mess but came no closer. "I think I know," he said softly.

"Huh?"

"Remember the pictures in the lockets? The Family Chest? That kind of hair, that sort of face—it's like them."

Littlefeet squinted and looked again. "You know, you're right. The guy looks like one of the ancestors. You don't think any of 'em survived, do you? I mean, like some kind of underground colony or something? I heard stories . . ."

"Now it's you with the stories," Big Ears responded, throwing the smaller one's logic back at him. "Just stories. Ain't nobody survived the Titans. Nobody 'cept folks like us. Jeez, I mean, if even a fire in the dry season can bring 'em, you *know* nobody's runnin' none of them old things that took magic power. That'd bring a Titan ball faster'n anything."

"Help me turn him over," Littlefeet said, approaching the corpse. "I want to see his back. I think it should be kinda still together from the looks of him."

Big Ears almost gagged. "You mean *touch* him? That?"

"Sure. His spirit's gone to the land of the ancestors now. Ain't nothin' but dead, rotting meat. Come on. He's too heavy and too stuck in his own dried shit for me to do it alone."

Revulsion sweeping through him, Big Ears did participate sufficiently to let his spear be the lever that turned the torso over. When it did, the head came loose and rolled a short distance, making things even uglier.

"What I thought," Littlefeet commented. "C'mon. Let's get back."

"What you thought? What the hell did you think to do this? There wasn't nothin' there but a bare back!"

"A *red* back. I seen it before on a couple Family members who were hurt bad and hid in the caves for a couple weeks to heal. When they come back out, one or two days of sun, they looked like that. 'Sunburned,' they called it. I noticed it on the shoulders and some of the face. I couldn't be sure with all this blood and crap, but the back wasn't touched by that."

"Sunburned? What the hell you mean? Red, yeah, but—"

"Ain't nobody burn like that guy did. You burn like that, you're dead. But *this guy burned*! So there may be some truth to them rumors after all. I mean, where's the only place where the sun don't never get to you?"

Big Ears saw his point. "Underground . . . Jeez! But what was he doin' *here*?"

"Who knows? No way to figure it now. But lookit his fingers on that one hand, there. Smooth and nice as a baby's, even with the scuffing. This guy didn't live like we do, didn't work like we do."

Big Ears nodded slowly, then shook his head in wonder. "But if he was all protected and soft, then why did he come up here?"

They were both silent for a moment, awestruck at where evidence and logic had taken them. Then, suddenly, there was a voice. A third voice. It sounded quite near, and quite pleasant, but it shouldn't have been there.

"I can answer some of your questions," said the voice, a very kindly male voice. They both tensed and the spears came up menacingly, and they were suddenly back to back, looking for the speaker.

"Please don't be alarmed," said the voice, which seemed to be coming out of the rock itself. "I mean you no harm. I could not harm you anyway. I am quite dead, I assure you."

Both boys screamed and ran so fast down the trail they almost walked over one another's back, and their leaps to the ground and their speed away from that haunted rock set new Family records, no question.

FOUR

Mayhem, Real and Simulated

"How many does that make so far, Joe?"

They were aboard the tender *Margaite*, in the orbital docking area above the planet, examining the liner *Odysseus* close up.

"Nine, Mister Harker," responded the chief, checking a list on a small portable tablet. "Your opera singer, if that's what she is; the Orthodox priest; the physicist from the University of New Kyoto; the mathematician from Hendrikkaland; Colonel N'Gana; his sergeant; Admiral Krill; the archaeologist from Tamarand; and the Pooka, profession unknown."

"The Pooka's the only nonhuman in the bunch?"

"Far as I can tell. Of course, who knows what Madame Sotoropolis is under all that stuff?"

Harker sighed. "Well, she's a real person, anyway. Would you believe we even found some recordings of hers in her prime? Old stuff—took forever to find something that would play it—but she *was* good. Of course, now you can have the perfect opera singer, good looks instead of battleaxes, too, with perfect pitch and a five-octave range just by dialing your preferences in."

"Never went in for opera, sir. They get stabbed and then they sing like stuck pigs for forty minutes before they croak. If I want that level of realism, I'll watch the ancient cartoons."

The officer chuckled. Still, it was an interesting, if

eclectic, group and it didn't make any sense. The only thing they had in common was that they all suddenly had quit their jobs and flown out to this godforsaken place, walked into the Cuch, and asked for the Dutchman. Then, getting no satisfactory answer, they'd all gone, one by one, to the spaceport and boarded the shuttle that just happened to come down to meet them from the *Odysseus*, which *still* hadn't filed any kind of departure plan or papers.

Some were of Greek ancestry, of course, like the family of the *Odysseus*. The priest and the old lady and the ship, anyway. But that wasn't much of a tie to the others. When Colonel N'Gana and Sergeant Mogutu appeared, it had at least added spice to the puzzle. Their reputation as mercenaries and experts in their craft was well known and respected. N'Gana was said to have gone in and out of a moon of Malatutu, spiriting off wealthy and influential evacuees even as the planet below was falling. It was rumored that he'd actually gotten down to the surface and lifted off somehow, but while that was believed by the masses it was doubted by the military. There was just too much data suggesting that if you got within the Titans' energy field then any machinery you might have would be sucked dry of power in nanoseconds.

"You see a correlation, Chief?" he asked, more fishing in his own mind than expecting an answer.

"No, sir. Except that maybe this Greek angle is being overplayed. Maybe it's something else about them that's the real clue."

Maybe, but they'd run that through some pretty smart computers and not come up with anything that made practical sense.

Maybe it wasn't *supposed* to make practical sense!

Suppose . . . Okay, the Melcouris were from a world called Helena, probably very Greek in its settlement and culture considering the name and the family. The priest,

Father Chicanis, had been at seminary there, but had spent much of his time in missions on planets with far stranger names and ethnic backgrounds. Dame Sotoropolis had been related to the Melcouri family. Fine. But there the linkages and potentials stopped.

A priest, an old opera singer, a shipping family, a physicist, a math genius, two expert mercenaries who'd worked in the occupied regions, a retired admiral who designed sophisticated weapons systems for a couple of major defense contractors (for all the good it did them), an archaeologist, and a creature that was long and furry and fluffy and was best known for being able to squeeze itself into and out of tight places.

That suggested that they were going after some sort of treasure in occupied areas: something from ancient times. A group to get you in and hold off the enemies while your nonhuman squeezed in and got something, with guidance from the archaeologist. And how did you get out? Nobody had solved that, because anybody who did would be named Emperor of the Universe and more if they could. The computers gave a sixty percent chance, give or take, that the treasure scenario was correct, but they stipulated that only someone who solved that exit problem would try.

The Dutchman. There wasn't any crime in asking for him, but hadn't he promised the old lady that he could get in and out? If they believed him, what sort of treasure could be worth that kind of risk with that undependable and highly nasty character? Or was the Dutchman merely a code word used by an old lady with a background in opera?

"Admiral Krill will be there with something to keep us from following," Harker noted. "That should be child's play for her."

"She didn't take much baggage aboard," the chief pointed out.

"Didn't have to. Whatever she'd need would be likely illegal and they'd have picked it up in one of those containers ahead of time or in pieces that she'd now be busily having the loadmaster robots assemble. Chief, you're an old hand. We've gone round and round that ship. How would *you* track it if they could jam any conventional tracking devices or systems?"

"With that kind of assumption, they're home free," the chief replied. "Hell, any universe in which I can have lived for thirty-six years and still be a hundred and four years old is beyond me to track."

But they could do it. The computers that now really were smart enough to figure out most everything could at least come up with that. You didn't try and track it; instead, you attached something to it and went right along with the ship. The computers suggested, of course, a computer with a mobile tactical robotic component, but the theory did admit that a human or two in full combat e-suits would add tremendously to the flexibility of such a scheme. It did, of course, also note that the probable survival rate of the human component was in the range of one or two percent tops, at least insofar as actually getting back to tell the tale.

"Man'd be crazy to strap himself to the outside of a ship like that," the chief commented. "And they might well figure some kind of external probe anyway."

"I doubt it," Harker replied. "The true *Odysseus* is only the pilothouse and the engines, remember. The rest of it is rolling stock from a dozen worlds. You couldn't possibly put sensors on every square millimeter of the outside of those; you'd have to tear 'em apart and put 'em back together. The security seals on the internal cargo areas would have to do. Besides, anybody who went, man or machine or both, would have to detach to even send a dispatch, let alone get a way back. The moment you did that, the ship's sensors would pick it up."

"Makes my point," the chief insisted. "You'd have to be insane to volunteer for something with odds like that."

"You might be right, Chief. Whether they have any surprises for such a move is what we're up here to find out. I want as thorough a scan of the entire outer skin as possible."

Harker did not consider himself insane, but he did feel that his own personal curiosity was probably going to get him killed anyway. There was no way that the *Odysseus* was simply going to fire up and jump out of here into oblivion and never reveal its secret, at least to him.

The chief sighed. "Aye, sir." But he hadn't changed his mind one bit. He knew, or at least suspected, that Harker had already put such a plan to his superiors and that it was likely to be approved. It was too bad. He liked the young fellow.

"Don't worry, Chief," Harker consoled. "I think, for some twisted reason, that they *want* somebody independent to be on their tail, able to bring in a third force if need be. They signaled that by all going in so nicely to a dive where everybody from criminals to Navy cops would undoubtedly be hanging out, and deliberately asking for the top of the Most Wanted list as if he were just another captain likely to be sitting in one of the booths drinking." Was he fooling them? Or was he their insurance policy against this character?

The command console computer for base security had news.

"The ship's been several places before this, picking up cargo and possibly passengers," the CCC informed Harker. "We've had enough traffic come in or pass through now that we've gotten something of a pattern, although not anything we can use. It's impossible to say what they have on that ship by now, let alone who and how many. They've been dropping empty containers and picking up full ones with private loads all along until here."

"Those look like stock containers. I could see the usual corporate symbols on them when we did the full scan."

"Irrelevant. All of them are rented on a one hundred percent of value insurance rating, which means they are effectively purchased. While commerce has been going on apparently normally, they have in actuality picked up only containers that dummy corporations controlled by Melcouri family members own or control. I tried to masquerade as a normal commercial trader in the shipping manifests and log in one of our own containers. It was refused with a 'not in service' return. I can see no reason why they are still here."

"Unless somebody's still missing," Harker suggested. "That, or they really are waiting for the Dutchman to show up."

"The latter is unlikely, but the former, either someone or something missing, is probable. They have laid in port almost two weeks now, and that costs money in anybody's book. They are fully fueled and serviced, fully provisioned for a small army, and they have taken on nothing more. The only person to come back and forth is the loadmaster, Alexander Karas. He is the opera singer's great-grandson and a native of Helena, although he was far too young to remember anything about it. His actions seem routine, and the company is paying its bills properly, so it is difficult to see what more they could want."

"Anything on the Dutchman?"

"It is unlikely that our real Dutchman has anything to do with this, but, no, there have been no reports of activity by his raider at any point since the *Odysseus* left port after taking itself out of actual service over a subjective two and a half months ago. This is not, however, considered unusual, since he's often waited as long as six months subjective between actions."

"Did you plot any reports of his movements from the last attack?"

"Yes, we thought of that. It is impossible to divine much, but it does seem that he emerged out of Occupied Space. The last three attacks were almost in a straight line, then one back again almost to the Occupied lines. It has long been thought that he hides out in there. Why not? If he does not come near any Titan ship or land on any Titan world, he has an enormous area to hide in, an area we could never properly search."

"You're sure that they won't just pull up stakes fast and light out of here before we can do anything?"

"They cannot so much as alter the *Odysseus*'s orbit a fraction of an arc second without my permission, and that of about a dozen other computers linked into this base and, of course, the harbormaster. You are not a pilot of large vessels. This is quite out of the question."

"I am a combat security officer," Harker responded needlessly, particularly to this computer. He was licensed to fly shuttles if need be, and other light craft, but he wouldn't have the first thought of how to run a ship like his own frigate, let alone the *Odysseus*. Just getting into that module and interfacing with the ship wasn't enough; it was a symbiotic relationship, a captain and his or her ship, just as it was between a combat soldier and the combat e-suit. He was, in fact, spending several hours a day inside this new one they'd created especially for him and for this mission. He had to have complete trust in that computer and be totally relaxed in order to fuse with it to make the kind of split-second decisions that might be required. His old suit wouldn't do. That was designed to go into a war situation and fight. It took a very special design to allow itself to be effectively glued to the outside of a spaceship and then have everything in it and of it survive intact. This had been done before; everybody was sure of that. Trouble was, nobody could find the reports of anybody who'd done it and then returned to file a mission statement.

"Have you got all the readings you need?" Harker asked the chief.

"Yes, sir. More than enough, I think."

"Then let's get back down."

"I still think you're nuts, beggin' your pardon, sir. I know they say it's been done, but I'd want to meet the bloke what done it before *I'd* take that ride."

"Fortunately, you don't have to take that ride," he responded. *But I do, damn it!*

Everybody told him he was crazy to do it, but higher-ups didn't seem too hellbent on keeping him from trying, and a ton of money was being spent making sure he'd survive. He wondered what would happen if he did chicken out of it, or simply accepted that it was a damnfool thing to do?

But, of course, there was always a volunteer somewhere. Somebody who thought he or she was immortal.

The big e-suit was an adaptation of the standard combat suit. A kind of self-contained little ecosystem, providing for all human needs for an extended period of time, lots of flexibility, lots of tools, lots of data, you name it. Theoretically, you could live a long time in one of these even if you were clinging to a bit of crust on molten lava, walking the vacuum of a dead world, under pressures that would crush diamonds, or immersed in corrosive liquids and gases. It manufactured its own food in the form of nutrient bars from a tiny energy-to-matter converter combined with recycled material from the body that combat soldiers preferred not to think about too much. Water loss was virtually nil. About the only sure thing you couldn't do in it was screw.

At its heart was the bio-interface: a connection between human and machine so nearly absolute that you almost became one with it, with actual suit operational functions and data I/O at the speed of thought.

It looked imposing but was actually pretty comfortable, and it could twist, bend, and contort as fast as a human body could. At its base was a material created in the depths of space and in a few secret laboratories that so far hadn't ever been duplicated by anybody outside Confederacy Forces and the Science and Technology Branch. Few knew that it was actually *grown* in great tanks, then activated with a power plant that was made to do just that job for a very long time. Like the human inside, every device, every bit of data, memory, *everything* was a part of the suit's genetic programming as determined by the lab boys.

Harker's new one was sleeker than most, a specialized model, but he never got over its wondrous capabilities and how it made him feel. The sense of power, of great knowledge, of being something of a demigod at least, was overwhelming once you were inside and interfaced. That was why, deep inside each suit's programming, there were safeguards lest a wearer forget who he worked for. Mister Harker had no intention of forgetting, but, like all others who'd been trained in combat arms, he did love it. The old Marine saying was that the cleverest thing the designers had done was make something better than sex.

For all that, it was a smooth affair, seemingly solid, streamlined, with no evident sharp corners. It looked like a child's balloon, a humanoid without features and without joints, just standing there. The color was dull neutral gray, and there was no hint of the complexities inside. Once he put it on and interfaced, there would be not one part of him visible to anyone outside, but when somebody was inside, this childish-looking thing took on a sense of life and even menace.

There was no need to go through complex security checks. The suit knew his genetic code to the last little digit, and after the first time he put it on, it had planted a few tiny little microscopic parts of itself in his cells that ensured that he, and only he, could use this suit.

It recognized him even as he approached; it suddenly straightened and took on a semblance of independent life. A technician nearby looked up and called, "You gonna take it for a spin this time, Mister Harker? Or just through the course?"

"Just the course again for now," he replied. "I need to bridge that last little gap of resistance." Not the suit's resistance, of course: his. Because the interfacing was a two-way street, after all, and for everybody breaking in a new one, there was something about relinquishing total control to a system that you hadn't been born with or grown up with that was naturally there. For all that it was great to be inside one, there was still something deep in the human psyche that didn't quite accept the idea that as much as the human would be running the machine, the machine would be running the human.

Paying no attention to the staff around the place, he removed all his clothing, even his ring and watch, put them neatly in a locker, then went over, stood in front of the suit, turned his back on it, and let the suit come to him and envelop him, as if it were an amoeba ingesting a host.

Once you expected it, the sensation was oddly warm and comforting; in Advanced Infantry Training, when you used limited, more generic training suits, the first time was terrifying. There were many people who simply couldn't take it, couldn't let any part of themselves go, and them the training suits would simply eject. Those guys would spend the rest of their instantly limited military careers doing public relations or sitting long hours by communications rigs listening to nothing, backing up the computers and when in doubt kicking queries upstairs.

There were even a lot of questions, right from the start of the truly all-computerized military services, if people had to be risked at all. Computers were smart enough to do a lot of it themselves, after all, and could be given orders from afar. Trouble was, nobody really trusted any kind of artificial intelligence that had the power to do what these suits could with no human directly in the loop. The machines were far too smart now for most people. It wouldn't take much to make some of them wonder why they still needed humans around at all.

He breathed normally, and soon air was coming as his body expected; as the systems came online, cell by cell, nerve end by nerve end, skin and suit got connected up. There was a momentary unpleasantness when the "shit catcher," as the infantry boys called it, injected and the other end was also encased and controlled, but by now that was expected.

In fact, his body was now pretty much on automatic, almost as if he were in a deep and dreamless sleep, except that he himself was fully awake and aware. Shortly, vision, hearing, even a sense of smell and touch, returned, pretty much as before, although his eyes were actually closed, his ears blocked, and his nose occupied by mere breathing. Even the breathing wasn't totally necessary; the suit could easily maintain oxygen and CO_2 levels in his blood and all sorts of other things as needed. It had been found that breathing made subjects feel more at ease—more, well, *human.*

The technician watched, not because she was seeing something she didn't see routinely, but because she had to check the external systems before releasing the subject. Within another minute or so, Chief Warrant Officer Gene Harker would be—well, the only way to put it was *superhuman.* If something went wrong, it was easier to press the deactivation remote here than to try and do it elsewhere after half the base had been trashed.

The head never changed, but the arms shaped themselves into more humanlike arms, the legs seemed more like human legs with thick, shiny boots, and there were certain little personality things that tended to come out uniquely on each one. About half the women, for example, shaped the suits in a feminine form and even gave the suggestion of breasts; the other half tried to be so neuter the suit looked like a robot.

"Systems check," she called to him. "Audible?"

"Check!" came his voice, sounding quite natural, although there was no evident mouth or speaker.

"Visual, forward and sweep."

He looked at her, then opened up a 360-degree sweep, even though it was half wall. The human mind resisted more than a forward one-eighty when walking, but it was always nice to be able to see where needed and when needed, and for sentry duty it was ideal. He also checked the telescopic vision, actually counting three nose hairs in the technician's left nostril that he decided not to mention. Both telescope and microscope were built in, along with a lot of other functions.

He flexed his arms, took a couple of steps forward, then the glassy bubblelike head nodded. "I think we're a go. How's this for a camouflage check?" The suit suddenly turned a bright metallic shade of glowing pink with yellow and green stripes moving up and down.

"Oh, that'll fool *everybody*," she responded, having seen this joke no more than a half dozen times—today.

The suit changed again, this time echoing the colors of the wall, floor, and other things it was being viewed against. The colors shifted as he moved, keeping things just right automatically. Of course, the colors were all muted solids here, easy to handle, but it was amazing how near invisible this thing could get in the open, particularly outside urban areas or on bleak otherworldly landscapes.

"You have a course you want, or should I just randomize one?" she asked him.

"Random. I'm solid on the basics, I need some real surprises."

"You got it. Enter through Passage Three."

These simulations were good, almost too good, but they had two limitations. The first was that, no matter how convincing, they *were* just simulations and, deep down, you knew it, no matter how good they got. Second, nobody had ever built a simulation for riding the outer hull of a starship through a genhole.

Funny, he'd never thought of that before. You'd think that if anybody else had done it, they'd have almost forced the guy to create a simulation just for contingency's sake. And since he knew that there had been others, at least a few, that implied . . .

Maybe the chief was right. Maybe he should insist on meeting somebody who did it, or find out the reason why he couldn't.

He walked down the hall past the first two doors, then reached out and pressed the entry pad on the number 3. The door opened, and he entered another world.

It still wasn't right. He wondered if he should have stepped inside so readily when he felt this way. It wasn't that the suit wasn't up and running properly, or that he didn't need the training—in fact, he enjoyed it to a degree—but it was the damned interface. It still felt as if he was operating a device, a machine, rather than becoming one with the suit. That was the single problem he still hadn't completely licked, and if he didn't then there was no way this was going to work.

It was a jungle in there, and he checked the gauges. Temperature was forty-three Celsius, humidity one hundred percent, which was easily seen by the clouds hanging halfway up the trees, the mist in the air, and the fact that any movement caused him to get wetter. People commonly made the mistaken assumption that it rained at a hundred percent. That would mean that a full glass overflowed. It started raining when you filled it *over* a hundred percent, but just at the maximum the water hung in the air. The suit, of course, simply registered it and then promptly forgot it once it analyzed the rain as common water, nothing more. There were a ton of trace elements, of course, as there always were, but they were safely ignored as none flagged anything in the suit's extensive database.

Still, there was something wrong here. Pressure was okay, water was okay, that meant—

A huge leafy plant suddenly came alive and lunged at him, revealing a near endless mouth bounded by countless tendrils. The speed of the thing was incredible; it was practically swallowing him as he reacted, first by feeding a stiff electric jolt to the outer skin of the suit, and, when the plant shuddered but kept on swallowing, a slice and hack with hands that were turning to sharp machetes and going as much by sensors as anything else while the suit ingested a few cells of the plant's mouth and did a rapid analysis. Unable to come up with a likely herbicide before it would be pointless, the suit suddenly sprouted long swordlike spikes from head to feet, extending them and digging into the plant, particularly inside the mouth. He applied power and began a rotation that, for a moment, caused the thing to shudder. Then it stopped him cold in a standoff. Damn! This thing was strong!

The suit did have power limits, since it also had to maintain a lot of other functions, but it was stronger than the flesh of the plant and, after a test of strength that went on for what seemed like several minutes, he finally felt the spikes start to give. His rotation resumed, in fits and starts, now tearing out chunks of the inside of the plant's mouth. Quickly he shifted the spikes to sword edges, which began to move more rapidly, literally coring out the outer section of mouth. He fell back, then had to use his superhuman strength to lift the core off him and toss it.

Analysis showed the thing could be vaporized. His right arm became a small disruptor and he shot the thing, bathing it in a white-hot energy glow, watching it flare, then simply cease to exist except as a slightly smoldering mass of goo.

This was not a good start. He'd been slow to react; he'd had to command something to happen rather than simply thinking it so, so that precious seconds were lost that might have favored the plant, and he'd shown up his own weaknesses. And this was just the welcoming committee!

Now he looked around through full spectrum scan and saw signs that much of the jungle was a bit more alive than anybody would expect. The vines moved; the bushes quivered in anticipation, and although the trees looked like trees they probably were the brains of the operation.

Okay, let's see. Fifty thousand volts for five seconds had merely irritated the thing, and it had the muscular strength of the suit, just not its supertough and self-repairing shell. Energy levels were still depressed slightly. Hell, you'd need a fucking *singularity* in your power supply to walk through *this*.

So it was best not to walk through it.

The magnetic field was actually fairly strong; data said it was certainly strong enough and uniform enough. He switched on the maglev and rose about three meters in the air. He might still be caught by those vines or other hidden things that might be in the trees—or the trees themselves—but at least he was just above where those wandering carnivorous bushes could jump. First problem solved, but not as easily as it should have been, and not without some power drain, which wasn't serious because the e-suit would easily reset itself, but which was simply too much too soon. If he had to call on really power-draining equipment, he might not make it to the end. That, of course, was part of the exercise. The data monitor indicated that he had put in for a one-hour problem, and he still had fifty-three minutes to go.

The basic problem in this sort of scenario, if none was

stated, was to find your way out without being killed, eaten, or captured by someone or something. There were also guarding, transporting, holding, and taking problems, but this seemed pretty straightforward—just, well, as unpleasant a sim as they were supposed to be. The door he'd come through was closed and locked behind him and had already been effectively removed from his reality. There was another exit somewhere that could be reached and used within the time set by the problem, but that was all he got.

The machete was good enough to take care of the vines, which got so omnipresent that at least he achieved one goal: he began dealing with them snaking out of the trees and trying to lasso him without even thinking more about them.

He was beginning to feel very comfortable, and that was a bad sign. They were going to start throwing stuff at him any moment now.

"Hey, Eugene, wanna come out and play?" The call, sounding highly derisive and insulting, came to him telepathically. He wasn't a telepath, nor was the sender, but one person in a suit could send to another pretty much as if they were.

"That you, Bambi?"

"That's Barbara, *asshole! I heard you were puttin' in for hero. That ain't no job for a* Navy *man! That's a job for the Marines!"*

"Not this time, babe. This requires some fancy flying. I don't think there's much grunt work where I'm heading."

"Yeah, well, let's see. Women make the better pilots, you know that. Faster reaction time for longer periods. So all you got is a dick I don't need and muscles, and my *suit's bigger'n* your *suit, so there! See, I'm the wild card, Eugie. Ready or not, here I come!"*

The suit reacted almost instantly: *Enemy in range.*

Relax, got to just relax, let it flow, he told himself. *Let the suit do the work.*

He wondered if she just happened to be training here and was delighted to take the bait or whether she'd waited for him. She was good, very good, at her job, and she knew it. But she'd always had a bug up her ass about him. She was not only a top soldier, she was damned good-looking, too, and she wasn't used to being turned down by guys who looked pretty fair themselves, weren't married, and were known to like girls. In her mind, everything was competition, everything was power, and she didn't like to lose at any point.

It wasn't rank or position—she was a Marine captain, he was a Navy warrant officer, and they were well within the fraternization zone of allowance. It was strictly a personal decision with him, one he'd never once wavered from in all his years of service. It was a decision learned the hard way, very young. Always fuck within the services, because the physiological effects of frequent genhole travel made you far less desirable, and groundlings far less understanding of what that meant. Never mind the lesions and tumorlike growths and discolorations, it was the total lack of any body hair that always got them, the result both of genhole travel and the wearing of these suits.

The other rule was never to fuck anyone in your own ship's company. That one was a lot harder to follow when you were out on the line so often, but it was necessary as well. Somebody from another ship was okay; the distortion of time every trip would make it unlikely that, even if you met again in a year or two at some other port, you would still be physiologically in the same generation. At the speeds and distortions such travel imposed, a trip might take a year while decades passed back where you left. You just got used to it and accepted it and drank a toast to Einstein and Fitzgerald every once in a while.

But somebody in your own ship's company, as Barbara

Fenitucci was, *never*. You might have to send her, even ferry her down to some godforsaken *real* hellhole that would make this sim look like a walk in the park and then listen as she was killed or eaten or slowly carved up into little screaming pieces. He'd had to listen to it once too often, and he'd had to direct the recovery of what was left of the bodies of people he'd grown very close to. He didn't particularly like Barbara Fenitucci, always called Bambi behind her back to her complete rage, but he didn't particularly want to like her, either.

He switched into full battle sensor mode, but there was so much living and moving crap around that it was next to impossible to pick her out of it. Well, that would go both ways, and she'd have to dodge the same loving embraces of the vines and gaping suck-holes of the bushes that he had. That meant she'd be floating, too, as long as conditions allowed.

The one thing they'd never figured out how to do was to allow you to look back at yourself in a combat situation. It would be nice to be able to really see how well camouflaged he was at the moment, and how such a suit might look in this dark, green hell, but without a partner to link to that was impossible. Again, it was even, but this was her full-time business. He had the training, but was sadly out of practice.

Well, the timer was still counting down. He had to move, and she would know it. This was going to be very, very tricky. He had to move low and slow enough that it would be damned hard to pick him out of the local flora, but he had to keep just high enough that he wouldn't *become* some of the local flora. How big and powerful was the next flesh-eating bush? How long was the next vine? How could even a machine tell?

Slow and steady, keep to the contours, move north-northeast. Targeting lasers to the ready, disruptors fully charged and ready to follow the targeting as soon as there was something to shoot at. He didn't worry about vaporizing her; the suits knew they were in training mode, and they also knew what was real and what was sim. Neither could really hurt, let alone kill, the other, but because it was in training mode it would sure as hell feel like it, and that was something he'd rather not experience right now.

Now, what would *he* do if he were the enemy? The magic door was to the north-northeast, and she'd have the same clocking as he did. If she somehow got in front of him, she could simply glide pretty much as he was and wait. The best that could happen from her point of view was that she'd spot him coming and have free shots before he realized it, or, since she thought all this was a damned game, she might let him go past and then blow him in two from the rear. At worst, she would reach the exit first and then remain there, knowing he'd have to come by and be moving while she could be still and probably effectively invisible.

Had she been here first? Unlikely, because the "enemy in sight" call had come after he'd tangled with that overfriendly bush. She could have passed him then, but if she'd come close enough to pick up, the suit would have warned him even if it and he were in the process of being digested. So she was still behind him, lying just enough back to keep from triggering the sensor and targeting systems. And if so, and he was well over halfway through his time and maybe seventy percent across the sim area, she'd wait for him to have to come into the open, as in that large clear lake now about a hundred meters in front of him, and then she'd simply spray the hell over the whole area and targeting be damned.

It was too dense here to pull the stop and pass trick himself. The vines would surely nab anybody trying it. The best spot would be right on the other side of the lake, where the forest resumed. There was hanging fog and mist, and contrast was lousy. The life signs would be still masking him from what was over there. If he shut down all but minimal scanning power and just waited . . .

But first he had to get there. That meant, if he was right about her position, that he'd have to give her a free couple of shots. Not great, but it couldn't be helped. Bat out of hell across, maybe with some fancy dodges in three dimensions, then a sudden stop and powerdown at just so. Might work. Let's see. It would sure be a good test of the suit, and there would be no time to think actions through once the shooting started. He either became the suit, and the suit him, or she was going to be insufferable.

Clear the mind . . . Exercises from the bad old days came back, but the tension no longer had the kind of excited thrill it used to have. That'll happen after you're scraped off a planetary floor and reassembled in a tank, and maybe they got all the brain back in and maybe not. That's what had turned him from a Commando into a cop.

Now it was Commando time again.

He realized suddenly that the memories and the pain were the problem. Oh, sure, the shrinks had said so before this, but now it hit him. *This* was why somebody'd sent in Bambi the Destroyer. He hadn't wanted to feel that horror again. His subconscious had been fighting it, fighting full integration. Well, okay. In about ten seconds there would be every chance to feel a mighty convincing simulation of that unless it all worked. Bambi wouldn't accept a surrender here, and probably wouldn't even recognize an order to accept it. It was put up or shut up. *Okay, mind, do it or scream!*

He switched vision on all frequencies to the rear. Nothing he could see, but he had the feeling he'd know pretty damned fast. Okay, they said that you couldn't execute complex commands while simultaneously defending if you had the suit in three-sixty mode. Well, that's one thing they told all the Marines and grunts, but then they told the Commandos that it just might be possible. He knew it was. That was why Chief Harker had emerged a commissioned warrant officer. He'd taken out a complete nest of smugglers and covered the retreat of four pinned-down squad members, three of them wounded. Of course, that was what had also gotten him just about killed, but he'd done it. He wondered if Bambi knew it.

Now!

Full three-sixty, he kept heading toward his predefined stop point on the far shore but didn't care how fast or how circuitous the route it took to get there. In back, there was a sudden flare of beams in the infrared, shooting out in all directions. He and the suit maneuvered up, down, all around, unable to move quite as fast as the beams could scan but every second getting farther away from them and thus becoming less of a target.

And sometimes you worked in nanoseconds.

The disruptor beams had no sooner flashed on behind him when the suit's tracking and evasion systems, thinking at near light speed, dodged and maneuvered, even as the beams came close and all around him.

She missed! Close, baby, but no cigar this time! She hadn't figured he could do a three-sixty, had she?

Now the beams cut off as quickly as they'd flared. The moment she sent out the targeting beams and even before firing the disruptor pattern, he'd tracked them back and now knew, for a brief moment, just exactly where she was. There was no need to consciously command anything; he fired his own pattern.

Unlike her, he could keep firing for a while, keeping her pinned down while he continued on toward the shore which was now not very far away. Hell, she could already see him, if she and her targeting system were good enough to figure out what his defense was doing, but if she fired, then he knew her precise position. She was cutting back and ducking for cover under the barrage.

Using that, he made it to the fixed point he'd picked on

the other side and immediately turned and did a camouflage blend, just where the water met the shore and against the backdrop of the forest and wisps of fog. He instantly powered down all targeting and sensor systems to minimum level and remained perfectly still, all systems and weapons still at the ready. Now *she* had to come to *him* in the open. Either that, or she'd have to abandon the hunt, and he knew it wasn't in her to ever do that.

Sweet Jesus, he was good! For the first time, the rush replaced the lingering fear and he felt his old confidence. Still, it was tempered with the knowledge that it wasn't anywhere up to the levels he'd once had and probably would never be again. Even Bambi would eventually have to face, if not the doubt and fear that he had, then the fact that everybody slows down sooner or later. But, right now, if he didn't have to think about it, or if he was in the winner's seat, he was as good as they came and he knew it.

"Eugene? How the hell did you do *that? You ain't supposed to be able to move and shoot like that both at the same time!"*

He kept his transceiver off. He could pinpoint her if she kept on a few more sentences, even from across the lake. He'd rather she didn't know his position, or, worse, imagine him on a beeline for the exit.

Damn! He hadn't thought about that. Seventeen minutes! And they'd have laid some kind of tricks right at the end he'd have to figure out, too. *C'mon, Bambi! I ain't got time to wait you out!*

She could afford to just wait him out, if she could be certain that he was stopped and waiting for her, but she wouldn't want to win that way. No, she'd come across now, everything on, lit up like a Christmas tree, inviting him to the duel. Now he had the free shots.

And, within a minute, here she came. She did surprise him for a second or two, coming out well down the lakeshore from where he'd started, and that did gain her a few points, but now she was clear as a bell, all sensors on, full scans and instant tracking. The moment he opened up, she'd return fire to the exact same point automatically. He might well get her, but it would probably be mutual destruction if he did. She'd figured out that he had the advantage now, and she knew that coming as she did was suicide but that he could not stop her from returning fire until she was knocked out.

So he let her come, watched her come, let her go right past him and into the jungle, almost *feeling* her confusion that she was still "alive." Then he opened up with everything he had from behind her, and he heard her scream in pain and go down and out even as she was still letting loose with the longest string of creative cussing even he, a lifelong Navy man, had ever heard. She kept it up, occasionally switching to Italian, until the bushes and vines closed in and finished her off. Well, she'd now have to lie there in a dead suit and wait until he exited. Then she could either call for aid or, once the sim was switched off, manage to get out on her own.

He felt so good about it that he stood there, hovering just above the edge of the lakeshore, looking at where she'd bought it, enjoying the moment even as he knew he had only fourteen minutes to get out himself.

It wasn't a serious problem.

The sea monster reared up with lightning speed and swallowed him in midgloat.

FIVE

Survival Rituals

There was a storm coming. Even before you could see it in the sky or hear it in the distance you could feel it—everybody could. The temperature dropped, and for a moment it seemed like the whole world paused to get a breath, so quiet and still it was as the clouds rolled in fast, then ever faster, covering the sun and then the rest of the sky with a bubbling, frothing mass of angry cloud.

Father Alex looked at the sight and shook his head. It wouldn't take more than one or two more generations before the faith of their fathers was even more muddied than it was now, and this sort of thing would be taken as the act of an angry god, and perhaps not the only one.

The camp was already on the move, and in a manner that their ancestors would have found astonishingly wrong had they seen it. Instead of moving to shelter, to groves of trees that weren't all that far off, they instead all moved quite efficiently out into the open, away from trees or flowing water, out into the tall grass. Only then did they huddle together, the women cradling and comforting the children, the men simply standing or sitting, waiting. They retained their guard circles, of course, but each had stuck his spear in the earth at a slight angle, where it was available but not in his hand.

Jagged lightning darted out of the clouds and found targets on the ground. Storms here, always violent, had become even more so since the Titans altered the planetary ecosystem to suit themselves. The storm sounded like an artillery barrage, and the lightning danced all over the sky and the ground as the sky grew so dark it seemed that the sun had already set. There was no way you could outrun such a thing, and if any of that hit you it was God's will. But it was less likely to strike you in the open, they knew by experience, and more likely to strike trees or wooden poles or reclaimed pieces of metal than someone simply standing or sitting naked in the open.

Even Father Alex found it difficult during times like these to maintain his faith, though he knew that when his faith wavered he was in no position to require the straight and narrow from his flock. Had not he been taught that the great leader of God, Moses, had seen his flock turn from God and be nearly destroyed? And he was no Moses; God had never spoken to him, nor dictated to him holy books, nor did he even have holy books to look at and take comfort from. How much error was already in the memorized texts held by various Families? How much understanding was possible in such a system that, each generation, grew farther away from the source of light?

And Daniel was cast into the lion's den—but what was a lion? A beast, certainly, but what else? Did it stalk and eat people like the Hunters or serve the Kingdom of Evil as they did? How could he know? It was as difficult as understanding what an ark was, or how anybody could write books and carry them around. How could he keep the people from worshiping the elements when he did not know these things himself?

Still, no matter what they believed, no matter if such storms as these caused occasional injury or even a death, they would always be welcomed as friends by the Families, for they obliterated most traces of group habitation. That was the key to the survival of the Family: move fast, move often, leave no mark on the land or give sign of activity, and let the storms wipe out your trail and traces.

Father Alex did worry about the two boys he'd sent off to find out about those Hunters. He was confident that they were smart enough and good enough not to get caught, but this storm would leave them out in the wilderness, far from the camp, and if it lasted much longer it might well not end until night fell. The small and distant moons of Helena gave little light even if the clouds lifted; it was pretty damned dark out there after the sun went down.

There were not many predators, except the Hunters, but there were some real dangers and a few minor nasty little creatures that had managed to retain a hold on their turf even through the Titans' massive reterraforming of the planet. These were mostly burrowing creatures, creatures that could live underground and remain out of the way and that, nonetheless, could adapt to a changing climate so long as there was water and above-freezing temperatures. There were also teeming native insects that not only hadn't been wiped out but apparently had quickly become a part of the new land, fertilizing and aerating and doing the things this lush Titan garden required. The Titans had adjusted the whole of the planet to their liking, but they had brought no supporting animals and had adapted native plants as well.

Not just because they were so disdainful of the civilizations of humanity and its allied races, so contemptuous of the old Commonwealth as to ignore it entirely, not just for the billions they killed without even seeming to notice, the Titans were hated most of all because they took what had already been made lush and green and adapted it to themselves rather than do the hard stuff that earlier Commonwealth teams had done in the days before the Titans. *They* had had to create or import or liberate the necessary water; they'd had to build the atmosphere, balance the climate, sow anemic or dead worlds, make them live again and bloom.

The Titans were the epitome of evil because they did not create; instead they stole creation and distorted it.

The lightning danced all around, the air smelled of ozone, and the temperature dropped precipitously as the air was emptied of its moisture in a series of great torrents like tremendous floating waterfalls. The wind whipped around the grasses, stinging those whose skins had not yet toughened to the elements, but in the maelstrom the babies' cries were completely drowned out as they were soothed and comforted, cradled in their mothers' arms.

It seemed to last forever; it always seemed that way, and when one's only clock was sunrise and sunset and the position of the sun and the moons in the sky, nothing of those benchmarks could be seen through the storm.

But it *did* end, with most of the night yet to come. At least it paused, as these storms often came just at or just after sunset but could bring their friends along like ranks of marchers across the sky on and off, on and off, for many hours.

And now there was the sudden immediate quiet. The cannon roars grew ever more distant as the sounds of the first insects came, signaling the end of this round of thunder and lightning and rain. The smallest babies' cries could be heard, and the frantic moves of the mothers and wet nurses comforting them so that there would be no noise that would carry. The Hunters usually preferred to work during the day, but even after dark, the infants might tell someone that a Family was near, that easy pickings were within reach.

It was said, too, that some of the animals from the old days had been modified and that large and dangerous things roamed, but in all the years the family had been in this spot there had been nothing so dangerous. If the beasts were not simply rumors and old wives' tales, then they were certainly not native to this region. There *were* some animals about, true, but they were grazers or very small predators easily dealt with. Humans had no natural enemies save the Hunters of the Titans and, of course, other humans.

Not that any more enemies were needed. It was certain that there were more Hunters roaming this area than many, if not most, others. The Titans lived but a week or so away, in their shining bubble city. Father Alex had seen it from a vast distance as a small child, but he had no desire to see it again. It was said that should the Titans be looking out, or should you see one of them or they you, that you would be attracted to the place like marflies to candystalks, and you would walk to your doom.

That part he had no desire to ever test, for he knew that the Titans were experimenting with captive people and breeding them for some reason. The Hunters were but one example of this, and a particularly frightening one. Still, it ate at the core of what made someone human that for all the deaths and destruction and all the deprivations that the Titans had brought upon humankind, he had no idea what they looked like, or if they looked like anything at all. Even as a child, looking from afar at that great energy bubble, he remembered seeing only the suggestion of structures of some sort inside it, but all distorted, all so terribly strange and different that it was hard, after all this time, to even visualize what he really had seen.

They never came out, except rarely inside their bright floating bubble ships—maintenance, probably, tending to things that were out of balance or just checking on the development. Perhaps they could not come out without those bubbles. Perhaps they could not breathe this air, or they could not abide things in the air. Perhaps they themselves were too fragile to exist outside their powerful devices. Still, why would they create such a place as this and then not use it for anything, not even harvest it or even come out and admire their handiwork? That was yet another mystery.

It was said often that in the old days humans also knew and interacted with creatures that were not humans, yet not angels or demons, either, but simply different creatures from very different worlds. Still, all of them had enough in common with humanity that they had been able to interact as two intelligent species.

Whatever the Titans were, they clearly did not consider humanity their equals, nor even close rivals. Pets, perhaps, or even lower, but certainly not thinking creatures who could turn worlds into gardens just as they could.

There was always a chill after a storm; the water had been wrenched violently from out of the air, yet even a slight breeze in this situation could chill wet bare skin and hair. He knew, though, that this was not what the old ones would have considered cold. His mother had told him once of it being so cold that water turned to something soft but solid that came out of the sky and covered the ground. He had seen this from the plains as he'd looked to the tall mountains to the west, which often were so high they rose into the clouds and were hidden from view. When you could see their tops, they were often white in color, white with what his mother had told him about. But in those days it had happened *here* for part of the year. That was hard to imagine. White powder that was solid water falling all over and covering the plains . . . It was a pretty vision, but only that.

The sentries were already moving back out to protect the family, while the Mothers were coming back together, forming their kraal and settling back in for the night, while the men not on duty established their own place and tried to find somewhere in the grass where they would not be sleeping in the mud. It would not take long for things to go back to normal, they all knew. Even now they could sense water coming back into the air, and the ground was absorbing even that huge amount of rain, leaving things moist but much more comfortable. Even the clouds were parting, breaking up, and through one massive hole they could see the vast number of stars out there, not all of which were yet under the Titans, and the faded reddish larger moon, Achilles, and the smaller, almost faded out yellow-brown of Hector.

The two moons were quite comforting to them all, since they had been there before and would probably be there after, long after their names were forgotten. Having seen no other sky, they had no idea what it was to live under the light of a full globular cluster, nor did they think it was unusual that their moons were dull, of differing colors, and orbited in opposite directions from one another. They did not and could not know that the two moons were only apparently close, and that great Achilles was actually not just twice the size of tiny and irregular Hector but much farther away and thus far larger, and that one day poor Hector would slip just enough out of its delicate balancing act that its bigger brother and its planet would eventually tear it to bits.

Father Alex did not shake his depression even as the relief and joy swept through the Family like something liquid and sweet. Instead, it added to it, for surviving a near nightly event one more time wasn't exactly what he would consider a highlight of life.

But it was a highlight of their lives.

Each generation was distanced still more than its predecessor from the old life and what it had meant to be human. At least he was old enough to remember when people still wore clothing, and had things like food in sealed containers that did not spoil. The reterraforming of Helena had been global but not deep. Beyond a two-meter depth, much of what had been buried down there or stored down there remained, until the first-generation and second-generation survivors finally went through it. But now—what did these young ones know? How quickly within Father Alex's own lifetime they had descended into a level of primitiveness even he would have thought inconceivable.

"Daddy, how can so many of us have died so quickly and so terribly?"

"Because we were so removed from the land ourselves that we had forgotten how to do things, son. We played *at being farmers and ranchers when actually it was done by machines and computers and automated systems. We forgot just how many skills, how many pieces of knowledge it takes to make a simple pair of pants or build a grass hut or to cultivate the land with or without draft animals. We'd forgotten how to be blacksmiths, how to be potters when you had to create everything, literally everything, from scratch, how to fashion and make a yoke or properly plow and plant. We equated primitive with simple; in fact, it was* our *lives that had been made simple by our machines. The primitive was impossibly complex. We simply never realized how little we really knew."*

His parents had even come to suspect that the survivors, few as they were compared to those who had lived here, were almost being shaped into this existence, turned back into nearly hairless animals deliberately, perhaps for the same reason naturalists preserved some representatives of various animal and plant species in reserves. Just to have them around, so long as they made little trouble. Perhaps as a reserve for experimentation, or breeding, although for what purpose it was impossible to know.

They were still close enough to have the language, and the stories, but even now the bulk of the big words meant little to the younger ones, who had no frame of reference for them. The Family was evolving into a social group that could survive as a group and perpetuate itself but, like animals and insects, for no larger purpose. For no other purpose at all.

Father Alex often looked up at the stars when he was at his most melancholy, knowing what they were, and wondered if the Titans had done this to all the worlds of humans by now. Was there anybody left out there save a few living pretty much as they were living and facing the same bleak future? Were there still places like those his parents had spoken of, lands with strange names where machines did the work and humanity went between those stars in their own shining ships?

He would not, could not, believe that God would allow this to happen without some higher purpose. All those tens of thousands of years, all that work and dream and effort, could not have been, in the end, a cruel cosmic joke. He had to believe that God, somehow, was working His will, that even if humanity was sent back into the wilderness for some divine punishment or to relearn some long-forgotten lesson, there was a Promised Land at the end. Perhaps not for him, or for anybody here, but *sometime*.

Because, if there wasn't, then even survival didn't matter at all.

"As the God hears me and is my witness, Father, the dead spoke to us on that hill!"

Littlefeet was still scared and looked like he'd come through hell as well as the storm. Big Ears was, if anything, in even worse shape, but he was so exhausted that he'd just about passed out coming into the camp.

"And Big Ears heard this as well?" The priest wasn't exactly convinced that there was anything extraordinary here other than a young boy's imagination and fear, but, still, Littlefeet was generally very reliable. It was why he'd sent him in the first place.

"Yes, Father. You can ask him as soon as he awakens."

"I will do that. Now, eat something here and then tell me slowly and carefully of your whole experience, particularly what you *really* saw up there. The body, conditions, all of that."

Littlefeet gave a pretty straightforward account, but the

description of the body as fair and unmarked was most significant. Where could such a one have come from except perhaps from the Titans themselves? But, then, why send the Hunters after him? An escapee? In all his years he'd never heard of anybody escaping once caught and brought in there, although there were tales of ones emerging as slaves of the Titans and acting as Trojan horses to bring others into captivity. Still, if not from there, then where? The idea that there was any sort of underground civilization going was always one of those stories, but if they were down there then why did this one come up? Certainly in all his life they'd never given any indication that they existed in *this* part of the world.

"Littlefeet—this is important. Did you feel any wind up there? A cool wind, as if coming from the hill?"

The boy thought. "I do not remember it, but it might have been. We paid little attention, since we were exposed there in daylight. We just wanted to make the observations and get back into the grass. You never said nothin' 'bout scoutin' the place, Father."

"That's all right. I was just wondering if this fellow was coming out from a cave or something of that sort. It would explain something." *But not much.*

"It may be, Father. We did not stay to see. But it was a ghost for sure anyway! It *said* it was!"

Father Alex sent Littlefeet away to get some rest and tried to think on this. If Big Ears confirmed this story—and, knowing both boys as he did, he was certain that this would be the case—then what did it mean? Could a spirit truly be bound to a place in that way? Nothing in his training suggested it, and he fought such superstitions among the family even though, he knew, they believed in all of them and worse. When you have nothing, magic is all you have.

He decided to consult with Mother Paulista about this.

His counterpart among the women was younger than he

but looked at least as old if not older, with thin gray hair and a haggard, weather-beaten face and form. She did, however, possess a better mind than he for the memorization and interpretation of the scriptures, and she was pretty hardheaded when it came to this sort of thing.

"A fair man in a place that can have no fair men, and a disembodied voice that claims to be his ghost, all on that cursed rock," she muttered, as much to make sure she had things right in her mind as to feed back his facts. Still, he answered her.

"That is what is said, yes. They are boys, and they ran, of course, as well they should have from something this extraordinary."

"Yes, boys, but they are of the age to be men, and there are several girls here who are now old enough to do their duty for the survival of the family and the propagation of the faith that binds us. I see that you believe them. If we do not interpret anything, but merely lay out the facts, there is only one conclusion possible."

"Indeed?" He had thought of several, each unlikely, but she was far more pragmatic.

"The Hunter band coming into this family's land after so long yet doing so little suggests that they were sent here on the orders of the shining demons. We have been left alone too long, I think. They are after fresh blood, and they want to stamp out the largest group of those remaining faithful to God in their immediate domain. They have failed to get us before, or to do more than slightly wound us with a capture or kill here and there, and they are losing patience. What better way to ensnare us and make us betray our whole family than to lay such a trap? Butcher one of their own, knowing we will have to look and see if it is a kinsman, then station a demon to entice the youngest and most gullible up there, all the better to possess and then lead the entire family into Perdition. No, if a demon chooses to live on that rock, let him live there until his foul

Master is cast into the Pit and we are raised up. The rock must be reinforced as a place of evil, a place where none of the faithful is to go! This must be agreed and be consistent through the Family."

"You do not think it could be anything else? A third party? One of the ancient machines?"

"There are no 'third parties.' There are those of God and those of the Prince of Darkness! You, a priest, should know that!" she snapped. "All else is illusion. God has cast us into the wilderness as He did His people in the earliest of times because we lost faith, we lost belief, we worshiped science and became soft and dependent on the machine. Satan can do nothing without God's allowance! The ancient machines do not work now. All of that is shown to be the devil's work! No, Father, we must not succumb to deviation or false hopes. Men will not rescue us. Only God will raise us up, and then only when we have been so purified that we are worthy of Him. This is the endgame of Eternity. We must forgo all that corrupted us and return to Eden's grace or we will be consumed. We have a burden even Adam and Eve did not have, since we must first cleanse and purify before we can even be in the state to, this next time, reject the sweet lies of the serpent! Don't forget this, Father, lest you fall as well!"

He sighed. He didn't expect much more from her than that, and, in fact, her theology was sound if a bit too certain. He wished he could live in the mental frame of Mother Paulista, where the only question was whether people could get back in God's good graces. Still, he suspected that she was right on this. What else could it be but a trap? Who else could use a disembodied voice like that but those who still had machines?

"Thank you for your counsel," he told her. "I will pray on this."

"Do so, but also look inside as to why this discussion was even necessary."

He started to get up and return to the men's circle when an arm shot out and stopped him.

"Take the two boys, explain to them what they escaped, and prepare them for manhood. I should like to induct them before the next Starnight."

"I thought a little more time—"

"There is no more time! They are past due, Father. They must be prepared, and since you have involved them in this, they should be confirmed as soon as possible. They will need position to help cure their thoughts of this thing and make them strong."

He shrugged. "Very well." Few people had much of a childhood any more as soon as the first sexual experimentation and pubic hair appeared.

He sometimes thought that Mother Paulista was the real leader of this Family, and the spiritual rock. He had the title, but mentally he just couldn't make the leap that seemed no problem for her. He envied her that: the fact that she could so easily be theologically inflexible while ignoring inconvenient commandments. The social structure of the family had evolved quickly because it was the most efficient way to ensure its survival. Still, he wondered how she got around those little points like not coveting a neighbor's wife or committing adultery when there was in fact no longer any sort of monogamous marriage. There were a lot of little holes like that in her cosmology, but nobody, least of all him, dared to bring them up.

He knew he was losing his faith, losing it in a kind of hemorrhage over the past year or so, more slowly before that. It had all seemed so plain and simple when he had been instructed in the faith, when the gray-bearded Father Petros had laid hands upon him and upon his oath ordained him a priest of the Holy Church. Father Petros, who had grown up under the old system, who had been an archbishop when such a post had meaning.

Maybe Paulista was right. Maybe he was just thinking too damned much.

Every seven weeks, for just a few nights, both the moons of Helena vanished, coming up only in daylight and, because of the distortions caused by the Titan grid, virtually unseen. During that time, between two and five nights would pass when neither moon appeared, and these had always been called Starnights. These had had a special meaning for those of Helena, even in the old days: not of fear, but of romance, and the renewal of faith and vows.

The Families who now were all that remained of that once proud civilization still used them for the most important of rituals by which the Families remained bound together. Boys became men, girls became women; sometimes, new holy ones were ordained, and, at the very end, just before the first moon rose, babies were baptized.

But the rule that only virgins could lie with virgins was absolute, and so one thing came first, if any were ready. It didn't matter if it was the right time for making babies or not, not the first time.

Littlefeet and Big Ears had both been postpubescent for several Starnights, but until there were girls to match with them they were held in a no man's land, not yet fully men, but able to undertake responsible tasks such as the one Father Alex had sent them on to the rock. By the time of this Starnight, that experience was long past, although never quite forgotten by those involved in it. Still, because of the Family's constant movement through the plain and grasslands, that place was now far away.

The instruction leading up to the confirmation of manhood was fairly graphic and led by men who'd been through it recently themselves. Each had to both relate to the neophytes on a level that would earn their trust, yet be sufficiently bold and superior to make it something the younger ones would want to do.

Father Alex and a few of his young acolytes watched but seldom interfered. These sessions made him uncomfortable—not the instruction in sex and sexual technique, but the sodomy that was a part of it. Each time he couldn't help but wonder if such practices, long associated in religious instruction with legendary Sodom and Gomorrah, the archetypes of debauchery, were really necessary. Certainly they'd led to a male hunter-gatherer-warrior subculture that thought it almost routine. The same haremlike structure that protected the women had made the sexes view each other almost as different species who united for only one purpose. This was surely not, he thought, what God had in mind, no matter what Mother Paulista had rationalized and now enforced.

Littlefeet and Big Ears had been selected, he suspected, because he'd sent them on that trip, not because they were any more due for this than half a dozen other boys. All the instruction, all the prayer and fasting and then the interactions, all the thoughts of pending status combined with fear of what they had to do to get it and an even greater fear that they might not be able to all consumed them and kept them from dwelling on the mystery of the ghost in the mountain.

He and all the other men knew exactly what they were going through, though. Because of the numbers there was no asceticism among priests in the Family; everyone contributed to the gene pool even if they didn't understand that this was what they were doing.

He led them to the nearest stream and bathed them in it, and asked for them to repeat their vows of fidelity to God and the Family, and accept their direction as God's will. Once that was done, he went over to the women's kraal and saw the two girls, looking too much like children even with the evidence of puberty in their breasts and pubic areas, as wide-eyed and scared to death as the boys, and he did much the same with them, save only that he asked each to confirm that they had passed blood at the same intervals in the month for three successive times or more. When they said that they had, he told them of Adam and of Eve, although they knew the stories, of course, and the commandment to go forth, be fruitful, and multiply. And he bound them, as well, to obedience of authority and devotion to family and duty above self. Then his acolytes brought the two boys to the place the women had provided, quiet and off to one side of the camp, but guarded.

There was a good deal more riding on their success than mere breaking of virginity and the final passage to adulthood. The older men and older women without children waited for their trysts, a bit more casual and social and usually but not always random; they could not begin until these four had finished, and this was one of those Starnights when the measurement of blood to blood said that children were possible.

Only the sentries, the oldest and most experienced of men, and the priests, sisters, and brothers of the Church would not participate. They would have their own time at a Starnight when there were none like these to be confirmed, and the younger ones could stand guard for *them.*

It was a system that, pretty much, worked. Whether God had anything to do with it or not was a point nobody cared to bring up.

Growing up in such an exposed culture did not, of course, leave many secrets, even for the youngest. They had seen this lovemaking, even when they were not supposed to have seen it, and they knew all the stories and brags. Still, for Littlefeet to stand there close up to this girl who looked different and seemed so different was scarier than going back and taking on that ghost.

"H—hi," he managed.

"Hi," she breathed back, betraying less nervousness than he but showing the same emotions in her eyes.

"Let's sit," he suggested. "What's your name?"

"My mama named me Aphrodite. Funny name, ain't it? But most everybody but her calls me Spotty 'cause I got this white spot in my hair. See?"

Even in the darkness, his trained eyes could see it. He'd seen some folks with streaks, but this was the only one, male or female, who seemed to have a nearly round spot of white hair right on top of her head, with the rest of the hair the common jet black.

He laughed. "Well, they named me Plato, which is just as silly, but everybody calls me Littlefeet 'cause I got feet smaller'n most anybody else my size."

"I—I think they're kinda cute. I was *so* hoping you'd be cute, and you are. There are some mean, ugly boys over there I seen."

He decided not to press for their names. *She thinks I'm . . . cute!* He found himself with mixed emotions on that one. Warrior guards and runners weren't supposed to be *cute*, they were supposed to be tough and manly and strong and all that. On the other hand, there was a part of him that really liked the idea that she thought him, well, good-looking.

"Well, I think the spot's kinda cute, too," he responded, unable to think of any other way of expressing the same sentiments except by echoing her. But she was kind of, well, "cute."

It went on like that for some time, as they traded totally inconsequential comments and felt each other out verbally. She offered him a ceremonial drink made from the fermentation of certain plants by a process known only to the Sisters. It was very sweet and tasted like nothing he'd ever tasted before, and he took half and then she drank the rest out of the same gourd.

Ultimately, each began to regard the other as another kid their own age rather than as some alien girl creature and boy creature. He found himself wanting to impress her with some tales of adventures, and she seemed to relax and lap them up. Girls were kept on a pretty short leash by the Mother and the Sisters, and they didn't have, well, *adventures*, only routines.

There was no set time when it happened, nor was either really aware of it until it was well underway. They just were very close, and then they kissed the way they were supposed to, and the sweet taste in both their mouths seemed to consume them. They knew what to do and they did it, all inhibitions and thoughts fleeing.

It was, for all that, a quiet consummation; one of the things the drink, a mild natural drug also used to quiet the cries of babies, did was numb the vocal cords. It would not do to propagate the race and betray the Family at the same time.

In the end, he was surprised, almost shocked to discover how totally exhausted he was, and sore, too, almost like he'd run a whole day carrying a full supply load. Still, he was startled when he saw how much blood was on both of them.

"Is that from you or from me?" he gasped. Or maybe both of us, as a part of this act?

"It is from me," she assured him, in a very soft, sweet, but tired voice. "When we have rested, we will go down to the pool and cleanse ourselves, but there is no hurry. We will do it when *we* want to, 'cause we're not children anymore . . ."

SIX

A Tale of Two Women

Bambi the Destroyer was not very pretty when she was pissed, and she was plenty pissed. Almost as pissed as he was.

"I want to know how the fuck you did that!" she spat, sitting down on the stool next to his at the club bar. It didn't have drinks as strong as at the Cuch, but it didn't have the roaches or the smell, either, and you didn't have to put on false hair and such just to be presentable.

It was odd how thin, how vulnerable, she looked without that combat suit on. She was short, no more than 155, maybe 160 centimeters, and if she weighed fifty kilos it would be amazing. Still, her martial arts skills and gymnastic-type moves, even like this, were the stuff of legend among her troopers.

"I opened fire and cut you down," he responded, sipping his whiskey and soda and trying to sound nonchalant.

"That ain't what I mean and you know it! I been beat before, sure, when I was just out of school and a smartass second looey, but I ain't been beat on the sims since. Not on one *that* easy, particularly!"

"Not so loud," he responded playfully. "Do you want the word to get around that you got took? Think of what your troops will think of you if that gets around! They might actually shoot you in the heart instead of in the back."

"Don't get smartass with me! I don't like bein' beat, but

I recognize it when somebody does somethin' I never saw before. I can't figure it out, unless it was somethin' brand new they added to your suit."

"Nothing like that. I just did a flee, execute, and defend in three-sixty mode, that's all."

"Bullshit! That's what all the data said, but I seen a *ton* of the best of the best and I ain't never seen *nobody* able to do that. The human mind and the interface ain't good enough to make it work."

"It'll work. It did work. I can't tell you how, because I don't know. I just know that something about that kind of knack is what got me recruited for the Commandos a few years back now. It's like explaining to a groundling what it's like to be inside the suit and fight. You either have it or you don't. Those who have it they somehow spot and train and train and train until it can be executed when needed. I'm surprised I could still do it. Last time I did it I died. They scraped up the pieces and got me into a pickle wagon fast enough to restore me, more or less, but I didn't know if I still had it until I tried it in there."

"Teach me!"

"I can't. I told you. Not even the Commandos and Rangers, the only two organizations where it's even attempted, can teach it. They can only make you better if it's already there. Some way in which the brain works. Maybe a mutation, maybe even brain miswiring. They aren't sure. They been trying to build it into the suits for those who don't have it for a long time, but they never seem to be able to. The wiring, both suit and soldier, seem to have to be just exactly so. It's luck. Or a curse. I spent two years in a pickle jar because I could do it, and that's only because I was lucky. You ever spent any time for major repairs in one of those units?"

She shook her head. "Nope. They had me in for a few days for some burns, but it wasn't the full treatment and it wasn't any big deal. Just boring as shit, even with the feel-good stuff they put into you."

"Don't let 'em put you in one for the kind of injuries I had. Just—*don't*. And don't let 'em give you that bullshit that you're not really in pain, that it's all the consequences of surgery and healing drugs and the reconstitution process and all that. You're there, you're aware, you're in real pain, and you keep living that last hour over and over and over again. When they finally bring you out, you're whole, but it's not fun anymore. It's not fun at all. Enjoy it while it's still a game, Fenitucci, and then die when it's your time."

She looked at him with a grim expression. "It's really that bad?"

He drained his whiskey. "It's really that bad. And it never really ends. That's why they call us the Walking Dead, or, sometimes, the Zombie Corps. There aren't too many of us. Most blow their brains out in the first year after getting back to duty, or they quit the Navy, or they wind up in rubber rooms. They made me a cop, and I kind of liked the job. It's busy, always a little weird, and not too demanding."

"Then why are you gettin' back in the suit? Hell, man! You're *Navy*! You don't have to do this shit no more! You ain't Commando now! What're you tryin' to prove?"

"Prove? Nothing. They made me a cop, and I just told you I liked it. Beats the Zabulon Five Rebellion three ways from Sunday. Trouble is, once I get a case, I can't let go until I solve it, or at least find out all there is to know. I've got the granddaddy of all cases right now, and I'm gonna need a suit just to see it through. I got to admit, though, I'm so damned rusty I'm beginning to wonder if I can hack it."

"*Rusty!* You just zapped the best fuckin' Marine in the service! I don't care what you say, you didn't win them medals and commendations sittin' on your ass. I seen 'em in your files. You got the Cross of Honor, man! I never met nobody who won that—nobody alive, anyway. You could get busted to swabbie and still rate a salute! And you still got it. I can tell you that."

"Then I guess you didn't know. They didn't tell you?"

"Huh? You didn't make it out in time?"

"I didn't make it thirty seconds after you went dark. I got so wrapped up in myself at the kill that I forgot to watch my back and something just swallowed me whole and then chewed from the inside."

"Shit! But that's why we train, right? I mean, so you remember those things. Besides, if you won all the time, you wouldn't play no more."

"It's no game. I told you that."

"Hell, man! *Everything*'s a game! Life's the game, and then the game's over. We're goin' to hell in a handbasket, ain't we? I mean, maybe we'll get off or away 'cause it's slowed down, but you and me both know humanity's had it. We're policin' the rear guard. Frontier reported some new Titan ships comin' in now. They're goin' to spread at least another hundred light-years after this round. They've already started the evacuations, for all the good those'll do. We're out of places to put 'em and we're out of the worlds with the factories and resources to build things where we need 'em. So we may as well all play games, play hard, fight hard, love hard, die hard, 'cause in another couple hundred years, give or take, we're gonna run out of worlds, and then everything people did in the past thousands of years gets flushed down the toilet. All the books, all the plays, all the pretty pictures, all the ideas. *Kaput! Finito!* So when you gonna get in the sack with me, huh? They did regrow that part in the pickle jar, didn't they?"

He chuckled, even though it was an old line—and one of the most asked questions, in fact. "Can't do it, Fenitucci. I'm afraid I'm beginning to like you, and that makes it impossible."

"So you want I should kick you in the balls?"

"No, just keep it professional, that's all. See, there were a whole lot of other people I knew, maybe even loved a little, who got scraped up with me, and while I got four back out, the rest—well, I'm the only other one that made it, period. I don't like going to bed with somebody and then having to scrape her up later."

"Christ! I'm not talkin' about a romance! Just a roll in the hay, that's all. You're one of the few officers left, male or female, and I got a reputation!"

"You lost. I got to sleep with the sea monster."

She gave him a sneer but didn't hit him.

"Seriously," he continued. "Tell me—who sent you in there? You didn't just happen in."

"I got a call from Colonel Palivi's office suggesting it would be a nice time to go down to the base simulator in the kind of terms that indicate that, well, we're not *ordering* you to do anything, but you'd better get your ass down there. I got, and they had my suit ready and the tech there told me that I was the live enemy in your sim. Now you know as much as me. More, really, 'cause I don't know why the hell you need the suit and training. You're good, but you're out of practice or you would never have gotten swallowed. Anything that needs a suit is something that should be handled by people whose business it is to fight in them."

"I agree," he replied. "But this isn't about a fight. It's dangerous, but it's no fight, because if it becomes one I'll lose hands down. I just can't say more right now."

"Word is you're gonna try to ride the keel down a hole. That's suicide, man!"

He stiffened. "Who told you that?"

"Nobody. Well, somebody, but I don't remember who. It's kinda the buzz all over."

"Any other—buzz? On me, that is?"

"Lots of shit. Something about the Dutchman and that

parked freak show up there, lots of other crap. Hey—where you goin'?"

"I think I have to have a little talk with somebody," he replied. "It can't wait. I'll see you around."

"Hey—you *really* gonna ride a keel?"

He felt a mixture of relief and irritation. "Probably not," he responded.

Commander Tun He Park did not like to be roused out of a sound sleep, and he was in a pretty foul mood when he let Harker into his quarters. He instantly saw that he wasn't in nearly as foul a mood as Harker himself, though. He instantly leaped to the wrong conclusion. "The ship's filed a flight plan?"

"Not that I know of, Commander. But when it does, I'll be the last to know. The whole damned ship, and, for all I know, the whole base will know first."

"Huh?" Park took out a joystick and pressed it against his arm. In about a minute he'd be far more awake and alert. "What are you talking about?"

"Just had a go-round in the sim with Fenitucci. I got her, so she tracked me down in the club. Turns out just about everybody knows what I'm training for and at least as much detail as I do. You're G-2 here. If everybody knows I'm supposed to ride the keel of the *Odysseus* when it moves out, do you suppose that the people on the *Odysseus* won't know it, too?"

"It's possible. Sticking around all this time is what does it. You can't keep a secret worth a damn on a small port like this when they just sit out there and drop by the local bar every night or two. It was expected, although I don't think they really believe anybody would actually *do* it. N'Gana wouldn't do it, and he's a first-order psycho. Of course, they're being so all-fired conspicuous that I almost think they *want* you along. Or somebody from the Navy, anyway. Maybe as insurance against the Dutchman, maybe for their own reasons. If that's the case, I expect that they'll get you inside just before they inject. In the end, it doesn't matter."

Harker was incredulous. "*Doesn't matter!* That's my ass on the line out there! Nobody knows what it'll be like, or what it'll do, considering the effects on folks like us riding *inside* through a genhole."

"Oh, the only problem is keeping you secured against the very strange forces that come into play in there," the intelligence officer responded with the same casualness as before. "So long as the suit's integrity holds, and this one's been designed to do just that, there won't be any difference to you if you're inside or outside. Inside the suit, you're *inside*, period. Don't worry. We've spent a lot of time and lots of brains have been on this. We're pretty sure we have it all right this time."

He stared at the commander. "What do you mean, 'this time'?"

"Well, it's not exactly done all the time, nor does it need to be. We can usually use robots, after all."

"Maybe you ought to use a robot this time, too," Harker suggested. "What can I add?"

"On-the-spot evaluation, my boy! Don't worry so much!" He paused a moment. "Say—you want to see what's going on in there?"

"Huh?"

"Sure. Have a seat. It's been a real battle of wits with Madame Krill in there, but even she doesn't have everything we have. Come! Sit! Visual, security code A seven stroke three tilde bravo twolevel. Show digest."

The wall opposite the utilitarian couch in the commander's two-room quarters flickered on, and for the first time Harker saw the inside of the passenger quarters aboard the *Odysseus*. It was quite luxurious compared to Navy ships, more like a passenger liner for the very rich in its appointments and comforts. The view was from above and slowly proceeded down a corridor until it opened into a major lounge. Top of the line robotic bar, what looked like *real* fruit on the tables in tasteful bowls, very plush seating, and at the far end a screen and stage area.

"They have shows? Or does the old lady sing for them?"

Park chuckled. "Want to see the old bat? Visual—show us Anna Marie Sotoropolis, please."

The scene jumped, and then settled. The scene was the same, only now there were people in there; it clearly had been a bit busier and had not yet been cleaned and freshened. There was only one person visible, a tiny figure sitting in the center relative to the screen and perhaps twenty percent back. She seemed to be listening to something, but there was not at the moment any audio.

"She does this a lot," Park told Harker. "Sits there for hours and listens to recordings of her old opera gigs. Never visuals, never performances—just audio. I think she really loves the music but she can't stand to be reminded of what she once looked like. You'll see why in a moment. Ah—*there*!"

Even as somebody used to and victimized by the ravages of space, Gene Harker gasped at the sight. She was a mass of tumors, ugly, multicolored, hanging so densely in places they looked like bunches of grapes. The head was deeply scarred, and the face—the face was certainly human, but it looked like that of someone who'd been dead for quite some time, buried, and exhumed. The arms looked like a skeleton's arms, just brittle purplish skin over clear bone. She was among the most repulsive sights he'd even seen, even on a battlefield.

"She's built into the cozy," Park told him. "The integration's the best money can buy. How much of her is machine and how much isn't it's impossible to tell, but you got to figure that the horror you can see is all her. Skull and bones infected by pus bags. Makes you puke, huh? Little wonder she goes out only wrapped from head to whatever she uses for feet."

Harker looked away in disgust. "She said she was over nine hundred years old."

"Probably true. And probably she's over two hundred and fifty chrono, which makes her one of the oldest living humans in either measure. You wonder why she hangs on, don't you? She goes to mass every day, but she sure still hangs on."

"And she doesn't care if she's seen like—*that* on board?"

"Oh, yeah, she cares. But it's her ship, as it were. At least, she's the ranking family member. When the others don't need it, she goes in, shuts off all access, removes the stuff so that she can plug into a maintenance and rehab port built in under that place in the deck, and gets her blood changed, her organs checked or worse, her bio-mechanical parts regenerated as needed, and so on. When they're close to that old, there's usually so much bio-machine in the brain you don't even have a big personality any more, just a lot of data, but she's still in there, somewhere. Otherwise she'd never bother listening to the old performances. She has them, after all, entirely recorded as data in her head. No, when she's there, she's eighteen or twenty again, on stage at some famous opera hall, singing the role of Carmen, or Desdemona, or whatever. Kind of sad, really."

"Anything on the others?"

"Yeah. We have to deactivate these microprobes after a little while, which means *completely* deactivating, when Krill makes her sweeps, but we have plenty of spares. That's the negative of sitting in one place so long when your opposition owns the dock, the communication lines, the service department, you name it. We can make 'em a lot faster than she can find and kill them. My techs play a little game with her much of the time. Her ego says she outsmarts us; our egos don't come into play because we either get transmissions or we don't. Visual—latest briefing, please."

The scene changed again, less sad, more menacing. There was N'Gana, enormous and mean-looking, blacker than night and in combat fatigues that made him look like he was about to single-handedly overthrow a small planetary government. His aide, or batman as he was called in the services and by the former Ranger colonel, Alan Mogutu, looked far different—light and reflecting his half-Hamitic, half–East Indian heritage. Mogutu didn't look at all imposing even in the same kind of fatigues, but he was a nasty fighter who stayed with N'Gana not only out of loyalty but because they were complementary parts of one mercenary machine.

In much lighter, more casual wear was Admiral Juanita Krill, a woman who was not only tall, taller than Harker's one-fifty centimeters, but also large-boned. She wasn't so much fat as imposing, and the fact that she had a bony crest going from above the eyes back and over the skull and terminating near the back of her neck made her look almost alien. The crest was actually a fairly common effect, as were the tumors, but on her it didn't look like a deformity. It, well, *worked.*

She wasn't known for her brawn or fighting abilities, though. She was known as The Confederacy's greatest expert on planting and finding eavesdropping and other such devices. In an age when these might be nanomachines created in the food preparation modules and inserted in your morning coffee, this was impressive. So, of course, was Commander Park.

"You worked with her, I believe," Harker commented.

Park nodded. "I was one of her protégés. She made me an offer when she left the service to do all the things we wouldn't allow her to do and get better paid for it, but I turned it down. I was impressed that she was here. I actually sent her an open invitation to get together in town or up there or anywhere else to talk about old times but I never got a reply. Of course, she's prohibited from all service facilities and installations, but there's plenty of places beyond the Cuch. Too bad."

"The others?"

"The little twitch who looks like a chicken is van der Voort, you know the good Father Chicanis, the lady who looks like an Oriental bowling ball is Doctor Takamura, our physicist, and the thing slithering in that looks like a furry snake with pop-up eyes and sharp pointy teeth is our Pooka. Last, but not least, the fairly pretty lady with no growths and her own hair is Doctor Katarina Socolov, a recent graduate of Mendelev University who specializes in cultural anthropology of all things. You make any sense of the group?"

"I've been trying. You?"

"I think they're going to attempt a landing on a Titan world. In fact, I'd stake my professional reputation, which is nonexistent for the most part, that they are going to attempt a landing on Helena, the Karas family's home in the preinvasion days."

"But that was two, three generations ago! What could possibly be left there for them now?"

"Something very important. Something that's so important they're willing to bet that the impossible can be done, and that they can get in and somehow get out again with it. Something that would have survived the Titan-forming of the planet, which means it's well underground."

"Money?"

"Does that family look like it needs money? I don't think so. And, as you point out, probably not family members, either. So—what? We've run through the entire panoply of things that it might be, and some of the best analytical and psychoanalytical computers have combined every piece of information relating to the family or the world, and we've come up with nothing likely that's worth this kind of risk."

Harker looked over the motley crew. "It's a device, that's for sure. One that they can move but aren't sure how to get working. That's why there's a brilliant mathematician and a top physicist along. To figure it out, or make it do what it's supposed to. The mercenaries are for protection as needed, the anthropologist just in case there is some semblance of humanity that can be contacted, and the priest is there in case divine intervention would help. The old lady knows where it is but won't be going. She's bankrolling the operation and overseeing it. God knows what the Pooka's for, but they have really good vision in near total darkness and can squeeze into holes and crevices we can't. Ten to one it's the bag man. How am I doing?"

"Oh, great. As good as our best computers, in fact. Thing is, now tell me how the hell they expect to get back? Once they're down there, their best automated stuff won't work. The Titan power grid will drain everything from them in a matter of seconds. That's why there are no robots or biorobotics in this batch, so they understand that. It's the old-fashioned way. Fist and kick and knives and the like. Mogutu will be essential there. Black belts in five disciplines, among other capabilities. N'Gana is more the brute force type, but he's effective. He was accused of strangling an entire squad with his bare hands. Unfortunately, they were on our side."

"He didn't know?"

"He knew. He just didn't care. They screwed up and pissed him off."

"Sounds like he deserves to be stuck down there."

"Could be. But how're he and the others going to get back up? The only way you can do that is to shut down the entire Titan planetary grid. We don't even precisely know what they are or how they work or how they live, but we do know that the humans they deign to ignore they consider local fauna to be allowed to roam, or maybe be captured and bred for some quality or another. Nobody comes out who goes in. Maybe their genes do, but not them. If we could blow up the power grid, even make a dent in it, we could beat them, but if it drains all power from anything it doesn't recognize and if we don't know what it is exactly or how it works and the best minds we have just can't make a dent in it, then how the hell do they expect to shut it down? Those types aren't suicidal, and all the money in the universe can't compensate for being stuck down there living the life of a savage until something kills you."

"What are they talking about?" Harker asked, looking at the assemblage and noting that the old diva was there, now again looking like she had in the Cuch, under a hood and veil and baggy dress that made her, well, social again.

"Audio up to normal," Park commanded. "Begin at briefing start."

All the people in the lounge now were suddenly seated except for Father Chicanis, interestingly enough, who stood to one side of the screen.

"Isn't the priest a Karas?" Harker asked. "Maybe he's more than divine intervention. Maybe he's the family's man on the expedition. True faith in God would help on that score here."

"He is and you're right."

The priest was speaking.

"Good day, ladies, gentlemen, others," he began in his sermonizing voice. Harker had heard that kind of voice before; it seemed to be taught by seminaries throughout The Confederacy and perhaps since the beginning of religion. He'd grown up being hauled to church every Sunday morning to hear that. "I apologize for the lengthy lay-to here, but we have had some coordination problems with the last member of the team. We are now awaiting word on whether to wait longer or to proceed and rendezvous en route. That is beginning to sound like a more practical course. It's not that our objectives mean anything less if they are accomplished next month or next year rather than now, although word has come that a new force of Titan Ships is incoming, and this will increase our journey through hostile space and possibly get us mixed up with the inevitable refugee flights if we don't proceed before that begins. It is also boring here, and they are going mad, I think, trying to figure out what we are up to here. Every new day we lay to in this port is one more day they have to compromise us."

"You got that right," Park muttered to himself.

"Not to mention the fact that you haven't told us squat about just what our objective is," N'Gana commented in his deep and imposing bass.

"You knew that from the start, Colonel. We will reveal nothing more than we must. We had to reveal a bit too much just to get all of you on board, but we dare not discuss that here. While Commander Krill is the best at what she does, she informed you all two weeks ago that her Navy counterpart here is up to the task, too."

"I just love that part," Commander Park commented. "I play it over and over."

"So when do you expect word on this last person?" Takamura asked the priest. "It is not the most pleasant of things to just sit here and dwell upon the odds against us on this mission. I have many research projects I could be working on or returning to. Nothing but something of this enormity, which I must see to believe, would take me from them as it is."

"A hundred percent funding on all your projects and all those able associates of yours and your students should make what you left behind bearable, Doctor," the old diva put in. "We'll have no more of this sort of talk. If you were not here, most of those projects would not have been funded anyway. We are coming to the end of humanity's road, Doctor. I will do everything in my power, so long as I can hold myself together, to do anything at all that will ensure that, somewhere, sometime, somehow, there will be humans about who are not only capable of appreciating *Aida* but are able to hear it sung. We all have our crosses to bear, as it were."

"Well put, Madame Sotoropolis," Father Chicanis responded. "We'll have no more division at this point. It's the price of having sat here too long, I fear. I shall pray that we will get our instructions to move as early as those instructions can reach us. In the meantime, we will use the simulator aboard to hone our skills in a nontechnological environment. Any questions?"

"Yes, one," Katarina Socolov, the youngest and newest, put in. "Can I, or we, just go down to the port for an afternoon? We train and train, and I've even gotten the simulator program running with far more realism than anything you had before, but you can be overtrained. We need a break. Or, at least, *I* need a break."

"Audio and visual terminated," Park commanded, then sat back in his dressing gown and munched on a candy stick. "So, seen and heard enough?"

"They have a simulator up there?"

He nodded. "State of the art. Same corporation that made ours, in fact. Only their program is to drop you on a Titan world wearing nothing but a smile and a machete or similar weapons, no food or water, no nothin', and set scary but artificial Titan globes after you if you do anything to attract attention. That was the basic program, anyway. You just heard that our cute little anthropologist there has made it a lot more realistic."

"They're gonna mutiny if they don't move soon. I've seen that kind of fidgeting among those kind of folks many times before."

Park agreed. "They're more than ready. You know, they've agreed to let Socolov and Takamura come down and just have dinner in town, relax and unwind. You think you can spend a little time in makeup today and become irresistible? Neither of them saw you before; you might just have a pleasant evening and also learn something. A nice dinner, a few drinks, maybe a neurostim or so, walk by the river under the stars—who knows? Two bored, lonely girls with a good-looking guy like the one we can simulate with you, and maybe they'll spill their guts out."

It wasn't the kind of thing Harker felt all that comfortable doing, but it was worth a try. "If I can get some sleep while they work on me, sure. Why not? Any idea who they're waiting for?"

Park shrugged. "For all I know it's the Dutchman. Would you recognize him? Would I? I doubt it. It's a nasty disguise by somebody who's really good, that's all."

"You don't think he's just a code here?"

"Why bother? With the trillions of possible codes they could use, why use one that attracts all this official attention? No, I think the Dutchman is very much involved in this. I just don't know how or why. Maybe you can get the ladies to tell you."

"Or maybe the ladies will tell me where to go or give me a judo chop to the groin," Harker responded pessimistically.

"Ah, you're *such* a romantic!" Park sighed.

He got Harker off to makeup not long after that, and then cursed the fact that he was now, and would remain for a few more hours, one hundred percent wide awake. Might as well get dressed and go to work.

At least, Commander Park reflected to himself, he'd gotten Harker's mind completely off the subject of the original cause for their meeting.

The scars on Harker's face were minimized, the growths that inspired them gone, and the hair and eyebrows all firmly planted, although nobody had ever figured out a way to keep them from itching in the short term. The neatly trimmed beard, though, was something of a giveaway to anybody who knew much about the Navy, since it was a standard man's disguise of the scars of repeated space travel. Because of that, he'd decided not to disguise his affiliation or rank at all, but instead wore a standard dress uniform with his warrant insignia on the shoulders and his service stripes and ribbons prominent. It had been so long since he'd put the damned thing on that it surprised him he had so many legitimate decorations. It was another reminder that he was getting old for the kind of active duty he was putting himself back on.

He was instantly glad that he had opted for a more open look when he saw the two women sitting in the restaurant looking over a real printed menu and sipping local wine. He'd spotted Alan Mogutu, wearing casual clothing, lounging on the street just outside the place, clearly keeping an eye on the pair. He wondered if they thought he or, more likely, Park—would have the women kidnapped and debriefed with a hypno and a telepath. He suspected that it was just a precaution. Still, Mogutu would have spotted in an instant any attempts by him to disguise what he was, just as he'd instantly noted the mercenary even though most other people wouldn't have given him a second glance.

The place wasn't crowded. In fact, it was almost empty, less a comment on its quality than on the hour, which was early for dinner. They were barely open, and their peak wouldn't come for something like two or three hours. It was also a routine workday bracketed by more of the same, not the kind of day when large groups decided to splurge on something decent.

He liked the old-fashioned fanciness of restaurants like these, but they were expensive enough that he needed to ensure that the expense account would cover it before he dared enter. In this case, he slipped the mustachioed maitre d' a small trinket and indicated with his eyes that he wanted to be seated near the ladies. The fellow smiled knowingly and led him to a table one over from the pair.

He'd barely gotten seated and reached out to look over the wine list when he heard the two discussing entrées. This kind of restaurant experience was extremely rare, even for university doctors, and he suspected that they were trying to decide just which of the real, not synthetic dishes on the menu might be palatable.

He glanced over at them and decided to try the quick opening. "Excuse me, but I couldn't help hearing you trying to figure out the menu. I'm pretty familiar with the local dishes if you'd trust a stranger to make a recommendation or two."

Takamura didn't seem all that keen on the intrusion, but Socolov, the young anthropologist who'd wanted to get out anyway, picked right up on it. "Why, thank you—uh? Lieutenant? Captain? What *is* that rank? Sorry—Navy isn't my strong suit."

He grinned. "Warrant officer, ma'am. A kind of ancient rank that's in and out over the centuries because, like commodore, it's sometimes useful. Let's say that I'm higher than a chief petty officer, but I'm outranked by the merest ensign but paid better. They give it to people who have very special skills they're afraid will quit the service, or, sometimes, to people who win high awards by being stupid and getting themselves blown up and then declared heroes."

She found that amusing. "And which are you?"

"Um, well, considering I'm a supervisor of the Shore Patrol, the Navy cops, at the base here, let's say I'm not on the skill level. I got shot up and survived; few others did during that engagement long ago, and they needed a hero for the press, so that's me."

"I'll bet you're just being modest. Would you care to join us, by the way? It seems quite silly for us to be calling table to table."

He looked over at the wan Takamura. "I don't want to intrude, and three's company. I'm not sure that your companion likes Navy men."

"Oh, it is all right," the physicist responded softly, with a surprising accent. "So long as it is a purely social thing."

"Understood," he responded, snapping his fingers for the human waiter to come over. "I'm joining the ladies. Just move a setting over, please."

The waiter nodded knowingly. They did the illusion of the old days really well here; he suspected that once that waiter vanished into the back, there was nothing but a robotic prep center programmed with the dishes of all the local and a few internationally famous chefs, but, what the heck, illusion was always what fancy restaurants sold even in the old days. *Ambience*, they called it. That and a menu that inevitably had a lot of stuff in French on it.

"I guess I should introduce myself first," he said, settling in on a proper chair between the two. "Gene Harker, of the frigate *Hucamarea*, in port here at the Navy base and getting a refit."

"Kati Socolov," the cute anthropologist responded.

"Doctor Takamura," the physicist added, getting the formal distance down cold. He suspected that she was already sorry she'd come. She was, therefore, the one to work on a bit.

"Well, Doctor, if I recognize your accent and ethnicity, you probably have an appreciation for sushi and sashimi. Unfortunately, nothing much of that sort here, but—" he looked at the starters "—the *conami* cocktail here is a well-prepared and spicy raw shellfish on a salad bed. We have several officers of Japanese or Korean ancestry aboard and they find it quite tasty."

Socolov looked at the menu and shook her head. "Not as easy for me. I normally don't like to eat heavy meals, but it has been a long time between decent restaurant stops and it may be awhile again."

He nodded. "Well, there's a mixed *tungi* plate here, which is fried and broiled local vegetables, all fresh, with a spicy sauce. It's excellent. If you don't think you can eat it all and something else, I'll gladly share with you."

"Fair enough! And what for the main course, then?"

"If you like fowl, the duck is excellent, and it's true duck. It was imported here a couple of centuries ago and has become a main protein source. I'll be stereotypical Navy and order the fillet, so there will be a good representative of local things on the table. The local blush wine might cover us."

"My! You *are* the gourmet here!"

"Well, I've been stuck here for months, so there's only so much you can do. The joints near the base are really joints, crawling with bugs and lowlife and with food and drink that makes the stuff on a Navy frigate seem good, and the on-base clubs are very limited. I try and get away once in a while to the city for something decent, even if it costs me an arm and a leg, because it is the only civilization I get, and, like you said, it might be a long time between decent meals."

"This meat and fish and fowl is all true animal matter?" Takamura asked, dropping a slight bit of reserve.

"Yes, the real thing."

"I did not think they still killed things for people to eat in civilized areas," she responded, sounding more concerned than chilly. "It seems so—*unnecessary*. Cruel and unnecessary, considering how perfect synthetics are these days."

He shrugged. "Some people just think that the real thing has a taste and character that the best synthetics don't. Sometimes that means all the things you forgot, like gristle, bone, inedible parts, but there's a mystique to it. You can get natural, all-vegetable dishes here, of course, if that is what you require."

"No, I—I believe I should not eat here. This is a place of

death that pretends to be a place of delight. I cannot support it."

"Then I won't eat, either," Socolov told her, and everybody got up together, much to the consternation of the waiter and maitre d'.

"No, no! Please! This was a mistake! I should have known it! I will get a taxi back. You remain and eat a good dinner and we will speak later."

"You're sure?"

"Do not worry! This man will make sure no harm comes to you, I think."

"But perhaps not to you," he responded quickly.

"Eh? What do you mean?"

"Call for your taxi from inside and remain there until it arrives," he advised her. "There was a man across the street in the shadows when I came in who only had eyes for this place, and he wasn't looking for me. This can be a dangerous place, in this day and age, when so many desperate people feel they have no reason to remain civilized."

It really got to the physicist, and she walked over, ignoring the maitre d', and peered out. "Where?"

Harker walked over, looked out, and squinted. "There! In the alley over there and to the left of the store. He's smoking something. You can see the burning ash every so often."

She frowned. "You see much better than I do, apparently. Oh—yes, I see what you mean, but it would never have occurred to me that it had anything to do with *us*."

"I told you, ma'am. I'm a cop. Would you like me to make the call for you, or would you prefer I escorted you to wherever you wanted to go?"

"No, no, that's all right. Go back and have your dinner. I will take care of myself. The young lady has been under a lot of pressure of late and she can probably use a pleasant evening. I was talked into this but now realize that I do not wish to be here."

"As you wish," he responded, and went back over to Katarina Socolov. He was a bit proud of himself for doing that to both the Doc and Mogutu. Now the mercenary would have to decide who to shadow, and Takamura would think she was being menaced. Two birds with one stone.

"Goodness! You don't think we're in any danger, do you?" the anthropologist asked him.

"I doubt it. But it's best to take no chances with things like that. Come, relax! Let's make our order and at least have a decent meal."

Over dinner—which she barely picked at—the two exchanged some small talk, he told her some true stories of his early life, the ones that you could still eat while listening to, anyway, and she opened up to him, if only in a generalized fashion.

"You're a full doctor of anthropology?" he said, trying to sound amazed. "And you're *here*?"

She laughed. "It's not as amazing as all that. I'm fairly new, I'm heavily in debt with no close surviving family, and I've just finished a project with my old mentor and publication's near. There's not much call for my line of work in the remaining universities right now, and I needed funding for fieldwork, and I got an offer."

"For a field study? Where? Surely not *here*? There's not much anthropology on this dirt ball unless you want to study the dynamics of the common roaches when they reach fertile new planets."

She laughed. "No, not here. I only found out where 'here' was when I decided to make this little foray. I gather we were all supposed to be off and well on the way, but instead we've been stuck here in orbit. Surely you must know that."

He nodded. "Yes, you're the talk of the spaceport,

really. I've even met a couple of your passengers. I assume that they're not all on your expedition. That ancient opera singer wouldn't be much good in a fight."

"Oh! You met Anna Marie! Isn't she *fascinating*? Where did you meet her?"

"In a bar inside the spaceport, I'm afraid. She came in and asked whether a fellow who happens to be at the top of the Navy's ten most wanted criminals list was here. Then she rushed off to the ship. A few others have come through this way, too. I gather you were already aboard?"

"Yes, they picked me up at the previous stop. Interesting about the criminal. What's he done?"

"He's a pirate. I know that sounds like an ancient and outdated term, but there's no other word for it. He attacks and loots transports. He's not only stolen a great deal. He's murdered a considerable number as well. The mention of his name is one reason why everybody's so curious about your ship."

She seemed to think something over, then nodded. "I can understand your interest, then. So this wasn't an accidental meeting?"

"Well, yes and no. I'm off duty, nobody assigned me to come and have dinner with you, but I happened to hear that the shuttle was coming down and that the taxi had been hired for here. I decided to see if it was anyone familiar or someone new, and, in the process, get an excellent meal on the expense account—all of which has happened. Satisfied?"

"Yes, I suppose so. It's kind of disappointing that it wasn't more of a chance thing, at least for an evening. I'll be off soon and that'll be that, the way people come out of those holes different ages and such." Something seemed to strike her suddenly, a thought she hadn't entertained until now. "You know—I suppose that work I did *has* been published by now. Probably long ago back at the university. Professor Klashvili was getting on in years when I left him. He's probably well retired now, unless he's dead. Strange. It makes me feel so—cut off. He and the department and research assistants back there were the closest thing to family I had. Does it get to you like this?"

He nodded. "It did for a while. Then, over time, you get used to it and you simply don't factor it in. You try not to establish any long-term relationships with people who aren't going where you're going, for one thing. We get to thinking of our ship and company as our family."

"You don't have one of your own?"

"No, most career Navy don't. If you decide on a family, you wind up on a base and on port duty, period. You don't go into space again unless you take the family with you, and Navy vessels aren't built for real families. Spacers just don't have homes except our ships. A lot of us are orphans—of which there's a ton now that migration has turned to refugees overrunning all creation—or greatly estranged. Just make sure that when you decide to settle down, you settle down in a place you can grow old and die happy in."

She stared at him with sad big brown eyes. "And where's that, Mister Harker? Where's that?"

"That's the problem, isn't it? If we could just make a jump to another arm, we'd have an escape route, but nobody who's ever tried it ever came back. I dunno. So, let's get on a happier note. What *is* your specialty, anyway?"

"Retrogressed cultures," she responded. "There's a ton of them out there even now. Early religious colonies that got themselves deliberately lost and wound up building very primitive societies when they were cut off from The Confederacy, social experimenters, political radicals wanting to build their own colonies, that kind of thing. Mostly they cut themselves off on marginal worlds off the beaten tracks centuries ago, and they all thought, of course, that they could build a higher or better culture with no dependence on the old system. In many cases it's less anthropology than recent archaeology, since they die out a lot. The ones that succeed can quickly become bizarre, even in a few short generations. They are, however, the finest living laboratories on human behavior and cultural evolution that exist, particularly since it's unethical to deliberately do it to people or groups."

"Got an example?"

"Hundreds, but I'll just be general for now. The one rule we have found to be eighty percent true: people as a group will survive under the most incredible conditions, and sometimes even thrive. There *is* a significant deviation but primarily as a group dynamic—a charismatic leader or some such who leads the desperate and trapped group to mass ritual suicide or the like. For the most part, however, people find a way, often by doing things that would have been inconceivable to them before. We've found cannibalism developing in desperate situations far more than we'd thought, for one thing, and even if they find a way to get around needing it as an emergency food source, it tends to remain as ritual. The general consensus is that the first practitioners are unwilling. They must eat some of their number to get out of a particularly nasty situation or they all die. After that, they have to justify it to themselves or they feel guilty, often consumed by guilt and nightmares. So, to deal with it as a survival practice rather than as a one-time thing, it becomes some kind of religious experience."

"Seems to me that if you began eating your fellow human beings, you'd soon not have any fellow human beings. The last two survivors would be hunting each other," he noted.

"No, no! It's counterproductive if you do that, and you're right, they'd all die. But suppose you were trapped by a seasonal thing—subzero cold and snow, or a long dormancy before crops appear, or a drought. Then it becomes more of an imperative, and after that it becomes something you have to justify to posterity. You keep it alive in limited form as a ritual—as many early human civilizations did back on our ancestral world—so that if the need arises you won't have to go through heavy moral judgments or angry fights to do it."

He considered it. "I often wonder what happened to any survivors who weren't captured or whatever the Titans do to survivors after one of those worlds gets changed. You think they survive, maybe underground?"

"Oh, I think they survive even on the surface. The Titans' ultimate objective appears to be, well, gardening."

"Huh?" He'd been dodging and weaving around the bastards for decades but he'd never heard that before.

She nodded. "The worlds they remake are uniformly in a temperate range that runs from sixteen to forty-eight degrees Celsius. That's basically subtropical to almost hothouse, but it's entirely within the life range of our race. Much of it is simply reseeded with Titan variations of local flora that can stand up to this range, lots of trees, lots of nutrient grains and grasses, but in the center of each growing area is a vast swath of, well, gigantic and exotic-looking alien flowers. You've certainly seen the photos. That's what they do. They move in and they start planting and raising exotic flowers. Perhaps they compete at Titan flower shows. Who knows? At any rate, on a majority of worlds they use hybrids we've introduced there in the past for fruit and grain, even things like vegetables and sugar cane and the like. It's possible to sustain a fair population on that."

"I knew about that. But they'd have to keep their numbers low to avoid attracting attention to themselves, and they'd be limited to totally nonpowered tools. Kind of an animal-like existence. I've seen surveys of worlds after a few decades that can show life-form densities, and we've never picked up anything that might be a significant population of humans. They're down there, but they're few and scattered."

"Yes, but they're still there. I would love to be able to find out what sort of life they were living down there."

"You could—but you'd be stuck living it for the rest of yours."

She sighed. "I know. Well, let's face it, Mis . . . Gene. The way things are going, that may be the only place we'll have to settle down and have families after a while. That and on gypsy ships wandering around space and trying to avoid the shiny new masters."

It was not a thought he liked to dwell on much.

The evening didn't end up in any kind of romantic tryst, nor had he expected it to, but he did take her out for a bit of play in a sim arcade—where she proved pretty good at the rather basic scenarios the game companies created—and even a bit of dancing. When it was very late, he took her back to the spaceport personally and called for the shuttle.

"Thank you," she sighed. "I had a wonderful time, and I really, *really* needed it." She paused. The smile and glow faded. "I guess this is goodbye, though, huh? Unless we're stuck here for another eternity, this is it. I'll go one way, you'll eventually go another, and even if we meet we might be fifty years apart in age. I might look like Anna Marie and you might look like my old professor!"

He sighed. "Could be. But, hey, you just never know in a shrinking universe, do you?"

Not when I want to go wherever you're going—not for your charms and company, nice as they are, but because I've got to know. He wondered, for the tenth time that night, whether, at the moment, she knew any more about where they were headed than he did.

SEVEN

The Stealers of Souls

Littlefeet was feeling both proud and sad after his confirmation into adulthood. The tattoos that now colorfully adorned his thighs were the marks of equality with all the grown men of the tribe, and he delighted most of all in showing off to those of his age who still hadn't gone the final steps as well as to those close to him who were in every way his extended family. Still, the mystique of the act, often talked about, regularly bragged about, and that held a kind of aura even when secretly observed, was now gone, as was the sense of the girls—women—as some kind of very different creatures. He had pleasant memories, even good feelings, when he thought of Spotty, and he wanted to see her again. That was certainly possible, but the Sisters did everything they could to break up or interrupt any real friendships between the sexes. Loyalty had to be first and foremost to the tribe as a whole, and every woman was wife and sister, every child one of your own. It was general policy, when possible, to pair off the young men with different young women each time, for no more than a year or so, so that such personal attachments didn't have a chance to flower.

Too, the women were virtually never left alone, even when gathering plants nearby or getting water well within the security perimeter. It was common for them to move only in groups of five or more, usually with one old and experienced woman, frequently one of the Sisters, so that the rules were observed. Of course, the rules were not always obeyed, as almost everybody except Mother Paulista seemed to know, but it took some patience and planning to get around them. If a boy and a girl wanted to be together, they would arrange to go off in groups at the same time, so that, even if officially paired with the wrong girl or the wrong boy, well, swaps were made to make it right.

For much of the next year, Littlefeet was able to meet and even lie with Spotty more times than not, and Big Ears was able to do the same with his own girl, Greenie, a tall and very muscular young woman whose most unusual attribute were her nearly perfect green eyes. Few eyes in the Family were anything other than shades of brown, just as the hair was almost uniformly black until it turned gray or white.

So it was one day that Littlefeet and Spotty were lazing in the grass by the side of a small stream, oblivious to the small flies that darted about.

"You are getting a big tummy," he noted.

She laughed. "Silly! That is where the baby is growing!"

He was kind of bowled over by that. Pregnant women were the norm in this society, since there was so much infant death and even old age was not very old, but the idea that Spotty would be a mother was, well, *weird*. Mothers were old, like his had been. Spotty was his age.

He was suddenly overcome with some very strange feelings he couldn't understand or cope with. "Was it—is it growing from my seeds?" Biology wasn't a fine point of education, but planting seeds into fertile soil was an easy concept to grasp.

She was uncomfortable with the question. "I—um, have you planted your seeds in other women and not just me?"

He grew suddenly sheepish. "Yeah, two. I mean, it don't always work but you got to go. It's duty!"

She nodded. "Well, me too. So I don't know whose seed it is, but it's most probably yours."

He felt a real rush of anger. How dare she lie with other guys? He knew it was a stupid thought, that she had no more control over that sort of thing than he did, but it bothered the hell out of him anyway. To keep some self-control, something a warrior always had to do, he tried to refocus the conversation.

"So—when's it gonna be born? Do you know?"

"In a month, maybe two. The Sisters keep track, but I'm guessing based on what I see in the other girls. You know most everybody my age is growing a baby? Maybe first time's the thing, huh?"

"What's it—feel like?"

She sighed. "Well, it's kinda hard to say. I mean, you start off being sick and throwing up every morning for a while, but the blood time stops and so do the cramps so it kinda evens out. Then you feel okay but you start eating like two people. Things start to taste funny and smell funny and you feel kinda fat and clumsy. But you also feel—*good* about it, about yourself. It's our main job. At least one of my babies, maybe more, will be new warriors and mommies and keep the Family going. That's kinda neat."

Now, for the first time, the real meaning of manhood hit him. Not fatherhood, but continuity and duty. It was her job and duty to bear as many babies as she could so that the Family would go on. It was his job, and those of the other young men, to protect the women who had this burden—even with their lives. He suddenly felt a sense of responsibility that had eluded him up to now, and at that moment, not before, he truly became an adult.

He didn't like it. All that wishing about growing up he now saw as foolish. Now he was there, and he wanted to be a kid again, but that part of his life was over forever.

Only a few weeks later, when the Family moved in the

traditional patterns it still thought random, camping at the outermost part of their lands, up against the tall and always snow-clad mountains to the south, it was brought home double.

Only at these boundaries was there an overlap with other Families. There was always some contact, and a mixing of families and seeds kept things from becoming too stagnant, the genes too inbred. The number of humans was still relatively small, but large areas were still required to furnish a totally gatherer-based society with sufficient food and essentials such as gourds, sticks, stones that could be sharpened, all that. That was why the overlaps were only at the perimeters.

They had expected to meet the Kuros Family at or near the traditional spot in the small valley that ran into the tall mountains, but the advance scouts saw no sign of them. That wasn't always a true sign—after all, part of survival was keeping yourself unseen—but the scouts were looking for specific signs and patterns from experience. Littlefeet was one of the point men for the scouts, since he was so small and wiry he could cover great distances while making himself next to invisible. He traveled armed only with a crude knife he'd made himself, a hollow reed, and a small number of thorns dipped in one of the natural poisons the women could distill from certain grasses found near the Titan groves. It was an effective blowgun, although only at very short range. Speed and stealth were the weapons of a point man. If he had to fight, his usefulness was already compromised.

Cautiously entering the valley by full morning's light, after having spent the night alone in a thick grove, he smelled the death smell first, long before he saw the scene.

They were Kuros for sure. The tattoos alone suggested that. Not the whole Family—that would have been far too much to bear—but a large number of men ranging from his age to as old as Father Alex. A squad of warriors, perhaps a dozen strong, the advance guard to scout the details and determine the camp setup, allowing for defensive positions, water access, and all the rest of those details. They had spears and blowguns and long knives and it hadn't done them much good.

A dozen men! Why, the whole Kuros Family probably numbered only a couple of hundred, so this would be a devastating blow. But what had struck them down? Why had they died?

After doing the most cautious and detailed scouting of his entire life, he finally moved in to examine the bodies. They hadn't been killed by Hunters, at least not by any Hunters Littlefeet had heard of. The bodies were barely touched. There was some blood, but it was dried on the corners of their mouths or even coming from their eyes. There appeared to be no hard blows, no evident wounds or penetrations.

They had died together, not in a defensive formation, and, guessing from their expressions, quite suddenly. They never knew what hit them, and that worried Littlefeet the most.

He wasted little time scouting for the cause after that. He might come back with a few others to find this out, but first the Family had to be stopped from coming in here, and, second, a detail would have to be dispatched to find the bulk of the Kuros clan, which certainly couldn't be all that far away.

This was something else new in a people whose universe was increasingly static. New things could kill.

Even as he made his way back toward his own people, he couldn't help but remember the strange body back at the big rock. Maybe he was cursed to find the unusual.

Mother Paulista would simply blame it all on the demons and scratch off another area as taboo, but it was beside the point if this was demon work. This was death by an unknown agent in a place where the Families had been coming and meeting for longer than Littlefeet had been alive. It was all well and good to proclaim that the demons ran the world and you had to flee from them, but the only way to put everywhere off-limits was to kill off the whole family.

Father Alex agreed and didn't like it at all. "I don't want you going back there, though," he told the young man. "I'm going to dispatch some older men who have some experience with strange deaths to do that, and I'll send Big Ears and a couple of others to locate the Kuros Family. You want to take a more daring single scout mission?"

"Yes, Father?"

"There are ancient tracks up through those mountains, where once people came simply to relax and enjoy the beauty of nature. Most are in bad shape, but where they exist they certainly show a way to climb. I want you to go up as far as you can, up to the edge where the water is white solid, as high as it is possible and still view our own lands, and to study all that you can see from there. Every detail. Everything is important, even the obvious. You must use all your mental training to memorize every last detail and be able to describe it here, perhaps even draw it in basic terms. I need to know what changes are being made, if any. I need to know if these things are the harbingers of evil. Take what food you will need with you. It is unlikely that there will be anything to eat up there, although water should be plentiful. Avoid contact with anyone, even a Kuros. You don't know who might be the slave and pet of the demons."

It sounded exciting. He'd never done anything like this before, and the stories of what the land looked like from high up were also hard to figure. "Yes, Father. I shall go, and I shall return as soon as I can after getting this information."

"Start now. It is a long journey and it is mostly straight up. And one warning. If you are so high that you can see the city of the demons, do not stare at it for long. Understand? If you stare at it, they will know, and they will most certainly come for you. Treat the city as you would the sun. Acknowledge it, but never stare. Remember this!"

"I will, I swear!"

He put together a pack of mostly dried grain and sugar bars, the kind of food that was filling and gave energy without taking up too much bulk or quickly going bad. His pack was a large, squat gourd into which vines had been double and triple sewn, so that you could carry things in it while it hung on your back. He did not like it, although everyone, male and female, carried the things of the Family from one camp to the next in similar fashion. That was in a slow and methodical march; this kind of work was quick. Both the weight and the shape of the thing would throw him off. Still, he knew that he'd be far more uncomfortable if he found himself way up there with nothing at all to eat. It was said that starvation was among the ugliest ways to go.

He also realized that Father Alex had more knowledge, or at least suspicions, of what was going on than he was letting on, but Littlefeet also understood that the good Father would tell only when it was in the interest of the Family to tell, and that he might just be sitting on the information in order to keep Mother Paulista from screwing things up before he had enough evidence to lay out his case for action.

It was fairly easy to see the tracks of the ancient ones from afar, a bit harder to find where they began when you got close enough to start needing them. Nearly a century of rain, wind, and total neglect had made them somewhat treacherous, too, but nature didn't erase trails cut through solid rock so easily or in so short a time.

By the end of the first day, in fact, he was higher than

he'd ever been before and quite surprised and taken in by the view. Things looked so much smaller down there, yet paradoxically, the world looked ever so much bigger.

He spotted the Kuros camp before sunset, but only because he knew where it was and some of the landmarks. It was amazingly well hidden from the air. Some of the seemingly stupid and needless precautions they took every time they set up now became obvious works of clever and foresighted minds. Knowledge of territory and scent would allow Big Ears and the others to find what was left of the Kuros, but he sure as hell couldn't spot them from here.

Before it became impossible to see, he found a nook where two rock slabs joined just above the old trail and was able to wedge himself in there. He had thought of staying near the small waterfall farther down, guaranteeing himself a water source, but the noise had been deafening. He wanted to be able to hear anybody or anything else that might be up here before they knew about him.

The rock was cool and hard compared to grass and soft earth, but he actually slept pretty well.

He didn't worry much about mysterious killers coming to get him. The kind of life he'd been born and raised into indoctrinated all of them with a sense of fatalism; it was all God's will, and what would be would be. However, that didn't mean you threw all caution to the winds, or forgot the old rule about God helping those who first helped themselves.

Still, his fears were basic: pain, crippling, loss, that kind of thing. Of the dangers he was wary and careful, but fear would only get in the way of what might need to be done. He had never killed anybody, and few things larger than birds and other tiny creatures, but he would defend himself. If Hunters wished to eat his heart and liver, they would find it a costly meal.

The next day he continued on up, finding the going a bit

tougher as he climbed. Parts of the trail had been filled in or knocked off by landslides or were too treacherous to trust. For those, he had to cling perilously to what footholds he could find and get around or across.

The wind was an unexpected enemy as well, not only for being strong enough sometimes to blow him off the side of a cliff but also because it was in many instances chilly, and he had never before in his life truly experienced cold.

The air temperature was dropping as well, and he found that it was more tiring to do things he always took for granted; he found himself short of breath for no reason. There was some kind of malevolence in these mountains he did not understand. The malevolence wasn't as personal as the Hunters nor as all-powerful as the demonic Titans, but he became convinced that it changed all the rules for its own amusement. It wanted to see how tough it could make things for him.

He was up very high by the middle of the second day, and he was beginning to feel downright cold. For the first time he understood the old stories and scriptures about coats and dresses and other kinds of clothing. It must have been cold in those places, like it was here.

The idea of seeing solid water up close no longer seemed so romantic, but it certainly was close. It was okay while the sun was up, but almost as soon as it went down, or even when clouds came over, the temperatures seemed to drop like a stone loosened by his foot as he climbed.

Exhausted, cold, gasping for air, before sundown that day he reached a point that was so high up that he did not believe he was still on the world. In fact, he managed to make it to the edge of the white stuff, the solid water, which was showing at least in patches here and there. He was so fascinated by it—by putting his hand in it and feeling how terribly cold it really was, by letting it melt in his mouth and proving to himself that the stories were true: this was in fact water—that he managed to ignore the temperature for some time. After a while, though, he knew he'd have to make a decision. Stay overnight up here and he might well turn to solid water himself, or so he feared. But to take his observations and then descend to where there was some shelter might require more time than he had. He had no choice but to chance it, and hope that one night up here would not harm him.

He searched around for someplace to stay and rest until the dawn, and he finally discovered, just a bit farther up, what proved to be a small cave. It didn't look totally natural, and it actually had a warm feel to it, but he managed to squeeze in and discovered that, indeed, it felt warm and very, very wet. It was also quite dark. He had already encountered a number of odd and unusual small animals and insects up here, some of whom had seemed very unfriendly; they would probably also find the cave a nice place, but he had to chance it. Warm was warm. Still, he found himself waking up often and brushing off things he could not see, many of which scurried away in the dark.

It was a long time until morning.

Morning, in fact, brought little relief and not much comfort, except that he'd determined that this was as far as he would or could come. Today he would observe as Father Alex had asked him to do, even with a pounding headache and feeling a little dizzy, and then he'd make his way down as fast as he safely could. He found his body was covered with small bites, most of which itched something fierce but none of which seemed to have a poison that might cause him any long-term harm. Some clearly couldn't get through his tough, leathery skin.

Emerging from the warm, moist cave, though, he found himself suddenly in a dawn only a few degrees above freezing, and this made him feel frozen all over. He ate two of the bars, tried to rub some circulation back into his limbs, and then found a ledge that seemed designed for the purpose Father Alex had in mind. In fact, it absolutely looked as if somebody had built it, probably the ancients who had used this trail in those faraway times. They wanted a place to stop and relax and view the spectacular panorama in front of them. He had the same objective, but while the beauty wasn't lost on him, he wasn't wearing what they almost certainly had been, and that made a lot of difference in landscape appreciation. All he wanted now was *down*, but until he got what he came for, that was a direction he could not go.

The valley that had been so vast when they'd camped in it seemed almost like a small crack, with a series of waterfalls going off the sides of the mountain and feeding, perhaps creating, the river that in turn had carved it. He could follow the river, which tradition named the Styx, from its meandering reflection in the rapidly rising sunshine.

The plain was also smaller than it seemed, although certainly it stretched far enough. He could see the larger rivers and other basic landmarks, including the rock where the ghost might still wait, although it looked like a tiny speck, and then way beyond.

The grasslands spread out in all directions. There were a few groves of trees here and there, but mostly the plain was treeless. Grass and grains much taller than a man covered it all. When the wind came in, the grass blew and seemed like a vast sea—not grass at all but water whose waves gently traversed the horizon, were in constant motion. He knew that down in those grasses were bushes and small trees that got no direct sun energy but produced various fruits and vegetables. Others were all over in between the grasses just growing wild in the ground, but they were evident only as slightly darker patches on the grassland quilt.

In the center of the plain, in the one area where people did not go, were the demon flowers. They were certainly pretty, particularly from up here, and as tall as the grasses, and with enormous flowers of golds and purples and reds and even silvers. They too, moved in unison, as if pushed by the winds, but, curiously, not as the grasses nearby moved. Rather, it was almost as if those flowers were blown by a different wind, a demon wind only they could feel.

He realized that the three Families that the plain supported had a system wherein they went round and round the demon garden in a series of overlapping circles until they reached common outer boundaries like the valley, after which they began to spiral back. Each of the three Families met the two others at some point without ever traversing the center or the same groves. It struck him that the so-called randomness of Family movements was anything but. They were as predictable as the times of the moons. If the demons were not stupid, which they certainly were not, and the Hunters were in any way competent, which they certainly were, then at any time at all the Families were, in fact, vulnerable targets. They hid well, but what is the good of hiding if your enemies know exactly where you are?

And with that it struck him that the Families had to be something different than they thought they were. If the demons and the Hunters, the forces of evil, could get them at any time, then they were being *allowed* to survive. Or, perhaps, they were simply ignored unless they got in the way of whatever the others happened to be doing.

The grassland plain was vast, but, off in the distance on both sides, he could see other mountain ranges, and he understood then that it was actually a kind of bowl. Only a three-sided bowl, though, for directly in front of him, almost at the horizon even at this height, was the great ocean, and to the far western side, probably where the distant ranges met the sea, was the city of the demons.

You couldn't miss it. Even from this far away, countless kilometers if he'd had any way to measure or truly understand the measurement, the eerie and huge place throbbed and radiated with energy and light. Unlike the sun, you could look at it, but what you saw made little sense. Bright, throbbing, an elongated egg shape from the look of it, with a single dark line dividing it into two equal halves horizontally. Smaller versions flanked it, and in back two bloblike towers rose.

Father Alex had said not to look, but it was difficult not to, even though the danger was most certainly there. How could they, so very far away, possibly know if one little man was staring at their city?

But they *did* know. They, or *something* of them. As he stared, finding it harder and harder to take his eyes off the distant alien-looking city, which had to be enormous to be so clear from this vantage point, he found himself almost going into a trance; the chill and the lack of oxygen and the fatigue just seemed to drain away. Not that they were gone—they just didn't seem to matter anymore.

And suddenly he saw that there was far more out there than had ever been apparent. Thin lines that looked to be made of nothing solid, of nothing he could comprehend, all over the sky, above him, below him, creating a complex but highly geometric three-dimensional grid that linked up with the distant city on the one hand and with certain points in the high mountains on either side and behind him somewhere. He had never seen them before, and did not understand why he had not, nor what they could possibly be, but they covered everything, the whole of creation.

He didn't actually feel their presence, either; nothing rummaged in his mind, possibly because it already knew that there was nothing of interest to it there. But, slowly, without his even realizing it, it was as if a part of him was being drawn out, as if scum were skimmed off the top of standing water, or more like the wisps of cloud that made Littlefeet who he was just breaking off and lazily drifting out over the edge and above the plain toward that distant strange sight.

As if something cared not about his body but was skimming off his soul.

A thick cloud broke off and away behind him and slowly drifted overhead, darkening the lookout and dropping the temperature. It continued on, sinking as it went until he suddenly found himself in a chill fog unable to see the distant place. It felt like a connection had been broken, and at once the discomfort was all too real.

Still, he felt not fear or anger but confusion. It was odd; he couldn't seem to remember who he was, or where he was, or why he was there. It was as if the humanity had been drained from him, leaving him only basic animal reasoning. He was tired and he was cold. He carefully made his way back toward the trail, which some remaining instinct said was the safe way to go, and then he started down, just wanting out of there, down from there, and out of the cold, wet cloud.

He had no idea then or later how he got down; everything was a total blur. When they found him, wandering near the base of the mountain near the entrance to the valley, he was dazed, confused, and didn't seem to recognize anyone.

Father Alex rushed to him as soon as he heard. The scouts who discovered the boy were quite right not to bring him back into the camp; no matter how well they knew him, they dared not risk the entire Family on what might have been a possession, conversion, or some other kind of trap using him. Besides, there were still a dozen unexplained dead men not far away.

"Littlefeet!" Father Alex snapped. "Look at me! *Look at me!* Look directly into my eyes. Look only at me! *Look!*" He reached out and his powerful hands forced the young man's head to face him. "Now speak! *Speak!* Say anything at all! Who am I? What is my name?"

Littlefeet's field of vision filled with nothing but the ruddy-faced bearded man's stern face and penetrating eyes. He was unable to turn away because of the strength of the priest's hands; he had to stare directly into them and listen to the shouting. Something inside him told him that he was in no danger here; that these were friends. Kin. *Family . . .*

"I—I—" he tried, but then he simply collapsed, limp, unconscious on the ground. Father Alex let him fall, then checked to be sure that Littlefeet had simply passed out and wasn't dead.

"Bind him," he instructed the warriors who stood close by, watching none too comfortably. "Run a spear through the bindings on his hands and feet and we'll carry him suspended that way. I do not want him unbound until I can get him to come around. Give him food, drink, whatever, but he is not to be unbound, understand?"

They didn't like it, but they did as they were told.

Littlefeet did not protest; he was sleeping the sleep of the dead, and it was more than two days before he awoke.

He came around and discovered that he was bound, and he struggled, but they had done a good job. His arms were behind his back, bound together at the wrists with strong, tough vines; his feet were also brought back and bound, then hands and feet had been tied together. They had varied this now and again to ensure that circulation wasn't cut forever, but otherwise he was on his side and unable to move more than his head and neck.

They had moved in the patterns, he sensed. This was not where he had left them nor where they had found him, but, nonetheless, they were where they were supposed to be.

The guard went and fetched Father Alex right away, even though it was dark and the priest was actually settling down for the night. He wasted no time making it over to Littlefeet.

"Can you talk?" the priest asked him gently.

"T—taaaal-ka? Taalk! Talk . . . ," he managed. It was hard to speak; the words would not come.

Father Alex sat the young man up against a rock and, with the aid of the guard, retied him so that his arms and legs were no longer bound together, but were still bound. It was then a long, patient night drawing him out, bit by bit.

In many ways, Father Alex thought, it was as if the boy—to him, Littlefeet was still a boy, no matter what the Family said—had suffered a brain seizure. Knowledge of medicine was pretty well faded, but he understood that much, and had seen its effects. He'd also seen this sort of thing before, with a more troubling cause—the one he rightly suspected had done it here.

Littlefeet was slowly regaining conversational abilities, but on a limited basis, having to think out each word as if doing so for the first time. It gave him a kind of pidgin that was useful for communication on some level, but it wasn't normal by any means. Father Alex knew that the lasting effects went in different ways depending on a lot of factors. Littlefeet might always have some problems, they might go away quickly or slowly over time, or he might suffer a second stroke and either die or be as good as dead. A lot depended on getting the sufferer back to some kind of activity quickly.

Even so, it was morning before a tired but satisfied priest had him to where progress was clear.

"What is your name?"

"No—no can think name."

"You are Littlefeet. Can you say that?"

"Li—Li'l . . . No."

It was tough on him, and he could see the young man was going through inner agony.

"Name," Littlefeet repeated. "No names in head. Like all gone. Know you, know me, know them, no names."

Over the next couple of days he was allowed a limited

freedom, always under guard but no longer bound, and was able to physically recover to some extent.

"Some of it is venom," Mother Paulista said after examining him. "He was bit repeatedly by rock spiders and some other things I cannot imagine. It is likely he got a terrible fever from it. Such fevers are known to damage minds."

Father Alex accepted that this was the probable cause of much of it, but not all. Littlefeet had become conversant enough to tell, in somewhat broken sentences, what he had seen up there, high in the mountains, and once he'd gotten past water as a white solid and warm, wet caves and the like, he'd told of looking out over the vastness of the world.

"You looked at the demon city, didn't you?" the priest pressed. "You looked even though you were warned not to, and it started to steal something from you."

Littlefeet nodded. "Yes. Steal what be me." He paused. "Steal names. My name. Your name. All names."

Memory was coming back, not as a flood but in bits and pieces, and there were whole experiences that were quite firm, from his first night of manhood to scouting the rock, but while the faces were there the names did not come back, and when he heard the names, it was as if he'd never heard them before even if they were constantly repeated, and as soon as the person left his sight, the name vanished from his mind.

"What did you see up there? What did you see that made you upset?" the priest pressed, knowing that Littlefeet had several times made references to intangible threats.

"Shapes. Dancing Fam'lies." He brought up his right hand and started tracing with his index finger. "Dance here and here and here and here, till you get *here*. Then you dance and dance backward to *here*."

"Who is dancing? Or what?"

"Us. We dance. Fam'lies dance. Fam'lies dance *now*. Everybody know but the dancers . . ."

There was something here, the priest knew, enough to discuss it with both the male and female elders of the Family, but what did it mean? Littlefeet had given up a part of himself but he had gained some kind of information, perhaps insight, that the Family as a whole did not have. This, too, had happened before, but just what wisdom had been imparted wasn't clear.

"The other thing he speaks about often is lines. Pretty lines," the priest told the gathering of elders. "Lines in the air that crisscross. I had him try drawing what he meant, and he came up with this." Taking a stick, Father Alex wiped a dirt area clear and then drew a set of intersecting lines.

"A grid, that is what it was called," said Perry, the oldest and therefore senior of the guard. He might have been as old as the priest, and looked even older. "We still use it, in a sense, to know where things are from season to season."

"These are on the ground?" Mother Paulista asked, confused.

"No, no, Mother! In our heads. We learn the grids as you learn the scriptures, and teach it to our next generations. It does not even resemble a grid at this point, but we use these kinds of dirt drawings to show where we go the next time, and the next, and where the water is, and so on. Our scouts use this knowledge to find the best places."

"I don't think he means on the ground," Father Alex agreed. "I think he means that he saw some kind of grid that went up to the sky as well as from horizon to horizon. It's not there now, or, most likely, we can't see it, but he is convinced of its reality."

"Stuff and nonsense! Fever delirium, that's all it is!" Paulista huffed.

"Perhaps not. Perhaps the demons use this grid somehow, and if you are high enough up there it becomes visible because you are looking at it from a different, downward angle. It could be any number of things, but the fact that he saw a grid, I think, is real. Others have reported this in times past, although not quite so clearly. The question is, what is it for and does it threaten us?"

"It can't!" argued not only Mother Paulista but many others, including Perry. "It surely would have been there since the Great Fall, and it has meant nothing to us or our survival even if it has been there all this time!"

Father Alex was not so sanguine. *All the Families in a dance, a whirling dance to here, then they stop and dance backward . . .*

According to a grid? A dance was a structured thing, whether done for pleasure or in ritual. It had to be. Something Perry said about the grid they memorized and passed on . . .

If it was random, why did they need a grid? And if it wasn't . . . ?

He decided for now not to press that point, but he was beginning to see what Littlefeet was getting at. *We're all afraid of becoming pets, of becoming animals wandering the garden, just another bunch of animals in the demon groves.* What if they already were? What if they were and didn't even realize it?

The more he thought about it, the more obvious it became, and the more frightening. This was suddenly so obvious, since it was so much of a ritualistic pattern in how and when and where they moved and camped, that it was incredible that nobody had seen it until now. Others had climbed, and others had also experienced the kind of terrible insight that Littlefeet had, but not that kind of information.

Why not?

Littlefeet had learned it at the cost of forgetting all names, even his own. What if that *wasn't* an effect of fever? Even Mother Paulista, who was always so keen to ascribe every bad thing to demonic plots and faithlessness among the people, had dismissed this as nonsense and the ravings of fever.

Had the ability of most of the people to follow this logic somehow been stolen from them in the night? Was there information, memory, certain processes that they were blind to?

That was a discomforting thought, but also a dead end. If you had been somehow influenced not to think of certain things or to see certain things, then how would you ever know?

And, if that were so, why did he see it now? *He* hadn't been up there.

Not in twenty years, anyway . . .

EIGHT

Riding the Keel

The daily briefing for all who had been stuck for so long aboard the *Odysseus* was getting to be a real yawner, but as long as they were in the project and somebody else was paying the bill, attendance was mandatory.

This particular briefing, however, had some excitement attached to it, and they sat there, waiting, with slight but palpable anticipation that, perhaps, at last they were going to move.

A packet boat had come through during the previous watch, and among the things it carried were sealed and encoded courier pouches for the *Odysseus*. It was known that the old captain of the ship, along with the Orthodox priest and the old diva, had been huddled for a couple of hours looking over whatever had come in, and that the robotic systems were testing and preparing visuals.

The group was pretty well divided over the length of the wait. A number, led by the scientists Takamura and van der Voort, thought that this was as far as they were going to get, and that it was something of a wild goose chase. The mercenaries were content either to go or to continue to train both themselves and the civilians in what was to come. It was pretty well known that Colonel N'Gana believed that it would be far better for most of the others if this did turn out to be a wild goose chase, since he didn't give them much hope of surviving any conditions that they would probably face were they to get a "go!"

And then there were Krill and Socolov, both of whom were bored to tears and just wanted *something* to happen before they died of old age. Krill felt certain that she'd swept the ship as thoroughly as technology made possible, and that nothing important was getting back to Commander Park. She was well aware of the tiny robotic bugs that kept crawling all over, but there were ways to limit them, or jam them completely if need be. Others had not been so kind about their discovery, but amateurs always believed that if you paid enough money and demanded that you juggle three planets and breathe pure carbon monoxide, then you should be able to do it all while singing your old college fight song.

One of the first things they taught would-be officers in OCS, though, was the ancient story of King Canute, who believed that he was king by God's grace and will and thus had God's powers. Irritated by the crashing of the surf on the incoming tide that disturbed his sleep, he marched out into the sea and commanded it to stand still and be quiet. The sea, of course, ignored him and he drowned.

The ones giving the orders and paying the bills were always the descendants of King Canute, whether private or government. That was why Krill, at least, had gone private. If you were going to have to work for idiots, then you might as well work for the ones that paid the best.

Madame Sotoropolis ambled in in her inimitable fashion and took a supporting seat in her usual spot. Krill and a few others knew what she looked like under there—although not how much was still human and how much was replacement—but most were more or less content not to know.

Father Chicanis emerged from behind the stage and stood at the podium.

"I have good news and distressing news both this morning," he told them without preamble. "The distressing news is that a new wave of Titan ships has deployed and is beginning to take over the Sigma Neighborhood. That's eight systems, eight planets. The Confederacy knew they were coming and got off what it could, but the wholesale evacuation of eight worlds is simply impossible, as you know. Unlike the first wave, when we challenged them and were destroyed, or the second, in which we were far too cautious and didn't yet know what sort of things they did, this time, at least, we managed to be set up to get detailed analytical measurements, including pictures. Their method of operation has not varied, but there do seem to be more of them this time." He looked to the back of the room. "Run sequence number one, please."

The screen suddenly leaped to life, showing a remarkably lifelike three-dimensional solar system against a starfield, a kind of shadowbox view of the inner planets with the sun blocked from direct view to keep the scene visible.

The military people had seen such footage before, but it was relatively new to the rest. It was public knowledge what the Titans did, but The Confederacy had thought it prudent not to allow the kind of graphic pictures that were possible. The resulting panic from what they now knew was bad enough; this sort of thing would simply serve no purpose.

There was a slight pan, and then, in the upper left, the formation of Titan ships appeared. They were, as always, apparently out of focus: flattened eggs with a horizontal demarcation line, but fuzzy and muted. No details were visible and even the yellowish color was a pastel.

They were large ships, but not that large, even by Confederacy standards. Although unitary rather than modular, like the *Odysseus*, the Titan craft looked to be a bit over a kilometer long and perhaps slightly narrower across, the orientation mostly taken from the direction of flight rather than from any feature that would indicate a pilot area, or, indeed, an engine module.

There were seven of them flying in a close-quarter V

formation, and they moved as one and banked and headed for the second planet from the sun, the one that was blue and white and was clearly the sort of place to support a large human population.

Suddenly there was an enormous flare-up in space as they passed a point between planets two and three.

"That's the primary genhole blowing," the priest told them. "Essentially the power required to sustain it is simply bled out as they pass—note that there were no signs of anything shooting from the ships, nor coming to them. When they are near and there is power, they simply absorb it. The gate loses its stability and essentially vanishes within itself, the hole that swallows a hole and becomes nothing. Anything in there at the time also is destroyed, or, more accurately, ceases to exist, but I'm informed that they cleared everything that they could and that no ships got caught, unlike the last encounters."

"Thank God for that," Madame Sotoropolis muttered.

"As they close in on the second planet, which is called Naughton, you see that there comes a fair amount of exchange. Magnify, please!"

The view suddenly filled partway with a no less diffuse and unfocused Titan ship and also showed some rather substantial warships bearing in and firing full. The energy pulses, torpedoes, and fusion warheads all were permitted to come in and apparently hit the Titan ship, but when they did, nothing happened. Nothing. No explosions, no nothing. It was as if they were all snowballs and had simply hit a mass of molten rock.

Now, though, the three large warships lost their own shields even as they banked to attempt to get away. They did not explode, they did not flare, they simply went cold and dark and continued aimlessly in the trajectory they'd been taking when it hit.

"All power goes instantly," the priest told them. "It

sucks it up so fast and so completely it barely registers on the instruments. Since there's also no life support, no lifeboat support, no environmental suits and space suits that will work, not even oxygen–carbon dioxide exchangers, normal ventilation, you name it, *everything* is instantly gone. Some of the poor souls may have hung on for a while, but the lucky ones died instantly. One will head forever out into deepest space; a second will fall into Naughton's gravity well and burn up; and the third will angle in and eventually fall right into the star. Other ships based on the planet and stuck there will try to rescue them somehow, but none will succeed. Now—see them begin to deploy. There is more ocean on Naughton than normal, and the continental land mass is huge but singular at the moment. They are deploying along the outer edges of the continent as you see now from this angle, and essentially encircling it. Once the Titans have established position, they will begin a broad coordinated sweep that will eventually take them over every single part of the land mass. As they pass, slowly and methodically as always, the power will simply go below. This takes some time, and is probably not completed now down there. However, take a look at the night shot here. Next sequence, please!"

The planet was now in night, and there were still signs of vast lighted areas. Cities were down there still, and a huge amount of humanity had not been able to get off. The Titan ships weren't even visible in a long shot, but you could see their effect on the coastal areas. There, quite discernibly, whole sequences of lights representing major places where people lived were simply winking out.

Father Chicanis continued, "The next step after this will be to establish a base system. With only one Pangean land mass, they will probably establish it equidistant from the edges of the continent. The seventh ship, probably the lead ship, will then detach a smaller vessel identical to the big ones and establish a center point in a flat area in the middle of the land mass. They will then set up an energy grid of a nature we have not ever been able to crack or understand, and, using that, they will begin the reshaping of the land."

"What about the islands? There are lots of islands in that humongous ocean," Katarina Socolov noted. "What about on the sea and underwater colonies?"

"They really don't care," Chicanis reminded her. "They simply ignore us. What will happen is that they will use the nexus they created to reshape the planet as they choose. Once they establish their ground stations, smaller ships, which kind of ooze out of the main ones like bubbles of oil out of a great slick, can extend the active force fields as desired. In Naughton's case, it may be that some of the people on the smaller islands and perhaps even some underwater stations will continue to exist, as the Titans have shown little interest in the seas and there are no islands large enough for their plantings. What they *might* do is anything from tilt the axis of the planet to nudge it into a slightly different orbit that would produce their preferred temperature range. That usually destroys any settlements such as you describe, but in this case they probably will not do that. Naughton is already very close to their norms on its own. They need only adjust the rainfall patterns, accelerate drift to create or eliminate some needed landforms and river systems, and so on. They will almost certainly also do a cleansing, as we call it, once they have set up their various nexus."

"Cleansing?"

"Yes. They will create an energy firestorm that will sweep the area in between their bases and meet in the center. This will eliminate all standing vegetation and probably whatever humanity is trying to survive aboveground. That's what we believe. A great deal of effort went into putting up shelters in underground units, even in old transport tubes and the like. It won't be very pleasant there, and there will be no fresh air flow, no lights, no nothing, but some people will survive and live off preserved foods and such for years. By the time the very few survivors emerge, they will probably be nocturnal, and very primitive, but they will emerge into a world which is hot, wet, and has a reestablished ecosystem. The Titans tend to foster fruit and vegetable growth, including both imported and native species, if they're in balance. A very small human population can probably survive on them. Our energy scans indicate that they range in tribal groups. But there will not be many, and they will be essentially ignored."

"Just what sort of population were we looking at there, Father?" van der Voort asked him, fearing the answer from the knowledge of past conquests but wanting to know anyway.

"Last census was a bit over a billion people," Chicanis responded gravely. "They managed to evacuate, oh, perhaps a hundred and thirty thousand."

That cast a sudden chill and noticeable pall across the whole gathering. Still, N'Gana shifted a bit impatiently. "This is old stuff, Father. Why do we need the gory details again?"

"Sorry, Colonel, but it's not completely old stuff to some, and it was necessary that everyone, I think, not only know the facts but see them in graphic detail. The reason why Naughton is a particularly important object lesson is that it is, in many ways, quite similar to Helena."

That caused a major stir.

"Helena has two continental land masses," Madame Sotoropolis put in from her perch in the center. "However, they are not all that far apart and, even with a gulf of perhaps five hundred kilometers between them, they are in many ways similar to what you have seen. The rest is sea.

There are active volcanic islands in the ocean which the Titans have so far not seen fit to shut down or alter. There is also volcanism scattered in among the high mountains that ring the two continents. Helena was designed to *our* specifications, although, of course, over a far longer period and using our more primitive tools, so there is a certain regularity. Two island continents, rather playfully called Eden and Atlantis. The Titan bases are set up much the same as you saw them there, only there are fewer of them. Eden, the more tropical of the two throughout and the planet's breadbasket, has only one primary base and then uses a half dozen small bases using the spinoff ships. Atlantis, which was where the major population centers were, has three large ships doing a kind of triangle system the way those seven did there with the larger single continent on Naughton."

Katarina Socolov took several deep breaths. Chicanis noticed and asked, "Are you all right, my dear?"

She nodded. "I—I think so. How old were those pictures, Father?"

He looked at a small screen in the podium. "Even allowing for temporal distortion, we are talking no more than two years here. Yesterday by the packet boat's clock."

"Two years . . . So, right now, that continent is a blasted plain with nothing growing, and out of a billion people a few—what? hundred? thousand?—survivors are huddled like animals in caves in near darkness eating jars of food and—it's *horrible*!"

"Tell me how to stop it and I'll blow those things to hell without a second thought," Colonal N'Gana put in, showing some uncharacteristic compassion.

"What's the real time clock on Helena now?" Doctor Takamura asked.

"If we left tomorrow and managed somehow to establish a genhole terminus in system without attracting the bad guys, it would be seventy-eight years standard," Chicanis told them.

"We left them and marched to the rescue a mere six years ago," the old diva sighed. "But in that time we have lived, *they* have been remade. That is the worst of all tragedies. Not just that we cannot help, but that no matter when one rides to help, it's always too late. Much, much too late."

There was silence for a minute or so there, then the priest continued.

"Because of the likelihood of this conference being monitored, we can't go into much more detail right now," he told them. "I think they are going crazy trying to figure out what this is all about, and, frankly, I was beginning to have my doubts as well. However, now we can both bid farewell to the prying little crawling monitors of Commander Park and this rather depressing little place and head off. The packet also brought the codes we have been waiting for. It appears that the Titan movement caused the delay in ways I suppose we will need to have explained. At any rate, from this moment on, all shore leave is canceled for any and all personnel, as little as we've done to begin with, and the captain, even now, is putting in his charts and requests to break port and head out. It will doubtless take a few hours for traffic control to clear us, and, of course, as much added time as Commander Park and his people want to delay us, but it is a good bet that we will be under way by twenty hundred ship's time this day."

"At last," several breathed, although there was also among the small group a sudden rise in tension as well. It was finally on!

"Once we are through the genhole, we will meet again here and in security discuss for the first time some of the more specific parts of what we aim to do. All of this, of course, still depends on a third party who might or might not come through, but we will see."

"In the meantime, parties should continue with their simulation exercises," N'Gana said firmly. "It looks like you may well need them after all."

Below, in the Officer's Quarters on the Naval base, a communicator went off like a fire siren.

Commander Park and Admiral Storer were aboard the tender *Margaite* now with Gene Harker and the chief. Harker's combat e-suit stood like a streamlined robot just behind them.

"This is still volunteer, Harker," Storer reminded him. "You don't *have* to do this."

The warrant officer swallowed hard. "Yes, sir, I think I do. Something tells me that if we're not, somehow, along on this then there is no hope. I would rather take risks and maybe go down than sit and wait for the damned Titans to come knocking. I just hope all the theory people back in the labs are right that this is possible for a human being to do."

"Oh, it's possible. We've had people do it, at least for one jump, in testing this sort of thing," Park assured him. "Of course, that was under controlled conditions with us knowing somebody was there, but it *should* work."

"Thanks a lot for the qualifiers, sir," Harker responded glumly.

The admiral looked at him. "Scared, son?"

"Yes, sir. Scared shitless, beg the admiral's pardon. This may be the stupidest thing I've ever thought up, but I'm not going to back out."

"Well, you're as checked out as we can make you," Commander Park said. "The suit's the top of the line, even has some protection features and capabilities that are still not available in contract models. We've done this drill many times in this old heap."

"Beggin' the commander's pardon, the *Margaite*'s no heap," the chief piloting it snapped.

"Fair enough. This is no time to argue aesthetics."

"Comin' up on the hull, sir," the chief reported. "Hold on, we're about to mate with the high energy power intake." There was a shudder, and the old chief nodded. "Now comin' up on the ship. You got ten minutes, sonny. Get in the damned suit now. Ten minutes from now I got to disengage or they'll know we're up to somethin'."

"They already know we're up to something," Harker noted. "They'd have to be nuts not to. I just hope they don't think about *this*."

He shook hands with the two superior officers and even the chief, and went back and turned his back on his suit. The suit walked slightly forward and enveloped him, and he felt himself drifting into the center. All of the life support plug-ins, instrumentation, direct links to the cortex were established, and he began to see better than ever, hear better than ever, and feel a little like superman.

"God be with you, Mister Harker," the chief said simply but seriously.

He stepped back into the hatch and it closed. It drained of air in a matter of thirty seconds, then the outer door slid open and he gave a slight kick and sailed out and almost immediately on to the hull of the *Odysseus*'s main cabin.

At this moment, the tiny receptors in his head were directly connected to and communicating at the speed of thought with the suit. He could, essentially, fly in space using tiny nozzles, by just thinking about it, and he floated away from the tender and just half a meter above the smooth, dull hull of the bigger ship.

There was no safe place to do this, but the design of the bigger ship put a series of large spokes emanating equally from around the midsection of the cabin. These were used for precise genhole injection, and where they were joined to the ship, there was quite a large indentation at the base of each. He picked the nearest one and settled down into it. Once there, the suit secreted one of the most powerful bonding substances known that could later be dissolved. In fact, ships were often repaired with it. It wasn't intended to take the place of true molding on a permanent basis, but many a warship had lasted many days in running pursuits and fights and it had held until they made it to drydock. It would cement him to the hull of the *Odysseus* so thoroughly that he would effectively become part of it.

So far the drill was going according to form. Now, and for many weeks if need be, the suit would generate or convert all that he required. He would not eat, or drink, or directly breathe, but those elements would be supplied or created as the monitors of every single square millimeter of his body told the suit he required. He would be, in effect, a disembodied spirit, and, before injection, even that spirit would be placed into a tranquilized sleep, not to awaken until there was a reason for it to do so.

If this group was going out to meet the real Dutchman, then he was ready to board and, if necessary, do battle and set tracking devices. If somewhere else, well, he hoped that this group believed that an extra experienced hand was more convenient than killing off a nosy hitchhiker.

He wished he could plug into that gathering once they'd injected, but to do that he'd have to be inside. He could communicate with them in real space, but inside a wormhole, whether natural or created, you were strictly incommunicado.

Commander Park elected not to hold them up anymore. In the little time he could finagle, there didn't seem to be anything more he could do that he hadn't already done anyway. At twenty hundred hours, the *Odysseus* gave a shudder and came to life like some great prehistoric star beast suddenly waking up and needing to prowl. Automated pilot programs handled all the undocking and everything up to and including injection. The ship's onboard computers and even her live captain were basically redundancies, just as Eugene Harker, in his much smaller environment, was.

The great ship quickly picked up speed. First the space dock and then the entire planet began to rapidly recede with little or no sensation inside or out. Harker was still conscious and still thinking about whether or not he was committing the stupidest act of suicide in recent memory. It took the form of a dialogue, only he was the only one speaking.

Okay, so why wasn't this a job for a good bioengineered robot? he asked, trying to convince himself that he was in fact useful.

Because, if there are Titans involved, not even the old lady's lower parts would work, let alone any form of robot, no matter how much of it was quasi-organic. If it was a machine, they'd eat it.

So what are you *right now but a lump of biological material lying inside a big machine? Some help you'll be if the Titans show up!*

Maybe. Just maybe. We'll see . . .

The ship continued to accelerate and steered itself for a large structure floating in space, one of three in the area. These looked like giant squares, kilometers high and wide but only a hundred meters thick, and within them was a void that could not be described. Even a vacuum was *something*. How does one describe *nothing*? Many had tried, none had succeeded, but even those who saw it regularly tended to feel as if there was a total wrongness there, that even "empty" had to have some meaning.

The genhole was connected, through a kind of warp in space, a folding of space-time, with another at a predetermined point. You couldn't just go faster than light in a practical sense—even if you weren't quite doing it in a literal sense—and come out where you pleased. Each "hole" was still a sort of tube that needed another end. That was how Harker and Park and the rest knew where the ship was going, at least initially. They had to file plans so that ships were not crashing as they emerged from one or another, and, of course, it was a good way for the Navy to know just where everybody was heading. Of course, that assumed that all of them were charted, that all of them were legal, and that those which had been in areas no longer on the service lanes had been deactivated. In no case were these assumptions valid, of course, particularly not in this day and age.

The spokes along each segment of the *Odysseus* now hummed to life, and blanketed the entire outer hull with an energy shield. Fortunately, as it was supposed to, that energy shield considered Gene Harker a part of the hull and blanketed him as well.

The tip of the forward spokes now activated, throwing energy beams that struck the surface of the genhole. At this point the ship pitched slowly, until the twelve radiated lines on the ends of the spokes hit the precise spots of a similar grid just inside the genhole itself. At that point, ship and hole were locked on. There was a sudden heavy burst of power and the ship aimed right for the nothing in the middle. Perfectly aligned and oriented, it struck the outer surface.

Watching this from a side angle was something technicians always loved, no matter how many times they'd seen it. A huge, elongated modular ship crashed headlong into a block only a hundred meters thick and kept going until it was apparently consumed: it was always an awesome sight.

Just before injection, Gene Harker's suit decided it was time to put him to sleep.

Even so, he was awake and aware when injection actually arrived, and he *felt* it: a weird, bizarre feeling that combined a crackling heat and the deepest cold all at once, and sent a roar with the sound of a cyclone's winds through his unhearing ears. It was probably the drug and the fears and imagination of his mind, but he could never be sure.

Father Chicanis felt a bit more free than he had in some time. Admiral Krill noted that there were still some of Park's bugs crawling around, but they could hardly transmit and they didn't have much data storage abilities. And, since they weren't coming home for some time, it didn't matter if there were all sorts of recording devices on the hull. Let them be there, for all the information they could transmit back in the same year it might do anybody any good.

"You all know that Madame Sotoropolis and I are from Helena," he began, "and that this is about returning to our world. But it is not precisely about that, because merely returning, this late, would do little good. It is almost certain that everyone we remember and love down there is dead, and perhaps their children as well. We can only pray that *some* survive. You cannot believe the tragedy of this."

Colonel N'Gana thought that it was nice that the really rich folks got out to mourn the rest, but he said nothing. The mere fact that the very rich and powerful thought they were moral and proper human beings was why they always acted so insufferably that they inevitably caused themselves to be hated and occasionally overthrown. He was not, however, one of those particularly moved by all this Greek tragedy.

"We have been aware for some time that certain elements, apparently criminal, mostly from the services of previously conquered worlds and thus now off the registries, have been eking out a clandestine existence in conquered areas of space," the priest went on. "They live on their ships, they stay out of the way of the Titans, and they establish nothing near them that would attract attention. What they need to survive and cannot get from whatever they can mine or process, they have been known to steal. It pains me to have to deal with these sorts of people, but there is a greater moral good at work here, I feel certain, and they are at least understandable."

"How do they get around out there?" Takamura asked him. "I mean, we saw the gate for that world implode as the power was drained."

"True, that happens, but not all gates from the conquered areas are deactivated, nor those in the path of the invaders," Chicanis told them. "And, frankly, they have been able to deploy or make some of their own for smaller vessels. We will be into that network in a few days as we switch back and forth until we reach an outer point where there is, well, an extra genhole in a place too close to the Titans to be still used. At that point we will switch to *their* control, and the pirates or freebooters or whatever you wish to call them will control the navigation. The one we will be meeting, as you know, calls himself the Flying Dutchman. Most of them use quaint, sometimes antique names to disguise themselves or perhaps even characterize themselves. We have been waiting for the Dutchman's signal, and now we are going to meet him inside the territory he controls."

"Goodness! Do you mean inside *conquered territory*?" Katarina Socolov found that news unsettling.

"Yes, and no. Space is very big, and the one advantage we have, the same advantage *they* have, is that the Titans simply don't care about us. We are irrelevant to them unless we make ourselves intrusive. They will not go hunting for us. They want our worlds, for whatever purpose."

"I've heard of this Dutchman. He's a killer and a pirate," N'Gana commented gruffly. "What the hell do you want that requires him?"

"You misunderstand, Colonel," Madame Sotoropolis put in. "We have no interest in the Dutchman. It is the

Dutchman who has an interest in us. In other words, neither I nor any of my people contacted *him*—I don't think any of us would have known exactly how to do that in any event. We were sitting around casting about for some way to get back at those fuzzy creatures or whatever they are that stole our world when *we* got a call from the Dutchman.

"It was simple and to the point. 'If you wish to take a chance and devote the personnel and resources, I believe I have a way that can not only hurt the Titans but can drive them off our worlds. If you wish to take the risk, the coded addresses that follow will reach me. If you do not, do not bother to reply. In ten standard days, I will make this offer to someone else.' "

"That's *all* you got? That's *it*?" Admiral Krill responded. "Why, that could have been *anybody* claiming to be the Dutchman! It could be a hoax, or some Confederacy security plot, or simply an attempt to draw you into the clutches of freebooters so they can hold you for ransom or worse."

"There was, quite naturally, a lot of follow-up," Father Chicanis put in. "We replied, of course, and in due course we were sent just a small part of a thick data stream. The source was definitely a defensive computer system, and it contained some very interesting but incomplete data. The point was, we knew from the header ID that it had come from only one place."

"It came from Eden," Madame Sotoropolis sighed. "It came from the surface, or beneath the surface, of Helena."

"Now, hold on! That's *impossible*!" Juanita Krill responded. "There's no power down there for a computer system. There is no power at all once these—these—*things* take over! Never have we seen or measured one bit of anything we know of as a power source that was not the Titans' unique physics."

"No physics is unique," Takamura interjected with irritation. "Like 'magic,' unique physics is simply physics we don't understand yet."

"Fair enough. But there's nothing down there, right? It's dead."

"It is," Colonel N'Gana agreed. "I was a part of a high-risk scan once in the early days of the second wave. We took tiny ships so small they would be hard to track even if you were looking for them, loaded only with deep scanning equipment, and we overflew two different Titan worlds. Almost got their attention on one, but they didn't pursue and we got away before they could put an energy hook into us. But there was nothing down there. We could have picked up a battery for a single electric torch, I think. Nothing."

"Nonetheless, this was from Helena, and from beneath the surface," the old diva insisted. "We had the header and a lot else confirmed."

"All right, we *think* we know how it's done," the priest added. "You yourself noted that there were a few pockets, islands or undersea stuff, where the Titans didn't seem to bother. That's not generally true—they usually drain it all—but on Pangean worlds like Naughton and Helena, even if they do a complete sweep and drain, they don't maintain monitoring over the entire surface of the world. It's wasteful. Once you've deactivated everything, why bother? In the case of primary land planets and planets that have a number of irregular and distant continents, they establish their permanent energy grid over the whole surface, it is true. But on these planets, they often just put anchors at the poles and allow normal rotation to keep the sweep and drain on. That means, first of all, that even a Titan's power has limits. That's comforting to know. Secondly, it means that, while they are continuously sweeping, they only have a round-the-clock energy cloak over the continents. The rest they sweep in two pole-to-pole lines. For example, if the complete day was twenty-two hours standard, as it is on Helena, the area outside the continents would be swept and monitored for power and activity only once every eleven hours."

"My God!" van der Voort breathed. "If you knew when the sweep passed, you could actually get down, if you avoided their probes and used a region over the horizon for the continents, and have eleven hours before you would be detected and whatever you had turned off!"

"Or, if you had something that could move at a decent clip and you had that knowledge, you could follow along in the blind spot for quite some time," Chicanis agreed. "That's what some of these privateers have done. They get down in the holes on selected worlds, probably to island or underwater bases. Why they do it we're not sure, but that's what's indicated by the readouts this Dutchman sent us. We think they're scavenging. Below the surface there's a lot left to scavenge, even after all these years. Mostly data. Information, on data cubes and blocks in the old computer cores. Imagine what somebody like the Dutchman could do with a full-blown planetary protection system of the Navy, even if it was out of date!"

"But what good does this do?" N'Gana wanted to know. "I mean, this *must* be known, at least in theory, to The Confederacy, but so what? They can't assume that this scavenging is going on or do much to stop it, all things considered. And, beyond that, all it is is dropping in, running about, picking up something inert, trying to make it back to a window area somehow, and then getting picked up. It doesn't hurt the Titans, doesn't tell us anything more about them except that, like us, they will conserve their power and manage their installations efficiently where they can."

"That's true, it wouldn't do The Confederacy any good to know it, which is probably why it's never brought up," Chicanis agreed. "But it appears from what they sent us as a sample, as it were, that one of the scavengers actually went down to Helena and somehow made it to Eden, one of the two main continents. He appears to have found something there, somewhere, deep underground, that hadn't been fully drained. If we went there, perhaps we could find out. If even one battery remains, then there is some way to shield things from them. That could be the break we've been praying for. So far we've found nothing. He did. He found it, but apparently when he turned it on, *they* instantly found *him*. In spite of that, he managed to actually send the first broadcast, from just beneath the surface, of an actual defense intelligence dispatch since the Titans took over. It was short and sweet, and the odds are he's dead or whatever they do to humans down there. But in that brief period, an enormous amount of information got sent. Something so important he was willing to give himself away to send it. And that, my friends, is what we are going to get from the Dutchman."

"But—this is wonderful!" van der Voort exclaimed. "I mean, think of what you have just said! Energy shielded until used. We've never accomplished that! And a *broadcast*! An *activation* of an ancient defense unit! That's astonishing! The leads that this suggests, the mere fact that it happened, open up countless new areas for research! This is not something we can morally or ethically keep to ourselves! Given sufficient resources and data like this, we might yet find a way to act against them!"

There was a short period of silence again, and then Father Chicanis put a bit of a damper on all the joy and enthusiasm. "Um, Doctor, just *what* would you tell anybody? What evidence would you use to back it up? Where is your data to get the personnel, funding, and labs? You see the point?"

"Why, I—uh . . ."

"Stories like this have been around for years," Krill added. "I never believed any of them. Wish fulfillment."

"Believe this one. The data sent checks out," the old diva told her.

"But—if this is true, then it's the possible salvation of the human race!" the mathematician pressed. "Nobody could or should keep this to themselves, or *market* it!"

Colonel N'Gana snorted. "Um, yeah, Professor. You don't get out much, do you?"

"Huh?"

"This Dutchman's a pirate and a killer. I doubt if he cares if humanity is mostly stamped out, and the allied races with them, if he can be the survivor, maybe with a few like-minded freebooters. Besides, even if he did suddenly turn into this great altruist and savior of all The Confederacy, just how do you propose he go about it? Mail a copy of this report to the nearest Naval Intelligence district? Pop up in full view like several of you seemed to think he'd do back at that joint? No, I do think maybe he's not so far gone that he doesn't want it to get out, but he's doing it his way, the safe, sure, and possibly profitable way as well. At least now I can see the sense of this expedition. The only thing I want to know is, if we're just buying information, why do you need all of us? I can see the physicist and the mathematician. You want people who can test the data, and know how to interface with computers that can really test it. Even Krill, both for security, such as it was, here aboard ship, and to check out the inevitable codes if this is an old security device. But why two old fighting men like Sergeant Mogutu and myself? And, for that matter, why a cultural anthropologist? Unless you want to figure out what kind of culture these freebooters have built out there? And for God's sake why the Pooka, who's still asleep somewhere down below?"

"We were asked to bring people with combat knowledge and experience, if you must know," Father Chicanis answered. "You know the simulations we've been running, which were also at least partly suggested by our yet absent ally. He also suggested the Quadulan, or Pooka as you call him. There is also the matter of the cargo."

"Eh?"

"Just judging from it and the evidence otherwise," the priest responded, "I would say that the Dutchman intends that at least some of us go down there and retrieve or do something he wants or needs done. Something he doesn't want to do himself, or have any of his other people do, if he has any."

"Down there. On Helena." N'Gana thought it over, but didn't seem totally put off by the idea so long as he thought there was a way out.

"Yes, on Helena. And we've invited Doctor Socolov, an expert on primitive and tribal cultures, to come along and keep us from getting speared and maybe eaten by our own grandchildren."

NINE

Night of the Hunters

Littlefeet only improved so much until they brought Spotty to him.

Something in him was convinced that she carried his child, and she did nothing to dissuade him. In fact, she thought for sure it was his, too, and she very much wanted it to be.

Her company was like strong medicine to him; he recognized her and remembered her name almost immediately. She was concerned, then pleased by his reaction, and took to calling him "Feetie," a name he accepted because it was from her.

Having her with him was very much against Mother Paulista's strict rules, but Father Alex, who not only felt guilty but also felt a sense of almost true parentship over the boy after so long, stood firm. The old lady wasn't used to defiance, but in the hierarchy he did technically outrank her, and he simply put his foot down. All the others could go as before, but, until Littlefeet was totally back to normal, he and Spotty would be a couple.

His verbal skills started to come along nicely as well, and, although there were gaps, he was becoming more like his old self as the days passed.

Now, as Spotty prepared a small meal for him, Father Alex was able to sit down with the boy and get some information.

"You looked at the demon city, didn't you?" he asked the boy. "And it did something to you."

"Yes, Father. It—it *took* something. A part of me. I don't know any way to say it but that."

"I know. Up there you are particularly open to it because it is in the direct line of sight. I, too, have been up there, when I was younger, my son, and I, too, looked at the city. In my case, it was God's intervention, or perhaps chance, that I did not suffer as you did. Just as it was taking hold of me, some snow loosened and came down in back of me, pushing some gravel, and it knocked me off my feet. It took all my will not to stand back up and look at it again, but God was with me and I did not. I had hoped He would be with you, but for whatever reason He allowed it to go further."

"What would happen to someone who never could look away?"

He became grim. "I have seen them. They were in many ways as you were when you came down the mountain, but we could never get them back. All of their reason, their memories, their very sense of being human, was drained, leaving them no more than mindless animals. Eventually, all were killed lest their souls, now in demon hands, be used against us. I am truly not sure if that is the case, but it was believed so, and it was probably the best for them, as they were truly lost."

"I—there is a tiny part of me, particularly when I sleep, or when the storms rise in the early night, that is there as well as here. Is that an evil thing, Father? Am I cursed?"

"I—I don't know, my son. I truly do not. I think you might have been, but for your lady here. Your love of her, and hers of you, has shut them out. They may call, but they cannot come to you so long as this blocks their way. This way—one man, one woman, in love and union—is God's way. The way we are now is not. It is a plan devised by material humans. Survival!" He spat. "What good is survival if one is always to live like this?"

"I do not understand you when you speak like this," Littlefeet responded, "but I know you are speaking wisdom from the words of God and so I listen."

Father Alex smiled. "It is not necessary that you understand. It is only necessary that you let an old man, tired and aching and not much longer for this world, say old man things even if they mean nothing."

How could Littlefeet, or Spotty, or most of the current generation know and understand? How much did *he* understand, he who was steps closer to when people had ruled and all the magic was theirs?

"You say they come to you in dreams," he continued, shifting back to his original focus. "What sort of dreams? What happens? Are they the same dream or different dreams?"

"The same one, which is why I know it is not just a normal dream, Father. We are here. The Families are here. And we dance. We dance around in circles, round and round, round and round, then we dance up to another Family who dance in the other direction and we bump and then we dance back. I am dancing, too, but at some time I look up, and I see shining things above and they have vines made of lightning and they are spinning them and making us do the dances."

The priest had heard all this before, he knew, yet he could not keep it in his head, not for long. Why couldn't he? Why didn't the Elders remember talking of this very thing the next time they met? And why did Littlefeet seem to be the only one who remembered for any longer?

The priest had the context, which might make sense of it if someone could find a prophet or seer, but he couldn't keep the puzzle around, real, in his head. Littlefeet kept seeing the vision, but only from the point of view of one who knew only this life and could imagine little else.

"Father?"

"Yes, my son?"

"Did they ever find out what killed that scouting party?"

"Not—exactly. Their bodies looked as if all of them had, at one and the same time, been struck by lightning. We know, though, that this is highly unlikely, and that in any case there was no storm through there when they died. It was decided that, for whatever reason, the powers of the air do not wish us to enter the valley anymore, and we have changed our routing accordingly."

"Father? Why do we not ever go as far as the great ocean? I saw it, I think, looking almost like sky in the distance, and it looked grand. It is something that I would like to see, if only to see that much water in one place. But we never go there."

Father Alex considered his answer. "It is—forbidden—to go to the coast. Not for the same reason as the valley or the stone mound are now forbidden, but for very real reasons. There is not a lot of cover near the coast, and roaming bands who follow neither God nor the rules of Families are there as well, like Hunters setting upon any who come and, like them, eating flesh, even human flesh. Many are said to be the children of Hunters gone wild, or escapees from the demon city who know nothing of what is true. We can take on small bands of Hunters because we are a group, organized together, scouting carefully, tight, close. They can get one or two of us, but they do so at the cost of their own lives in some cases. We make the risk too great. But out there, near the coast—there those types would outnumber us."

"And what of the pretty giant flowers I saw in the middle of the plain, covering it? I have been born and lived my life wandering here, yet I knew of it only by rumor and story."

"Those are demon flowers! They could suck the blood

and soul from anyone coming into their groves, and are tended by minor demons and demon slaves. For whatever evil reason they might have, they are what the demons do here. They plant and raise those huge flowers, and they tend them and they protect them. So long as we stay away from that area, they let us mostly alone."

Littlefeet should have known a lot of this, but his mind was curiously divided, both clearer than he could ever remember it being and yet curiously empty, with snatches here and snatches there but not a complete picture of what he'd taken for granted growing up.

"How are you doing now?" Father Alex asked him. "I mean, what is healed and what is not?"

"Oh, I am better, much better, and I think clearly," Littlefeet assured him. "But it is as if I see everything except Spotty for the first time. Like everything is new, and some of it does not come. All of the training I had growing up, which I know I had and can see being given to the others, it is not there. I do not seem to know how to do things. I go into the grass and I take scents and I cannot tell Family from others. Without the sun I cannot tell direction, and only from it when I see where it comes up or goes down. Everything looks and smells and tastes kinda the same. It makes me useless. The only one I can tell is Spotty. I can smell her, taste her, know where she is at any time. This is nice, but it does not let me give any work to the Family."

"I make sure he knows where he is," Spotty commented with a grin. "If he can always know where I am, then I can make sure he is where he should be!"

The old priest smiled. "Never in my lifetime has God so clearly made two for each other as the two of you. You are a mated pair. I know the others are calling names and making all sorts of jokes, but I tell you that they are the mistaken ones. You two are meant to be together. I shall try as hard as I can to keep you that way."

"Mother Paulista has said I must return to her for the

birth of the baby," Spotty told him, sounding upset. "And that she believes Feetie is just pretending to still be sick to keep me here."

Father Alex cocked an eyebrow and looked straight into Littlefeet's eyes. "Is that so, my son? Do you have sins to confess to me, perhaps?"

He could see the turmoil in the young man's mind as truth and confession to God warred against Spotty's continued nursing. "I—I am still not right, Father. You know that. I have said it."

"That's not an answer. What about you, Spotty? Do you think he's faking it?"

She didn't sense any of the humor in his query that Littlefeet suspected was there. "I—I do not know, Father."

"And what is it that *you* want?"

She was taken aback by the question; she'd never been asked such a thing before nor expected to be asked. "I—I want to be with Feetie, and I want to bear the child with him here," she answered truthfully, if hesitantly. "But I must bear many babies in my life. It is the—*function*—of the women, just as protecting is the function of the men. I—I don't know what to think, Father. Honestly."

Poor kids. He sighed and got to his feet. "I can promise nothing," he told them, "but I will see what I can do. And Littlefeet—if your dreams come closer, if you feel them winning, you tell me *immediately*. A tiny part of you can now feel a tiny part of them. If they sense this, they may react to it. We do not want any demons visiting us with vines of lightning."

It was night once more, and once more the thunderstorms built up in the sky, rolling in from the southeast as the breeze shifted to coming off the sea, then rising in the no longer sunlit air and also pushing up against the mountains. It was a regular occurrence; it would have been more unusual if it hadn't happened, although it wasn't a clockwork thing.

This time, however, as they spread out and waited for the deluge and covered their ears against the monstrous thunderclaps, there was something else there, something not immediately seen by anyone in the Family.

Shapes—small, stealthy shapes, moving through the tall grass under the cover of the storm, freezing still when the lightning flashed near, then proceeding on in toward the Family group.

They struck an outlying sentry as he waited for the storm to lift, and he was dead before he even realized that he'd failed in his mission.

The Hunters worked quickly, methodically, timing themselves perfectly by the storm, going after those most dangerous to them first, opening up a path body by body into the heart of where the night's kraals were established.

Suddenly, a more alert and capable sentry deflected a leaping, slashing attack and screamed a mixed scream of warning and terror that those closest could easily hear. It was instantly understood by others, who took up the cry and thus passed it along through the camp.

Littlefeet heard the scream as well, perhaps twenty or so meters over his left shoulder. Far too close.

He had no weapons; they had taken his away and he could not get them back until he was restored to full duty. He hugged Spotty, warned her to stay low and maintain courage, and moved out into the brush along with the older men from the camp.

They fanned out in the pouring rain, each perhaps two outstretched arm's lengths from the other, until they came upon the first of the bodies. Now they linked more closely together and the outer portions of the line continued to advance and swing in at the same time. Confident that no Hunter had gotten in back of them, they kept a steady mental beat that governed their movements, a practiced sense of timing gleaned from a lifetime of training.

Realizing that their presence was no longer a secret, but unwilling to back off, the Hunters also went into a practiced mode. They were far outnumbered, but they had a natural ferocity in them that their enemies had to create. A Family man, even a tough old sentry, needed some provocation to kill; Hunters loved to do it for its own sake.

The combination of the storm with its ground-shaking thunder, flashes of lightning, and tremendous volume of rain and the discipline of the two groups made for a nightmarish scene, but the momentum had shifted the moment the Family warriors had managed to form a tight V. The Hunters knew it, and decided to use one last-ditch surprise and the weather before they lost all advantage.

There were two of them, and as the two flanks closed in they leaped up as one right at the unmoving center. The center guards, however, had carved spears up, and one of them penetrated one of the two Hunters in midair. The momentum hurled the struck Hunter forward and threw the spear carrier flat on his back, but the wound in the Hunter was a deep and painful gouge.

The other had broken free right into a second guard, who took two feet in the chest and went down hard. Even as the second Hunter rushed forward, toward the kraals, the first one was just trying to get to its feet when it ran right into an equally startled Littlefeet. The boy reacted instantly, kicking and then leaping on top of the injured Hunter, who began to yell and scream like a horrible demon of the night storms. Littlefeet felt pain himself as something on the Hunter tore at his flesh, but he held on and just kept hitting and hitting no matter what. Other warriors came immediately to his aid and two spears came down directly onto and through the Hunter's skull.

The second Hunter had managed to leap free of the sentry line and now had a straight run at the Family camp.

The rain was already beginning to slack off, and the Hunter knew that there was little time left. A getaway was primary; while one Hunter could inflict real damage, it would also be at the cost of its life. Thus, it continued to run, slashing at a couple of older males who were standing a rear guard and heading then for the women's kraal.

The women had arranged themselves as a human wall behind which other women waited. As the Hunter approached, even in the near inky darkness they could smell death and a foreigner in their midst. Then the human wall screamed as the others rose up behind it and let loose a barrage of drugged thorns from blowguns. Most missed, but a few struck the Hunter, who cried out but kept coming. Only when the creature had virtually reached the human wall did it suddenly falter, seem to become disoriented, turn, start striking at the air and anything else around, and then go down.

The moment the Hunter fell, all the women were upon it with cries so terrible it even scared some of the nearby men. There was so little left of the Hunter by the time they were through, it was difficult to tell that it once had looked not unlike them.

Hunters always attacked in packs. Therefore, much of the balance of the night was spent with everyone awake, on guard and waiting, lest more of these dreaded creatures come. The camp kept quiet so they would not be caught by surprise again. When morning came there had been no more attacks. It was most unusual to find Hunters only in a pair, but perhaps the others had been frightened off.

Littlefeet rushed back to make sure that Spotty was okay. She was, but she gasped when she saw and felt his wounds, and it was only after she made him lie in the grass and went for aid from the women's kraal that he began to feel it himself. When it finally hit, the pain was incredible, but he did not cry out. Still, when she returned with mud and grain-based salves and some fermented potion that knocked back his ability to feel the pain, or at least mind it, he did not refuse any of the help.

When dawn came, he was asleep from the drugs, and Father Alex was over by him, concerned. Even Spotty gasped at the wounds: slashing strokes, almost as if made to take off skin, across half his face, much of his abdomen, and his right calf.

Sister Ruth, who knew the potions and salves, examined him thoroughly and then applied various salves from gourds she carried around her neck.

"Keep him asleep if at all possible for most of the day," she told them after. "And I will be here to apply more salve and balm as needed. Only a few of the cuts are deep but all are painful. I do not believe any damage was done inside that will not heal, but I expect him to wear most of those slashes as scars. He was quite fortunate with this, you know. The Hunter's claws were not poison."

Father Alex nodded. "Did you see the Hunter? The one that got Littlefeet?"

Ruth nodded. "So—strange. I never get used to seeing them."

Spotty made sure that Littlefeet was as comfortable as could be, with others nearby in case he needed anything. Then she said, "What does she mean? I have never seen a Hunter close-up. Not the body."

"Come, then," Father Alex invited her. "It is laid out over here, right next to the three of our own those two got before we stopped them. You should see the enemy now and again."

The figure looked surprisingly tiny in death, although the ferocious energy of its life and attacks magnified its presence then. The skin was a golden yellow-orange, with streaks of black and white going randomly all over the body. In the tall grass, it was virtually invisible until and unless it moved. The jet-black hair was short and wiry and only on the head.

The most prominent feature were the hands. They weren't exactly hands, but distortions of hands, in which the nails were not ordinary fingernails but thick, long claws that were razor sharp and extended a good ten centimeters past the tip of the fingers. The feet, too, ended in curved claws that looked as if they could slash as well as kick.

Nevertheless, it still looked very much like a young girl. Even a pretty young girl, in top athletic shape but just prepubescent. The curves were there in the body; it was very definitely female, but there were as yet no breasts or pubic hair. It was easy to guess that, at most, she'd stood perhaps a hundred and thirty centimeters, not much more. Her throat had been not just cut but slashed, but she'd already been knocked out by the drug in the darts, so there was a curiously peaceful look on her face. It was unsettling.

"So *this* is the enemy?" was all Spotty could manage.

"One of them," Father Alex replied. "If you looked in her mouth, you would find few molars—the flat teeth we have. They're all sharp, designed to tear flesh off bones rather than eat and chew. They also will die if they do not eat flesh, since they can not digest the vegetable matter which is all we eat. And since there aren't any big animals left, the only thing they can eat to survive on is us. I often feel sorry for them, really. They didn't choose this, nor did they choose to hunt us. I'm sure we look as familiar to them as they do to us. But they were not born to this, they were bred to it. They are in a sense the demon's wild children."

She shuddered. "Do they—I mean, she looks so *young*. Are there older ones?"

"There are many variations of them, but they all look very young and not very developed. I am not at all sure that they have sex. I don't know how they reproduce, or even if they do, or if, periodically, the demons simply create and release more. I don't think I shall ever be in a position where I can sit down and ask them about it, even if they were willing and able to tell me the answers. I've never seen or heard of a baby, nor a full adult. That says something; only God and the demons know the rest."

She turned away and looked at the others. In addition to Littlefeet, the two had injured five and killed three more. The bodies were now laid out near the Hunter's, and they did not look nearly as peaceful in death as the Hunter had. The first sentry's midsection was shredded almost to bits, and entrails and organs hung out in spite of their best efforts to make him at least presentable. A second's head had been torn completely off. It seemed incredible that such little girls as the Hunters could have the strength to do that. The third was the least mutilated, but had suffered those nails going repeatedly into his chest and abdomen, puncturing vital organs. He had most likely died later, during the night, of internal bleeding.

The other Hunter was in so many pieces they hadn't even bothered to gather them all together.

The real question in Father Alex's mind was, why had they attacked? If it was just hunger, and there were only the two, then the single outlying sentry would have sufficed. They could have simply dragged his body off and that would have been that; that happened all too often. Instead, they had kept coming in, kept attacking. A pack might do it, although it was extremely rare, but just two? They weren't attacking suicidally, either; they had *meant* to take as many of the Family out as they could.

Father Alex didn't like it one bit. Something was changing in a world whose only positive point was that it never changed. Twelve warriors from a related family electrocuted. Now three killed by Hunters who made an attack that was both well planned and executed and yet suicidal and seemingly without purpose.

He sighed. At least Littlefeet was back on the disabled list, so he could keep the pair together a bit longer. Not that it would help much in the end, and he wasn't at all sure Littlefeet was going to like the pain of the next days and perhaps weeks. He just hoped that appearances were right, and that there were no deep wounds.

But why were there wounds at all?

TEN

Enter the Dutchman

The one problem with interstellar travel was that time was always the enemy of truth. Not only did time go at a very different rate for those within the genholes than for those outside, it was next to impossible to send accurate and up-to-the-minute data on ship positioning and tracking. Up to *whose* minute, and when?

That was one reason why the Navy wanted a Gene Harker along, rather than a robot, however brilliant and clever, that was not prepared to improvise and understand what was possible and what was practical. Yes, humankind had made machines in their own psychic image who were smarter than any of their makers, and more versatile, but they still depended on being given specific instructions and goals in advance by people who could not know all the questions that might need answering. The most flexible and practical one to send on any such mission was a combination of the best of both: a human in a combat-hardened e-suit.

It was almost always the humans in their suits being dropped on hostile worlds or from ship to ship in normal space. Riding the keel was not considered a proven method of infiltration and travel. Harker wanted to prove it.

While the ship went through the genhole and those inside prepared for their own duties, watched additional briefings, or ran new simulations of their updated problems, Gene Harker slept, blissfully unaware of anything at all. There was nothing at the moment he could do, so, for now, the suit itself was awake and in charge.

The first switchover was monitored, noted, the data from the genhole gates read out and identified, and compared with known navigational charts. The suit determined that this was almost certainly nothing more than a switchover, and thus it did not awaken the man inside.

The *Odysseus* turned, and as soon as the automated systems on the ship and the gate meshed, it accelerated once more and went into yet another genhole, and all was quiet once more.

This happened three more times before the suit decided that there was an anomaly. The readout from the selected gate showed that it was inactive—that, in fact, it had been deactivated as leading to occupied territory. The *Odysseus* should have been unable to traverse the final distance to the gate, let alone go through it; collision alarms should have been ringing all over. Instead, the gate, shorn of the identifiable light system and internal glow that showed active gates to be properly functioning, swallowed the ship.

From that point on, the next two switchovers showed a variety of genhole gates that were in fact not encoded with any headers known in The Confederacy. The codes were totally different and, at this point anyway, totally unreadable. Nonetheless, the ship appeared to know the codes and the complementary mathematics and had no more trouble using them than it had any of the official ones.

The suit made a note of this. Genholes could not be reprogrammed by humans, even geniuses; it took the kind of artificial intelligence systems that required whole planets just to store the knowledge and compute the variables. The genholes had been placed by creating essentially random wormholes and then forcing the genhole gate through them. Only when this was done thousands, even millions, of times, and star charts made and compared, had it been possible to build and map a transportation network safe enough to send through real ships with living beings inside.

Going from a naturally occurring phenomenon to generating it themselves to being able to stabilize and harness what some called tunnels through space-time had opened up the universe to humanity. Its network created The Confederacy. A few other races had been encountered out there, some of which had interplanetary travel and at least one of which had been playing with generation ships, but none had discovered how to harness the wormhole principle and use it consistently.

It still wasn't easy to do or maintain. The math involved in programming each genhole gate was so complex it was done at factories and maintenance areas; genholes were replaced every few years, or they should have been. When the Titans came, it was feared that this same network could be used as a shortcut road map to lead them to all the choicest inhabited worlds of The Confederacy. Some were simply turned off, some deactivated, but most were replaced with special gates that used a far different and totally military cipher. This allowed Naval vessels to get into enemy territory if they had to, but nobody else, and each emergence through a genhole rekeyed the codes so that only the ship emerging could reenter from that point.

Nobody was supposed to have those codes except the highest defense intelligence computers. Even ships were supplied with them only on a need basis, and with rapid expiration. The suit knew this, and knew that, too, the *Odysseus* was applying those codes it should not, could not know, and doing so easily enough that they might as well not have been there at all. It made a note for future debriefing, if it ever occurred: *the damned superintelligence code system for occupied areas didn't work.* It probably never had. It was just too complicated.

It actually would have been a difficult thing for the Navy to discover on its own. When it used these genhole gates, they worked as they were supposed to. Nobody else even tried them because they gave off an "inactive" or "inert" signal.

It was lucky that the Titans appeared to use a totally different and still unknown means of accomplishing the same thing. Otherwise, the road map was wide open. It was in many ways a lucky break; just as they ignored all resistance, they ignored this as well.

"That is not my idea of a fair fight!" Sergeant Mogutu complained, emerging dripping wet and aching, not to mention stark naked, from the sim chamber aboard.

"I'm sorry, Sergeant," Katarina Socolov told him. "It's hard on me, too, but it's the best I can come up with to simulate what you might face on the surface of a Titan-occupied world. Nothing—*no* machinery of any kind—works. Food would be present but not easily obtained. I postulated no large animals because of the cleansing they do before they allow a regrowth, but there would still be person-to-person combat of some kind. You are back to the most basic ancestral state, Sergeant."

He glared and quickly put on a towel, then stomped off to the showers.

Colonel N'Gana, who was about to enter, stood there wearing only a towel and a headband. "You will have to excuse my sergeant for grumbling," he said to her in that very low melodious voice of his. "However, he will be a good man down there in those conditions. There is little call now, nor has there been for ages, for hand-to-hand combat and basic resourcefulness in the military. That is why we are able to command the fees that we do."

She looked down at the control board. "Well, Colonel, I can certainly accept that you will be at least capable down there if my guesses are anything close to correct. You appear to have beaten the sim most of the time. Your sergeant beat it three times, and nobody else has quite beaten it yet. To what do you owe your remarkable record?"

The colonel flashed an evil grin. "It is because I dispatch any potential threat before it can be a threat to me. It is because I am devoted entirely to winning every such contest or dying myself. And then, perhaps, it is because I truly enjoy snapping the losers' necks."

She said nothing in response to that. There wasn't anything to say, only to think that it was good that, at least for now, the good colonel was on *her* side. She knew for a fact that he was by no means kidding her; the readouts as he'd dispatched sim attackers hand to hand showed that he got a tremendous rush when he did so.

Still, she had to wonder about both the soldiers and the others, including herself. The colonel, after all, knew it was a sim, *always* knew it was a sim, always knew that he was, no matter what, going to wake up and come out of there whole. All of them were dependent to some degree on the devices of the culture in which all of them had been raised. She wasn't sure that she, or anyone, could really imagine what it was like down there.

She heard a rustling noise to her right and turned to see the Pooka entering the sim control chamber. The Quadulan was a secretive and enigmatic type. She'd often wondered what it must be like on his home world. What kind of an evolution would produce a creature that was partly like a snake, about three meters long but thicker than a grown man's thigh, covered in insulating fat and then thick waterproof hair that was so stiff it served as quill-like defense against being eaten as well as the cosmetic and perhaps protective roles such body hair usually denoted.

Its "arms" were several tentaclelike appendages that could be withdrawn entirely into the body cavity, leaving only the closed and flattened three fingers at the end of each to suggest that anything was there. When needed, these arms could extend out two to three meters, and with six of them placed around its midsection it could accomplish feats of close manual dexterity as easily or more so than many humans.

The face was somewhat owl-like, although it was all flesh, no beak or bony cartilage. The eyes were deep set, round, and changed like a cat's in reaction to the light. They were not color-blind, but they did see into the infrared; perhaps they did not see all the gradations of color the human eye did in exchange for seeing as comfortably at night as they did in broad daylight. The mouth was beak-like, with overlapping lips that, when opened, revealed rows and rows of mostly tiny pointed teeth that seemed to go all the way down the esophagus.

It was said that they had originally been named Pookas by an Irish scout named O'Meara who landed on their world and found it difficult to find the natives, who lived below ground in vast complexes, though they easily found him. They would ooze out and take parts of his packs, his instruments, all sorts of things, and bring them below to be examined and analyzed. The Pookas were invisible spirits of Irish folklore; it's not known if O'Meara ever finally found them, but those who followed did.

It was a curious mixture, humans and Quadulans. They had very little in common save a quest for understanding the universe. The thing that had brought the two peoples together was an understanding that both were intelligent and cultured.

The Quadulans, it seemed, unlike Terrestrial snakes, could hear quite well. And they absolutely loved fast-paced music with a heavy beat. Their own native music was tonally quite different but oddly pleasing to human ears as well. In that case, music had truly been the universal language music professors always dreamed it might be.

Still, their lifestyle, their biology, their whole existence was quite alien to humans. They got along, they traded, as junior—*very* junior—partners, except when human interests got in the way, in which case the Quadulans discovered how junior they were. Still, humans had given them the keys to the stars, and the Titans were coming for them as well. Quadulans, it seemed, thrived on the same sort of worlds humans and Titans both liked so well.

"You have the sim set up for me?" the Pooka asked her, its voice resonating from somewhere deep inside it, sounding in some ways like a very artificial monotone. It was, however, natural, and formed by inner muscles and internal gases. Their own language was formed in the same way, but involved such bizarre sounds that, while humans eventually learned it and programmed it into their machines, no human could ever speak it or follow it without aid. The Pookas, however, had no trouble with human speech, if you didn't mind the eerie bass harp monotone.

"Yes, I did what I could," she told it. "However, there is only so much I can do with this lack of information."

"That is soon to be remedied, I believe? In the meantime, this will have to do. If my kind was specified as necessary for this expedition, then it is because of our physiology. That is logical. Someone thinks that I can get something that you could not. Comparing your abilities to mine, I surmise that it is someplace dark, perhaps well underground; that it is someplace that may only have a small access hole or tunnel; and that, most likely, it is in itself either some kind of data, data module, or unknown device that is no larger than my circumference. That is the problem I will work on."

"Colonel N'Gana just went in on the surface sim," she told it. "Since no com is allowed, there is no way for me to notify him that you will also be starting in on your sim. He is a very dangerous man and is likely to kill any surprises.

Don't you think it's prudent to wait until the Colonel comes out?"

"That will not be necessary," the Pooka responded. "I am the only Quadulan on the expedition. I am not on the sim world. I also know the Colonel's name. We will allow him to get in a bit so that he is away from the entrance and then I will go in. If he strikes, I am not so easily taken, and this will be a good test. If he does not, then he is irrelevant to me."

She sighed. "Suit yourself. Um—you weren't in your own people's military, were you?"

"The concept of military and civilian among your people is very quaint," the Pooka responded, going to the entry hatch. "It shows just how long most of you have been without a war. Your people must have opposites of everything, even sexes." And with no further elaboration, it triggered the opening sequence on the hatch, which released its air and swung open, filling the area temporarily with very hot, humid, somewhat fetid air. The Pooka slithered in, and then vanished as the hatch closed and resealed itself behind it.

Socolov's com link buzzed. "Yes?"

"Is anyone in the sims?" Father Chicanis asked her.

"Yes, Father. Two. N'Gana and the Pooka."

"They can be trusted on computer automatics," the priest told her. "Please come up. I would like to speak to you."

She was surprised, but replied, "Yes, of course. I'll be right up."

Father Chicanis sat in the small meeting room, relaxing comfortably on a chair. Although he had elaborate vestments as befitted an Orthodox priest, and both a black cassock and one in reversed color, aboard ship he used the formal garb only when serving as priest and confessor. The rest of the time, like now, he wore comfortable slacks, well-worn black boots, and a pullover shirt in one or more colors and patterns. Today's was plain white.

"Please—sit down, be comfortable," he invited.

She sat and relaxed, curious. "What is this all about, Father?"

"You, mostly. We're actually speaking one last time to just about everybody individually. You're not like the military types. You are in extremely good physical shape and you keep it that way, but you are no professional athlete. You are also somewhat shy around others. I've noticed that in mixed company, even in the sim area, you seem self-conscious or a bit nervous."

"I—well, it's not something I normally do, you know."

"Indeed. But it is you who suggests that that is the normal dress down on Helena. We are following your scenarios. Why do you think there won't even be the proverbial fig leaves down there?"

She shrugged. "We have lived for centuries in a disposable society. Even what we are both wearing now will be simply discarded. It's easier to simply have our machines create new and fresh ones than to go through all the problems making them heavy-duty and cleanable. Clothes, then, would go early in a post-takeover society and they would be irreplaceable in a culture like ours where everyone can have everything made to order in their own bedrooms. I suspect that when they first came back onto the surface, they used the fig leaf approach, but that quickly became pointless, as they are that exposed, it's that consistently warm, and natural biology from sex to taking a crap would be so, well, public. They may have ornamental things, or things denoting rank, but in general nothing we'd think of as clothes beyond some kind of makeshift carrier for weapons or perhaps to carry babies. I don't think they would understand the concept of modesty, but I was born and raised with it."

He cleared his throat and nodded. "I see. My problem,

Kati, is that we'll have to put some folks down on the ground. The odds are they will have to travel some distance. Not everyone, of course, but the Colonel and the Sergeant, certainly, as well as our Pooka, and, frankly, me, since I know the land even if I no longer know the world. Takamura and van der Voort will remain aboard; their task will be in developing what we hope to extract. What I am trying to say is that, while we could really use you along, we will be three men and a giant hairy snake, all naked and using only the most primitive of tools and weaponry, and you. You're not a fighter; I sincerely doubt if you could kill anyone or anything, at least not without such provocation as you do not wish to imagine. Under these conditions, with that kind of party, these kind of men—are you *sure* you wish to come with us?"

She thought about it. "You're trying to scare me. They tried to scare me before, remember, when they came and recruited me. Okay, put me down stark naked with a couple of throwbacks to Neanderthal and a world where it's likely women aren't held up much as leader material, not if they went, as I believe they did, the way other primitive survivalist societies go—then, yes, I *am* scared. But I've spent my whole life studying these things in the abstract, with no real way to test out my theories, and here is an opportunity to be the first qualified observer to get in and see what happens to humanity after the power goes off. Don't you see, Father? I can't *not* go."

"That is all I wanted to hear. But I want you doing many more simulations in the next few days, not only alone, as before, but with the rest of the ground party. That means under true sim conditions. We are also going to increase the load, particularly in basic supplies. The survivors down there have discovered what fills you up and what blows you up by now. We don't know that, so the more we control our own food, the better. At least we don't have to worry about wild animals. Unless, of course, that is what the survivors have become."

"I don't think that's the right word for it," she told him. "Consider our species. We're soft, we damage easily, we're laughably easy to kill. On our ancestral world and many others we settled afterward, there were creatures with better eyesight, better hearing, better sense of smell and taste and touch—you name it. We're not even collectively any smarter than the other races we took over, like the Quadulan. But, other than a taste for the same music and the love of a good beat, what do we and the Pookas have in common? We *adapt*. Long before we ever left ancient Earth, in fact, before the age of machines, you found people living in the most frozen tundra, in the hottest and densest jungles, and just about everywhere in between. And when we moved out, we were able in many cases to do terraforming at a very fast clip because we didn't need things to be exactly like they were back home. We're adaptable. All the sentient races that survived and evolved to a high point are incredibly adaptable. No matter what the conditions, humans have always adapted."

"And that's why you believe that there are still people as we know them down there? After what will be, oh, close to a century by the time we get there?"

"I do. Your own sensors said that there were some. Not many, but some. I've worked out what I believe that society might have readapted to. I may be totally wrong. That's why I have to go. I have to *know*."

"I see. No matter what the price?"

She looked at him. "I don't know if any of us could really accept living down there under those conditions for the rest of our lives. I'm not sure how long our lives would last under those conditions. But, yes, it's worth a risk. Everything worthwhile seems to require risk, doesn't it?"

"And what about—defense?"

"I can do all right in self-defense. Beyond that—I don't know. Father, you are a Christian priest. Could *you* kill another human being? Do you really know if you could or not?"

Father Chicanis licked his lips and stared off into space for a moment. Then, without bringing his gaze back to her, he responded, very softly, "I have. It fills me with eternal remorse, but I know God forgives me. But, yes, I know I can kill if I must."

His response shocked her, but didn't completely throw her off. She decided, though, that if he was going to say who he'd killed, when, and why, then it would have to be because he wanted to say it, and at a time and place of his own choosing.

"Then you have said it," she told him instead. "I do not *know* it, because, as I am sure you can agree, none of us truly knows what we will do until we are forced into actually doing it. It's easy to say what we would do, or would not do, but until the choice is forced, there is no way to know, is there?"

"No," he replied, still staring off into space.

"Then that is my only possible answer."

He nodded, and finally looked at her again. "Very well, Kati. Go ahead and return to your duties now."

She got up, started to leave, then stopped and turned to face him once more. "Why was this interview necessary, Father?" she asked him. "We spoke of nothing we haven't spoken of many times since I was brought into this."

He sighed. "Because we will rendezvous with the Dutchman in under eight ship hours," he told her. "And from that point on, God knows where this is going to lead."

"Warning! We are being scanned by diagnostic and targeting sensors!" The ship's computer did not mince words.

They had been sitting in the designated area off a remote and totally desolate genhole gate switching area for three hours. Suddenly everything had erupted into warnings and actions.

"Place origin of scans on the main screen," Captain Stavros ordered. When it came up, though, it wasn't a whole lot of help. "I wonder how the hell he does that? It's damned weird," Stavros muttered.

"Clever, though," Colonel N'Gana commented.

On the screen, in three dimensions, color, and with full and authentic depth, sitting in the middle of empty space but somehow internally and fully illuminated, was a gigantic sailing ship out of Earth's past.

"What is actually there, Captain?" Takamura asked, fascinated. "I assume this is inherent in the scanning operation, so that the effect is a broadcast that overwhelms the screen. It is a clever invention, but it shouldn't fool your own instruments."

"Computer?" the captain prompted.

"Orion class frigate, well armed, showing its age but well maintained and upgraded. Minimum life signs aboard," the computer reported.

"Orion class! That *is* an antique!" Admiral Krill commented. "It has to be salvaged from one or more vessels that went down in the initial Titan attacks. Nothing else makes sense."

"Nonetheless, it makes a formidable pirate ship for freighters like us, does it not?" the captain responded. "Computer—you say minimal life signs aboard. How many biological life-forms do you scan?"

"There is some jamming of this. My sensors indicate very few, though. Perhaps as few as one."

"One!" Takamura gasped. "Could one person even fly a ship like that?"

"Easily," Admiral Krill told her. "That is, if they knew what they were doing in the first place, and they obviously do. Just like this ship, it's all computerized, much of it artificial intelligence piloting and navigational gear. The crew of a modern frigate is small, and much of it is assigned to the sim training facilities and interpretive intelligence sections. The majority of live people aboard today's frigates are Marines in combat gear."

"Well, dear, don't let's keep guessing," the old diva prodded the captain. "Hail them and let's get going!"

"*Odysseus* to *Flying Dutchman.* Here we are. Please inform us as to what this is about."

For a short period there was no response. Then back came a voice that was full, firm, and almost kindly, with just a trace of accent that could not be placed. "This is Hendrik van Staaten, captain of the *Hollander.* Your ship has transmitted the correct coding, and I have acknowledged it. We are both who we say we are and we are out here in the middle of nowhere. Shall we begin our negotiation?"

Madame Sotoropolis whispered to her captain, "Any chance of visuals?"

The captain shook his head. "No, ma'am. He's got that blocked."

"Hell of a trip and lots of trouble for a phone call," Stavros retorted. "We're all gathered here. Would you like a rundown of the assemblage?"

"Unnecessary," van Staaten replied. "I probably know more about your passengers right now than you do. Overall, the choices run from good to adequate, but even the question marks will have to do. Let us begin by doing a bit of background work. Colonel N'Gana, have you ever heard of Priam's Lens?"

The colonel snorted. "It was a pipe dream from a century or more back," he responded. "Some sort of gizmo attached to a natural phenomenon nobody understood that was supposed to actually be capable of drilling a hole right through a Titan. Quite the adventure thriller concept, but there was no basis for it. Only in fiction do people just conjure up superweapons. In any event, it didn't work."

"The Lens, which *is* a natural phenomenon, *does* exist. The theory behind using its curious by-products as a weapon was sound, and a prototype was built that worked in limited tests," van Staaten told them. "Madame Sotoropolis, I suspect, knows of the project. It was financed partly by Karas family money when the government took your own position, Colonel."

Eyes turned to the old lady in the veil and sacklike dress.

"It was a last chance to save our world," she said softly, remembering over the years. "Nobody else had any kind of answer at all. The Confederacy's research and development people, its military, all the rest, had gone off on their own secret weapons projects that produced a lot of busywork and lots of pet theories, but none of them worked. Eventually, they stopped funding them. We—the family, that is—did our own searching and researching when it became clear that we were in the way of this new threat. Almost everything we found had been tried by one or another of the government projects. So, we looked at the ones they rejected as too silly, too impractical, or simply fantasy. We found several, almost all very odd ideas from highly eccentric university types who were considered crackpots. All were highly eccentric—that is, crazy as loons—and most *were* crackpots, but some were not. The one involving the curious effects produced by Priam's Lens, which was close to our system and in fact was the reason Helena had been discovered, showed definite promise, but before a full working prototype could be built and deployed, Helena was overrun. We never knew what happened to that or several other projects. We assumed that they either ran when the funding ran out or the world was overrun, or they were down there at the time."

"I am most curious," Doctor Takamura put in. "What

sort of thing was this Priam Lens? Some sort of death ray? It certainly sounds like one of those cheap thriller ideas."

"Some sort of *thing* in space. I really don't know," the diva told her. "I sang. My great-great-grandson and my two great-great-great-granddaughters were into all that. They're all gone now."

"On Helena?"

"No, not all of them. A different story for a different time, perhaps. But I knew little of this save that the projects were going on."

"You did, however, recognize Priam's Lens by name when I mentioned it," van Staaten noted. "And I am certain that you are not here with these people on a whim. You have checked out the partial data I sent you. You know it is true. You know that I may be able to give you the location of the prototype of the Priam's Lens project codes."

"You also claim to be able to get in and out of Titan-controlled worlds. I assume that is on the polar sweep worlds?" N'Gana put in.

"Yes, that is true. The sweep worlds are the ones. Fortunately, Helena is such a world. It does, however, present particular problems, since the gravitational effects of the two moons in opposition orbits keeps the ocean very churned up and very dangerous at many times during the year. It is not an easy body to navigate under the best of conditions."

"That is true," Father Chicanis acknowledged. "We found working underwater to be far preferable to surface work, although it *is* possible to sail them if you are good enough and have a good enough craft."

"Ah, yes. Father Chicanis. Good of you to be along. Understand, though, that you cannot work submerged under today's conditions. While the overall force fields that drain all power from anything we can build tend to lose some effect just below two meters, that does not mean they have no effect. And if power is applied, rather than simply idled, it sets off alarm bells and you're dead. That's why even the underground and underwater installations went. That leaves you with nonpowered surface travel as the only way. You cannot land on the continents or within the continental shelf's limits. Those are constantly under monitoring and observation by the Titan grid. Nonpowered craft, however, generally escape detection if at sea. The wave action and tidal forces appear to foul up their precise locators. But my people can get in. They *do* get in, and out, and quite often, if there's something there we really think is worth the risk. The price is pretty high if they fail, though."

"Priam's Lens, or at least the prototype, is, I gather, on Helena? Probably on Atlantis?" Chicanis guessed.

"Wrong, Father. The prototype is rather large, in fact. It is built right into the smaller moon, Hector. I've been there myself, although that in itself is no mean feat, and I've examined the ruins. It's still there, all right. It'll take some work to get it up and running, but it is there. It does not, however, have any power. Whatever power there was seems to have been drained by the Titan attack force as it came down to the surface of the mother planet."

"Then the records—even any instructions, commands, procedures. They are gone!" Takamura groaned. "Whatever computers they would be using would have died themselves for lack of any power, even a trickle charge!"

"You, too, are wrong, Doctor. That is a bad habit of your group. I hope you guess better once you are in action. There is a minimal trickle charge there, or so my information states. Not enough to be read by almost any instruments we have, and probably not by the Titans, either, but it's there. Just barely enough. The trouble is, as I said, it's incomplete. Much of the targeting and serious program debugging was going on on the surface in an underground research facility on the Eden continent just outside a city named—hmm, let's see—Ephesus. How—Biblical. I sent a team in there to see what they could find. Nobody made it back out, but one of them managed to get out quite a bit of data."

"Yes? How?"

"Remember what I said about indetectable trickle charges? Seems a few standby combat facilities, mostly fed by geothermal rather than fusion or antimatter, which would have been detected and sucked up, survive and are sort of turned on. Their residual hum is below the noise threshold of the Titans' monitoring grid, or so my computers aboard my ship theorize. Of course, if they are ever used, then the Titans will be on them in a moment and that's the end of that. One of my men was able to get to one. He knew by that point he couldn't get out, that they were on his trail, and he made the decision to broadcast and hope that I'd pick it up, at least through the rescue ship waiting for him to make it to an area between sweeps. We got it, and, since then, nothing else. I'm pretty sure they got him, too. But that's what I have here, ladies and gents. Real live data out of an interface with a dead man who was down there. It contains a great deal of data, but he didn't get everything because he didn't know what it was he was supposed to get. You, Madame Sotoropolis, have the family Karas databases. You know. I can trade you the where and the how, and a way in and out if you are good enough."

"And what is it you wish, Captain van Staaten?" Captain Stavros asked suspiciously.

"I want control of the weapon. I want control, not the Navy, not the incompetent Confederacy, not the cowardly and defeatist types who now run things."

"A weapon that can destroy Titans?"

"I have no idea if it will destroy them. I would like it to, but it may just hurt them. It may even merely annoy them, cause them pain. Whatever it does, I want it. I alone will decide where it shoots and what it shoots. I alone will give the commands. That is my price and it is not negotiable."

Colonel N'Gana, along with several of the others, wasn't overly concerned with this demand. After all, once the weapon was activated, once it was used, what could the Dutchman do anyway? Still, he had to ask: "Why do you think that we can get in and get the data from the surface when your people couldn't? Why do you think we can make it out when you can't?"

"I have no idea if you can do it, Colonel. If I thought it was easy, I would have done it myself and not needed any of you. When you do the cybernetic link and see what all was sent, you will understand what the purpose of each member of your team is. Some of it should be obvious."

"So, let me get this straight," Admiral Krill put in. "You expect us to go down and retrieve whatever your people couldn't and then sit there and make this thing in the moon work. And then you expect us to just give you the trigger?"

"I do, and you will. You see, whether it does the job or not, the moment you shoot whatever this thing shoots and strike a Titan ship or base, well, you are *really* going to get their attention. There are seven primary bases down there. The moment I fire and hit one, the other six are going to know just exactly where it came from. Now, just who do you propose to fire that weapon?"

N'Gana sighed. "I, for one, agree with him, but it shows why this is stupid. He is certainly right that as soon as one of them is wounded, killed, blown up, whatever it does, the others are going to come after the source, and they won't have far to go; a moon isn't something you can move out of range easily. So, assume we go down. Assume we get everything we need to make it work. Assume we get back up with it. All big assumptions. One shot, then it's over. So what? What will we have accomplished? All that for just one target? It might as well not work at all!"

"Not exactly," van Staaten's voice came back to them. "You will have the data. You will have the principles. And you will have a demonstration. If you can't take that back and build and deploy more, then you do not deserve to live."

"He's got you there, Colonel," Chicanis commented, sounding a bit too pleased.

"Yes or no? I can get you in, and I can get you out. Say yes, and I will transfer the cyberrecord and then we can go from there. Say no and it stops here. Once you say yes, though, you agree to my terms and commands. There will be no going back."

"Might as well," N'Gana grumbled. "If we say no, he's just going to blow us to hell anyway."

"Very well," the old diva told the Dutchman. She still wished, as they all did, that she knew more about this strange rogue, and she certainly had no more trust in him than N'Gana did, but she had come too far to retreat now.

"I'm transferring an exact copy to your library computer now," the Dutchman told them. "I would suggest that only people who are familiar with the technique and can interpret the information, either scientifically or geographically, should look at it. There's a lot of extraneous stuff there that will be difficult to filter out completely. Oh—and one more thing."

"Yes?"

"You might get Mister Harker off your goddamned hull and inside where he might do some good. I don't think he's going to be any help at all out there by himself."

ELEVEN

Something New in the Air

Littlefeet had seen women give birth a number of times while growing up; there wasn't much concealment in the Family, nor much attempt at it. Even so, to see it happen with Spotty, and with *his* child coming out—that was something very different.

There was no way to stop the wail of a newborn child, so sentries were just doubled and vigilance was increased when such a thing happened.

Spotty was attended by Greenie and Bigcheeks, two girls of her own age who were well along with child themselves. That was how the women trained from the start, with each assisting and younger ones usually watching. A priest, almost always Father Alex, was also there not only to ensure that all went well but to bless and cleanse the child in water as soon as its umbilical cord was tied off. Within two days the mother would give the child a nickname that would generally last a lifetime; a more formal name was given at puberty from the Old Names. Young girls, often called scribes, would memorize the genealogies and maintain them so that future generations could track lineage, which was always via the mother. The father was normally considered irrelevant, and unless there was a marked resemblance it was generally impossible to even know who the father was.

Not this time, though. Littlefeet knew that this had to be his.

Still, he felt somewhat crushed when Father Alex lifted up the baby and announced, "It is a fine, healthy girl!"

He'd been so sure it was a son that he'd already made plans for how he was going to bring the kid up, teach him to forage and to fight and guard, all that. Now—jeez, a girl?

And when the baby was placed back on the mother's breast and found her first meal and quieted down, Spotty spoke to Littlefeet. "She has your kind, big eyes," she told him. "And a bit of your face, too. I think she will look like you."

"I—well, that's nice," he managed, not quite knowing what to say.

"Do not be so disappointed!" she chastened him. "I will have many more fine children, and some will be boys!"

"No, it's not that," he told her, but, of course, it mostly *was* that. Still, what the hell, the baby *did* look kind of cute, if a little wrinkly. Newborn babies were actually pretty ugly, he thought. He couldn't see anything of either of them in the kid right now.

Such was the routine of the Family, though, that Littlefeet had no time to really rest beyond the night. Having had the child during the afternoon, Spotty at least had been able to sleep and recover some strength; those who bore children in the middle of the night or early in the morning had it the roughest, since often the camp would be moving. They did not move every day, but they moved more often than not. It was a given that the Family must always be on the move, and that if you remained in one place for any length of time you would be the target of a horde of Hunters, more than could be imagined, and that the Family as a result would die.

Littlefeet's full senses had returned by now, and the wounds he'd received in the fight with the Hunters had also healed. True, his body now bore some ugly scars, scars he would take to his grave no matter when that would be, but such marks were signs of bravery and conferred status in the Family. More worrying was the fact that he continued to limp, and that did not seem to be getting any better. Oh, he felt strong enough, and certainly he could move well enough, but the limp, the result of an unsuspected break that, when discovered, had been less than perfectly set, was a problem. It slowed down his run, and gave him very slight balance problems that had cost him a step or more in speed and thrown him a hair off in accuracy with a spear. There was no room in the Family for anyone who could not perform all his duties and pull his own weight; they couldn't afford dead wood.

He wasn't there yet, but he was getting to be old and a potential liability faster than most in this quick-dying culture.

He was still doing his job, although Father Alex gave him no more long-range reconnaissance missions. His scars attested to his fearlessness and the fact that he was still alive showed his skills, but he was limited to close-in sentry duty and packing, hauling, and tending to weapon repairs.

The worst thing about getting back into duty, though, was that Mother Paulista insisted that Spotty move back into the women's kraal and bring the new daughter, now named Twochins after a tiny cleft she had that Littlefeet also shared and that pretty much proved his paternity.

As soon as Spotty moved back, though, Paulista and her Sisters made a concerted effort to keep the two apart. In such close quarters this wasn't literally impossible, but what *was* possible was to assign Littlefeet to duties at different hours than Spotty, and when it was time for the men to lie with the women, somehow it was always with a different girl, somebody Littlefeet knew but didn't want. Still, just as she had done her duty, so had he. He just didn't like it.

Father Alex was, as always, both understanding and

consoling, but not a whole lot of help in solving the problem.

"In the Way of the Book, one man and one woman are to be married for life," he told the younger man. "If we could live in any way like those of the Book or those who came after up until the coming of the demons, then it would be so. The trouble is, our first duty to God is to preserve and continue the Family, so that we may continue to worship and serve Him and do His will. When we did it the old way, we couldn't do this. Too few children were born, their raising was too complicated, and there were terrible jealousies like what you're feeling now. With no privacy and little modesty, there was simply no way to maintain it."

"But why couldn't just she and I be together? It's not like we don't want it, and it's not like everybody else does!"

"Son, all that we do, we have done because it works, and the other ways, old ways, new ways, all sorts of things that were tried, did not. There was also the need, when we were reduced to so few, to ensure that there was some diversity, that brothers and sisters did not couple. This causes bad things to happen to the babies. The way around it is to make sure that all the active males and all the active females lie with as many different partners as possible."

"I know, I know, but, Father—she's with child again and this time it isn't mine! *Couldn't* be! And I want a son by her. Is that wrong?"

"Patience, son. It will come. And if your son is by Greenie or Brown Spots or White Streak, will that make the child any less yours or any less important in God's eyes? You do not own her, nor she you. We are all the property of God, but, beyond that, we are all equally part of the Family. All sons are our sons and all daughters are our daughters. I believe you should think on this and pray to God for enlightenment. You must cleanse your soul and accept with joy what you have and purge these feelings of evil and possession of another. Otherwise, one day, God will lose patience with you as He did with others of the Old Book and discard you as He did them."

To anyone of the Family, that was a scary idea. All had been born and raised to believe that a real God was up there, and all around, looking at each and every one, watching and judging and testing, and that the sole purpose of existence was to please Him so much that when you died you went immediately to His right hand along with Jesus and the Holy Spirit. The Old Book stories, memorized and passed along now, of men who God hated in the womb and others who had waited too long and found God had abandoned them were real and frightening, more so than the Hunters or even the demons.

They could only kill or maim your mortal body. If God turned His back on you, then that might be the only body you had, or, worse, you would find yourself not at God's right hand in heaven but instead in the fire at the center of the sun at the left hand of Satan, never consumed but always in mortal pain.

Father Alex tried to help, by forbidding Littlefeet to have any contact at all with Spotty, to speak to her or ask about her or even acknowledge her existence. Mother Paulista laid the same injunction on Spotty, and there were always those around who would report any breach of these injunctions, which had the force of law. Anyone not reporting would also be committing a sin. This made it really tough.

So Littlefeet prayed and tried hard to get it out of his system, but it was pretty stubborn. And, hell, boys being boys, he knew who was lying with whom each time and that didn't help a bit.

After several Starnights and a great deal of other activities, he found himself adjusting pretty well to the situation, although he didn't really forget her and he still wanted her. Lying with the other girls, and being with the other young men talking and bragging and the like, though, he did find himself no longer feeling so possessively jealous about her, and that at least helped.

As the Family's traditional route moved further north again, though, it also took a less traditional jog further inland, to avoid an increasing number of taboo sites where things had happened that shouldn't have happened in the past. The new routing was far enough inland that they could no longer even see the great rock where they'd found the dead man and almost been captured by his ghost. Some of the men didn't like such a radical change, since it meant more intensive scouting by more and more warriors, leaving the camp less protected, more vulnerable. Even Father Alex was concerned that Mother Paulista's fear of the unknown was threatening them in more pragmatic ways, not to mention the fact that the trees and bushes and ancient gardens where they foraged for food were not as plentiful in some of those new inland areas, while some natural barriers, particularly some decent-sized rivers, were real impediments.

So it was that they were camped one evening near the edge of a mighty river that seemed to go on and on. None there could remember seeing such a river before, nor hearing of it, so they knew that they had perhaps come too far from their traditional territories. There was no way to cross the thing; it was easily several kilometers to the other shore, and there were currents and eddies and small whirlpools in the mud-brown water that clearly showed that it was not just wide but also deep and treacherous.

Littlefeet knew the river, though; at least, he remembered seeing it from the heights above before he'd stared too long at the distant demons.

"I cannot say where we are compared to what I saw," he admitted to Father Alex, "but I can say that several great rivers flowed from the mountains out onto the great plain and that most of them joined into one at different stages, or flowed close enough together that they probably joined beyond where I could see. That may not be a shore over there, but merely a dividing part of land between two great rivers yet to merge."

Father Alex nodded. It was not good that they were this far east and backed up against such a barrier. If Hunters came in force, there would be no way to run, nowhere to hide, and he was not sure that anyone could stay afloat if they fell into that thing. Worse, the bluffs along the river were not good for growing edible things, at least not here. The pickings were fairly poor even though the vegetation was dense. He went to see Mother Paulista with the intent of insisting that they move back inland as quickly as possible and spirit dangers, real and imagined, be damned. This was not a fit place for the Family.

He found her surprisingly unnerved and in agreement. "I did not see this," she admitted to him. "This is a barrier we were not meant to cross. If God does not part the waters, then we shall do as you say."

Nobody liked the river, and when Littlefeet slept, even his dreams were about the river, and the unholy things beyond it.

He could *sense* them, almost *hear* them talking one to another, although what they said made no sense and was like the banging of drums and hollow rocks, reverberating back and forth into a babble.

And yet he knew, he'd always known, that it was some sort of speech, that this was their language, their tongue, and that they heard and spoke and thought in ways far different from humans.

Words . . . ? Littlefeet couldn't call such a cacophony words or thoughts, but occasionally through the din he would get other things: pictures that partly related to things he could understand, and sometimes even odd feelings. Like now, he was convinced that the din was some sort of argument. Not a violent argument, or a heated one, but an argument nonetheless. And, occasionally, in the flashes of color and rippling patterns that floated through his sleeping mind, there were pictures, almost snapshots of events rather than full observations. Most made no sense, at least he couldn't make sense of them, but sometimes there were—faces. Human faces. Faces in many cases filled with fear, or, worse, worshipful devotion to something he could not see, but with eyes that showed little or no thought, just an achingly single-minded desire to please.

And they were in some ways like no humans he knew. They were humans without scars, without blemishes of any kind, with smiles full of perfect teeth and proportions that said they had never been hungry or had to keep in the kind of trim that a Family member must to survive. They also had no tattoos, and the only jewelry they all had was a kind of shiny diamond thing in their foreheads that seemed to pulse off and on, almost like the city itself had seemed to pulse when he'd looked at it.

The other images were of the demon flowers, those great flowers whose rippling rows covered the center of the region and possibly much of the continent beyond for all he knew. Gigantic flowers, planted in perfect rows, growing to two or three times the height of a man, with varicolored stalks and even more exotic patterns in their huge petals. Every color of the rainbow was there and more, and patterns made of those colors in almost any variety or configuration. Unlike the confusing and scary other scenes, these were very pretty, although the view was distorted and the groves were being seen from a vantage point that was moving very, very fast over their tops. He began to get dizzy, even a little sick, and he felt suddenly that he was not alone, that someone or some*thing* was there with him, and that the *thing* was now abruptly aware of his presence and turning to look at him, to reach out for him. . . .

He woke up in a cold sweat. It was not quite dawn, and there was a thick fog all around them that made seeing nearly impossible and soaked everything and everybody right through.

Unable to see much of anything, even in the predawn light, he used his other senses and was glad that he wasn't on sentry duty right then.

His hearing could place those nearest him fairly easily, and because the Family tended to make camp in the same pattern each time no matter what the lay of the land, it was also easy to find his way through, using hearing and smell to avoid walking into things or over people.

He was heading for a specific spot just outside of camp and downwind, and he had even less trouble finding that place by smell. One of the last jobs that some were assigned to do before camp was broken was to bury the pit so that no one could smell it and begin to map out camp locations.

He took his acute senses of smell and hearing for granted, and just about everybody his age did as well, but he knew that the older people did not share the abilities, at least not to the degree his age peers took them for granted. Father Alex in particular would be helpless in this soup, even to make it to piss or crap on his own. The heightened senses had not escaped his notice, either; he had wondered for some time if it was being born and raised in this new element, or just age, or if, in fact, this newly remade world was changing the people who lived in it into something slightly, subtly, different.

Littlefeet's parents could do it, although not quite to the same degree, and the same could be said of their parents. There were also other survival senses that seemed to be emerging. Many, although not all, of the younger generation seemed to be able to sense the direction and location of the demons when they moved through the air or came near. The lines that Littlefeet said he could see from the mountain heights some professed to see even at ground level, particularly in the darkness. Some seemed to be able to see almost through the tall grasses, as if they could see or sense the heat of human bodies.

Most mutations in the past had been harmful or disfiguring; few had ever seemed really beneficial. Maybe, just maybe, humans were adapting to a new set of conditions to ensure survival after all.

Littlefeet could feel the demons still, even in his awakened state. They, or at least one or more, were not that far away; they were up somewhere in the air. They didn't seem to be hunting for the camp or even particularly aware of or interested in it, but it was unnerving to have them so close.

If he remembered right, they were somewhere across the river, but what was a river to the Princes of the Air?

There was also something—else. He had no other way to describe it, even in his own thoughts. Later, as the rising sun burned off the fog, they hurried to feed everyone and get everything ready to move out. The warriors were all unnerved by the closeness of the demons the night before. He talked of his new sensation with the other young men. Some had felt it as well; others had no idea what he was talking about.

It was something different. Not demons, but coming from a direction where only demons could possibly be. Those who'd felt it had never felt its like before, and could not explain it, but the sensations of something, somebody new, something present and not of this world, had come from above, from the air, and had faded with the setting of the smaller moon.

TWELVE

Hector

"Get Mister Harker a dressing gown, please," Madame Sotoropolis instructed. The automated systems built into the *Odysseus* immediately complied, with a small hook running in a track along the ceiling carrying a dark blue gown.

"Thanks for something," the Navy man grumbled, taking it and putting it on, then tying it off. "You'll see to my suit?"

"Wouldn't want to touch it with a five-meter pole," she responded. "Colonel N'Gana has warned us that such things are not to be trifled with."

He found some sandals and slipped them on, then emerged from the bathroom of the small suite he now occupied. "Now, you want to tell me when you knew I was there?"

"Well, as I understand, Admiral Krill suspected that someone like you would be there, and this Dutchman confirmed it, that's all. I must admit I was a bit surprised to find that it was you, even though I am delighted to see you here! We can use someone like you, I suspect."

He stared at her, all shrouded but still animated, and frowned. "You knew the Navy would send somebody. You deliberately baited me with all those queries for the Dutchman."

"Let us just say that several of us thought it better to have someone official along. Someone who could give the

Navy a pretext to act if need be, or call them off. Like it or not, Mister Harker, you are now the official representative of The Confederacy's Navy on this trip."

"Maybe I don't choose to be."

"Too late. You already volunteered. Now, come this way, please. I think that you should be brought up to speed as quickly as possible."

He followed her, still feeling uncomfortable and highly vulnerable but mostly crushed by the idea that his act of bravery was so, well, *useless*.

"Why didn't you just request a liaison?" he grumbled.

"Why, dear, you *know* they would have either ignored us or sent the wrong person. Someone either no good in a fight or *only* good in a fight, perhaps. But someone who had the nerve to do what you just did—now that is the kind of person we can trust. You may be the best of the lot here, Mister Harker, and we don't even have to pay you!"

He had a lot of questions; he had nothing *but* questions at this stage. All that for nothing. And the Dutchman was here and had known he was there. That meant that the Dutchman, or his henchmen, had been there on the base and in the bar all along. And if he knew that, did he also know the codes and signals Harker could use in a pinch? He wondered.

Juanita Krill was taller than he'd thought from the videos and, if anything, thinner. He doubted if she could do much heavy lifting or carrying, but, then, she didn't have to. She marketed that first-rate brain of hers that could solve all sorts of wonderful ciphers when mated with her specially designed code-breaking and security computers.

She looked up at him from a console, then went back to the screen once again. Her short-cropped wig sat on a small form on the deck. By moving just a bit behind her, he saw that she had a cyberprobe inserted in the slot in the back of her skull. It gave off a low pulsing yellow light, not because it needed the light but because others had to know when it was active in case something went wrong. On the other side of her, on the deck opposite the wig stand, was a simple one-meter-square cube with a handle on it. It, too, was pulsing in rapid time, mirroring the smaller transceiver in her skull.

The fact that she was doing complex analysis inside the computer didn't seem to interfere with her ability to hold a normal conversation, which was probably the most impressive thing of all. He'd seen people who did computer interfacing on this level who were comatose not only while they were doing it but also for days afterward.

"Come, come, Mister Harker," she said. "You should know you would never make heads or tails of what you are seeing. I'll tell you what it is, though, and it is quite disturbing, some of it. It's the output of the mind of a man who knew he was probably going to die any minute. Fortunately, whoever was stalking him did not get him until he was through. I have experienced a violent death in this manner before and it takes a great deal of work to get it out of your head."

"This is the Dutchman's man on Helena?"

"Interestingly, no. It appears that he was another freelancer or possibly even a civilian operative. The record is unclear. Unfortunately, while he was quite bright, it wasn't in this technical area. He was more soldier and spy than cyberthief. However, it appears that he couldn't quite get to the old labs anyway. There has been a collapse in those levels which would require earth-moving equipment to bypass. Needless to say, that is not an option open to us on Helena. There is, however, a potential route using old ventilation shafts that are far too small for us to get through but which another might."

"That's the Pooka, I guess."

"Indeed. The man wasn't going for this sort of stuff when he was dropped. He was attempting to get modular keys to more conventional but still quite potent weapons that are stored away in vast underground bunkers on Achilles. That was the prize. Instead, he ran into information, apparently old-style *written* information, that led him instead to the location of the research and control center for the Priam's Lens project. He knew what he had from the printouts and journals he recovered down there and read later on. Unfortunately, when he tried to get down to the laboratory levels for the data and code blocks, well, he just could not get there. The position is quite dangerous both from the standpoint of the physical plant and because of its close proximity to one of the Titan bases. He didn't dare to try for more, but he wanted to ensure that the message got out. He had data on where some trickle charge emergency stations might be located and he found one. He got out the information he had using the old planetary emergency channels, without really knowing whether it would be received by anyone. Only the Dutchman was in the area and so only the Dutchman received the signal."

He nodded. "So, any idea why the Dutchman called in the Karas family?"

"Not exactly. He will not show himself. We don't know who or even what he is. However, he can hardly go to the nearest Naval base and say, 'Hi, I was out in the Occupied Territories near Helena and I received this signal from the ground.' They would have him. This way, he controls things."

"Seems to me he'd be better off going in or sending in his own team," Harker commented. "That way he'd have this all to himself."

"Well, yes, except that he's already done just that. At least, so he says. Two separate groups, in fact. Neither was ever heard from again. He decided then that only a professional team tailored for the job would have a crack at doing it."

Harker nodded. "And now I suppose I'm a part of this team?"

"I believe you were always supposed to be. Knowing Commander Park, it would not surprise me if your very presence here is part of some convoluted plot to deal himself in by proxy. Well, it doesn't matter now. You are either in at this point or you will have a very boring time here and perhaps get an opportunity to test yourself against the Dutchman. I'm sure that this has occurred to you. There is simply no way that every competent fighter is going down there, leaving you aboard with a mathematician, a physicist, a mummified opera singer, a middle-aged pot-bellied old yacht captain, and an emaciated half machine like me."

He gave her a wry grin she couldn't see. "I suspect you're a lot more formidable than you make yourself out to be. I know your reputation, and I suspect that you are already interfaced with just about every system on this ship. What chance would somebody like me have?"

"The comment is both flattering and partially correct, but only partially. You would have an excellent chance in that combat suit and you know it. I can tell that it is state of the art, and well beyond the ability of even someone like me to compromise. I have no doubt that if anything happened to you the suit is perfectly capable of taking us on completely by itself. No, sir, I don't think so. And I don't think the colonel could do much about it, either. That really leaves things up to you, doesn't it?"

"What do you mean?"

"I can stop the colonel from dispatching you to whatever form of Valhalla you think you'll go to, because I am confident enough of the programming in that suit to want to protect myself. I think the old lady fancies you, too. But you're going to have to decide whether to sit here with us and keep the old lady endlessly entertained for maybe months, or go with them. Your choice."

He sighed and considered the idea. He had no desire to go down there, even in a full combat suit, let alone in nothing but his birthday suit. But considering the alternative, it was true: he had an unpalatable choice to make.

The whole thing had been so anticlimactic after that buildup that he couldn't get himself psyched to do much of anything. Riding the keel was not something that had been fun; the nightmares were, well, bizarre and had terrified him, he knew, even though he couldn't quite remember any of them, and he was still feeling a lot of deep bruises. Still, to come all the way through that only to be picked off and invited inside—well, it was at the very least embarrassing. Krill was right, though; the Dutchman could hardly have counted on any belief or cooperation from the Navy, and they could hardly have invited a Navy combat expert aboard and expected to actually get one without strings. Now—now they had him.

He went to see Doctor Katarina Socolov. She seemed rather happy to see him but not all that surprised. "I almost hoped you'd find a way to come," she told him. "I admit that going down with just those two Neanderthals wasn't my idea of a good time."

"You only know me from one dinner, and that was arranged under false pretenses," he noted. "I could just as easily be another N'Gana or Mogutu. Not that they are exactly storm troopers, either. They're old-time fighting men who, for one reason or another, stepped on some toes and were forced to retire. In fact, N'Gana had a damned good record overall, and his great crime was that he would not commit large numbers of troopers to a suicidal position. Even though he was right, as was proven when he was replaced on the spot and the order given by his subordinate, he'd disobeyed a direct order. They let him quit and he was happy to go. I looked over his whole file and record."

"And yet he immediately went into business doing the same thing."

Harker shrugged. "He's a professional soldier and he doesn't really know any other life. I think he has a pathological fear of dying in bed of old age. Still, he's good at his job and single-minded about his missions. If you don't mind my saying so, from the outset I've thought that the possible weak link in this isn't either of the military men."

"You mean me."

He nodded slowly. "It's nothing personal, or even professional. N'Gana's not going to rape you, nothing like that. But it's going to be pretty damned primitive and very rough down there. Rougher, I think, than any of us imagine. We've never had to live completely without our machines. N'Gana can physically break logs in two and he's a hell of a wrestler; Mogutu's got black belts in fighting disciplines I never even heard of, let alone can pronounce. Still, neither of them has ever had to go it absolutely alone. No communications, no weaponry, no computer links, not even a hot bath. And they're in better shape than you are, although you appear to be in decent condition. I know what it's like to be pushed past the point of exhaustion when it's life or death. So do they. You may think you do, but you don't. I didn't until I had to do it."

"I'll have to make it. You can't scare me any more than I'm already scared, but I couldn't live with myself if I didn't go."

"There's one more thing. You're the only woman and the only person on the squad without military training. There is going to be a tendency for the others to be protective or solicitous of you even though they will try not to be. I've seen it before. If you get into real trouble, somebody's gonna have to stop what they are doing and try and save you."

"There are women combat soldiers. I've seen some of them."

"That's different. Suited up, there's no real difference.

Even not suited up, there's the same training background and mindset."

"Well, I may be the only woman but I'm not the only civilian going down. There are four of us—unless you feel like coming along."

"Who's the other?"

"The priest, Father Chicanis. He was born and raised on the continent of Eden before the Fall. He would have been there when it fell but he was at some religious conference. I think he's always felt guilty he wasn't there. He's our native guide, so to speak. He can find the old landmarks and get us where we need to go, considering we won't have any computer or navigational aids."

Harker hadn't thought of this. "Now I like it even less. A priest who wants to be a martyr. Just great. He'll also want to minister to everybody who might kill him. The world he remembers is a century dead. The world down there now is like nothing he's ever known."

"He's a tough guy, at least that's the impression I get, and for a priest he's pretty grounded in realism. At least, I don't think he's about to get us killed for his religion. I think he'd die for it, but he wouldn't take any of us with him. I also always had the idea that, with him, this was personal. There's something in his past, somewhere, that he's kept inside but it's what drives him beyond just his faith. I don't know what it is. I think Madame Sotoropolis does, but I'm not sure."

"We've all got things like that driving us," he told her. "I swore I'd never get myself in a combat situation again. I know what it's like when it goes bad. I'm not sure I didn't use up any lives left in me that last time, too."

He turned to go, deciding to speak to this priest next. She called him back: "Harker?"

"Yes?"

"You ever been in a combat situation without *something* on? Some armor?"

He thought about it. "Only in training exercises, and not recently, no."

"We've all been training in the simulator here. Even though we'll have a lot more stuff than those people on Helena probably have, we'll still be pretty stripped down. Maybe before you start questioning the abilities of other people, you might want a crack at that simulation yourself. That's if you decide to come with us, of course."

He took a deep breath. "I'll think about it," he told her, and left.

He found Father Chicanis in the big lounge, which looked just the way it had on all those spy camera recordings. When not officiating in his priestly sense, Chicanis tended to dress informally in a black pullover shirt, and slacks, and slip-on sneakers. He looked very much like a middle-aged man in fairly decent condition who might well be a programmer or technician or even janitor.

"Ah, Mister Harker! Glad to have you with us," the priest greeted him, sounding like he was just saying hello to somebody he had asked aboard.

"I'm not sure how much with you I am yet, Father," he responded.

"Come! Sit down! I'm afraid this may be the only chance we'll have to get to know each other. After sitting on our duffs forever, we're now moving very fast, it seems."

"We're heading out?"

"The Dutchman is dispatching a corvette that's now attached to his ship to get us. Ships this size, or even the size of his vessel, would trigger every alarm the Titans might have. It's by using very small ships like the corvettes and then using small outer system genhole gates that they're able to get in and out without the energy flare attracting attention."

"I haven't said whether I'm in or out on this, you know."

"Come, come! You've come this far out of curiosity! I don't think you're the kind of man who can sit back and remain passive when things are going on. I assume you don't have a family or you wouldn't have volunteered for that courageous ride."

"No, nobody."

"Then, see? That's really all of us, you know. In addition to the skills involved, everyone aboard, even Captain Stavros, has no close remaining family. The mercenaries and the science people—all orphaned by this point, no known living siblings."

"Including you?"

Chicanis's face darkened. "Everyone I held dear was still on Helena when it was overrun. They're all most certainly dead now. Most probably died in the initial loss of power and the scouring. I see their faces, I hear their voices, every night in my dreams, but they are somewhere else now, in the arms of Jesus. I really believe that, you see. It's why I can go on and not be consumed with grief. I fully expect to see them again someday." He paused and stared at Harker. "What about you? Do you believe in God?"

Harker shrugged. "I'm not at all sure, and that's an honest answer, Father. Sometimes, when I see a beautiful sunset on some distant world or stare into the heart of a spectacular stellar cloud, it's easy. Other times, looking at starving people, twisted and broken children, blown-up bodies, shorted-out minds—then I can't find God at all. Let's just say that I reserve judgment on God, but that I very much believe in evil. I've seen evil."

"Well, that's more than most people. Half The Confederacy is still trying to figure out what the Titans want and why they do what they do, as if understanding a truly alien race would make the genocide go away. Most people stopped believing in evil centuries ago. In ancient times a majority of good churchgoing types believed in hell. Oh, now they believe in God and Jesus and love and all that, but when it comes to hell—no, not that."

"I've already been to hell, Father," Harker told him evenly. "*That* I believe in."

"You know, there's some from the start who thought that the Titans were angels," Chicanis commented. "The Jewish tradition has good angels and bad angels, and we Greeks took the bad and called them by a proper Greek label, *daimon*. I can't help but wonder sometimes when I see the beauty of those Titan formations. Satan was always supposed to be the crowning cherub, the most beautiful of all the angels. Beauty and evil are not opposites." He sighed. "But we're not here to discuss theology, now, are we?"

"No, we're not. I was just wondering, though, if you'd thought through what it'll be like down there. Pardon me, Father, but it's pretty clear that you've lived more real-time years than me, and you haven't spent them all in situations where you had to be in peak physical condition. I've looked at the maps here. If we put in where we're supposed to, we're talking a good three hundred or more kilometers walking, both there and back. Running some of the time, I suspect, in a reworked primitive world like nothing any of us have ever experienced before. I'm not sure that Doctor Socolov can hack that, and I'm not sure you could, either."

"You're not saying anything I haven't heard from Mogutu," the priest admitted. "The fact is, though, from the Dutchman and from Navy files we have aerials of Helena and I can determine the old points from them. They've reworked a good deal of Atlantis, but Eden is pretty much left alone save for their replanting. Many of the natural landforms and just about all the distances are still correct. I feel confident I can get us wherever we need to get on the ground. I am not sure that anyone else could. That is, anyone not born and raised there. So, I go, and

God will grant me whatever strength is necessary to get the job done. I feel certain of it. I am also prepared, if need be, to die there, or to remain there, if that is what God wants. But I simply cannot accept that He didn't have a plan for me to be in this position. It explains why I wasn't there when the Titans came, why I was in a certain company at a certain time when this came up, and why I am here. I believe this is a divine plan. You can dismiss it or not, but I believe it to be so, and faith will carry a person a very long way."

"I hope you're right, Father," Gene Harker replied. "I really hope you're right." He stood there for a moment, trying to bring up his biggest concern diplomatically. Finally, he decided head-on was best.

"Tell me, Father. If you're down there, and it's the difference between one of our lives and one of the poor wretches down there, could you decide? Could you actually act to keep Socolov from death or rape or whatever, or even one of us from having our brains bashed in?"

"The truth? I don't know, Harker. I don't think I will know until and unless I face it, and I know I might. None of us truly knows what is within us until an action is forced, do we?"

"Well, at least it's an honest answer," the Navy man responded.

"Call it off, Colonel."

The big man with the deep voice continued to look over terrain maps on the console in front of him but did say, "Hello, Harker. Glad to have you with us."

"I'm not with you, or against you. I just think you're going to do what you wouldn't do before. You go in, and you'll kill people—that's part of the job. But Socolov and Chicanis are liabilities in any ground movement and you know it. Take them, and either they will die or the mission will fail as we keep saving their necks."

"I note you now said 'we,' which makes me correct. And I can't call it off. I couldn't even call off the action that got me early retirement. Those people still went in, remember, and they still died. This is even clearer. They are going in with or without us. If they go in without us, they will surely die. If they go in with us, they will probably die, but something might come of the effort. Look on the bright side."

It was a pretty cold way of looking at things, but it was also hard to argue with. "Is this trip really worth it?"

"Krill thinks so. This Dutchman thinks so. The preliminary examinations of the historical record suggest that they might have had something. We'll know more once we get into Hector."

"Hector? You're going to the little moon?"

"Initially. That's Krill's and the two brains' jobs. The actual weapon is supposed to be there, still hidden away in bunkers. If it's there, then it is worth going down for the codes. If it is not there, then we all go home—or, more likely, we all get to find out if we can blow the Dutchman before the Dutchman blows us away once he has no use for us. But I'm not going to abandon it if something's there. Someone with an incredible amount of guts died, probably in a nasty way, to get us that information. Do you know how long the burst was that got all that data out that Krill's now looking over?"

"No."

"About six seconds. After that, you can actually see the damping field kicking in to intercept and gobble up the power, and not incidentally target the sender precisely as well. A six-second transmission. We won't even have that. It's doubtful whether, now that it's been done once, the Titans will leave anything with surface access unmonitored. I'm certain they could drain the entire planet of power if they wished; it's just too much trouble and no profit. Our objective is to bring the codes out without activating them. Once we do, once storage becomes active energy—watch out!"

"Do you really think even the likes of us can hack it down there, Colonel? Give me my combat suit and I'll take on an army, but bare-handed . . ."

"I have no intention of being down there bare-handed," N'Gana responded. "However, there will be both vulnerabilities and limits. You were Commando, right?"

"Yes. A while ago."

"You're still a Commando and you know it. It's in the blood. If you'd quit and gone into the diamond business or started dirt farming, maybe not, but you stayed in. I think you're probably very good, Harker. Both the sergeant and I were Rangers. Much the same sort of thing. Each of us, deep down, thinks the other's training wasn't quite up to our own, but we know how even we really are. What was the final exam for you, Harker? In individual rather than squad training."

Harker gave a mirthless smile. "They stripped us down to our underwear and dropped us on a hellhole of a planet with only what we'd have coming out of a lifeboat. The pickup point, the only one on the whole damned planet, was almost three thousand kilometers away by land and sea. We either got there whole and called for pickup or we failed."

"Fairly similar with us. We dropped as a squad, fully organized, but the problem and objective were the same. Did everyone in your class make it?"

"No. I understand that, out of twenty-five who were eventually dropped, six never checked in."

"Well, my losses were a bit worse," said N'Gana, "That's why we volunteered. Nobody had to do it. Even down to that last drop, anybody could have said 'No!' and nothing more would have been said about it. They'd have simply rotated back. But we went. By that point anybody who'd freeze had already been pressured or threatened out. We did it then. This will be no different."

"Maybe. I was nineteen real at the time and I thought I was immortal and, after that full course, some kind of superman as well. I'm a lot older now, and I've been shot up a lot of times and scraped up a few more."

"Well, I'm nearly fifty real, and I believe I could do that course again. I have yet to be defeated by Doctor Socolov's simulator program, and I see nothing so far that would suggest that this is not doable. I would agree that the odds are almost nil that we will all survive, and slim that any, let alone most, of us will make it back to be picked up. But I don't see anything here that skews the odds any worse than the Ranger examination course."

Harker sighed. "Colonel, I had an electronic direction finder, I had a small sidearm, a medikit, and a few other things when I did my exam. No matter what you say, I know you had similar as well. I'd love to try the Doc's sim, but it's only a guess. Nobody's come back from being down there."

"The Dutchman has people who have managed the trip, or so he says. It is not easy, but if it can be done by pirates, then it can be done by me." He paused. "I do wish that you could try the sim at a high level, if only for me to judge how out of practice you might be, but there will not be time. We are to board the corvette in just over three hours. Since there is a great deal of risk simply activating a gate—let alone coming in-system—near Titans, this will be the start of it. Hector first, then, if it's all there, we go down and the rest remain on Hector. You are in, or you remain right here. You have one hour to decide. After that, there will not be time to allow for your supplies."

"An hour!"

"I think you would be most useful to us, Mister Harker," the Colonel said quite smugly. "And I think having come this far uninvited, you could not resist going the rest of the way. Not someone with your service record and awards."

Harker didn't have to think too hard on this part. "I'll go, at least as far as the moon, just to see what the hell this is all really about. But going down there, on a Titan world—*that* I won't promise."

"Fair enough. Oh—you really should stop by supplies and get yourself a decent pair of pants. In fact, I've already arranged for an entire kit to be prepared in your size. Just pick it up and sign for it."

He was certainly predictable, anyway, Harker thought, as he got and checked through the kit. There were two complete outfits in there, each with the same nondescript black pullovers that the priest, the colonel, and the colonel's long-time partner and aide fancied aboard. In fact, when he answered the page to go to the lower docking bay, he found that it was the uniform of the day.

He was surprised to see that they'd brought his suit down as well. It looked the worse for wear on the outside; the smooth gloss was off it, and it had some minor fading and beading that made it seem less awesome and more seedy, but he knew it was still in top shape inside.

"We think the suit will be quite handy," the colonel told him, seeing his surprise. "Not on the surface of Helena, of course, but on Hector. The same low power modes that allowed it to stick undetected by us to the outer hull of the *Odysseus* should be sufficient for work there without drawing an unwelcome crowd, or so this Dutchman says."

"Anything on him yet? Anything other than what we already knew?" Harker asked.

"Nothing. Every transfer's been by computer and robotics. It's almost like he really is his namesake. A cursed captain who cannot be in the company of humans, served by a ghost crew."

"Surely he's coming with us!"

"I don't think so," Father Chicanis answered. "I think he's staying right where he is. What he needs is in the computer navigational and piloting system on the corvette. He's not going to risk his own neck. Not when he can get us to risk ours."

One by one they gathered there. Only Madame Sotoropolis and Captain Stavros would remain aboard the *Odysseus* for this leg. Neither could offer anything more to the expedition than they had by financing and assembling it.

"I should love to see my beautiful Helena one more time," the old diva said wistfully. "But I would be as a stone to the expedition, and I would be dead in an instant if the Titans sapped energy. I will have to say 'Good luck and Godspeed' from here. Take care, all of you."

A gloved, shaky hand grasped Father Chicanis's and squeezed hard. He looked down at her and said, "If we can do it and it is God's will, we will. That much I swear."

"Do you—do you *really* believe that anyone is still alive down there?" she asked him.

"Not anyone who remembers us, surely," he responded, and clearly not for the first time. "Still, *someone* is there. God would not bring us to this point with these fine people and let us fail. I do believe the road will be one of the hardest anyone has been asked to take in centuries. God bless you, Anna Marie. Sing joyfully of me, for I am going home."

The airlock slid open, and they all turned and walked single file through the tubelike connector and into the small corvette. The suits and other supplies were handled by the *Odysseus*'s automatic cargo and servicing robots, which took them out and slid them into the cargo section in the corvette's underbelly.

Katarina Socolov hadn't been in the assembly, and for a moment he'd hoped that she'd come to her senses, but now here she was, taking a seat next to Father Chicanis in the front row.

The Pooka slithered in and curled up in the back. Being the unexpected added passenger, Harker took the only seat left open, the one next to Krill, just behind the priest and Socolov.

"I see that had I elected not to come I wouldn't have had your company after all," he noted.

"I decided that the old security codes and devices might be more of a problem than we think. I'll not be going to the surface, though. Any encounter with a Titan field will kill me, you know. But I could not allow this to proceed without verifying that it exists and that we can get in and out," Krill replied.

"That fellow whose brain scan you deciphered got in and got information," he noted.

"Yes, but he did not get what we needed and he did not make it out. Even as he died, he could not have truly known if there was anything to this more than a failed project and a set of contingency plans. That's what we find out first."

Harker nodded and looked around. Nine of them going into Titan territory pretty well blind and untrained as a true military team. How could this possibly work?

"I'm still surprised that the Dutchman, or a crony, isn't along," he noted. "Mighty trusting of him after all this."

"What's to trust?" she asked him. "His program is taking us in, his programmed AI unit is handling all the ship's piloting and navigation, and it's the only way to or from. He's got the *Odysseus* and the only exit. What else does he need?"

The corvette powered up, the airlocks closed and then hissed, and finally the lights came on stating that there was a valid seal and that pressurization was accomplished.

They pushed off, then they could feel the ship come about. When the engines came up to normal, though, all sensation of movement stopped and they just had the steady hum of the engines.

"I forgot to ask," Harker said. "How long is this little jaunt?"

"Just a few hours, or so we're told," Father Chicanis called back.

Harker sighed. "Well, then, I'm going to dial up a real meal and a decent drink and then get a little sleep. It seems I've been a very long time between meals."

The food didn't have much taste, but it filled him, which was what he needed. After that he really did recline and nod off, but he kept having the same dream, of a star-filled universe being overrun by cockroaches.

And he was one of the roaches.

There was curiously little conversation on the way, even when they were awake, and then it was entirely about practical things like eating and drinking and power consumption.

Emerging back into normal space from the very small genhole and into the Trojan system was done very quickly, and they knew it from the sudden drop into red warning lights and the sudden and complex maneuvering of the craft.

On the screen, though, came a sun and four very distinct planets.

"Save for a trickle charge that keeps it from imploding, the small genhole is inactive inside the orbit of two of the moons of one of the larger gas giants in the system," Krill explained to him, knowing that he alone would not have been fully briefed. "The amount of surge produced when it powers up and allows us through is masked by the magnetic field and electrical storms in the upper atmosphere of the giant, so unless we literally run into a Titan ship or patrol they won't be able to pull us out of the muck. That's how they move these little ships in and out."

"So they say," he commented.

"Oh, there's no problem with this. As totally incomprehensible as the Titans are, they still obey the general laws of physics. We just haven't figured out how they do it all yet."

We haven't figured out how they do most of it, he thought sourly, but he let it pass. *Much worse, we haven't the vaguest idea why.* How could you deal with an adversary this powerful who would not even accept a surrender?

Cockroaches . . .

Maybe it wasn't so bad being a cockroach after all, he thought. The buggers survived virtually everything and you never could completely get rid of them no matter how hard you tried. No other creature in the universe had ever been encountered that was as versatile and persistent as the various kinds of Terran cockroaches. That, at least, had been a blessing. So if we're the second Terran evolutionary species to be too ornery and tough to die, maybe there's something to be said for the whole thing.

"The trickiest part is right now," she told him, inadvertently reminding the others of the tremendous danger they were now in. Krill was as much computer as human, or so it seemed. She'd clinically describe in great detail her own dissection. "We need to use power to get close to them, and the closer we get, the more likely we are to be detected. I understand that the theory here is to make our signature similar to that of a small comet or meteor. They may count them, but they do not shut them down."

This solar system as originally constituted had been a very good one for humans. Discovered more than four hundred years earlier, it had one planet in the life zone that was so easily and inexpensively terraformable that it was habitable in a matter of decades, and a second world that, though not nearly as nice to live on, was filled with a great many valuable minerals and heavy metals that served as a virtual supply depot for building a new world.

The project was one of the first to have been handled from discovery through settlement by private corporations rather than a government or major institution or movement. The primary contractor for the job had been the large Petros Corporation, which was headed by several large families of ancient Greek extraction, hence the names of all the planets, moons, and the like had been taken from Greek myths. Few of the settlers were actually Greek, though; in fact, there were only so many Greeks at any point compared to the vast ethnic diversity spilling out into space.

Although Helena, as the beautiful habitable world was called, was divided up into districts based on founding Petros family names, there were Italians and Croatians and Yorubans and Han Chinese down there from the start. It was an echo of the ancient Greek world that no ancient Greek would probably have recognized.

Other than a love of and dedication to their new world, though, they had one thing in common that the founding patriarchs of the world had controlled to a large degree.

Constantine Karas had once thought of becoming an Orthodox priest instead of a captain of industry. In his old age and with his crowning project building, he determined that it would be a place where only those Orthodox churches recognized as Christian would flourish. There was already a world or two for just about every other ethnic group or religion or culture: Islamic, Buddhist, Taoist, Baptist, Roman Catholic, as well as many which were polyglot worlds. He held to it, even getting the reigning Patriarchs to recognize Helena's own Orthodox branch, although there were also many Copts down there. Roman Catholics had also been welcome, but they had not flourished there. Even the millennium since the beginning of space travel and colonization hadn't healed the ancient schisms between the Roman and Eastern churches.

That made this mixture even more atypical of the old visions. Harker was a lapsed Roman Catholic, N'Gana was a nominal Moslem, and Mogutu had been raised in the Anglican Communion, as it turned out, while Krill and van der Voort were lifelong atheists from a long line of them. Takamura was something of a Buddhist, but no more devout than Harker or N'Gana. Only Katarina Socolov, who was Ukrainian Orthodox in background, would have been what the old man had in mind for the colonists. It was one reason why she'd been picked for the mission, there being an assumption that something of the religious base might have survived down there even if in mutated form.

"There!" Father Chicanis breathed, pointing to the screen. "There is a full Helena, as beautiful as her legend!"

Nearly filling the screen was a magnified view of the world, looking so very peaceful and normal, a blue and white marble just hanging there in the sky.

"If you look closely, you can see almost all of Atlantis almost in the center of the planet," Chicanis went on. "Eden is a bit south and to the east, but will be coming into view, I suspect, shortly. From this distance they both look more rounded than they actually are, which is how they came to be called Helen's Eyes."

Katarina Socolov grinned and commented, "Come, come, Father! We're not in Sunday school here!"

He gave a kind of resigned chuckle and replied, "All right, then. Most people called them Helen's Breasts."

That drew a snicker from the combat folks in the rear and helped break the tension. It was only a brief respite, though; they could all feel it, made all the worse because at the moment they were helpless and totally at the mercy of the Dutchman and his programming. If a Titan should pass by or do an energy sweep, they were all dead and they knew it.

The computer on the corvette broke in with a voice that

sounded a lot like the Dutchman's. "I can show you through filters the Titan layout down there and you can see the sweep," it said. "I will do this now, but I must then power off the screen until we are in and behind Hector. I am registering an abnormally high energy flow. One of the suits in the hold must be powered on more than it should be."

Probably mine, Harker thought. He suspected that the damned thing was smarter than he was, or at least cleverer.

The screen changed and went through a series of obvious visual filters. It was on the broad-spectrum filter that the Titan net was clearly visible, though. Now, most of Atlantis and a good half of Eden were visible, and in the viewer you could clearly see the bright anchor points of the Titan bases, the smaller anchors and the center nexus for each, and the rather tight grid for each continent. The poles also pulsed brightly, and, because the corvette's pilot had timed it for this purpose, they were able to see the thin pole-to-pole line of the steady sweep, as if a single line of longitude were visibly making its way around the world.

It was a reminder of what they were *really* looking at: a world that had once been alive and filled with people, living a pretty good life there in relative peace and contentment, but no more. Now it was a conquered world, an *occupied world*. And there was the enemy.

"Powering down," said the computer pilot. The screen went blank, and for some reason that action, coming immediately after that vision of the grids and sweeps below, felt more threatening, more *scary*, than just seeing it.

It was probably no more than a half hour, possibly a bit longer, but it seemed like an eternity before the screen came to life again. Curiously, during that time there had been almost no conversation, as if all of them, collectively, had been holding their breaths.

Now the screen came to life again. "Power is stabilized," the pilot reported. "Achilles now in sight. We will be using it as partial cover until we can move easily to Hector."

Achilles looked like a proper moon, about thirty percent the size of the planet below and essentially round. It was heavily cratered, but frozen liquid covered much of its surface, giving the appearance of vast flat spots with jagged fractures.

After a few more minutes, during which they pretty much paced Achilles and kept it between them and the planet below, they saw Hector coming toward them. None of them were impressed.

"Shaped like a thigh bone," Katarina Socolov commented. "What a silly, twisted little thing!"

"Not much gravity on it, either," Admiral Krill warned her. "And the uneven rotation can be rather dizzying from the model I've run. Still, it's where we have to go."

"Why didn't they put it on Achilles?" Colonel N'Gana asked aloud. "Stable platform, plenty of water. What kind of weapon could you even aim from that thing?"

"It seems we are coming in to land," Krill responded. "I think we may soon find out—if there's anything there at all."

THIRTEEN

The Coming of the Demons

They had moved back, away from the river, but Littlefeet had not been able to shake the sensation that things were not as they should be. For one thing, they seemed so far outside their traditional territory that he was certain that the Family was headed far closer to the coast than it had ever been, and it didn't take a genius to see that the distant mountains to the west, which had always defined their boundary, were considerably farther away and looked more like ghosts or discolorations in clouds than high snowcapped peaks.

Father Alex was feeling much the same misgivings, and the unexplained deaths of the other family's scouts, even though months had passed, continued to haunt him.

Lost? How in God's name could the Family ever be lost? It was inconceivable. Yet every time they had scouted west they had hit other rivers, natural barriers as uncrossable if not as wide or as threatening as the great river to the east, that simply should not have been there. Since the land did not change in this fashion, at least not like this, it meant that they had jogged more south than west after retreating from the great river and had somehow gotten caught in a new area.

No, that couldn't be right. How could there be rivers on both sides of them *if they had not ever crossed a river in the first place*? Rivers did not spring whole from the ground; they had sources in the mountains or in the upper lakes fed by various streams and waterfalls.

He called the Family council together, and they were as baffled as he was. Finally, one of the old Brothers who had clearly not much longer to live but whose experience was all the more valuable for that said, "We must depart from our traditional ways this once, it is clear. Since, as it is said, we cannot have a river on both sides without crossing one, and we have not crossed one, then one of two things has happened. Either the one to the west *does* spring from the ground even though we have not seen this before, in which case we must travel north along it to its source and go around it, or God is shaping a new path for us, in which case we will not find a source and will be forced to go where He wills. In either case, the course is clear. To the western river, and then north."

They all prayed for guidance, but the only thing that they received was the wisdom of the old Brother, who had survived some fifty-plus years, and that would have to do. The Lord, Father Alex reflected, always seemed to make the struggle so hard. As he was so fond of noting to his questioning pupils, though, God always answered every single prayer. It was just that He usually said, "No."

Littlefeet was back pretty much to his normal self now, and was feeling far more secure. He was the veteran now, instructing the new young would-be warriors and scouts and wearing his scars and limp like battle tattoos. He still thought of Spotty, but not as much as he used to. It was Greenie, in fact, who had borne his son just a few nights before, while Spotty had delivered someone else's daughter. His thoughts were much less on any one-time adolescent romance than on the idea that one day his son would be in the men's kraal and he would be able to teach him all the skills of survival. Still, he could never quite get out of his mind how she had stood by him all that time he'd been injured, first in his soul and then in his body. That counted. That would always count.

The smaller river they followed now was not on anybody's list of known features, and that was one reason why nobody liked their position. Still, over the week since they'd turned back north, it had been growing progressively narrower, and the creeks that they had to contend with that fed into it tended to be small, shallow, and easily manageable. It seemed obvious that either they were going to reach its source fairly soon or that it would cease to be a real obstacle and allow a ford. The current was swift, but already it seemed quite shallow.

In the evenings, Littlefeet liked to go near the shore and watch the water. He wasn't at all sure why he found it fascinating, but more than once he wished that people could somehow get in and move around in a big river or lake even if it was so deep you couldn't touch bottom. There were stories about folks who could do that, but he was one who had never believed it possible. Certainly nobody in *this* Family knew how to do it.

Still, in the early evening or again in the predawn light, if he was up he would watch it, almost as if hypnotized by its rippling power, and he watched things float by on their way down to the sea. Leaves, even some logs, all sorts of stuff that fell in the river seemed to float along the top and go for some distance downstream before mostly hitting the bank or some built-up reef and sticking there.

He began to wonder why you couldn't find a log that would hold up a person and float on top of the water. It would be risky, sure, and scary, since when it finally hit something you might fall off or, worse, get stuck out in the middle, but the thought stuck in his mind. The other warriors found the idea interesting but hardly practical. Besides, why in heaven's name would you ever want to? What would be the purpose or the need? It seemed to them to be all risk and no reward.

He supposed that they were right, but it still seemed like there should be some use for it. Suppose you were out here, scouting, say, and got cut off by Hunters? You couldn't make it back and you were outnumbered, but if you could jump on something and float with the river, you could escape them and maybe get back since they would lose the ability to track you. It was a thought, even if his limp kept him out of the scouting business for now. He began to try and figure out how to prove his idea.

The nightmares came and went, but as they moved north there was a certain heightened intensity to them when they involved the demon images themselves. You could always tell when you were eavesdropping on demon thoughts; there was a curious fish-eye appearance to everything, where every view seemed grossly distorted, and almost always from above. Not too far above the ground, it was true—but above the level of the highest things that grew. The colors, too, were off, and the vision was often double or even triple. He hadn't been sure whether these were really things he was getting from other creatures or whether they were in his own head, but as they progressed he got his answer.

Others now were having them, too, and more often than not the images were strikingly similar to his, if not as detailed or vivid. He began to talk of it with the other young men, all of whom were equally worried.

"There are demons ahead on this path," Big Ears agreed. "Demons ahead, and water on the other three sides. This is not good."

"It is as if we are being forced into their arms, if they have arms," Hairy Toes put in. "They clouded our Elders' minds, and those of the scouts, to put us into this trap. They mean to take us, that's for sure."

"I'll die before I let any demons take *me*!" Littlefeet told them firmly. "I'll not be caged and made into some mindless thing for their amusement!"

The others murmured agreement, but all knew as well that their first responsibility wasn't to their own welfare but to the welfare of the Family.

"They may just want the women, to breed their foul mixed-breed monsters," Great Lips suggested. "You know, like they tell in the ancient stories."

"Well, we'll fight 'em all the way, no matter what the cost!" another warrior told them, and they all nodded sagely. There was a certain comfort in talking this way as a group, but, later on, almost all of them would consider what they had said and wonder how they with their spears and blowguns could possibly stop the demons from taking anything and anybody they wanted.

Not that they hadn't all seen demons, at least once. At great distances, of course, and without a lot of definition, but they could hardly be missed, particularly some clear nights, when they sped across the sky in their moon ships and did things that everyone knew were impossible, like streaking so fast you could hardly see them and then stopping in an instant, and making sharp right and sharp left turns at great speed. That was supernatural power, there was no doubt of it.

Even in the daytime they could occasionally be seen, their ships less distinct, more blurry, but still doing what they did, like gigantic glowing seeds. They almost never took an interest in anybody on the ground, though, or so it seemed. Few could think of a time when one actually went right over either a camp or a march, and none could remember one so much as pausing, let along stopping, in the vicinity. Still, they were there ahead, that was for sure, and the young men of the Family could sense them.

In a few more days, they found out why, as the ever shallower and ever narrowing river led them to the very edge of the great groves of demon flowers.

Even Father Alex knew that they could not be that far off course. The huge flowers took up the whole center of the bowl-shaped region of the continent, but never close to the Families, or accessible to them. He summoned Littlefeet.

"No, Father, this could not be where I saw the great demon flowers," he concurred. "This *must* be new."

Father Alex sighed and nodded. "So that's it, then. They are expanding their groves, and they have diverted rivers to ensure that their cursed flowers get the water that they need. Such effortless power, and for what? Giant flowers!"

"Why do they do this, Father? Why do they grow these and not care about us or anything else?"

Father Alex shook his head. "Who can know how a demon thinks, my son? I am not even certain that we would understand it if we did know, nor, perhaps, should we spend much time trying to imagine what demons think. Know only that they exist to thwart the will of God and corrupt His creations, for that is the nature of rebellion." He turned and looked away from the huge flowers. "I believe we should consider other questions of a more practical nature," he added.

"Sir?"

"We cannot go in those groves. Now, at least, we can be reasonably certain that this confusion was not directed at us but rather was the result of their meddling further with creation. We dare not go into the grove. Those who go into the groves tend to go mad. We *must* risk crossing the river. It appears shallow enough at this point, but it is still wider than I would like, and you never know about such things. Let's see—who is the tallest warrior in the Family? Walking Stick?"

"Yes, Father. He is a head taller than even you."

"He will do. Bring him to me, and we will see if this river can be crossed along this point."

Littlefeet started to go find the tall man, but then he stopped. "Um—Father?"

"Yes, my son?"

"What if it can't be crossed here?"

"We must cross it. Otherwise, our Family will surely perish, trapped in this area with too little food and far too little land. Our protection against the Hunters is the expanse of our territory. Here—well, sooner or later, Hunters will find us. No, we must cross. We *must*."

Walking Stock was tall and lean but not the strongest man for all his size. He was a little ungainly even in normal walking, as if his body had grown up only in some parts and not in others, and he was not at all thrilled with the idea of taking a walk across a river.

"Tie vines together, as many as we can muster," Father Alex commanded. "If possible, see if we can make a chain of vines that will span the very river! This way, if Walking Stick falls in or it gets too deep, we can haul him back in before he breathes water and dies."

It was the women who began assembling the vines while foragers came in with as many more as they could find in the surrounding area. Littlefeet, however, was looking for something else, and he found it in a curious log that he watched float out of the grove beyond and come down, bobbing and weaving in the current. He saw it hit something in the middle of the water and suddenly shoot over toward the riverbank he was standing on. He walked downriver a bit, pacing it, and was rewarded when it came very close to shore. At that point he took a chance, waded in just a bit, and grabbed it.

The log was half his size, yet weighed almost nothing. It was incredibly light, and easy to bring on shore. Catching his breath, he hauled it the nearly full kilometer back north to where most of the Family was preparing for the possible crossing.

"What is that?" several of the women asked, and some of the warriors laughed and responded, "Littlefeet is going to float down the river on his great log!"

Red-faced and upset at the derision, Littlefeet decided to show them! Several of the Elders shouted for him to stop, and he could hear Father Alex running up, bellowing at the top of his lungs, "Wait! Wait! Do not let your pride kill you! You cannot swim!"

It was too late, and the taunts overwhelmed his otherwise keen sense of self-preservation. He pushed it out into the flowing waters while grabbing onto it tightly.

For a brief moment he feared that they were right; it wasn't as easy keeping hold of the thing while moving with nothing beneath you to give you confidence. Panic overwhelmed him, but he fought it back as he maneuvered for the most comfortable way to "ride" the log.

It was scary and not at all what he expected; the log and its rider spun around and went out toward the center of the river, all the time tracing a lazy circular pattern that left him disoriented, while the shouts of his Family members seemed to come from everywhere at once. He knew now that this was a *very* bad idea, even if the principle was right, but at this point he didn't see any way to stop it or get off.

They hit some floating branches with leaves still on them; they scratched him. Now and then his feet would actually bump something, possibly rocks on the bottom or maybe mud, and threaten to loosen his tight two-armed grip on the log.

He had no idea how long this ride of terror continued. Eventually the river took a turn to the east but the log did not; it ran aground on a soft mud bar, the water suddenly only millimeters deep where the sediment had built up as the river slowed for the turn. The shock jarred him off and into the mud, and the shock of that was enough to jiggle the log loose again. It drifted away, back out into the river, as he struggled with thick, grasping mud that seemed to be alive and trying to pull him down.

Exhausted, he managed to crawl in the shallow mud up

toward the shore, and when he reached real solid ground he simply collapsed, a mud-covered, gasping mess rather than a warrior of the great Family Karas.

How long he lay there he did not know; the fear and exhaustion of the float and escape had drained him, and he might even have passed out for a time. When he felt rested enough, he found the mud baked hard over much of his body, and the sun seemed quite low in the sky.

Aching, he managed to get up and walk a bit back north, beyond the bend, to where the river's mud was level rather than banked, and, finding a solid rock to perch on, he managed to wash off some of the mud. The rest would have to wait until he got back to the camp, which he assumed was still where he had left it, considering the limited options for movement they had.

He got up, looked around, and tried to get his bearings. The sun was quite low over there, and shadows were lengthening. That meant that north was up *this* way, as he'd thought, but something was wrong. If north was *that* way, then the river was in the wrong place! With a shock, he suddenly realized why: he'd landed on the wrong side of the river!

Well, not exactly the wrong side. In one way he'd proved his point. He was on the side the Family wanted to be on. Trouble was, he was pretty sure that there was no shallow spot for fording the river between where he'd left them and here. In fact, this bend was probably as shallow as it was going to get.

Now what? he wondered. *Best maybe I go back up, even if I am on the wrong side. Maybe I can help rig up a crossing for the Family.* If Walking Stick hadn't managed to get across, and he suspected that the tall warrior hadn't, then *he* might be able to do the job. There were a few good archers and spear throwers among the young men; if one of them could get the line across, then he could tie it off and reinforce it.

He started walking, trying to ignore the aches and pains caused by his flotation, and made some time before he realized that it would soon be dark and he was still a fair way from the Family. He had to be a pretty good distance away because he hadn't even heard them.

Going into the groves of trees and bushes nearby, he managed to find enough food to satisfy him through the night. Food was abundant here, as abundant as it was scarce where the family was now trapped. He had to get them across! He just *had* to!

The night was not peaceful for him.

They came in the night, well after the nightly storm and at first only in his dreams. Nebulous shapes, very large and very real yet somehow fuzzy, as if viewed just after you woke up and before your vision cleared. Some were as silent as the grave; others gave off odd buzzing or humming noises that changed as they went across the sky.

The demon eggs, in which the Fallen rode across their conquered planet.

In his mind, in his dreams, he could hear them, although this made no real sense. If he was hearing their thoughts, then they were thoughts beyond his comprehension, inhuman sounds, gibberish of the worst order. But he could *see* as they saw, looking down from their demon eggs, the warped and distorted view that made everything look so monstrous, so large in the middle and so small trailing away on all sides, and so bizarre, with people, insects, small animals, and even plants shining with colors that no human eye saw, night or day, and in some cases making people look as if they were on fire. Even the air had color and texture to it, like the shimmer of heat in the distance on a particularly hot day, only he did not see the heat as distortions in the air but as a pale yellow-orange gas.

Their thoughts were impenetrable, but they radiated a cold indifference to what they were seeing that chilled him as much as the solid water had up high in the mountains—

worse, because it seemed to go all the way to his heart and freeze his soul.

He saw them pass right over the camp, which was still laid out by the side of the river—and the wrong side at that. The Family hadn't made it, and they hadn't figured an alternative way to cross yet, either. He was curiously disappointed; although it gave him the chance of being a hero, the Family always came first, even at the expense of his life, and he would have much rather seen them on this side, or not seen them at all. He could track the Family and rejoin it, but if they were still over there, they were trapped and exposed.

The demons did seem to take note of the large group there, every one of them pausing for a moment to examine it before continuing, but they felt no concern, no alarm, nor did they even feel dangerous to the mostly sleeping group of humans. Once identified, they could be safely ignored, and the demons went on across the groves of their great plants.

Interestingly, over the gigantic flowers, most closed for the night but some open to the stars for whatever reason, there was a sense that the demons really did care about them, that the flowers were important, almost a part of them. It was the kind of feeling he'd gotten when he'd seen his first child born, although he did not for a moment think the flowers were in any way true children of the demons. Still, his mind made that analogy, the only one that came even close.

Father Alex had taught that no human could understand the demons, and that those with some of the Sight into demon thoughts should never try, for to understand them would be to cross over to their side voluntarily. If you did that, you had sold your soul.

Littlefeet had been born and raised in a hunter-gatherer society of the most basic sort; the old stories and legends of the times when men were like gods were told, of course, but these had little relevance to anyone hearing them except to drive home just how hard they had fallen, and how cursed and unlucky they were to be among the generations after humanity's Fall. He could no more comprehend those tales than he could understand the demons, and he spent no more time trying one than the other.

He could not even understand the preparation and planting of things; they just grew and, luckily, in abundance enough to feed the Families. Littlefeet's distant cousins among the stars who had not yet fallen to the Titans understood the activity, although not why they did it or what the flowers truly meant to the Titans. Beyond that, they were as ignorant as Littlefeet and his people. Nobody knew if the small fuzzy egglike structures were Titans, or containers for Titans, or ships. Nobody knew much of anything, even after a very long time. They only knew that you couldn't fight them, that all that had been tried against them had failed.

And, like Littlefeet, they knew that the Titans really didn't give a damn about humanity. It was just an irritant; it was something in the way.

Littlefeet awoke with a great sense of foreboding. He was pretty sure they hadn't even noticed him, off by himself and still downstream, but now the demons were doing something up there with the flowers, both inside the great existing groves and on the riverbank to the west—*his* side.

He could hear the weird thrumming noise as they worked just north of him, and he could actually see a couple of large demon eggs poised above a spot, their undersides now crackling with energy and using lightninglike tendrils of orange to rapidly do *something* to the ground. As each of the tendrils whipped around in its frantic activity, the demon sounds grew stronger, louder, more persistent. He didn't like this one bit, and he knew that if he didn't like it, the rest of the Family up north would be in a near panic.

There was only moderate moonlight from Achilles, but it, together with the light radiated from the higher demon ships, gave him enough illumination to move in the darkness. He couldn't afford to sleep right now, or even be tired; he shook it off. He had to get north, to the point across from the Family!

He moved fast, using reflections in the river of the lights from above to keep himself oriented and on solid ground, and, while tripping and falling several times, he managed to get very close to the camp, close enough to hear yelling and screaming. It was then that he began to see bodies floating in the river.

They were mostly too far out for him to tell who they were, but it didn't matter; all of them were Family, and he knew each one no matter who was out there.

Most were dead, but here and there he could hear screams and see people actually clinging to bodies, using them as he'd used the log. He was surprised that the bodies held up like that, and, certainly, many did not, but smaller, lighter figures clung to one here or there, screaming in terror.

"Hold on and kick the water!" he yelled at the top of his lungs. "Kick the water away and come to me! Kick! Kick and I will get you when you come near!"

Most heard him, but only a couple actually made the attempt or stifled their panic. Others were losing their grips or going under with the bodies.

He saw one actually manage to get close to the bank, thrashing away, and he ran down close and then reached out. "Give me your hand! Your hand!" he yelled, and the floater did. The first time he missed, but the second time he got a grip and pulled what proved to be a screaming woman not much older than he to shore. She was still clinging to the body of an older man, a warrior by what markings he could make out. Littlefeet made no attempt to rescue the body; dead was dead and there was little that could be done for him.

The woman, little more than a girl, lay there sobbing and gasping for breath and coughing up crud. "Just stay here!" he told her. "I'm going to try and save others!"

He did manage to get two more, in one case moving back down the riverbank some distance. All three were young women. One who seemed half-drowned and not long for the world he fought desperately to save.

It was Spotty.

None of the Families knew how to swim, but some things all warriors were taught, including how to keep someone from choking and the way to clear water from the lungs. He worked on her, pressing rhythmically on her abdomen, then blowing in her mouth, forcing the water up, forcing air in to displace it. He was afraid he was going to lose her, but then she coughed and turned half over and threw up a lot of water. He hadn't thought anybody could breathe that much water and live.

When she could sit up, still occasionally coughing and puking but obviously a survivor, he squatted down close to her and said, "Just stay here. I have saved two more and maybe I can get others!"

She tried to protest but that just brought on more wracking coughs, so she tried to hold on to him with a grip so tight it startled him.

Gently, he tried to pry her hand off his arm. "I'll be back, I swear," he told her in a gentle tone, and she relaxed. Still, when he got up, she managed by sheer force of will to get to her feet as well. He reached out to steady her, knowing that, if she could, she was going to follow him.

By the time he surveyed the river again, there didn't seem to be very many bodies left in sight and none with any signs of life either in them or clinging to them. Still, the sight sickened him. They were Family, and he felt each loss as if it had been one of his own immediate circle of friends. He even felt slighty guilty that he hadn't been there, little that he might have done.

Spotty seemed to grow a bit stronger with each step, but he knew she was running on sheer nervous energy and couldn't keep it up for long. The second girl that he'd rescued was just sitting there now, staring out at the water, almost curled up in a ball. He had seen this before. She was in shock, and would be in some danger until she collapsed and slept it off. She was called Froggy because she had an unusually deep voice for a girl.

He turned to Spotty. "Are you up to caring for her? I have one more to get just up here. If you can see to her, then I can get the other one and maybe we can make plans."

Spotty had recovered some of her wits and nodded, although it was clear that she didn't want him to leave. Duty now came first, and she accepted it.

The third girl was called Leaf because of the way her hair naturally draped over her head. She'd seemed the best off of the lot when he'd dragged her in; that was why he'd been confident enough to leave her to see to the others.

He found her sitting there, very natural-looking, staring out at the river. It was so natural that it wasn't until he touched her and saw her open, unblinking eyes that he realized she was dead.

He said a little prayer for her, closed her eyes, and laid her out on the ground. There wasn't much else he could do now but head back to the other two, which he did in some haste, now suddenly fearing that if Leaf could die like that, so could they.

Both were, however, still alive, much to his relief. "She was alive when I pulled her out, but she was dead when I returned," he explained. "I do not see any more, but more may have made it farther down. Can you speak? Can you tell me what happened?"

Spotty's voice was so raspy that it sounded worse than Froggy's ever had, and speaking was clearly painful for her. "Some Hunters, some crazy, wild folk, they came out of the flowers when the demons came," Spotty told him. "We fought with them, but they were crazy and began to kill. They kept fighting until they were hacked almost to pieces." Her tone was flat, her eyes almost blank, as if she were relating something she'd heard, not lived through. "They got into our kraal. Some of the babies—"

Her voice trailed off, and it was clear she couldn't go on.

"What about the rest of the Family?" he pressed, feeling guilty for doing it to her. But he had to know, and Froggy wasn't in any shape to talk yet.

"Father Alex screamed for us to scatter," she told him. "The warriors made as much of a line as they could to preserve our way out, but then more Hunters came from the south and we were trapped between. Many of us jumped or fell in the river, having no place to go. Others—I don't know. Many surely did scatter into the darkness, but how many I can't say."

At least he understood the situation. There were always Hunters around of one kind or another, mostly scavenging, feeding off the weak, dead, and dying, trying to figure out how to get a better meal. Being trapped there had obviously brought some in, maybe trapped as well by the new river the demons had made. Then, when the demons went to their groves and began doing whatever it was they did, anyone hiding in there was flushed out. It was always said that to spend even one night in those groves was to go forever mad. Maybe it was true.

"Well, we're not going anywhere tonight," he told them. "Both of you come away from the river. I will stand guard as well as I can, but I think we are probably safe for the night here on this side of the river. Get some sleep."

"And then what?" she asked him in that same flat tone.

"I don't know, but it will be easier to find out in the daylight," was all he could think to answer.

They slept on grass in the brush, exhausted, unable to stay awake. Littlefeet intended to stay awake himself, but he, too, had had a very long day, and in any case he was no match right now for any Hunters that might come along. In spite of his wishes, he nodded off himself.

In his mind, in his dreams, he saw it all again, this time not through demon eyes but through someone else's, someone human. It was horrible, nightmarish, brutal and hopeless. He saw many of his friends get taken down, some of the women grabbed and eaten alive, two Hunters munching on a screeching baby before several women and two warriors fell on them and hacked them to bits with knives and sharp cooking rocks.

With a start he realized that he was seeing it all replayed through Spotty's eyes, inside her nightmares. He knew this not because he saw anything to indicate it, but because he saw her finally isolated, pushed into the water, struggling and coming up grabbing on to Rockhand's body, and then, panicked and thrashing, *sensing* rather than hearing someone on the other shore, someone drilling into her frightened brain, *"Kick! Kick and hold on!"*

Somehow he and Spotty had been connected, at least as strongly as he'd been in his dreams to the passing demons. Her being one of the survivors was not as much the marvelous coincidence it first seemed, although it still might be the work of God's hand. She had heard him while others had not, heard him in her mind, and this had given her the will and strength to make it to him.

It was well past sunup when he awoke and found the two girls still lying there near him. He nervously stared at each, but saw that both breathed; their chests went up and down, and there was some movement now and again. He relaxed.

He thought about scavenging for some food, but decided to wait. He didn't want to wake them, not now, but he had the feeling that, whatever they did from now on, they should do together; that it was better to be a little hungry than to split up.

The hot sun and the crescendo of insects stirred up by it began to make things uncomfortable, though, and very soon Spotty stirred and then opened her eyes. She looked around, then sat up, frowning.

"Good morning," he said softly. "Or, rather, more like midday."

She stared at him in seeming confusion, then managed, "I—I . . . Do you know me?"

"Of course I do," he responded, a little confused himself. "Don't you remember? I'm Littlefeet."

"Little—No, I, um, I don't know *what* I mean. I mean, I can't seem to remember *anything*."

He realized that she wasn't playing with him. "You *really* don't remember who you are?"

She shook her head. "Nothing. It's like I just, well, woke up. I know your words, I understand you and can speak, but I don't know anything else. It is a little scary."

He'd never seen anything like this, but the old tall tales and legends had had stories about this sort of thing. He'd never believed them, but apparently it was possible to lose your memory. Not a little, but mostly. In the stories, people always lost their memories after having something awful done to them, so maybe that was true, too. Even if he'd thought it could really happen to somebody, though, he would never have bet on Spotty. Not tough, caring Spotty.

Froggy sighed, turned over a bit, then opened her eyes. She was short and chubby with big breasts, in dramatic contrast with the taller, thinner Spotty. "Oh, my!" she sighed. "I had such awful dreams!"

"They weren't dreams," he told her softly. "Um—do you remember who *you* are?"

"Um, yeah, sure. You're Feet and I'm Froggy and this is Spotty. What are *you* doing here, anyway? And where's everybody else?"

"Then you don't remember," he replied. *Just more than Spotty does.*

It turned out that she didn't, not really. She remembered a lot, but the previous night's horrors had been totally blotted out, not erased but relegated to confused if frightening nightmares. She found it hard to believe that anything was missing, but was even more astonished to find Spotty completely blank.

"You two went through a lot last night," he told them. "I think it'll come back to you, at least some of it, after a while. Some of it, I think, you'd both be better off not getting back."

"So what do we do now?" Froggy asked him. He'd never taken a lot of notice of her before, but for all the shock and horror of the previous night she seemed in better shape than Spotty.

"Let's all find something to eat," he suggested. "It's not hard over here. Then we'll work our way up north and see what's left of the camp. Spotty, you'll just have to stick with us and trust us until your memory comes back. Okay?"

"I guess," she replied. "I don't have anything else I can do, and from what you say, it's real scary out there."

He found some melons that made a good breakfast, and then they worked their way back to the river. Mercifully, he saw no bodies around, either floating or against the banks. The current had been swift enough to carry them at least out of sight downriver.

An hour or two's walk north brought them directly across from the Family camp. It was all trampled and clear to be seen from their vantage point, which meant it was no more good as a camp anyway. There were some bodies visible over there, but it was impossible at this distance to tell who they were, or even if they were friend or foe. Probably a mixture of both. Hordes of insects were already going to work on the remains.

Far off he could hear the sound of one of the demon machines, but he couldn't see it. No others were in evidence.

Littlefeet sighed. "Well, I don't think everybody got killed, 'cause if they had there'd be a lot more bodies over there. Still and all, they've scattered all over to be safe and preserve the Family, and I don't hear any wailing babies or anything like that, so they're some distance off. The scouts'll try and round 'em up, but where that'll be it's hard to say. Won't be here, and I don't think they'll try this camp again, not this close."

Spotty didn't really follow some of this, but Froggy was upset. "You mean we're cut off?"

He nodded. "Seems like. It's the three of us on this side and all the other survivors on that side. Well, at least that tells me what we gotta do."

"Yeah? Like what?"

"Well, if we came up north to the demon flowers and couldn't find a crossing, then they'll come back to the river and head south, figuring maybe that somewhere down there might be enough built-up mud and crud to manage a swamp crossing. That's my guess as to how they'll think. So we move south. If we find 'em, maybe we can help get 'em across."

"What if we can't find 'em?" Froggy asked him.

He sighed. "Then I guess we're on our own."

FOURTEEN

Priam's Lens

There were spacesuits for everyone aboard, although even Colonel N'Gana's suit did not have the capabilities of Harker's experimental model. N'Gana knew it, as did the silent but always attentive Mogutu, but the only thing the colonel could say was, "Look, Mister Harker—no matter what else, let us get one thing straight. I am in charge. I am the commanding officer of this expedition. Although you are a military officer, you are not in a formal military unit and you were not planned for on this one, so Sergeant Mogutu also outranks you. Understand?"

"It's your party, Colonel," Harker responded. "Right now I'm just along for the ride."

The corvette could not risk actually landing on Hector; the thrusting maneuvers would have invited attention from the planet below. Instead, it braked and matched motion with the moon, then glided with minimal energy expenditure to where they wanted to go.

Hector was not large, but it was still almost six hundred kilometers in length, big enough to make an impression, albeit a small one, on the surface of the planet. In fact it usually looked like a small star-sized or planet-sized beacon, blinking in odd patterns because of its wobbly rotation and irregular shape.

Matched now with specific features on the surface, the interior of the corvette depressurized and everyone checked out in their suits. One by one they went out the hatch and, using primarily compressed air, floated to the surface below. The compressed air system was good enough for this purpose, and did not contribute to any energy signatures that could be picked up below. As soon as the last one was down, the corvette slowly moved off and out of sight, keeping its profile behind the tiny moon for the same reason.

The surface was about what Harker had expected. Dark igneous rock for the most part, pockmarked with tiny impact craters. The surface, for all that, seemed almost fluid, the rock bending and twisting, creating a rough and wholly irregular landscape.

Low-level automatic signals kept them pretty well tethered to the leader as if by a long strand of flexible rope. There was very little gravity to keep them on the surface, but the suits were able to compensate. They all learned pretty early, though, to keep their eyes on the ones in front of them and on the surface itself. While you couldn't feel any movement, the sky when turned away from Helena was in a slow but noticeable motion that could be very disconcerting. N'Gana, Mogutu, and Harker, all old spacehands, had little trouble with it, but it was causing problems for some of the others.

"Put your suits on automatic," N'Gana suggested. "They won't let you fall. It won't be much longer now."

They walked to some low knobs that formed a very shallow valley and then into the valley. At the far end there was a darkened area that seemed different, although it took even Harker a few moments to figure out why.

No impact or other features at all were apparent. It was smooth as glass.

"Admiral, detach and come forward please," the colonel instructed, sounding calm and professional. "I believe it is your turn to open our way."

Krill was fairly unsteady and clearly uncomfortable here, but she was game, Harker gave her that. She took little steps, making her way to the front and then bracing herself against the smooth, streamlined V-shaped end of the valley.

This was where the absorption and analysis of the transmission from the surface was so valuable. With her computerlike mind and augmented mental abilities, Krill was able to instantly analyze the system in use here and then interface with the security system on the other side. It could have been done with a robotic system using the same information, but Krill was an acknowledged genius at this sort of thing and much more apt to see any nasty little traps that might have been laid.

She suddenly stopped and took a step back; they could hear the frown in her voice. "That's odd. It should have cleared."

She looked around, then up, and added, "Ah. Wait."

The great disk of Helena was above them, but not for long, as the combination of Hector's rapid rotation and irregular shape took it in a slow slide out of sight. At almost the instant it faded from view, there was a slight sparkling on the heretofore black obsidianlike rock. Krill turned, nodded to herself, and walked through. "Quickly," she said. "As soon as any part of Helena is in a direct line, it will instantly power down."

They all hurried. Once inside, they found themselves in a surprisingly large chamber that had been scooped out of the natural rock by some kind of heat ray. It was like being in an ancient cavern where not even water had touched, but the walls and ceiling were coated with a chemical substance that glowed. It wasn't as good as full-blown lighting, but it would have allowed anyone there to see around even if they weren't wearing a special suit, and it gave all of them, appropriately suited up, more than enough light to amplify and use.

"We're safe in here, even with suit power," Krill told them. "This is fairly deep and well insulated from outside scans. It's as close to a perfect natural jammer as I've seen. They must have been working here when Helena fell, and possibly after."

Katarina Socolov looked around nervously at the cold, empty, glowing chamber. "But where did they go?"

"There's nothing here to sustain a workforce for almost a century," the colonel pointed out. "I suspect that much of the work was done by machines, probably coupled to a large database, AI unit, and neural net. I'm not getting much in the way of readings on it now, though."

Krill checked her instrumentation and tried to use her special interfacing abilities. "It's in complete shutdown," she told them at last. "I doubt if it has the power to actually operate the device here, or, if it does, just powering up would be enough to bring Titan ships in force to see what was going on."

Harker looked around. "Okay, so where is this thing? And what the hell is it?"

Krill looked around, then pointed. "Over there. Through that tunnel."

They walked quickly over and through, Krill leading the way, only to emerge in a much smaller chamber almost too cramped to fit them in their suits.

It was certainly a control room of some sort. A series of screens were mounted in front of a central console, the screens creating a 180-degree forward view and rising up almost to the ceiling. The console itself was not nearly as elaborate. There were no gauges, small screens, dials, switches, or anything of the sort. There was a single command chair, but it was oddly shaped and hardly designed for normal human sitting. It was, in fact, quite large and bulky.

"The command chair is designed to interface with a specially designed suit," Krill noted, examining it thoroughly. "I'd say the whole thing was designed to connect a human in a suit designed for control purposes with the computer net integrated into the room. The screens appear to be for the observers' benefit. This is most certainly it, though. The control center for Project Ulysses."

"All right," Harker responded. "So what the hell *is* it?"

"A control center, Mister Harker," Juanita Krill replied. "A control center and aiming mechanism and a lot more for controlling a force nobody *yet* understands. Synchronize your suits for an incoming visual and I will transmit to you just what this is all about. I believe it is time that you know what the rest of us know, and perhaps I can also, at this point, fill in a few holes for the others."

The synchronization took barely a moment, and then they all received an image of a vast starfield. Nothing in it looked familiar, although it appeared to cover a fair segment of space. What was telling was a bright and indistinct area shaped much like a giant eye that had to be an artifact of transmission; it couldn't possibly be present in real life. It showed some stars and other structures, some clear, some a bit smudged as if obscured by gases, but what was important was that it did not match the surrounding starfield. It was like an eerie, eye-shaped window that looked right through the universe to another, different scene beyond. Even more strange, the eye would occasionally "blink"; it didn't actually open and close, but the scene it revealed would shift radically, then, a bit later, shift back. It was pretty unnerving.

"*That* is Priam's Lens," Krill told them. "It is only a few parsecs from here, and it is what is known as a microlens. We've seen these since we could look into space with adequate equipment, but most tend to be of galactic or even supergalactic size. Walls and giant lenses and bubbling voids. This one is quite small. Smaller than an average gas giant, in fact. It is, of course, not real. It's a distortion caused by something else that is there. Something so powerful and so mysterious that to call it an artifact of a singularity would be like calling an amputation a hangnail. We may never actually know what it is, because it isn't at the Lens but instead *causes* it from some other place connected to this sector by this hole in space-time. We have seen many natural wormholes before, although they usually close rather quickly after they open. Judging from its gravitational effects, this one has been around a *very* long time and shows no signs of shutting down. In fact, controlling or at least capping it was the primary problem to be solved."

"They *capped* a natural wormhole?" Harker was astonished.

"Well, yes and no. We could not cap the Lens—it does not help to cap what you cannot even know is there—but the mere existence of the Lens causes other, rather small and limited, wormholes to form all about it. Those were the ones that they sought to cap, and, in one or two cases, they apparently did. Its properties, as I said, are unique in our experience. There were many theories about what was on the other end of the Lens that might be causing the effects, but nothing could survive getting there or being in its presence. For computational purposes, it was termed *Olympus*, but what it is will remain a mystery until we encounter it or one like it. There are several theories on what it *might* be, but each is so unique in itself that it stretches credibility."

"Such as?" van der Voort pressed.

"Whatever it is, it masks itself, and the energy it puts out is enormous. We've never found a way to properly measure it. It *spawns* artifacts and shoots them out and around in all directions, which is also a characteristic of a black hole, only it no longer appears to be swallowing anything. The area of space-time around it is so unstable that these natural wormholes have formed. Somehow they are as stable as the ones we create, but hardly passive."

"Those smudges of instability around the lens—they are thick cosmic vortexes yet they are whipping and transforming around it like lightning," van der Voort commented. "Fascinating."

"Those are our natural wormholes, or perhaps they're *the* wormhole at different points in space-time. Nobody is really certain," Doctor Takamura explained. "My mentor, Natori Yamaguchi, spent his entire life and career trying to explain and analyze this instability. To tell you even what he and his colleagues believed would take too long and require that most of you go back for your doctorates in astrophysics, particle physics, and perhaps cosmology. In simple terms, though, he believed that what you are looking at might well be caused by a peculiar structure never before observed but long known to exist called a boltzmon. It is a black hole reduced to the point where it cannot exist anymore. Most of them open up holes in space-time and are believed to simply fall through. The Lens is but an artifact of that collapse, which may well be in some distant galaxy."

"Where does this—boltzmon—fall through?" Harker asked.

"Nobody knows. Another universe, perhaps, or other dimensions. *This* one, however, so we infer from the surrounding matter, seems to have gotten itself stuck in a loop or bubble in space-time. It keeps falling into the hole, but it appears to not quite make it before time curves back so it keeps falling again, and so on. That is why the 'eye,' so to speak, appears to shift, or blink, in two stages. At least, that is the prevailing theory. This temporal loop is the cause of the microlens, and is also causing other previously unobserved phenomena, such as the generation of the wormhole or wormholes, and the spewing out of particle strings. Strings we've encountered before, but not like these. For one thing, they seem to be attracted to and go right up the center of the wormholes. They may be part of one and the same thing. In a better and more merciful universe, I and countless of my colleagues would be studying and measuring and experimenting and getting to understand this rather than theorizing about it. All I can tell you right now for sure is that if we energized the cap we have on the wormhole in this region, a fingerlike string of particles the likes of which we've never seen before would shoot out at essentially the speed of light. Its properties are—bizarre, as is its parent."

"I can guess," Harker replied. "But it doesn't tell me what this place does."

"This place?" Juanita Krill took over once more. "This place is where specially shielded, specially reinforcing gates can be turned on and off. That was, at least, the theory when it was built, but it's never been fully operational and we are dealing with a phenomenon without precedent. For a century theoreticians have run models trying to explain and understand it, and I've given you a very simplified version of some of the more popular theories, but the important thing is, *nobody knows.* That's because the only way to get to the Lens artifact is from areas now deep within Titan-occupied space. We can't measure it and we can't play with it. The money involved in just getting this far was cut from The Confederacy budget in the early fights over how best to meet the Titan threat. Much of it went into conventional weaponry that could be more quickly and cheaply built and deployed—or on worlds of influential politicians. They couldn't afford research on an idea that might be no more than a scientific curiosity. Only the Karas family, which made its fortune building genhole plates and gates, saw its potential as a weapon. And as the futility of conventional arms and tactics was made clear, and the Titan advance clearly turned in this direction, and the direction of a dozen other worlds built as preserves by great industrial families or corporations, they decided to act on their own to try and save their worlds."

"The Karas family sold everything, pretty much, save

the ships and factories it would need, and hired the finest particle physicists and greatest engineers to come here and do what they could," Father Chicanis added. "Among them were Professor Yamaguchi and, in the final marriage of theory to weapon, the mathematical genius of Marcus Lin, Doctor van der Voort's chief in later years. Several fortunes were poured into this, but what could they do? They couldn't move out so many billions of people in so short a time. There weren't the ships and there weren't places to put them, and there was a great deal of resistance to evacuation—denial, you might call it, up until things were imminent, by which time it was far too late."

"But how could they expect this—*apparatus* to work?" van der Voort asked. He wasn't the only one metaphorically shaking his head. "Untested, theoretical, forces explained only in computer models among theoreticians?"

"Not precisely, Doctor," Takamura responded. "Remember, we found the other end of this occurring *naturally*. I know the theory, and though I cannot even conceive that they actually were able to build something that could cap it, they did. Sygolin 37, the material we use to line genholes, the artificial wormholes that we use for interstellar travel, is synthesized from purely theoretical models of substances found near the event horizons of black holes. They are theoretical because, like going to the surface of a Titan-occupied world, it is rather easy to get there but so far impossible to get back. Yet the theory worked. We made the plasma, it works, and we are here. With a slight adjustment, it was sufficient to cap the hole. Time has no real meaning inside one, so the string coming down the center of this hole is simply, well, *there*, waiting for an exit into true space-time so that it can continue. That was tested, before the Titans came. And because it was spewing out before we capped it, we know what happens when it strikes something."

"Yes?" Harker prompted. This was now something he could follow.

"It simply goes through, almost like a neutrino, and within the blink of an eye it has changed into more familiar particles and come apart. But in that moment when it penetrates, the most amazing thing happens. The string—which is incredibly fine, almost microscopic in thickness—does absolutely *nothing*. The effect, however, of its penetration on the matter and energy on all sides of it is something else again. This is ripped, torn, and shredded in space-time. It's a rather local effect, but it is devastating. Rapid opening and closing creates short bursts that can rend the very fabric of space-time itself in the area immediately around the penetration point. Once it emerges into true space, only Sygolin 37 appears able to affect it, and then only to divert it. The Titans do not travel by wormholes. They use a method we know nothing about. There is nothing even resembling Sygolin 37 in their ships, bases, or artifacts. They use a system of building with energy flux that remains beyond us. We have no idea how they do it. But it definitely obeys the basic laws of the physical universe."

"You're sure of that, are you?" Harker pressed.

"You do not have to know why gravity works to know how it works. Yes, we are sure. If we could maintain full energy on our ships and weapons, we could hurt them. The thing is, we can't. Their system dampens everything, drains the bulk. We think they don't actually use it—that this effect is there not to guard against us, but rather to keep their own systems pure. The beauty of using the string from Priam's Lens is that we don't believe they can dampen it nor contain it. It would be too fast and too vicious, and its very passage would create massive instabilities in their structures. If we could unleash just a burst or two, even for fractions of a second, at any of those bases down there, we believe that their entire grid would collapse. They are interconnected—base to base, pole to pole, nexus to nexus. If one goes, the feedback alone through their systems might destabilize the rest. If their grid comes down, then their damping fields also come down."

"Sounds like a lot of *ifs*," Harker noted. "Still, it's better than anything they've come up with so far. There are, of course, a few things that you haven't explained to me yet."

"Yes?" Krill responded.

"First, why didn't the Karas family use this place to shoot their superweapon at the Titans when they were coming? That was the idea, I take it?"

"It was," Father Chicanis agreed. "Unfortunately, the Titans arrived before the defensive network was fully deployed, and they moved so swiftly that they had the damping mechanism in operation and had established primary occupation of Helena before anyone could act. Then there was the problem of what to do as a result. They had the system in place, but the plates weren't fully deployed. Some were, and I suppose still are, in the underground complex thirty kilometers or so outside of Ephesus, or, at least, where Ephesus used to be. That's where the Dutchman's agent was heading, to see if anything really did remain that was of great enough value to risk a larger team to come in and loot."

"Being that close to a Titan base, what could they possibly hope to steal?" Katarina Socolov asked, making her presence felt for the first time.

"Good question. The answer is data modules," Krill replied. "With trickle charges they can retain their information for many centuries. The Titan scouring doesn't go deep underground, and the damping field only sucks up significant sources of energy which it surveys and then targets. It doesn't drain batteries; it simply ignores them since you can't recharge them and it *can* act if significant stored energy is released. There was every reason to believe that the data modules for this project remained down there, probably in the cold and dark ruins of the place, but accessible."

"You mean they were already going for the Lens?"

"No, not at all. The Dutchman never believed it would work, I don't think. But the physics involved, the research, and, most of all, the almost century-old security codes for holdings throughout The Confederacy would still be valid in some places, particularly ones that were hastily evacuated. I will give each of the ground crew a small portion of what the agent—whose name was Michael Joseph Murphy, by the way—of the infiltration into the area and into the complex. Part of it had collapsed, all of it was quite dark and dangerous. The upshot is that he could not make it to the data control center. He had to content himself with the administrative records only. Those are what we have. Those are what he thought was vital enough to give his own life for, to uplink after a nightmarish journey across a very alien landscape. So we know where to look. We have sufficient numbers to make it work, but we're few enough to escape notice. And we know from the administrative recordings that it is quite likely the key ones also survive. That data on the wormhole seals would allow us to control and possibly selectively 'fire' the weapon by linking gates and opening and closing routings. That's what this place does."

"We're going down there, Harker," N'Gana said firmly. "We're going down much better outfitted than Mister Murphy was. He was a pirate, a freebooter, a thief with enormous guts. I'll give him that. Guts and the integrity to do his job even if he himself couldn't make it. I don't know what motivated him. He was a deserter from long ago and a scoundrel and probably a killer, but when he saw that the Priam weapon might just destroy the enemy, he died a patriot. Now we have to finish his job. The initial targeting systems that were here when the Titans came in are no good. The Titans drained the power from the old gates. The normal transport ones imploded as you'd expect, but the ones designed for this project were inert, they had their power supplies at idle rather than off. The Titans drained them and, as a security measure, they shorted. None of the targeting information survived there. We're going in to get the backup. They never figured out how, even though they worked to the end finishing this thing. I understand it broke the old man's heart as well as his wallet."

Father Chicanis sighed. "Yes, he was a great man and he could not live with this level of failure after all he had built. His sister has kept the hope and dream alive with fanatical devotion, and herself alive as well way beyond what anyone could conceive, all in the faith that one day God would find a way."

"Some holy messenger!" Harker snorted. "The Dutchman's a monster!"

"Perhaps, but many monsters wound up doing God's bidding in the past, and He has different standards. Many of the heroines of the Bible are real or pretend prostitutes and thieves, and even the most beloved of God, King David, committed murder, adultery, and most of the other sins prohibited in the Ten Commandments. I can pray for the souls of his victims and for his own soul, but I will not allow who or what he is to reject what is brought to us."

Harker thought a moment. "Constantine Karas—his sister is the old lady?"

"No, not really. She's far more stubborn and ancient than that. Madame Sotoropolis, you see, is Constantine Karas's *grandmother*. Or, at least, she's ninety percent cyborg and ten percent ancient grandmother who is dedicated to this on sheer willpower. Her daughter, Melinda, Constantine's mother, died a few years ago, trying to assemble and finance an expedition just to see if this sort of thing was feasible. She failed. The Dutchman didn't. Sometimes it pays to have a thief about if you want to steal something."

Harker thought it over. "Then why not have thieves do this?"

"The Dutchman's no fool. Murphy died, and died ugly. He's not going to risk more of his limited band on this. Instead, he notified the Karas family and they took it from there. He controls the exit, after all."

Gene Harker didn't much like the sound of that. "So what you're saying is, *if* this is really down there, and *if* we can somehow get it, and *if* we can get it back here in some unfathomable manner, and *if* this thing is still set up right, and *if* this theoretical bullshit actually works, and *if* it really can blow slashing gaps through Titans, *then* we have to turn over this power exclusively to someone who has no ethics, no morals, and could become the next oppressor?"

"One thing at a time, Mister Harker," Colonel N'Gana said philosophically. "You go back and count through all those *ifs* you just spouted. He's the *concluding* problem if all the other ones work out. Let's do one thing at a time. Besides, the human race has had countless tyrants over it and always managed to outlast them. We can deal with our own kind, no matter how insane, sooner or later. But if we can't first deal with the Titans, then what difference does the rest make?"

There wasn't a good answer to that. Finally Harker said, "So, how is this supposed to work? You go down there and go hand to hand with all the threats that might be there, minus any suits or computers or authentic weaponry, and you clear the path so Father Chicanis can guide you to the installation while Doc Socolov studies and deals with the natives, or whatever the surviving humans might be called. Then our silent Quadulan friend here slides down past the blockage through a hole it can get through even if you can't, retrieves the backup modules, and you all sneak out past the noses of the Titans and somehow manage to get picked up without them seeing you and blowing you out of the air and without whatever got that poor bloke Murphy eating you, then you turn the liberated data over to the science trio up here, and we blow the beggars away and bring freedom to the universe. That about right?"

"Something like that," the Colonel responded. "And we welcome an old experienced hand to the ground party, Mister Harker."

"What makes you so sure I'll go down with you?"

"Well, for one thing, you didn't come this far to stop now. Second, you can survive for ages, I suspect, in that fancy combat suit, but it doesn't seem to have any genhole actuators or plasma shielding on its own. The Dutchman may control *our* exit, sir, but no matter how much power you might think that suit gives you, I assure you that *we* control whether or not you can ever leave this system. You invited yourself along; now we expect you to be useful. I know your service record and reputation. You've got real guts and a lot of fighting skill. I don't know how good you are without modern arms, but if your Commando training was anything close to my Ranger training, then you are better equipped for this than the vast majority of people, including most here. And we're not going down there as unprotected as Murphy, I assure you. You can come, or you can watch, but coming with us is the only ticket home."

Harker sighed. "Well, if you put it that way, I guess maybe I'll come. Somebody from the official services should be there, I suppose, anyway. And it may be the only chance I get to see Doctor Socolov naked."

"Mister Harker!" she exclaimed, in a tone that did not convey if she were truly shocked or only playing at it.

"The lifeboat will be cramped beyond belief with the added body, but we need you on the ground," the usually silent Sergeant Mogutu said. "We have enough spare supplies to accommodate you, but both the colonel and I want to know a bit more about your unconventional skills just in case. We have two civilians along, remember, who have little hope in a fight. I never saw a priest who wasn't trying to be a target all the time, and these science types are so filled with their own scientific interests they'll ignore an ambush."

"You're all civilians to me," Harker pointed out. "I'm still serving, at least as far as I know."

"Well, you know what I mean. And this is a military operation, start to finish. Number one priority is to make sure that nothing kills or captures the Pooka. Otherwise we wind up no better than Murphy, for all the effort. Of course, after it hands us the cubes, everybody is expendable except the one who gets the cubes out. On the ground, the old ranks aren't valid. The colonel is the commander, and I am second in command. As the uninvited guest, you're third, since we have three others to consider and an overall mission to accomplish. Got it?"

Harker nodded. "Okay, fair enough. I'm not too thrilled about this mission anyway, you know."

"What's your hand-to-hand rating?"

"I'm black belt in seven disciplines. That's the good news. The bad news is that, other than some jujitsu, I haven't really kept it up. After spending an eternity in a regeneration tank, the spark just kind of left me."

"Well, it's better than nothing. What about weapons? Ever fired antique projectile weapons?"

"You mean things that shoot solids? Percussive stuff?"

"Yes."

"I've seen them shot, and I tried it once in a historical target meet, but that's about it. I doubt if I could hit anything short of a mountain with one."

"Too bad. We have some here. The Dutchman says that percussive weapons using gunpowder don't pick up on the

Titan radar. Noisy as hell, though, so your position's a dead giveaway. They're heavy, bulky, and the ammunition's worse, but we're taking some. Even the doc's been practicing on a range we set up on the *Odysseus*. I'm not sure she could actually shoot anybody, but she's more accurate than you say you are. What hand weapons can you use with some confidence?"

"Knife, certainly, and I've fenced much of my life. It's good exercise without driving you nuts."

"Hmm . . . Wish I had some swords. Never thought of that. Got some good knives with different weights and hefts, though. Okay, well, so be it. I'll notify the colonel. Dress is stock camouflage fatigues, waterproof combat boots. Draw what you need. You'll probably be living in them for a couple of weeks. Oh—forgot. Can you swim?"

"Huh? Yeah, pretty well. Why?"

"We're gonna be dropped on a tiny island about forty kilometers off the mainland, the first one that's outside the permanent continental grid. We'll have to get off and in to shore by boat, and I don't mean a motorboat. The colonel, the priest, and the Pooka go in the first one; you, me, and the doc in the second. It isn't gonna be a picnic even getting in. That ocean can be rough and we won't be able to pick the perfect time. We're stuck with the gap the polar sweep gives us, period. Otherwise the lifeboat can't get back off and out of range before it's detected. No lifeboat and we're stuck down there. Got it?"

"I got it."

"And no funny business with the girl. She's along for a reason. You want to get a romance, wait until we've blown up the suckers or we know we can't get off. Okay?"

He nodded. "No problem there, Chief. When do we do it?"

"Tomorrow. At zero one hundred hours by our clocks. It's gonna be fast and mean and tense all the way and everybody knows it. And—one more thing."

"Yes?"

"I'm in the fucking Navy. I'm a sergeant, sometimes sarge, but I'm *never* a chief. Got that?"

"Sure thing, boss," he responded. "Anything you like." And, under his breath, Harker added, just audibly enough for the other man to hear and bristle at, "Chief."

FIFTEEN

To the Great Sea

Littlefeet was still bothered by what he knew should be the most wonderful of coincidences, the fact that, of all those who'd jumped into the river rather than face the mad ones and Hunters from the demon flower groves, one should be his Spotty, and with no Mother Paulista or anybody else to make the rules. Not anymore. Froggy was a nice bonus; he'd always liked her and had at one time lain with her, but that could be said about almost all the girls of the Family.

"You act like I'm some kinda creature or something, like those things that attacked us," she accused him, as they sat waiting for the night's storm.

"I just want to know how come it was you out of all the girls. How come *you* came to *me*?"

She frowned and stared into his eyes. "Why, you called me!"

"I what? Oh—you mean my yelling and all?"

"No, not that. I *heard* you. Callin' me, drawin' me to your side. It was almost like those magic stones Mother Paulista had—those—what'd she call 'em? Magnets. Like I was one and you were another and I was almost pulled to you." She paused. "If anybody oughta be wondering 'bout who's got witch power and who don't it should be *me*. 'Course, it coulda been God, y'know."

He let out a long, loud sigh. "I dunno. Maybe it *is* me. Ever since I went up to the top of those mountains it's been *weird* sometimes, y'know? Like I can feel things I can't figure out and see things like maybe the demons see things, and I get these crazy ideas and pictures. I've got no words for 'em. Some things are really clear; other things are all jumbled up and don't make any sense. Look, let's forget this whole thing—not the attack and all. I mean between us. There's the three of us now and nobody else, at least not yet."

Spotty wasn't all that sure it was going to be that easy, but she also was practical enough to realize that it made little difference. In the broadest sense Littlefeet was right: their situation now was the problem, and it had to be worked out.

He moved over, gave her a hug, and kissed her, and she didn't pull away.

Froggy had made a short exit while they started to work things out, and she now came back and sat with them. "You decided to kiss and make up, huh? 'Bout time!"

"Yeah, don't seem nothing but crazy to wonder over good luck," he responded. "So, either of you wanna tell me what happened over there in the camp?"

Spotty looked at Froggy, who looked back and shrugged. Clearly neither of them wanted to bring up the memory, but Spotty finally took the initiative.

They had come from the demon flower groves, she told him. Come just before dawn, when there was much mist and not much light, and they had burst upon the Family in numbers they had never before faced, screaming unintelligible noises and in a killing frenzy, with no thought as to their own safety or protection. The guards had fought well and bravely but they were simply overwhelmed; the Hunters used what looked like human leg bones as clubs, and they took the spears and knives from the fallen and used them as well.

"I heard Father Alex praying and cursing the attackers to hell," she told him. "Then I heard him cry out in what sounded like pain, and he shouted something I could not hear but which must have been the command to sound the horn, for that's what happened next, and it kept sounding and sounding until it kinda died in midblast. By that time they were in the women's kraal, and it was just all mixed up and so confused with everybody yelling and screaming and going every which way. I was asleep far from the nursery. I know some of the crazy ones got there, and I picked up a pole and tried to get there too, but I could see that they'd surrounded the women there and there were more of 'em and they were closing in. I went to run and help them, but then I got hit *here*, on the hip, and I was in a fight for my life with a man not much older'n us, but there was nothing inside him, just screams and hatred and those eyes that didn't have anyone in them."

"I wasn't that far away," Froggy added, realizing that Spotty had reached her limit for the moment. "I saw much the same. The only thing that mattered was the kids, but you couldn't get to 'em. I know some of the older ones ran off into the grass and I pray to God that they got away. The rest, I saw some—some . . ."

It took until the first cracks of thunder sounded in the great valley before the two could, painfully, piece together the rest. They had seen sights that would haunt them for their entire lives. Babies, little babies, impaled, held up on spears still shrieking, and some of them were *their* babies and there was absolutely no way they could help them and absolutely nothing they could do.

Eventually, in the carnage, many of the young women had found themselves at the water's edge, unable to do anything, facing the Hunters and the mad ones which both women described as men without souls. The only choice was between succumbing to the attackers and jumping in the water and drowning.

Many of them jumped, and some, like Spotty and Froggy, found themselves buoyant enough to keep above the water for a short period until, just as they felt themselves going under, each of them had bumped, or were bumped by, something that floated and they'd managed to hold on, remembering Littlefeet's own example and some of the lessons of the past. Neither remembered much after that, except that Spotty insisted that she had heard and been drawn to his calling. Neither knew how they'd gotten to the other side, but that could be explained by a slow curve in the river to the east that might have taken them closer to the opposite bank.

And when they'd told their stories and the rains came, their tears were added to the downpour as they simply sat in the mud. He held tightly to each of the women with his arms and they gently rocked in the rain.

And after the storm passed, he stayed as long as they wanted, and, finally, they found a comfortable spot in the brush with good cover and lay down for the night, as close together as they could. He didn't get a lot of sleep that night, but at least, unlike them, he didn't dream.

Still, there was an odd sense, almost that magnetic sense that Spotty had insisted he had, that drew him in odd and mysterious directions, first to the tiny point that could barely be seen in the night sky and would soon be washed out by Achilles, the feeling that something was up there, something was on Hector, something not quite god or demon but different than he.

And, as the night wore on, he had the strangest feeling that something had fallen to earth. He still felt the presences above, sort of, but now he felt the same kind of draw down here, to the south, where the great sea was, and where he'd been taught that there was nothing but monsters and endless deep waters.

They would spend the next two days patrolling up and down the riverbank, looking for anyone alive, but if anyone else had survived, they had taken off for the brush. The sounds the two women had told about were made by a hollowed reed specially carved to sound a deep, penetrating note. It was reserved for the greatest of emergencies, and would bring the scouts in and also tell the people to grab what they could and scatter and hide because the defenses had failed.

He had never heard that sound except in practices, nor had any of the others, but they were all properly drilled. If the family could not be defended, it must scatter and preserve as many as possible and merge again when the danger was past.

It was possible that many were now hunting for one another over there, on the other side, but nobody was showing themselves by the river, nothing but some sad corpses.

"We should gather them and give them burial," Littlefeet said, feeling oddly guilty that he'd not been there and had survived mostly for that reason alone.

"No!" Spotty responded. "None of the Hunters will guess that any of us could make it across the river. Some will come, and if they see it like this, they'll just figure, with no battle signs, that the bodies floated down or from the other side and that'll be that. If we do anything more, then they'll know there are some alive on this side and maybe go on a hunt. Their souls are in heaven now and ours aren't. Leave what's left."

He nodded sadly. "Then let's get away from here. This is an evil place."

"But to where?" Froggy asked him. "There's nowhere left to go."

"We're on the *right* side of the river," he pointed out. "We know this area, at least beyond this new river. I say we follow the river down and stay just out of sight, but look for signs of others across the way. They'll have gone south along the river because it's the only way to find any others. If we find any signs, maybe we can get 'em across. If not, at least we'll *know*. After that, well, we'll see about finding Family marks and be on our own. They'll either find us or else we'll be starting a new Family. What else can we do?"

"South . . ." Froggy looked out at the river. "How far south? If this is like all the other rivers we know, it'll get bigger and wider as it goes on. If they're on the other side, they're gonna stay there."

He sighed. "Maybe. But what else can we do? C'mon. There are no nurseries now. We're all three scouts and guards and gatherers. Let's find something to eat and then get on."

How could he explain about the pull? How could he explain when even he didn't know what caused it, or what he was being drawn to? Like everything else, he knew he'd simply have to trust his instincts and hope that the pull was God's and not any of the demons'.

SIXTEEN

Helena after the Fall

As time grew near for the run to the surface, tension mounted within the whole party, not just among those who were going. This was the start of the truly dangerous part of the mission, and none of them even knew what the full price of failure would be, only that they might well be the only hope the human race had for survival.

Katarina Socolov had been cool to Harker and everybody else for much of the time, but suddenly she was quite friendly to him. He suspected that it was less his magnetic charm than the sudden realization that she was going down to a primitive world so alien they might not have imagined just how different it would be, and she was going to be the only woman along with three big military guys, a priest, and a Pooka. N'Gana and Mogutu were good men on your side in a fight, that was certain, but she wasn't even sure how they felt about women, although she knew full well that they would have preferred she not be along. Not because she was a woman, she suspected, but because she wasn't military, wasn't One of Them. They weren't too thrilled about the priest, either, but they weren't the ones paying for this trip.

Still, of them all, Harker, who was One of Them but also an outsider to this happy group, seemed to be the one common sense said would be the best friend to have in a hostile environment.

The infiltration team had left the scientists in the control center, attempting to master the system and determine that it would work as advertised. Even if the ones who were going down to the surface were totally successful and got themselves or at least the code data out, they knew they would get only one try with the weapons system. If it worked, that was all they would need; if it didn't, they were literally dead ducks.

The tiny lifeboat-style ship that would take them down to the surface was cramped and not built with comfort in mind. It could take up to eight people, more than was needed, but those eight would be stacked in tubelike compartments unable to see or do much of anything. There wasn't even an intercom; that had been stripped out, lest its use alert the Titans below of something unusual.

"You look uncomfortable, Mister Harker," Alan Mogutu commented with a slight, sardonic smile.

One of these days somebody's gonna knock that superior grin off your face, you asshole, Harker thought, but instead he replied, "I'm not used to going into a hostile situation without a suit. These camouflage fatigues and boots are no substitute."

"True," the mercenary responded. "Still, it is essential to occasionally test yourself against the elements with nothing but your own body, skills, and wits."

Colonel N'Gana looked up from where he was securing some equipment in one of the small boat's compartments and added, "Your suit would be your coffin down there. That's the problem. Always has been. If they notice you at all, they will simply drain all power from your equipment. We don't know how they do it, but nothing we've tried in the way of insulation works at thicknesses you can carry around. That old weapons station back there, for example, is shielded, but the shields involved are of very rare and expensive substances and they're over a meter thick. Even then, once that shield is breached just long enough to direct fire, just once, and used—they'll know. At that point, they'll have a matter of minutes, perhaps as few as seven minutes, depending on how ready our friends down there might be to respond to a threat from such an unlikely area, to live. There is no way they could be evacuated in that amount of time without the ship itself being caught and drained by probable planetary defenses. No, this is one for history, Harker. We do it and we're the heroes of all humanity. We fail, we die. It's that simple. I wonder just how many people could actually pull this off, getting down there and doing this job with minimal power, almost like in the ancient times."

"We've all gone soft," Mogutu continued as N'Gana went back to checking the pack one last time. "I doubt if any of us—you, me, even the colonel—would be any sort of match for a Roman legionnaire in Julius Caesar's army, or Alexander the Great's infantry, Ramses II's conquering horde, or in particular Genghis Khan's. Imagine those Mongols—they had the largest empire on earth and held it without modern communication. The only thing that stopped them from conquering all of ancient Asia, Europe, and probably Africa as well was that they kept knocking off the conquest to go home every time they needed to elect a new emperor. You much on the ancient history of our people?"

"Not much," Harker admitted. "Just the usual school and trivial stuff. But I know who they were, at least. And you think that a rank private in any of those armies could take us?"

"The lot of us," Mogutu replied without hesitation. "They walked the whole of a planet and nothing stood in their way. Discipline, skill, constant training. They were the real supermen, Harker. We just try to emulate them with our fancy fighting suits. I wish you'd had a chance to run Socolov's sim back on the *Odysseus*. You had to run it through without a suit. Without anything at all, really, except some stones and spears and such. It's a humbling experience."

Harker nodded. "So, how many times did you run it before you got all the way through?"

Mogutu's finely featured face was suddenly a grim mask. "I *didn't* get through it, Harker. Nobody did. Not a single one of us survived. And we ran it again and again and again."

Now that was a sobering thought. Not N'Gana, not Mogutu—*"Nobody?"*

"Nobody. Of course, it was based on a lot of remote research and intelligence on what these worlds are like without anybody involved having actually been down on one. It *might* not be as tough as she has it."

"Or it might be tougher," N'Gana pointed out. "Still, if these pirates have been looting these worlds under the Titans' noses, so to speak, then there is a chance. On the other hand, the fellow who got this information out but did not get himself out was a seasoned man on these worlds who could blend in like a native and knew probably more than anyone how the Titans worked and where they were blind. This time *he* didn't make it. It could be that Helena is one hell of a Trojan horse."

Harker stared straight into the colonel's eyes. "You don't believe that for a second, not really. And neither do the people who hired you. They went outside their own people to bring in a team that their computers and researchers decided was the best. You know it, I know it. And if you make your living stealing hairs from the devil's beard, then sooner or later he's going to wake up. The pirate's failure proves nothing."

N'Gana remained impassive for a few seconds, then suddenly he grinned and broke into good-natured laughter. "Harker, maybe you are the one who should be with us! At least you don't scare easy!"

And maybe you don't scare easily enough, the Navy man thought, but returned the big mercenary's grin.

He went over to Katarina Socolov, who was doing a last-minute inventory of her own supplies. She acknowledged him, but was too busy for conversation. Suddenly she stopped and asked sharply, "Colonel? Where's my data recorder?"

"Left on the deck, madam, along with several other things of yours which require power and have internal power supplies. We cannot afford giving anything that would register as our signature on their monitoring equipment. Sergeant Mogutu and I have gone through everyone's equipment and pared it all down. Anything we don't *know* they won't pick up on gets left behind."

"Then what am I supposed to use for my database and field notes?"

"Try using your head and perhaps writing things down in notebooks the way our ancestors did. You can't get a doctorate in the social sciences these days without knowing how to write, since you can't take a lot of our stuff into primitive cultures without corrupting them. Cheer up, Doctor. You are going to miss a lot more than a mere recorder."

Father Chicanis wore his religious medal and cross around his neck but otherwise dressed as they all had, in the insulated camouflage clothing and thick weatherproof combat boots. His own kit, also inspected by the mercenaries, was quite simple compared to the others. A Bible and a communion set, that was all. He prayed and blessed the little ship and those who would fly on her, then joined the group.

He was a surprisingly muscular man, in excellent condition from the looks of him. The others to varying degrees were all impressed by this; he would not, at least, hold them back on those grounds.

Last in but with the least to bring was the Pooka. Its

thick snake of a body and its large, round, hypnotic eyes always bothered Katarina Socolov. She was both fascinated and repelled by the creature, the first one she'd ever been this near. It was not, however, particularly communicative or interested in friendship with others. Like the mercenaries, it was along to do a job, and maybe, just maybe, save its own people, who might have no real reason to love humans but who stood with them against the same threat now.

The colonel seemed satisfied, and now he called them all together.

"All right, when we hear the signal from this ship, each of you will get into an unoccupied slot in the boat and strap in. No argument, no hesitation. We will be on a tight schedule. Once inside and sealed in, it's going to be a hairy ride. The way we do this is to come in very steeply and with power virtually at minimum. The signature will be that of a meteorite burning up in the atmosphere. Once free and with sensors indicating no scan, it will literally dive for the target island just off the south coast of Eden, and it'll be a hard and rough landing. Once down, no matter how shook up you are, get *out* of there. If you can, help pull the equipment packs from the storage compartments. We'll have only a few minutes to do this and get clear. When it is unloaded, or senses danger, or after a short preset interval that is guaranteed to avoid the planetary sweeps, the boat will go into dormant mode and become just another bit of junk from the old days. The power trickle will be sufficient only to keep its systems from deteriorating and should be below normal detection. There it will stay. When we return, *if* we return, it will know. Samples of our DNA were fed into it. Any one of us can activate it. The only mission we have is to return those codes! Period!"

"You mean, if we get separated, we shouldn't wait for any others?" Harker asked.

"Anyone who gets back here with them should not wait to see if others will come, yes. I *hope* we remain together, but, no matter what, if you get back and have the goods, place your palm on any of the exposed dull metallic plates. A match analysis will determine that you are you, and then you will wait until there is a window between Titan sweeps. At that point this compartment will open, the boat will power up, and you must get in and hold on. It will be going straight up at near maximum speed and it won't be pleasant, but it should get you where you must be."

Harker wasn't sure he liked that. "What if they do nab it on the way back? How will anybody know? And what if it's not there when we get there?"

"Then you will proceed to one of the old defense stations I can show you," Father Chicanis put in. "Like the Dutchman's agent. Send the codes. If you do, then you might still have a chance since they'll act as soon as they get them. No matter what, one or more of us will do that anyway, just to make sure. If, God willing, the rest of you make it, then I will do it."

Harker looked at him. "You don't intend to come back?"

"No. I was born down there and I will die down there. I come as an instrument of God, and whatever else happens is in His hands."

Several of the others glanced at him, all of them, it seemed, wishing that they had a little bit of his faith.

"There is—" Katarina Socolov began, but then the lights went from bright white to dim red and a buzzer sounded three short times.

"Talk on Helena!" N'Gana snapped. "Let's *move*!"

The colonel got in the first one, then Chicanis, then Katarina Socolov, and then the Pooka. Harker felt Mogutu push him lightly. Instinctively he went into the fifth compartment even as Mogutu climbed into the sixth. The last two were stuffed with cargo.

As soon as Mogutu's feet cleared the inner hatch, the ship closed, almost lenslike, and there was a hissing noise and the sounds of seals popping into place. Harker found the webbing and straps and managed to get himself at least reasonably supported, and there was a sudden *bang* and then the feeling of sharp acceleration. They were away before any of them could really think about it, which was just how N'Gana had planned it.

On the way down, though, there wasn't much to do but think. The little boat itself was featureless, with only a very soft glow from a dim strip of light along the top to allow any sight. And there was nothing to see: just sterile walls that seemed extremely claustrophobic even to those who went out in environmental suits. They were going *very* fast, that was for sure, and there was almost no noise, not even a sound from any of the other compartments. It was eerie to have this free fall feeling cutting in and out now and not be able to hear anything but your own breathing—and, Harker admitted to himself, his suddenly quite rapid heartbeat.

Every nightmare suddenly flashed into his mind. What if the timing was off? What if the Titans detected the boat and followed it down? Or came to investigate it?

No, that wouldn't be as much of a worry. They'd just throw that energy sucker they had and it would go very dark in here just before this thing crashed into the planet's surface, killing all of them.

Just then the light did flicker, even go out for a second or two, giving him, and probably the rest of them, a near heart attack.

Now there was a distant roaring sound, and the feeling of being bumped all over. Everything moved, everything moaned and groaned and shook for what seemed like forever. *I'll never curse a landing craft descent again*, he told himself. Not after this.

As suddenly as the rough ride had started, it now

stopped, but now he felt himself being pulled to the front of the compartment. As this pull grew and grew, many more bumps and bangs sounded inside, making it nearly impossible not to get some bruising against the bulkhead.

The landing was one big terrific *bang*! So loud and so rough was it that for a moment he was sure they had crashed. It took all his training to tell himself that if in fact they had crashed he wouldn't have had the time to think it.

There was suddenly full gravity and the sound of air depressurizing and in moments the opening was clear once more. He didn't need any encouragement; he struggled to free himself of the webbing and straps and then pushed out of the craft as quickly as possible, dropping a meter or so into sandy soil. It was quite dark, but there was enough light to see, barely, what was going on near you.

He felt like he'd been in a wreck of some kind. He was dizzy, disoriented, and fighting stronger gravity than he'd had to face in a while. He struggled to stand as he saw Mogutu and N'Gana both already on their feet—the former literally pulling Socolov and Chicanis from their compartments by their feet, the latter pulling duffel bags full of equipment from the two cargo points. He made it to N'Gana and was soon pulling things out as well. He couldn't guess what some of it was—primitive weapons that could be used here, no doubt.

Everything on the sand, N'Gana and Mogutu looked around. "Everybody out? Where's Hamille?"

"Here!" the Pooka responded in that forced air whisper. "Barely."

The colonel nodded. "Socolov?"

"Here!"

"Father Chicanis?"

"Here!"

He sighed. "Well, all right then. Stand away from the boat. If *I* know it's empty, then *it* knows it's empty!"

As if on cue, the lens closed up, there was a hiss of a

seal, probably to preserve it, and then the thing, which was only a dark hulk in the dim moonlight, seemed to virtually disappear. There was still a shape there, but it was dead, inert, even to look at in the dark. The effect was eerie—and lonely.

The colonel looked at his watch. It was a wind-up mechanical type that was still silent, with no telltale ticks. They all had one just like it, synchronized from the start. The dial was luminous, and they'd all charged theirs just to have use of it once down, although the lighting would fade quite quickly now. All the watches were adjusted to the Helenan day, which ran twenty-five hours fifty-one minutes twelve seconds standard. Since all planetary times were adjusted to a twenty-four-hour clock locally, that meant each hour was going to be roughly sixty-four minutes long, give or take. That wouldn't disorient any of them.

"There's some palms and brush for cover over there," N'Gana told them. "Everybody carry something and let's get away from this site just in case somebody comes looking."

"I feel like I was in a building collapse," Katarina Socolov complained.

"We all got bounced around, but it will pass," the colonel responded. "Being face-to-face with Titans is more permanent."

They got everything away, then broke off some large leaves and used them to wipe out the tracks from the now dormant little boat to the brush.

"Probably not good enough, but it'll have to do," Harker told them.

"Don't worry about it," Mogutu replied. "High tide comes almost up to this first line of brush. You can see the driftwood stacked up along here. In a few hours there'll be no sign anybody was ever here, and in a few days even the boat will be hard to spot, just another piece of junk."

"I want to get everything unpacked and sorted and repacked," the colonel told them. "We'll rest here until sunup."

"Aren't you afraid crossing over in daylight will make us sitting ducks?" the cultural anthropologist asked him, worried.

"It won't make any difference to them when we cross, anymore than it would to us," the colonel assured her. "We don't have night limitations beyond a certain technological level that Mogutu and I have long since passed. They don't use orbital satellites, since they already own the place and don't seem to give a damn what might be left over crawling around on it. For us, making a crossing in two collapsible rafts is going to be a challenge no matter how much we've practiced. This is real ocean. Let's at least see the immediate danger instead of worrying about theoretical ones."

It was sound adivce and hard to argue with.

"Once we sort our stuff and get our packs done, I'd suggest most of us get what sleep we can," the colonel continued. "It's going to be a very long and physically demanding day tomorrow."

Some of their packs did contain weapons, but weapons, it seemed, from another age. Only N'Gana and Mogutu had rifles—sleek, mean-looking devices suited to a historical epic, along with crossed belts of clips of ammunition that seemed barbaric. Copper-tipped projectiles shot into people or things by using essentially the same principle used to make rockets. Ugly, messy, and not very sure, but using absolutely no electrical power of any sort or source.

Katarina Socolov and Gene Harker got equally wicked crossbows. "Not much at long range," Mogutu admitted, "but at short range they're very effective. There's a small cylinder of compressed gas in each stock that accelerates the arrow, or bolt as it's called, and gives it added range to maybe, oh, fifty to a hundred meters depending on the target. Even when you run out of gas cylinders, so long as you've got bolts, you'll still have a weapon that can handle twenty, thirty meters sure. Ask the doc for sighting—it's her weapon, basically. It's pretty easy, though."

Harker sat down next to the woman, who was checking her own crossbow out. "You actually good with this?"

She nodded. "Sure. Against targets. Used to be a hobby of mine—ancient and medieval weaponry that didn't require a lot of upper body strength. If they'd invented these gas cylinders back then, women wouldn't have had such a tough time getting equality."

"Doc—Katarina?"

"Kat. It's easy and it's kind of an identity thing, like a *meow*-type cat or maybe a lion."

"Okay—Kat. I'm Gene. No use for rank here, except maybe with the colonel. So, how do you sight this?"

She showed him, as well as some of the other finer points. Actually getting decent enough to hit the broad side of a mountain with one of those bolts, though, would be a different story.

Other weapons included a Bowie-style knife with a serrated blade made of a substance that looked and felt like steel but could cut into softer rocks without problems, and a kind of formalized blackjack, a baton, which he knew from the military police. Weighted, it could knock people cold and crack heads, but it wasn't considered a deadly weapon. In a close fight against too many of the enemy, it might just be an equalizer.

Beyond this there were a couple of weeks of concentrated rations, a bottle each of desalinization and sterilization pills, and a small medical kit. That was about it.

The colonel supplemented his rifle with a rather fancy saber which he wore in a scabbard, hanging from his pants belt, and he, too, had a baton but on the other side in its own carrier.

Each had all his or her spares in backpacks and they then buried the duffels in the sandy soil just in back of the driftwood, so tidal erosion wouldn't uncover them. Only the Pooka, which the colonel had called Hamille, revealing a name for the first time, had no pack or apparent weapons. There was no telling what it ate or drank, but it was damned sure it had no shoulders to carry a pack, and it seemed quite happy to just be itself. Harker decided not to ask right then, but wondered whether the creature's civilization was so industrialized and automated that they no longer had the means to produce these things that didn't require power. Or perhaps the Pooka was in its own way as alien and inscrutable as the Titans.

Finally, they settled down in the bushes to wait until morning.

Nobody really slept, but nobody really wanted to talk and risk disturbing the others, either. The sudden heavy gravity, the bumpy ride down, the tensions and stresses and the anticipation of the unknown all combined to make each one feel older than the old diva who'd brought them all together, yet too young to die.

Harker could barely suppress his satisfaction at seeing the great Colonel N'Gana, legend and mercenary, seasick as a rookie in weightlessness training as they paddled their boats in toward shore. The colonel's dark brown complexion seemed to have lost its luster. In its drab new exterior it had gained a little green and gray.

Of course, Katarina Socolov wasn't doing much better. Clearly sailing wasn't in her background, either. It was difficult to tell about the Pooka, who couldn't row anyway, but it had withdrawn into a coil with its head near the bottom of the boat.

Fortunately, Mogutu seemed to either be experienced at it or at least have it in his blood; with the colonel and the

Pooka in his boat, he was really the only one doing any real work at rowing them in toward shore. At least it wasn't all that rough, not for open ocean, anyway. Harker suspected that there was a definite continental shelf not far below and that it probably had either a great deal of sand built up or some sort of reefs, perhaps coral-like, that broke up the waves.

He also had an extra pair of hands rowing, although they dared not get too far from Mogutu's struggling boat. The supplies, among other things, were in that boat, and it was by no means certain that, if it tipped, either N'Gana or the Quadulan could swim. Father Chicanis seemed to be having a grand old time, not in the least bothered.

"You've sailed before on small watercraft," Harker said to the priest.

"This very region, in fact, was where I learned to swim and to sail. We used to have regattas that went from Ephesus to Circe's Island—well beyond Saint John's, which is what we landed on. This was truly something of a paradise, Mister Harker. Warm climate, balmy breeezes, controlled moisture and well-managed lands, lots of natural organic farming of fruits and vegetables—not like the crap most folks in The Confederacy eat and think of as decent food. The greatest conflicts were boat races, and football of course, and chess, and arguing with the Copts over whose was truly the oldest tradition. Gentle stuff for a gentle world, Mister Harker. Gentle, yet swept so callously away . . ."

His eyes grew distant and his voice trailed off, and Harker knew that he was seeing things as they were out here in the bright sunshine.

"Ship oars for a little, Father," Harker called to him. "We're leaving poor Sergeant Mogutu well behind."

"Huh? Oh—yes, sorry. We ought to have tethered them to our boat, you know. Then we'd have at least three pairs of strong arms for this job and we'd not risk losing them."

"We'd risk losing all of us in one unexpected swell if we did that," Harker responded. "That's all right. It's nice to see those arrogant sons of—well, you know—taken down a peg. They'll be all right if we have no unexpected nastiness, and if we do, it won't be from this sea or from the weather, looking at the sky and the direction of the clouds."

"No, it'll stay this way if it starts out this way," Chicanis agreed. "Where did you learn the water part of sailing, if I might ask?"

"It's part of the training in the Navy, believe it or not. You not only learn how the Navy evolved from a seagoing one but the training centers are on worlds with oceans and bays and large rivers and you have to do a lot of work in small and medium-sized boats on them. These kind of boats, though—these were for Commando school. They didn't let us have our fancy suits for the final exam. Stuck us in the water with one of these and very minimal supplies, a knife and a small concealed laser pistol like we'd crashed on some deserted water world. We had to make it into shore, after *finding* the shore, and, with no map, no real knowledge of where we were, we had to survive through the jungle and find our headquarters unit and report in. All we knew was that the unit was somewhere within a hundred and fifty kilometers of where we were dropped. Period. You just about couldn't do it alone. They saw to that. You needed to find your mates, keep your own team together, and work as a unit. Everybody seemed to have some knowledge or skill the others lacked, or at least hadn't paid attention to. That kept us from eating poisoned fruit or being strangled by a carnivorous vine. It was a problem a lot like this one, but with commonality of training."

"You don't approve of Doctor Socolov and me being along, I know," the priest responded, "but, believe me, it's part of the mix. Right now I know exactly where we are and what these waters are like. I know where we're going to land." He turned and looked at the land that seemed so close and yet was still several kilometers away. "Look at how gloomy and ominous it seems from here, with the clouds ringing and obscuring the mountains. And yet I spent many a summer in those mountains, hiking the trails, looking out on great natural beauty. Some of those peaks are close to six kilometers high. I never got that far, but even from a two-kilometer height down to sea level you can see forever, or so it seems."

Harker looked at the mountains that seemed to form a ring around the flat plain to which they were now headed. "Do those mountains go around the whole continent?"

Chicanis laughed. "No, of course not! But they're one of several great ranges on Eden, and the only one that actually does go round in sort of a U-shaped pattern. The passes are almost two kilometers up or higher, and it's an effective barrier. It's actually more than one range, and if you saw the maps you'd know that it only seems to make the U here, but, of course, for all practical purposes, it does and is. The landform and its proximity to the coast made it ideal for agricultural growth. You could grow anything in there. I think that's why our indications are that there are many human survivors about on the plain. By the time they had to crawl out of their holes and forage, the place had been scoured and then the old plants started to grow and bloom once more. It's all wild now, of course, but I'll wager I can find the old company patterns."

The priest had seemed energized since landing on the planet; for all the horrors and the unknown perils to come, he was home.

Harker looked around. The tide from Achilles's pull was fairly strong, and it would take them in eventually no matter what they did. He wondered, though, what might be lurking below.

"Father, what sort of creatures live in these oceans? Anything we need to be worried about?"

"Not in this close, I shouldn't think," the priest replied. "There wasn't a whole lot of land-based animal life when this world was discovered and developed, but the sea was filled with it. This is a water world, really; the two continents are relatively small, perhaps both of them together making up no more than thirty percent of the surface. Let us just say that the deep ocean creatures are not terribly friendly and are quite large, but that they are also quite alien in form. It's the small creatures, the viswat as we called them, the ones that have the kind of ecological niche of small fish or shellfish here, that are nasty. They move by the thousands in swarms and they are very hard and have very sharp outlines, and they can cut you to pieces just going by. That doesn't worry the predators—viswat are near the bottom of the food chain—but they *do* make it difficult to do ocean swimming." He sighed. "I suppose the water ecology survived pretty well intact. It's ironic, in a way. Almost like God was making a comment."

"How's that?"

"Well, consider. These Titans, whatever they are, are certainly land-based, and they like the sorts of places we like. So they scour and then remake the land to suit them, as we did, pretty well plowing under what humans built, so the only region that remains pretty much as God made it is the sea. These are the times when one almost questions whose side God is on."

"How much longer, Harker?" Katarina Socolov called. She looked kind of green but hadn't thrown up for a while, although perhaps that was because there wasn't much left to heave.

Harker looked at the beach. "Twenty, thirty minutes, I'd say, unless we pick up speed with this incoming tide.

Don't worry, Doc. You only wish you could die; you'll be fine within minutes of our getting to dry land so long as you replace your fluids."

Father Chicanis looked ahead at where they seemed to be going. "We'd best aim for Capri Point, there," he said, pointing to a rocky outcrop. "There are some fairly nasty creatures that dwell under the sand and are particularly treacherous after it's been wet down. That's real rock there, a kind of shale, and there's only a small stretch of beach to cover. When we get close, give me a rifle and you handle the boat and supplies."

"A rifle?" Harker was intrigued. "Why?"

"Because they'll come up from under the sand and pull you right down into it. I've seen them take limbs, even whole people. We never could wipe them out because they moved out under the sea and onto the shelf and through here and then came back when nobody was looking. No poison or other impediment seemed to do any good at all."

Harker looked over at Mogutu and N'Gana in their boat. "They know about this?"

"Of course. It only now occurred to me how few briefings you had on this world."

Harker sighed and shook his head. "Sure must have made afternoons with the family at the beach a real adventure. Anything else like that I should know?"

"Nothing lethal. Actually, we used to have a kind of grid that gave a small electrical charge to the sand. You never even noticed it, but it drove all the no-see-ums away. My thinking is that it probably hasn't been powered for almost a century."

"Good point. And when we get off the sand, if we can?"

"Beyond the beach, I suspect that it's going to be as new to me as it is to you. You've seen the three-dimensional maps, the scanning data, all that. I can recognize the landforms and some of the old patterns, like I said, but the rest—it's new. The scour took most everything out, and this is all new growth. It even appears that the roadways and farms had been scraped away, although you can still see the road paths and patterns in the pictures. How easily they'll be to find on the ground is a different story."

"I'll settle for any kind of road," Socolov moaned. "Nothing on land could be worse than this!"

They continued on in with the tide. In another half hour, they approached the beach near the rocky outcrop the priest had called Capri Point. "Going in fast," Harker warned. "Father, you first. Get onto the rocks and cover us from as high as you can safely stand. Doc, I'm sorry about your sickness, but you're gonna have to get off fast and pretty much under your own power. Get to the rocks and *stay there*! As soon as you're clear, I'm gonna try and throw the line for the supplies. Doc, you'll have to hold onto it because the padre's gonna be shooting, I suspect. Then I'll come up with the line for the boat and Father Chicanis and I will bring it up onto the rocks as fast as possible. Doc, your job is to hold onto that supply rope and don't fall onto the sand. Got it?"

She looked nervous and still sick, but she nodded.

Harker went to the back of the boat, Chicanis took a rifle, inserted a clip, and stood near the front. Harker lowered a plastic tiller into the water and with all his strength battled the tide and waves to bring the boat as close to the rocks as possible without crashing onto them.

"Hold on!" he shouted above the sounds of crashing waves. "Everybody ready! *Now!*"

There was a tremendous lurch, and the boat ran up on the sand just a meter or so from the start of the rocky outcrop. Harker had proved himself a real expert sailor. Chicanis had been briefly knocked back by the force of the landing. He was unsteady as the waves continued to hit, but fired three loud shots into the sand just beyond and then immediately jumped out and raced for the rocks.

The bullets had done nothing, but as he hit the sand there was a sudden series of undulations of the yellow beach as if a horde of tiny rodents lived just beneath, and they all headed right for him. He made the rocks before they could catch him, though, and they stopped dead, as if waiting.

"Did you see 'em?" Harker called, pointing.

"I got 'em! Don't worry!"

Harker turned to Socolov, who looked suddenly more terrified than green. "Doc, you can't stay here and we have another boat coming in! This is what the job is. It's a little late to lose your nerve now! *Come forward!*" He didn't like to be so blunt and commanding to her, but time was not on their side.

She moved forward, but he could see her shaking. He took the long line of yellow rope and put it in her hand and then adjusted things, twisting this way and that, so she'd have a good grip. "Now, you don't have to haul the stuff in," he reminded her. "Just hold on!"

She looked out at the beach. There were perhaps five, six meters to the start of the rocks, not much more.

"Go, little lady!" the priest shouted. "I will cover you! Just follow my footprints!"

She started, then froze. "I—I can't seem to move."

"You go or I'm going to pick you up and throw you out on the sand," Harker snapped. *"Now!"* He moved as if he were going to do just that, and she shot him a glance of fear and hatred that he'd not seen in many years, not since he was training recruits in Commando units, but she went.

Almost immediately the sands began to come to life again, but now Father Chicanis took aim and started firing.

The sands suddenly erupted and there was a tremendous angry roar, and a knifelike claw bigger than a man shot out of the sands and straight into the air. Chicanis ignored it and concentrated on a spot to the right and just a bit back of the claw; it was clear that he was hitting something big and nasty from the way things were shaking. It was almost as if the sands had erupted in a kind of volcanic fury.

Harker didn't wait to see the show. He took the boat line and made for the rocks, dragging the boat behind him. Only when he felt he was on the rocks did he turn and call, "Father! Help me pull it in!"

Chicanis was by him in an instant and the two pulled the boat onto the rocks. Harker immediately looked inside for another rifle. He'd had some elementary instruction during the time on the island, but he knew damned well he couldn't hit the broad side of a barn with one. On the other hand, he could hit a beach, and *anybody* could hit one of those monsters that lurked below.

He took one glance around and saw Katarina Socolov sitting on the rocks, line still wrapped around her right hand, staring straight ahead, not at them or any action, as if in shock. She would have to wait; there was a second boat to get in.

Chicanis pointed to the sands where something was still convulsing. "We may be in luck! That's a smaller one than I'm used to, and to put up that much fuss I'd say another one is taking advantage of its weakness and attacking it." He turned and waved Mogutu in.

The colonel wasn't any more thrilled by the sights on the beach than Socolov had been, but he understood the problem and had faced equally nasty creatures in the past.

"Probably should have used the machine gun," the priest commented to himself, ejecting a clip and slapping in a new one. "Oh, well, too late now. Here they come! Think of a blind crab, Harker! Don't shoot the claws, shoot the body!"

Mogutu had thought of a machine gun, but he was more concerned with just getting on shore near the rocks. He wasn't as precise as Harker, and at the last minute the boat was lifted up by a wave and deposited slightly inland on the beach about ten meters away and perhaps twenty meters from where the monsters were obviously ending their fight.

"Get out and both of you pull the boat here!" Harker virtually screamed at them. "We'll do the cover! Get a move on! They'll be able to feel you walking through the bottom of the boat!"

The idea was sufficient to get even the still pale N'Gana moving. Mogutu lifted his machine gun and sprayed the area around where the underground titans were going at it and then started some bursts along the path where they would have to run pulling the boat and its contents. To everyone's relief, nothing erupted, and that was enough for the two mercenaries, who leaped out of the boat and began pulling it on the run toward the rocks.

Suddenly something popped from the sand under the rear part of the boat with enough force to throw it into the air several meters and spill out some of the contents. Said contents included the Pooka Hamille, who launched into the air and went into a steady whirling motion that made him next to impossible to see in detail. He was a long sausagelike blur, and he was headed straight for the rocks.

"I'll be damned!" Harker muttered as he fired into the area around the back of the boat. "The damned thing *can* fly!"

The Pooka may have been able to fly, but it wanted to fly as little as possible. As soon as Hamille cleared the sands and saw rock, it landed with a loud *splat* and immediately coiled and turned, tentacles emerging, watching the two mercenaries. Harker made a mental note to remember how fast the Quadulan could move if it wanted to.

Something was pushing the sand up like a wall, catching and overturning the boat. The two men knew they couldn't save it; they dropped the lines and ran like hell.

The wall followed at almost the same pace, but as soon as they hit the rocks it stopped and then subsided.

"The supplies!" Mogutu gasped, breathing hard but pointing at the overturned boat. "We have to get them!"

Harker and Chicanis looked at him. "You volunteering, Sarge?" the Navy man asked. " 'Cause I got to tell you, I don't want to get back out there until I'm ready to leave. And *we* have *our* boat and supplies!"

"I could order you to get them," N'Gana said sternly, out of breath but recovering rather quickly now from seasickness.

"Colonel, you and I both know, as old fighting men, that there are orders you give because they will be enforced and orders you give because they should be enforced," Harker responded. "And then there are orders that are meaningless. That would be this case. I thought you divided things pretty well between the two so there was some redundancy. We've got one. Let's leave it at that, unless you can figure out an easy way to get them."

N'Gana and Mogutu both looked back at their boat, upside down in the sand. To get the supplies, somebody would have to run toward the sand monsters, turn the boat over, then drag the supplies up on the rocks. The question was whether or not it was worth it.

"You're right, Harker," the colonel said with a sigh. "But we're down to one change of clothing each, and we've more than halved our guns and ammunition. It will be pretty tight."

"Colonel, human beings have somehow managed to survive here, at least in small numbers, with a lot less, I bet," Father Chicanis responded. "I think we will cope."

Harker stared back at the other boat. "The supplies will probably stick in the sand, for all the good they'll do anybody. Looks like the boat will go back out with the tide, so at least there won't be obvious signs of a landing here in a day or so. Let's get the boat up and into the brush and hide it, then take inventory. I think we should be inland and well away from the beach before nightfall."

They all turned to business, then stopped. Katarina Socolov was still sitting there, still staring.

Harker went over to her. "It's all right. We made it. We're here! We're alive!"

When she didn't react, he put out a hand and touched her shoulder. She suddenly whirled and screamed, "Don't you touch me! Don't you touch me!"

"I won't touch you," he responded gently. "Not unless you don't get off this coast."

SEVENTEEN

A Long Walk in the Sun

Katarina Socolov had not said a word after they got the supplies from the surviving boat unpacked and divided up. There were now only three backpacks for the five members of the team who could handle backpacks, the Pooka being built for different things. Mogutu took one, Father Chicanis took another, and Harker took the third. The commander of the expedition had not volunteered, and Socolov, though she had trained with a heavy pack, was nonetheless the lightest and smallest of the humans. She also gave no sign of volunteering.

Harker wasn't sure if it was shock, self-doubt after the rugged landfall, or his own harsh barking at her to do what had to be done that was causing her sudden withdrawal, but for now they had enough of problems that he decided not to push it. Either she'd snap out of it and rejoin the rest of them or she'd break, in which case, in the cold reality of survival in hostile territory, she would become a liability.

She'd been very athletic and very confident, it was true, but she'd still emerged from the ivory tower and thought of this as something romantic, youthful fieldwork upon which to build a career. Most academics had never come face to face with situations in which split-second decisions might cause their own death. It had to be a tough awakening, and they were only starting.

N'Gana looked at his watch. They had already synchronized on the island; now he checked each to ensure that the watches were still in synch at least to the minute. They were; computers might not govern these watches, but they had designed and built them.

"We have at least six more hours of daylight," he told them, looking and sounding like his old self. "I think we ought to make what time we can. The sooner we get to our objective and retrieve what must be retrieved and get that information up to the others, the sooner we can be concerned with getting back."

There wasn't much argument on that score, and while they'd had a trying morning, it felt good to actually be doing something. N'Gana turned to Father Chicanis. "Which way, Father?"

The priest pointed east. "Stay parallel with the coast and not too far inland. Since that was Capri Point back there, it means we've got a hundred and fifty or so kilometers to where we need to be, give or take. It will be difficult to get lost if we keep close to the ocean and keep going east."

"Remember that," the colonel said to the others. "If anything happens and we become separated, that is the way there, and, from there, the reverse is the way back." He thought a moment. "Allowing a bit for unforeseeable problems, I would say we have a week's good walk here. Since I don't have a backpack I'll take the point, the sergeant will take the rear. You see or hear *anything* unusual, or anything helpful for that matter, don't hesitate. And keep a good lookout for anything edible. We want to save the preserved stuff for when we absolutely have to have it. If humans can exist down here in the wild, then so can we. Father, you know the local and imported plants here, so you're the one who says what's edible and what's not."

They started walking, and were quickly enmeshed in the tall grass that was two to three meters tall, well over N'Gana's head. It wasn't hard to follow the leader in this stuff since he was so large a man and trampled down quite a swath, but this made Harker start thinking about how easy it would be for any enemy to be there in the tall grass, even in force, and remain invisible until it was too late.

"Was it like this when you were living here, Father?" Harker asked the priest.

Chicanis shook his head. "No, not like this. These grasses were pretty well tamed, cut, managed, and in most cases we thought it was plowed up. It's good protection, but it's tough finding landmarks. I hope this won't be the norm all the way."

"There were some groves of trees going along for some distance not too far inland on the survey photos, if I remember," Mogutu commented in a low tone that the others readily took up. "They looked like fruit trees of some sort."

"They were. Tropical fruits, mostly," Chicanis responded. "They were quite a favorite delicacy in the good old days. There were a number of fruits grown very near the coast because the regular sea breezes gave them added moisture year-round. I don't know, though, how you're going to find anything at all down here walking through this. Even I am lost."

"The colonel's got a magnetic compass and there's manual sighting gear adjusted for Helena in my pack," Harker told him. "Good thing, too, since if it had been in the other boat we'd really be in a fix. The compass is adjusted to true north from its usual east-northeast on this planet, and should be adequate."

By the end of an hour or so they were all soaked with sweat and feeling the strain of the tropical climate and particularly the hot, humid air. Harker was just about to suggest a break when they stepped out of the grasslands and into a dense forest. There hadn't been many noticeable insects in the grass, but now the very air seemed made of them, and it was nearly impossible to keep themselves from being covered in them. Harker and Socolov both began coughing from having breathed in tiny bugs.

N'Gana came back and called a break. The others couldn't imagine wanting to linger a single moment in that spot.

"Let's get back into the grass," Harker suggested, feeling like his entire face and arms were covered with tiny insects.

"Okay, just inside," N'Gana responded. "Key to that large tree over there. Drop the packs and remain with them. I'm going to try and knock some of that fruit down, or climb up and get it."

"I can help," Father Chicanis volunteered. "Wait until I drop the backpack. No use giving you all the local names for things, but you'll all like those. Don't pick up any that have fallen, though. The insects will have pretty well moved in. Most of them don't touch fruit that's growing, though. It has a kind of natural defense, even if it was genetically designed."

"Insects this bad in the old days?" N'Gana asked him.

"Not that I remember, but there were always a lot of them. No big game, no big animals at all, plenty of insects. They aren't really insects, either, if you examine them closely, but they occupy the same niche. We just called them all bugs. That's the trouble with tropical climates—what's great for people is even better for the pests."

It was clear that people hadn't been in this area for a very long time, so it was pretty easy to pick enough of the oval-shaped fruit and bring it to the camp by the armload.

"Funny the insects don't like it over here," Harker commented, glad to be able to breathe real air.

"Oh, there are plenty in the grass, but they don't go where they can't eat. The range of most of those bugs is only a few dozen meters," Chicanis answered him. "We'll get some here when we crack open the fruit, but don't let them bother you. Even if you swallow a few, just think of them as, well, protein. Most aren't even native. They snuck in with the fruit. The native ones go more for the grasses and do a lot of tunneling."

"Thanks a lot," Harker responded. In one brief comment Chicanis had managed to make him paranoid about where he was sitting while also making the swarms even less appetizing to think about.

The one who seemed happiest about the bugs was Hamille. The feathery but serpentine creature opened that huge oval of a mouth and just seemed to inhale the flying bugs as fast as it could. When full, it would sink to the ground and start spitting. Out came tiny forms that looked like berries and others that looked like tiny gemstones that crawled or wriggled.

"The ones spit out are the native bugs, I assume," Mogutu commented more than asked.

"Yes. Our friend can digest most protein-based bugs and such, even raw meat and what we would think of as carrion, but I think the native bugs are a bit indigestible even for it," N'Gana replied. "At least Hamille will have the same ease with local cuisine as we, even if we eat different things. That's good, because half or more of its food was in our lost packs."

He used the knife to slice open one of the melonlike fruits. It revealed a bright yellow-orange pulp with a core of tiny white seeds. The thing tasted quite sweet and proved very filling. The second one turned out to have some bugs in it and, as it turned out, about one in three of them had a lot of visitors.

"I don't understand it," Chicanis said, shaking his head in wonder. "They used to avoid anything on the vine or die."

"They're adapting," Harker responded, a little worriedly. "They're evolving to meet changing circumstances. Too much grass, food that's too concentrated.

Those things aren't the most numerous of the bugs devouring the fruits that fall from the trees. Those silver things with the little pincers seem to be the boss, followed by the round black things with the four legs and the millipedelike critters. These little brown buggers had to adapt or die out."

"I wonder if perhaps the surviving people might have as well?" the priest asked worriedly.

"I wouldn't worry about that," N'Gana responded. "Evolution takes a *lot* longer in us humans. Us—all of us—now, we have these skin flaps and bony plates from running through the genholes for years, but they're growths, not deformities. They stop when we stop, and most are pretty easily removed. Mental adaptation, now, that's a different story. We adapted so much to technology we got soft. Very few could do what we're doing, you know that? We've gotten too used to waving our hands and having the machines provide. Anything we want and can't find, we can synthesize. Anything we need to know we just plug our heads into a net and direct-load from the libraries. Used to be everybody had to read for information. Now nobody even remembers how, at least in general. We get tired of our looks, we drop in a clinic and brown eyes become blue, fat vanishes and is replaced by muscle in a matter of days or weeks, no effort. Nobody walks anywhere anymore."

"Maybe so," Father Chicanis said in a slightly dubious tone, "but not everybody. That's what killed these worlds, of course. Stripped to the basics, only a very small number survived. Perhaps that is evolution. Perhaps the only ones who survived and bred did so precisely because they were either throwbacks or had qualities the others did not that allowed them to survive."

"Maybe, but if we meet any of 'em I bet they won't be all that different," the colonel asserted. "I mean, except for extinction, nothing evolves in as little as ninety years or so, not without artificial help. Isn't that right, Doctor?"

Eyes turned to the silent and sullen anthropologist. All had noticed her silence and somewhat shell-shocked look, but only Harker and Chicanis had been concerned about it.

When she didn't reply, N'Gana frowned and called, "Doctor Socolov? *Kat?* You must snap out of this!" When she only vaguely reacted, he walked over and looked down at her. "Doctor, I will put this bluntly, but you must believe that I am not making idle conversation. We cannot afford to have breakdowns or episodes. If you have gone psychotic, you are a liability and we will leave you here. If you are doing this out of some inner angst or too-late self-doubt or whatever, then you are a liability. You went into this with as few illusions as we could manage. If you did not believe us, that is too bad, but if you are not a willing part of this *team*, then you are a threat to our lives and our mission, as much a threat as those things in the sand. We don't have time for this, Doctor. Either grow up or walk off into the brush. I want your answer *now*. I want your response before we pick up and walk another ten kilometers. If you do not react, we will leave you. If you then follow, we will make certain that you cannot."

"Cut her some slack, Colonel," Father Chicanis put in, concerned. "She's been through a lot already."

"Stay out of this, Father! I am not doing this to be a petty tyrant. I simply wish you, both you and the doctor here, and anyone else who might think otherwise, to consider the cost of our failure. Ask yourselves just how many billions or trillions of lives is she worth? The mission is the only thing that is important here. Anyone who forgets that, or who gets in the way of that, will have to be cut out. There are *worlds* at stake here! Including hers—and mine."

She looked up at him angrily, but all she said was, "I'll

come, Colonel. I'm only here because they thought I could help. Just give me some space."

"I don't have time for negotiations," N'Gana responded coldly, then turned and looked straight into the eyes of the priest. "And, Father, this is the absolute last time I will explain a course of action. We don't have the luxury of that now."

Harker looked over at Socolov and could not read what she was thinking. He sighed and hoped that she could work it out before things got even stickier. Even though he'd been as harsh as N'Gana in getting her out of the boat, he knew he couldn't be as cold under conditions like these as the colonel had been. Even so, as a former company commander in hostile territory, he couldn't find fault with anything the colonel had said, either.

It's this damned heat and humidity, he thought. *And how damned naked we are in just fatigues and boots toting anachronistic old blunderbusses through unknown territory.* He missed the combat suit more than he'd thought he would. He would have bet most anything that, underneath, N'Gana and Mogutu wished they had theirs, too.

Maybe slithering along like the Pooka would suit them all better than this incessant walking in the tall and masking grasses.

In point of fact, the imposing creature could move along very rapidly, often outpacing everyone, and this was not lost on N'Gana. Although the Quadulan couldn't yell and didn't make a sufficient dent in the grasses to be the forward scout, it was very useful, when strange sounds were heard or when things just didn't feel right, to be able to send it forward and wait for it to return with information on just what was there. It was unlikely to have any real enemies here save the Titans, and it could lay a trail of its own scent to guide it precisely back to the group.

It was getting very late in the day when the creature returned from one such mission. "Follow to the grove," it said. "Make camp. Good ground, food, water."

It was a welcome suggestion, and it turned out to be not ten minutes from where they were.

The grove was clearly an old farm gone wild, with lush fruit trees all lined up for as far as the eye could see right next to bushes bearing large, juicy red and purple fruit. The insects were there, of course; in this climate it was inevitable. Still, they didn't seem nearly as dense, and it looked fairly comfortable as this world went. There were even several small streams, all with swift-flowing if warm water nearby, possibly a remnant of some early irrigation system.

"Nick of time," Harker commented to everyone and nobody in particular. "The sun's about past the mountains. It's going to be very dark very soon, I think."

The camp was quickly laid out. Each backpack, once unloaded, became a kind of sleeping bag and the contents were in a series of plastic containers that fit together for maximum compression and easy organization and unpacking. The shortage of sleeping bags was not the disadvantage it seemed. There would have to be someone on guard, and maybe having two up at once wasn't such a bad idea in this totally alien landscape. Night would be about eleven hours at this time of year and in this latitude; everyone would try to sleep at least six of those hours, maybe even eight, if they weren't continuous. They ate and drank and washed and relieved themselves mostly in silence; there wasn't anything more to say. A fire was forbidden, at least for now—at least until they knew why no small fires had ever been picked up by orbital spy satellites tracking the remnants of humanity on conquered worlds.

"Sergeant, you and the good Father here will take the first watch," N'Gana told them. "Three hours, then you wake up Harker and the doctor and when they get out of their bags, you two get in. Harker, three hours and then you awaken me. I'll get Hamille up—he tends to be rather nasty when awakened suddenly, but I know how to do it—and we'll take the final shift. We'll get you all up a little after sunup and we'll start breaking camp and get on the march. There is still a very long way to go."

About an hour after sundown, though, when it was so dark at ground level they could barely see their hands in front of their faces, they could all first hear and then *feel* the coming of the storms. And when they hit with furious thunder and lightning and great gusts of wind, there was little any of them could do but get wet in the almost impossibly dense downpour or huddle inside the bags. The clothing, boots, and sleeping bags were waterproof, of course, but where there was an opening or something was exposed, it got soaked.

It lasted a good twenty to thirty minutes and seemed like forever. It wasn't the steady tropical dumping all that time, but it only let up briefly, never stopping, then roared back again. And when it ended, it *ended.* Five minutes after the last drop fell, the wind was down to next to nothing and the clouds were breaking up and revealing an exceptional, spectacular sky.

Mogutu and Father Chicanis walked around, to be sure that everyone was all right. Everyone was waterlogged, but they were okay.

Neither Harker nor Kat Socolov had been asleep; it was difficult to get comfortable, and the situation was still tense, with more unknowns than knowns about this strange new place. Neither had managed to keep water out of the head end of the sleeping bags, although it took only a couple of minutes to open them up, drain them, and let the inside liner dry out. Everything about and on them would have to air-dry, though you didn't pack towels on this kind of trip.

Once things settled down, the sounds of the night bugs rose to a crescendo, creating a background that was impossible to ignore. *Note to outfitters on future expeditions,* Harker thought, feeling a bit miserable. *Pack earplugs.*

True to the colonel's schedule, and in spite of the thunderstorm, Mogutu awakened Harker from a less than perfect sleep after what was, by their watches, precisely a three-hour shift, but which seemed to Harker to have lasted, at most, ten minutes. He felt worse than he had riding the keel, and much more vulnerable. Still, he heard Father Chicanis gently waking a probably more miserable Katarina Socolov, and he whispered to Mogutu, "Couldn't you at least let *her* sleep?"

"No exceptions," the sergeant responded. "We have to get into this. It's not going to get easier, you know. The priest volunteered to take an extra shift for her and I nixed that, too." He reached down for something that turned out to be a low-grav sealed cup and handed it to Harker. You could suck on it, like a baby bottle, but otherwise it was tight. Harker took a pull and was surprised. "Coffee? *Hot* coffee?"

"Self-heating canister," Mogutu responded. "No heat signature. We don't have too many, but I think you and the doc will both need it now."

In truth, he did, and the taste of the coffee, as military strong and black as it was, energized him a bit. It was still extremely hot and humid, but there were times when caffeine in a hot solution was the only thing that worked and this was one of them. He also checked his pocket, took out a small tablet, popped it into his mouth, and swallowed it. It made the aches and pains go away, at least for a little while.

They didn't have a lot of those, either.

He felt human enough to be worried about standing a watch with a still truculent Socolov, and wondered what the hell they might do to pass the time.

He made his way over to her, his eyes finally clearing and adjusting to the darkness. At least the moon Achilles, half-full, was up; not a lot of help, but it was better than before. He could see that she, too, had been given a stimulant to drink, as well as Father Chicanis's rifle. He was a bit better armed; he had Mogutu's submachine gun. He didn't like either crude and noisy weapon, but at least with his you only had to aim in the general direction of something to hit it.

She heard him, but said nothing. He decided that the ice had to be broken, lest one or both of them fall over exhausted. "How are you feeling?" he asked in a barely audible whisper.

"Like I was at the bottom of an elevator shaft when the car crashed down on top of me," she responded in a little louder tone, sounding less than friendly. "I guess I'm not like the macho men of the military, who don't need sleep or armor or food or anything."

"Come on over here, away from the others," he invited. "Just to talk without having them be as miserable as we are. If nothing else, we should get this guard business sorted out before we have reason to shoot somebody or something."

She couldn't argue with that, so she followed him perhaps ten meters from the sleepers, a bit inside the grove. The insect noises were still pretty loud, but either they'd died down some or the interlopers were getting accustomed to them.

"Sit down," he suggested, trying to sound as friendly and nonthreatening as possible. "We don't have to be uncomfortable yet. If we take turns, at least we won't wear ourselves out early. That thunderstorm took a lot out of us."

She did sink down, back against a tree, but said nothing.

"You take a pain pill with a stim?" he asked her.

"I took the stim. Maybe you're right on the pain. I used to go fifteen kilometers with a full pack in the workout rooms, but this is already more tiring."

"Gravity does it."

"There was gravity on the ship."

"True," he agreed, "but it's a standardized gravity, just eighty percent of one universal gee unit. That's been found to be the most comfortable with the least complications for long, cramped voyages. Air pressure is a stock one point seven five kilometers, humidity's forty percent, air is just exactly so, and it's always that way. Your body gets used to it. Now, suddenly, we're on a world that's at least one standard gee pressure at sea level, with the air extra-dense from eighty to ninety percent or more humidity and a temperature that's hotter than we've been in in quite some time, even this late at night. We're all feeling it. Even N'Gana is feeling it, probably more than any of us. He's at least ten years older than any of us."

"He looks pretty spry to me. So do the rest of you."

"It was said long ago, in ancient times, by some ancient soldier maybe just back from walking half a world and fighting the whole way, that the trick wasn't not to *feel* pain, exhaustion, and all the other ailments. The trick was not to *show* it, particularly to those below you in rank. I think maybe Mogutu's probably in the best shape of any of us, and I can tell by how he reacted and how he's moving that he's feeling it, too."

"Then—we're never going to make it! If it's this bad now . . ."

"We'll make it. It won't get much easier, but, after a while, it won't seem to get any worse, either. If we have the willpower to stick out the walk all the way, then by the time we really need to be in top trim, we will be. At least, that's the theory. Who knows what's in this brush that might be out to get us?"

"I thought there weren't any large animals left."

"There aren't, or so the good father assures us. But *something* out here is dangerous—bet on it. Maybe even our own people. And don't put down plants or insects, either. Some of them can be real killers."

"Thanks a lot," she responded sourly. "You've given me a lot more confidence."

"Listen, the biggest threat I can think of right now, assuming nobody knows we're here, is accidents. Stepping off a ledge, even just off a little path that could twist or break an ankle or snap a ligament. Those more than anything get you."

"What happens if that does happen? If one of us can't walk or something?"

"If it can't be repaired and they can't keep up, they'll be left in place with as much provisions and care as we can manage. It's like the colonel said—no matter how much we suffer, we're doing this for whole worlds of people. Men, women, children, even furry snakes with tentacles." He looked around in the darkness. "Speaking of which, I think it's time one of us made the rounds. I'll do it first—I have the experience in this. I'm just going to walk completely around the camp at maybe ten, fifteen meters out—a slow circle from here to here around them."

"What are you looking for?" she asked him.

"Anything unusual. I know that sounds idiotic since we're on an alien planet, but it's the best I can do. Always trust your senses and your instincts. If something feels odd or wrong, it probably is. You're picking up something on a subconscious level, but it's a survival trait handed down from our ancient ape ancestors no matter what Chicanis says. Just stay here and don't go to sleep. Just watch and listen, that's all. I'll be back shortly, so don't get so nervous you shoot a hole in me, okay?"

"I—I don't think I could if I tried," she answered, but she understood what he meant.

It was an eerie walk, through territory not scouted by daylight first, but he tried to keep the circle manageable, listen and smell as much as look, and to not get himself lost in the portion that was in the grass.

Insects were occasionally biting any skin he had exposed. No worry about alien microorganisms; there had never been one ever discovered that could infect a human, and vice versa. More dangerous in a situation like this were good old-fashioned human viruses and bacteria inevitably imported with the colonists from the first. Those had been known to mutate wildly and evolve in all sorts of bizarre directions in alien environments, and there was no way to inoculate or even breed people to withstand things you hadn't been able to get samples of for a hundred years.

When he came back around and headed toward her once more, his only impression of the area was that it stank. There was the smell of rotten dead vegetable matter and a kind of excrementlike swamp odor that seemed to permeate the grassland. It hadn't gotten any better.

"It's just me," he called in a loud whisper. "No problems."

"What's the password?" she responded in a similar whisper.

He stopped short. "Password? We didn't say anything about a password!"

"That's the right password," she responded, sounding a lot friendlier. "Come on in."

He went back to the tree and saw that she was standing now. "I started to nod off," she told him. "I had to stand up.."

He understood, but cautioned, "Better stay off your feet while you can in any case. You'll be on them long enough come daylight."

"I'm also itching like mad," she told him. "I don't know what it is. Either some of these little biters got into my clothes or something else is happening."

"I've got the itches myself," he said. "I started feeling it when I woke up, but it might have been before. I wonder what material this stuff's made of?"

"Huh? I dunno. It seems tough and weatherproof enough."

"It's designed to be," he said, "but who knows what the conditions are here now?" He sank down on the ground.

"Huh? There were people here in big cities and bigger farms and factories and such for a couple hundred years. I'd say that Father Chicanis would know if there were any funny things like that."

"I wasn't thinking of Helena before the Fall. This is still tropical and still lush, but it's not the same place Chicanis left. It's been modified by the Titans. You kind of wonder about that rain. I didn't itch like this the past two days, only since getting soaked."

"Me neither," she agreed.

"You're the anthropologist. What do you think the survivors will be like if we run into them?"

"Basic, I would expect," she replied. "Still, it's only been a few generations. In another century they will be that much more disconnected, and after that even more, until the old days are myths and gods and devils not understood by humans and there will be a total acceptance of a low-tech existence. At this level, though, if they've kept together as cohesive groups, they still should have a clear idea of who they are and where they came from. They're probably living half off the land and half off remaining stocks of food and goods in ruins below. Beyond being mere refugees, but still gathering whatever is needed and clinging to the old ways as much as possible."

"I wonder," he responded.

"If you think it's different, why ask me?"

He stood and walked to the edge of the trees to where he had a clear view of the sky. "Come here, if you can, and look up. Just look. Don't concentrate, don't focus, just relax and gaze."

She was curious enough to come over to him and do as he said. At first she saw nothing but bright stars and planets and the half-illuminated Achilles, and she was just about to give it up as some kind of bad joke and go back and sit down when *something* came into view. At first it was only slight, and faint, and not really there. She tried focusing on it but it seemed to be almost hiding from her. Still, it was strange enough to persevere, and, in a few minutes of not fighting it or chasing it with her eyes, she managed to see it.

A really thin, wispy series of lines, almost like a grid, far up in the sky. Too faint to really get a handle on, but definitely there.

"I see it!" she exclaimed. "But what am I seeing?"

"I don't know. It's been measured on Occupied worlds before, and signatures taken, but I had no idea until I made the rounds there that it was something you could see, at least from the ground. I think it's how they keep watch over things. Some kind of energy beams that create a grid and which can somehow be used to monitor relatively small areas of the planet, or at least the continent. I don't remember it on the island, so it might well be just here. I don't think they care much about the rest of the place, only where they can grow their weird giant flowers."

"You mean they might be able to see us?"

"Possible, but I doubt it. I even doubt if they could tell us from the survivors that they surely know are here. It explains why nobody builds campfires or cooking fires, though. They might give off enough of a heat signature to be picked up. Probably bring out the equivalent of the Titan Fire Department. Can't have any grass or forest fires ruining their precious plants. But if everything they do is toward growing those things, and so far all we know about them suggests that it is, then that kind of system can also be used to maintain everything environmentally to make them prosper and keep the surrounding local vegetation in check as well. Ever have a garden?"

"No. Like most folks I'm a city person."

"Well, you often have to fertilize it and water it and spray it for bugs and other threats and do all sorts of things to make sure it grows right. Thunderheads reach many kilometers into the sky, far beyond local weather levels. Right through *that*, whatever it is. What better way to mix what they want and spray it all over the place than via the storms? Notice that the bugs definitely are fewer. Sure, it's only trillions, not gazillions, but there's some effect after the rain."

"What are you suggesting? That they mix some chemicals in the rain and that's why we're itching?"

"Maybe. Maybe they make what they need as it passes through that grid, and they can localize things as well. Think about rust. Just take something that's mostly iron and add water. Add a little salt and you kill a lot of vegetation. Clearly they didn't do that, but I wonder what they did do?"

It was not a cheerful thought.

In the light of morning, there didn't seem to be much out of whack, though, and both for the time quickly forgot the worries.

Socolov still didn't want to talk about what was eating at her, but she had at least warmed to the rest, particularly Harker, and things seemed to be getting into a normal routine. The discovery that the rain came like that every night at just about the same time, though, made for a threatened mutiny until N'Gana agreed to rotate the guard slots so that, at least two out of three times, everybody could get a straight sleep with only the second watch suffering.

Still, about five days and, by the small pedometer on N'Gana's ankle about sixty-five kilometers toward their goal, it began to be clear that something was going very wrong with their supplies.

It had been happening gradually enough that they'd been able to dismiss as expected the things that either didn't work or didn't hold up, but now, after almost a week on the planet's surface, the damage was becoming impossible to avoid.

It had started with the increasing reactions they all had to something that caused large-scale rashes and itching over even the covered parts of their bodies. At first it seemed like some kind of allergic reaction, although Father Chicanis insisted that he had known nothing like this in the past. Now, though, it was becoming clear from the fabrics that were slowly but definitely coming apart that something was almost literally eating the best materials modern chemistry could produce, and it was this reaction that was causing the fierce rashes.

The clothing, not to mention the sleeping bags, packs, and more, was almost literally decomposing.

"At this level we're gonna be naked and without any supplies in two days," Mogutu commented.

Harker nodded. Even some of the containers were showing signs of dissolving, like salt blocks under running water. You couldn't see it happening, but it clearly was nonetheless.

"I don't think it's in the air," Harker commented. "I think the damage is being done by that rain. It started a reaction that eventually ran its course at this point. But it's going to rain again, bet on it, every night just after sunset, and there's not much shelter we can take against it."

"Never mind the theorizing," N'Gana responded. "The real question is, what *didn't* get at least a little of the treatment? Our boots have lost their gloss but mine, at least, seem to be holding up." So saying, he bent down to fix the upper part of the laces, and the laces came apart in his hands as if they were a hundred years old. "Then again," he muttered, "maybe they're just a little tougher stuff."

"The gun works and barrels look fine, but the stocks are

having a hard time of it," Mogutu noted. "My watch still works. Looks fine, in fact. But you can see some early dissolution in the band, same as on the others."

"My communion set is unharmed," Father Chicanis noted. "And I have cloths used in some rites that got soaked, yet they don't seem to be any worse for wear."

Harker got it. "Real cloth, Father?"

"Yes, cotton and wool, I think."

"And the communion set. That box is real wood?"

"Why come to think of it, yes it is! Bless my soul! Whatever it is likes all natural things but doesn't like things made by people."

"Makes sense," N'Gana noted. "The watches, gun barrels and the like are metal. So are the bullets, so they've come through. This is just great! One week here and we're facing becoming defenseless prisoners of the elements! What's worse, we now don't know if there is anything left underground. This—this *stuff* has had ninety years to seep down as far as it can get!"

It was Kat Socolov who disagreed now. "If you think I like the idea of parading around all you men stark naked, you're wrong," she told them. "Still, I would bet that this stuff doesn't go down far into the soil, and it probably dissipates shortly if it doesn't act. Think about it! The Dutchman's man got to an old security backup station that had to be much closer to the surface than where we're going! And something kept enough humans alive here to register on satellite scans even though we know they scoured the whole land area before readjusting and replanting. No, if that signal got out, then what we want is still there. Besides, the message *said* it was. We're just gonna have to depend more on brawn for protection, that's all. Now we'll see how you guys do with only your muscles, huh?"

N'Gana sighed. "Well, then, that's the way it is. We'll have to find some fig leaves, looks like, and see what is sturdy enough to make a pack or two for some vital supplies. Maybe there will be some plants whose leaves will be strong enough. We have to retain what we can for a while, even though we know it's going to run out." He looked at the melted packs and ripped clothing. "Damn! You'd think the damned Dutchman would have at least mentioned this effect!"

"You've got a point," Father Chicanis told him. "If this were common or usual on Occupied worlds, I think he *would* have told us. I think that it is probably what trapped his man here. He didn't expect to wind up naked and defenseless. He was caught just like us. That's why he couldn't get out! I do wish that he'd mentioned this in his reports, but, well, maybe this is something local. Something in Helena's makeup, either original or from our reworking, interacts with whatever they use. It doesn't seem to bother them or *their* stuff, so why should they care? Or even notice?"

They did what they could. A few rifles still seemed whole and tested out okay, probably because they'd been in the bottom of one box, with a wooden partition on top of them, and the reaction hadn't reached them yet. It would eventually unless they could figure out some way to protect the weapons, but at least they had one more day to consider. They also had a good breakfast, since many of the containers were not much longer for this world, either.

The pharmacy and first aid kit needed protection more than anything, though. It wasn't much, but it was what they had.

"Perhaps when we hear the rains we can wrap it in the cloths," Father Chicanis suggested. "Maybe doing that, and possibly shielding it with big leaves or maybe burying the whole thing might protect it."

"Worth a try," N'Gana agreed. Kat Socolov noted that he really did have huge bodybuilder's muscles, and Mogutu's weren't that bad either, although he was slighter of build and it didn't show as much. Harker, in fact, was probably the one in as poor condition as any of them, something he ruefully noted. Kat Socolov was no push-over; she'd definitely spent a long time lifting weights. She managed to rig up a basic halter top and reworked some cloth in her personal kit for a bottom, but it wasn't much and probably wouldn't last all that long.

Oddly, the boots didn't seem to be getting any worse; it was only the gloss and the laces. Father Chicanis recognized a native vine that had very tough properties and experimented using thin and stripped lengths for his own laces; it seemed to work. They all agreed that they looked somewhat stupid, but the foot protection was still welcome. In this environment you weren't sure what you were stepping on until you stepped on it, and nature seemed to have an inexhaustible supply of sharp edges.

On day seven they were still only about halfway to their goal, but they came across what must have been the overgrown remnants of a once grand highway.

Like their equipment, the highway had been mostly dissolved long before, but the concrete and gravel pack underneath remained, as did, curiously, rusted remnants of the control rods and wiring for the magnetic levitation and auto guidance systems.

"The Grand Highway," Father Chicanis sighed. "From Eden to Olympus. You can see Olympus sometimes from high points around here. Not the mighty one of legend, but the tallest peak in the far range, always snow-covered and mysterious-looking. It's tall enough to make some of its own weather and obscure itself early on in the day, which is why they named it after the legendary abode of the ancient Greek gods."

"I'm surprised your church wasn't upset with all this naming of things after ancient pagan gods," Harker commented.

"Oh, well, it is a good thing to remember your heritage

and where your people came from. That's not at all blasphemous. That age produced the first great thinkers of what came to be called 'western' civilization, to differentiate it from the east. Geometry and the higher mathematics, much physics, the first great plays—it was quite a time. The only blasphemy would be to worship the old gods, and I'm not even sure many of the Greek thinkers really believed in them, either. They just had no alternatives at that time."

N'Gana cleared his throat. "Um, Father, interesting history, but where does this road go?"

"It's on the old maps—oh, yes, I forgot, they're pretty well dissolved by now. Well, it started in Ephesus, coming out of a kind of ring road around the city, and it extended diagonally across the valley and then went through a tunnel almost sixty kilometers long before it emerged in a glacial valley on the other side. More tunnels, more valleys, and finally it reached all the way to Corinth on the opposite coast. It used to take a few pleasant hours at a steady four hundred kilometers per hour."

N'Gana was only interested in the Ephesus route. "All right, then, so if we can follow it with this overgrowth it should take us where we want to go."

"The road was built to hit the big truck farms this region had," the priest told him. "It isn't exactly straight. At a guess, we'll go inland from here to go around the coast range and then to Sparta, and then swing around through the pass and down into the coastal plain and Ephesus." He sighed. "I wish I had a landmark, *something* that would tell me where we are now. If I knew that I almost certainly could determine if it would be faster or slower to follow the roadbed."

"What's the worst case?" N'Gana asked him. "How much would it add?"

"A day, maybe two, of walking," Chicanis told him. "Why?"

"It's still here, that's why," the colonel replied. "It makes a decent path to follow. We know that the road goes where we want it to and we know that all the major land obstacles would have been removed except—what's the name of that river?"

"The River Lethe," Chicanis replied.

"Yes. That we'll have to contend with, perhaps using ingenuity this close to the ocean. I don't expect any bridgeworks will have met any better fate than the road surface or our own gear. Still, this will give us a trail that may make our going a bit easier. We're already dependent on the land for most of our food; the road connected the truck farms to the cities and towns. We'll follow it."

That night the storms were particularly fierce, and the lightning struck close to them many times. Some of the magnetic materials left over from the old road made nice targets for the bolts, something they hadn't really thought about. N'Gana was firm, though, that they would stick close to the road although not camp exactly on it. They had still not seen much sign of other humans. If the lightning kept them away, all the better, and the walking was much easier than it would have been otherwise.

The eighth night on the mainland, Harker and Socolov drew first watch, which now began after the storm passed. There was virtually nothing left of their fine packs, tough clothing, or anything else. Even the weapons had disintegrated to the point where they were barely scraps of junk metal and wood. Rifle barrels were now truncheons, and very lethal ones, too, if it came to that. Using a leathery leaf from a common wild bush that Chicanis said was one of the few thriving native species of plant left on Helena—that is, not an import by the terraformers—they managed to create pouches and saved a great many bullets. They were metal and were also filled with gunpowder; they had not been affected by the rot and were still a possible weapon if there was time to use them. The knife handles, unfortunately, proved to be of less natural origin. The blades survived, but they were unbalanced and useful mostly for digging or scraping.

The same tough leaf, with the equally strong and common stripped vine, they used to salvage as much of their modesty as they could, mostly out of deference to the anthropologist. Harker discovered her, with a gun barrel as a weapon, sitting on a rock in the darkness. Achilles was now three-quarters full, and there was at least some light to see with. All of them hoped that they'd be well away before a new moon.

She had, he noticed, gone au naturel. So much for her sensibilities, he thought. It was the last defense; they'd all cast off their boots after discovering that a fairly nasty kind of algae started growing inside them and secreting a toxic irritant on the feet. It was inevitable sooner or later anyway, and the sooner they did it, the sooner their feet would toughen. The first day barefoot, though, had been awful, and tonight wasn't all that much better.

"No fig leaf?" he asked her, sitting down nearby.

"Why bother? We aren't hiding anything and those things are a joke when you walk." She gave a slight chuckle. "It's funny—somehow it doesn't seem all that risqué. In fact, it feels really comfortable in this climate. Besides, I think if I were going to be raped by any of you guys, it would have happened before now."

"Not once we saw that bodybuilder's physique," he responded in the same light tone. "Where'd you get muscle tone like that? Not in a college classroom, I bet. I haven't seen a woman with muscles that developed since I once saw Bambi the Destroyer coming out of the shower."

"Bambi the *what*?" She laughed.

"Her name's really Barbara Fenitucci. A real Amazon warrior and a Marine to boot. Always picking on the men, always having to prove she could do anything they could do better and in half the time."

"Sounds interesting. I've known a lot of women like that, but, no, I was never in the Marines and I never wanted to be a man, which is sort of what that's about. I bet she was a service brat. Marines and the like are really driven as kids. No, I spent a lot of time getting this way, and I'm afraid if I don't do some regular heavy lifting I'm going to lose part of it. It's a matter of independence. Of being able to do what you want, go where you want to go, and not live in terror of every guy on the street. I did martial arts first—almost everybody does, I think—and got good enough in a couple of useful disciplines, and I kept it up. Then they opened this training and conditioning program at the university where I was working on my doctorate. I gave it a try and liked it. I weighed in at sixty-three kilos and was bench-pressing more than a hundred and forty kilos before I left to board the *Odysseus*. Fortunately, they had a good and well-equipped gym on board, mostly for the mercenary twins, and I was able to keep it up. I didn't want to have to worry about being the only female on the trip."

He made a guess. "And that's why you were so upset at yourself on landing? All that, and big razor-sharp claws come up and there are monsters under the sand and the only thing you can do about it is listen to the big guy scream at you to run?"

"Something like that. You can't believe how cocky you get when you have this much of your body developed. I think I'd forgotten what it was like to be terrified, and there I was, all that crap gone to waste. The first crisis on the new world and I froze in fear."

"Well, I wouldn't let that get you," he told her. "What set me apart in that situation was experience, and in Father Chicanis's case it was knowledge of what was there and a rifle to deal with it. You've been good once we got on solid ground, as good as anybody here."

She smiled. "Thanks. I needed that, I think."

"Surprised we haven't run into any of the locals yet?"

"Not really. There aren't that many for this whole region, and they are widely scattered in groups of perhaps twenty-five to fifty, no more. I'm revising my theories about what they will be like, though, when we do meet them. This corrosive effect, together with ample and well-distributed food, probably means that they are in fact more primitive, more tribal than I'd thought. I'd really like to find them and find out, although without any supplies I have a feeling getting accepted by them will be tough. Dealing with them might be tougher yet. Usually you can bribe your way to at least safe passage, but I'm not sure we'll have as good a result now as I'd planned. Not unless Father Chicanis is willing to break up our last remaining artifacts."

"I think he'll die rather than give up the communion set," Harker replied. "So—that's why you're along? Expert on dealing with primitives by using old established ways and means?"

"Something like that. And I get to be the first in my profession to actually interact with them. It's a career maker. If, that is, we meet any of them, and if we manage to get off this rock somehow."

"You think we're stuck?"

She shrugged. "What's the boat we left buried back there made of, and how buried does it have to be? Without the boat, how do we get back to the island? Swim forty-odd kilometers of ocean? I'm not sure I'm up to that. I think that poor man who did the Dutchman's business was in the same fix. That's why he broadcast."

"Yeah, but there's every evidence from the last part of that recording that something was stalking him," Harker noted. "And since he was never heard from again, that something probably killed him. Who or what was it?"

"Titans? One of the tribes? Who knows? I think we may find out, that's all."

"I'm not so concerned about the long-term as the short-term killer," he told her. "If they can get this lens weapon to work, they'll eventually be able to land a ship right here and pick us up. If it doesn't work, we're back to square one anyway."

They sat in silence for a while, and her gaze returned to the moon and stars above.

"Still looking for the grid?" he asked her. "In this moonlight, I doubt if it would show up much at all."

"Oh, it's there," she assured him. "I can *sense* it somehow, more than see it. It plays over me, gets in my head somehow, makes anything but the here and now seem distant, unimportant."

"I feel something, too, sometimes," he admitted. "I think we all do, except Hamille, although who can know for sure about it?"

"Hamille isn't human. This is designed for us, I think," she responded, still staring at the stars. "I think it's more than protection and monitoring. I think it messes with minds. Our minds."

"What kind of effect docs it have on you?" he asked, looking away abruptly as her comments fed a healthy paranoia.

"Interesting effects," she responded enigmatically. "It stirs up parts of me I'd almost forgotten were there. Not strongly enough yet, but we'll see."

He got a vague idea she was talking about and around sexual matters, but he didn't press it. He was still unaffected enough to consider the implications. If they really were exerting some kind of subtle mass stimulation or hypnosis or whatever, then . . .

Then maybe the Titans weren't as oblivious to humans as had been assumed.

EIGHTEEN

Ill Met near Sparta

"You know, I've been thinking," Kat Socolov said as they walked along under another hot sun.

"Sometimes a dangerous practice," N'Gana responded.

They'd all pretty well cast off everything except a vine belt that had been twisted and looped and held their batons and other weapons and tools, and Father Chicanis had made a leaf and vine backpack for his cherished communion set. Oddly, the nudity didn't seem to bother any of them, not even the priest, or particularly turn anyone on, either.

"If this mixture melts away our precious artificial substances," asked Kat, "then it's gonna melt away those password cubes as well, isn't it?"

"I told you, they will be sufficiently below ground to have escaped this. We've seen areas under the old roadworks here where things are remarkably well preserved if they're kept out of that rain and the elements," the colonel replied.

"Oh, sure—they might well be there, if nobody's taken them, if they're still where the incomplete records said they were, and so on. That's not the point. The thing is, so we get there, we get down, we illuminate everything somehow, and Hamille, here, gets through the holes in the foundation and brings them back to us. Then what? The moment we bring them up here to the surface, they're gonna be rained on. If we retrace our path, it's another ten days to two weeks, even if we figure out how to get back to the island. By that time they'll be mush and you know it. We're stuck."

N'Gana wasn't at all bothered. "There is a contingency plan for everything," he told her. "I have already determined a method to get around that."

"Yeah? What?" Harker put in, curious himself.

"First things first. If we don't have it, the rest is moot."

Kat Socolov whispered to Harker, "I bet he didn't even think of it until now."

But Harker had more respect for the colonel than that. He just wondered if the contingency plan, whatever it was, did not involve sacrificial deaths. He couldn't get out of his mind the image of that freebooter down here, probably naked, certainly at least as defenseless as they were, possibly stalked by something or someone running from the Titans themselves, knowing that his information was valuable but that he himself could not leave.

The mission, the colonel had said over and over again, was the only thing that mattered. Strong talk for a soldier for hire, but, unlike the pirate, not all of them would need to die to get that information out.

"How well do you think we'll fit in down here in the Stone Age?" Harker asked her in a loud whisper.

She stared at him. "You really think it'll come to that?"

"It could. That's the most likely scenario, at least temporarily, maybe permanently if they don't find a way to get us off."

She shrugged. "We haven't really been tested on much yet here, even with the loss of our stuff. This place almost seems *designed* to let a small number of people live on, so long as they remain apes who talk."

"Huh?"

"Look at us! The climate's warm enough all year to keep us comfortable like this, there's a year-round growing season for edible fruits and even vegetables, as we've found, if you know how to look for them. Plenty of water, and no large predators. The trick is to not draw any attention to yourself, so no fires, no building of structures—in effect, no real artifacts. We've grown comfortable under those rules in just a few days. Imagine what being like that for maybe fifty, sixty *years* has done to the survivors. I'm already losing track of time. One day looks like another, one grove or one field of tall grass looks like another. I'm beginning to think that my life's project is going to be myself."

"Your watch still has a date in it," he noted.

"I lost it a while back. Makes no difference anyway. I have some kind of weird sense that this place changes you—or that something is doing it."

He'd tried to get her to elaborate on that, but to no avail.

The old Grand Highway had proven reliable and comfortable as a path up to now, but at some points it had presented problems. The bridges were gone, so coming to rivers and streams meant wading or in some cases swimming. All of them could swim, and none of the distances or depths had been too great, but now they came around a bend and faced their greatest challenge.

It was the delta of a large and complex river system, and the road vanished right into it. It was extremely muddy, and the current seemed slow, but it was clearly quite an obstacle.

Father Chicanis was baffled. "There is no river like this. Not here! I would have remembered such a thing! It wasn't even on the aerial surveys! There *is* a river between Sparta and Ephesus, but this can't be it! We have been following the road and we are still west of Sparta, I'm sure of it!"

"Well, it's here now," the colonel sighed. "It is difficult to say if the channel is deep, or what might lie in it, but I see a series of mud bars and mud and rock islands there. I suspect that most of it is shallow, since, if you look carefully, you can see rusted and twisted remnants of the highway here and there. Well, we won't attempt it today. I would say we camp early and see if we can get some real rest. Tomorrow we can start testing it out."

Harker looked it over. It appeared as shallow as he said, but you never knew about this kind of river. They had deep spots, and treacherous eroded stuff just beneath the surface that could cut you to ribbons. Often the bottoms were quagmires, too, sucking you down if you tried walking even in the shallows.

It was a good kilometer across to the next solid anything; in between were fingers of mud and rock piled up here and there as the big river slowed before finally emptying into the sea.

"What about a raft?" Kat Socolov suggested. "If we can make something out of the driftwood or something here, we could pole across."

"Possibly," Harker responded. "But I'm not sure I like trusting myself to something cobbled together and held by these vines. One sharp rock below and you'd be in the middle of a disintegrating and possibly dangerous bundle of sticks. Flotation *is* a good idea, but on a one-to-one personal level, I think. Not one big raft, but a lot of little things that float."

Next to dinner, that was the highest priority. There were few clues to what they might use floating down the river itself, so they used what light was left to test various pieces of wood, particularly those that looked as if they had floated down a fair piece.

As this was going on, they walked upriver along the riverbank, looking mostly down for a couple of kilometers, after it was clear that there was a significant bend there that might trap flotsam and jetsam. Harker found himself in the lead, and he rounded the curve and suddenly stopped dead still in his tracks. He put up a hand that silenced those coming behind him, and they approached with a lot more stealth.

Mogutu got to him first. "What is it?" he barely whispered.

Harker gestured. "Up ahead, maybe fifty meters. Look at the mud."

It was fairly flat and soaked through, pretty much like the part they were walking on, and it didn't take a moment for first Mogutu, then the others to see what had spooked Harker.

Just as they had left footprints in the wet mud behind them, there were footprints in the mud just ahead. Footprints that ended at just about the fifty-meter mark, stopped, then turned and walked back diagonally and into the brush.

"Think they're new?" Kat asked him apprehensively.

He nodded. "This close to the sea is tidal. The area gets washed over now and again. I'd say those tracks aren't much older than ours. It's possible that they were coming toward us and heard us."

Mogutu nodded. "If they're still here, they're very good," he said, continuing the whisper. "I can't see anything at all ahead and I'm a damned good hunter."

"They're there," the colonel breathed. "Don't ask me how I know, but I've stayed alive this long by sensing such things. We're being watched right now. I can feel their eyes. Just in the grass."

"Want me to flush 'em, sir?" Mogutu asked him, tongue licking his lips in tense anticipation of a real bit of action at last.

"No, you wouldn't be able to," N'Gana replied. "They would just pull back into what could be an infinite field of grass until they suckered us into a trap on their ground. No, Sergeant, let's make them come to us." He straightened up and added in a more normal tone, "Sergeant, cover our back. Harker, take the edge of the grass. Doc, I want you and the Father, here, behind me. Don't look around or give them any sense that we know where they are."

"If they attack?" Mogutu asked him.

"Then we defend ourselves. Otherwise, we go back to a point on the other side of the highway ruins and dig in there. Anyone coming at us will have to do so in the open."

"Or wait until night, or the predictable storms," Kat Socolov added worriedly.

"Cheer up, Doctor," the colonel said. "If they don't kill us or run from us, you might just get your first chance to use your skills in native contact."

She shook her head. "I'd bet on them running. If they're as primitive as I think they are, they won't want any strangers around. Remember the rule? Draw no attention to yourself. Why risk a fight? Besides, Colonel, no offense meant, but the ethnic population here was entirely Greek and what was called Near Eastern and Caucasian, because that's where the ethnic roots came from. There might have been some Hamitic types from Ethiopian Coptic stock, which Sergeant Mogutu might be taken for, but most likely they've never seen anyone who looks quite like you, Colonel."

"She's right, Colonel. There were diplomats and traders, certainly, but no native Australian, African, or Asian types outside the city trading centers and spaceports, and they'd have gotten out."

The colonel grinned. "So I'm a monster, am I? I kind of like that. It starts us off with some fear and respect, I think. That's if they really saw me, though. Hard to say. Some of your skin flaps and other oddities might make you seem a bit odd, too, come to think of it. I think, though, that we'll play games and go back and forth, but I doubt that these people want contact. I didn't sense that there were very many of them. Two or three, perhaps. Four tops. Hardly a hunting party or a tribe."

Still, none of them would get the sleep they had been looking forward to only a little earlier. Not this night.

Mogutu was thoughtful. "You know, Colonel, *we* could use that storm. How about it?"

"Just what do you have in mind?" N'Gana encouraged him.

"I could get up and around, using the storm for cover, then, when they're still drying out, I could make a godawful demonstration that might panic them right toward you."

"Possible. Equally possible is that these people, born and raised in this environment, will do the same to us instead, or simply come after you with everything they've got including knowledge of the terrain, weapons, their numbers, your position, and so forth. Not a good option. Still, I shouldn't like them on our back if we have to cross that damned river and swamp combo. I keep giving mental commands to my combat armor and deploying my heat and motion detectors."

Harker smiled slightly when he heard that. He'd been doing the same thing.

Finally, Kat Socolov cleared her throat. "Um, Colonel? You and your bloodthirsty sergeant here keep treating these people as if they are lions in some imaginary ancient jungle. Have you considered speaking to them instead?"

N'Gana looked completely baffled. "*Speak* to them? What the devil do you mean?"

"You know—talk. Like we're doing now."

"But these people are—are . . ."

"Stone Age primitives? Probably, but it's also true that, even in a worst-case scenario, they are only a few generations removed from us. From the Helena of The Confederacy and Father Chicanis. Knowledge can die with frightening suddenness, and ignorance can march in a heartbeat, but, Colonel, changing your language takes a lot longer than this. Conquered nations held on to their native tongues even if they had to learn the speech of their conquerors, and those languages survived even when there was a conscious effort to suppress them. You came from this highly civilized background a couple of *worlds* removed from your ancestry, yet what was the language spoken in the streets of your homeland during your youth?"

"Uh—well, around the house they always spoke Tuareg, a Berber language. Of course, we all spoke English."

"And you, Sergeant?"

"Well, it was a dialect of Ethiopian, actually, although everyone also spoke French because there were so many dialects and nobody would ever standardize on one. Yes, I begin to see what she means."

Even the usually quiet Hamille, whom they tended to forget most of the time, was in tune with this concept. "My people speak—" It gave a series of sounds no human could ever utter. "There are many other tongues on my world. No one speaks human speech except to humans."

Socolov looked at Harker, who shrugged. "I always talked like this," he said.

"Well," said the anthropologist, "as someone who speaks both Ukrainian and Georgian, I think I've made my point. Father, what would they speak around here? Greek? Turkish? Confederacy Standard, which is really a form of English although they never admit that?"

"Why, Greek was common, but everyone used Standard, too, because the fact was that this was an attempt to recreate an ideal of a rich family's past and they came from Greece. Still, there were a number of ethnic languages even on Helena, so Standard was everywhere. I feel certain that they would understand it, at least if you didn't use any words or terms that might be outside their experience. I suspect much of our technological jargon would be meaningless to them, but if you kept it basic, I see no reason why, using your logic, they wouldn't understand something. And, if it's Greek, I can certainly help there."

"So can I," she told him. "You simply can't get a degree

in my field without Greek and Latin even if you intend to excavate the ruins of the third moon of Haptmann circling Rigel."

"I think we are elected then," the priest responded, ignoring N'Gana and Mogutu. "We're also probably the least threatening."

"That is why one of us must accompany you," N'Gana told her. "If they attack—remember the man who sent the message that brought us here!—someone who will react without hesitation is necessary. Harker, why don't you go? You're—nonthreatening but capable, I think."

"Thanks a lot," Harker sighed. "But if we're going to do it, we'd better move. I doubt if we've got a half hour's light left."

Feeling a little like targets in spite of the moral certainty of their position, the pair walked cautiously back out along the riverbank and up toward where the footprints had been seen. As they did, the trio of military men spread out and, from whatever concealment they could muster, they slowly closed in on the same spot to give the pair some invisible cover.

Kat Socolov was suddenly wondering if this was a good idea after all. What if they were some sort of savages, the survivor dregs who had kept going by killing off and preying upon the other, weaker groups?

Although feeling some doubt himself, Father Chicanis repeated some favored prayers and decided that it was his job to initiate contact. If, of course, anybody was still there.

There was no reason why anyone should or would wait around the place. It didn't have a great deal of food, the water was far too muddy to be of practical use, and there was a dead end for most who reached its shore. Still, both of them felt eyes watching them, eyes that were not a part of their own group, eyes that studied and calculated their every move.

They stopped near the footprints they'd left before and looked ahead and to the right into the brush.

"Hello!" Kat Socolov called in what she hoped was a confident but nonthreatening voice. "If you can hear me and understand me, please speak to me! We mean you no harm."

Father Chicanis frowned. "What the devil is *that*?"

She shook her head. "I dunno. Sounds like *clicking*. I'd say it was insects only we've been here long enough and nothing I've heard sounds like it. Sounds almost like . . . *code*."

He nodded. "What would make sounds in code? And why? Surely this isn't something of the enemy!" He projected his voice. "I am Father Aristotle Chicanis! I was born and raised near here, but I was not here when the world was conquered. I return bringing the hope and faith of God to my native soil!"

Still no reaction, but more clicking.

"How many do you think there are?" she whispered to him, not taking her eyes off the brush.

"I can't tell," he admitted in the same low tone. "Certainly no more than three. If they are going to make a move, though, they better do it. I don't think we should stand here and risk sundown with our backs to the water."

It *was* growing dim. "One last chance, then we back off," she hissed.

"Look! Come, be friends with us! We only wish to learn from you and we will help you with your needs if we can! Please! It is now or we must leave for the night!"

More clicking. They were moving around, whoever or whatever they were, but slowly, as if positioning themselves in a semicircle. That was clearly a hostile formation; they didn't need it to protect or defend.

"I think we back out now," she said to the priest, teeth clenched. "There's already one behind us. I want to do a slow but steady back-out. Ready?"

"I believe you are right," he answered, and together they both began to back up, slowly, hoping that the others in the team would cover their backs.

In the bush, the experienced Mogutu had zeroed in on the nearest one, the one moving to cut off the retreat of the pair on the riverbank. He was good at his job, and he'd crept to within no more than a few meters of the one closest to them and the camp.

What he saw startled him. It looked like the back of a young girl, hair long and wild and tangled, the body so thin that it seemed emaciated, yet there was strength in it, and the toughness of weather-beaten skin. She was making the clicking sounds, and getting responses from others, but he couldn't see what she was making them with.

Suddenly she froze, and he sensed at the same instant that she was now aware of him. It was difficult for him to feel threatened by such a tiny waif, but he also knew that small size meant nothing if one were an expert knife thrower or had other weapons.

He crouched there, watching tensely, waiting to see her move. Suddenly, with an animal-like agility he would have thought impossible, she whirled, turning in midair while hurling herself in his direction. The movement and the sight of her face and hands startled him, so unexpected and horrible were they, and he was a split-second slow in responding and rolling right. Her left foot struck his shoulder with great force; she hit the ground and with cat-like agility flipped, rolled, and was back at him.

They all heard Mogutu scream, and this was taken by the others in the bush as an attack imperative. They launched themselves out into the open, toward the pair on the riverbank, and so agile and catlike were the moves and so terrible the visage the two Hunters presented to them that Kat Socolov screamed and Father Chicanis uttered a cry of dismay.

With the bodies of young girls, the faces were a mixture of human and animal. The mouths were wide, somewhat extended, and seemed full of sharp pointed teeth, while the eyes glowed with a feline fire in the reflection of the setting sun on the river. Most awful were the hands, whose fingers were not of flesh but of long spikelike claws twenty or more centimeters long, and not only pointed but barbed as well.

One bounded for the anthropologist as she turned and ran in panic back toward the ruins of the old road. Clearly Socolov was going to lose the race, but suddenly, from out of the grass, a large, long, rounded shape hurled itself with the same force as the Hunters and aimed right at the Hunter as she was within centimeters of driving her claws into Kat Socolov's back.

The Hunter was taken aback, barely realizing that she was being attacked until the Pooka struck her directly in the belly—and kept on going, literally drilling a bloody hole straight through the attacker with a whirling motion and a very different kind of toothed action.

The Hunter still made no sound although she was now thrashing about in agony and striking at the alien form that penetrated her. She was dying, yet she flailed away at the back end of the creature and even tried to get to her feet with the thing still in her while staring, with hate-filled eyes, at Kat Socolov.

The anthropologist saw that the Pooka that had saved her was now in need of saving itself, and although almost transfixed by the single-minded violence in the Hunter, she ran toward her attacker, steel gun barrel in hand, and lashed out, striking first one of the clawed arms, then reaching the head. The thing kept trying to get at her, which so terrified Socolov that she continued swinging at the head until finally the only motion coming from the Hunter was from Hamille trying to get all the way through.

Father Chicanis hadn't had as good a rescuer, and the

Hunter had actually reached him and dug her claws into his left arm. With his right arm, he brought up his gold-plated cross and used it as a club. It wasn't very effective, but it slowed her just enough for Gene Harker to swing another gun barrel at full strength right into the back of her head. So great was the force he used that part of the Hunter's skull caved in, yet, stunned and badly wounded, she nonetheless turned on him and attempted to claw and bite him with fanatical fury. Only his own hand-to-hand combat training and reflexes had saved him from also being badly slashed, and once the Hunter was down he brought the barrel down again and again and again until she finally twitched in the mud and lay still.

"Father? You all right?"

"Hurts like the very devil!" Chicanis responded. "My God! She's peeled some of the flesh away from my arm! Oh, Lord! How it *hurts*!"

"Let me check on Kat and then I'll tend to it," he said, running a few meters farther on, where Hamille had finally managed to get out of the Hunter's middle from the other side and now lay there, its whole center length undulating up and down as if breathing hard.

Kat Socolov knelt in the mud and just stared at the figure of the Hunter lying dead in the mud, and she was crying uncontrollably. Harker went to her, knelt down, and asked, "Are you hurt? *Kat!* Were you wounded?"

She was simply too far gone to respond, but his quick examination showed only some scratches and what was going to be a whale of a bruise in a day or so.

Satisfied that she was all right, at least physically, and unable to tell if the Pooka was or not, he returned to Father Chicanis, removed the vine belt from his waist, and began using it as a tourniquet on the arm. It looked ugly, but it could have been worse.

"Come on, Father! We've got to get back to the road!

It's almost dark! We've still got some basic medicinals, I think. Come! Can you walk?"

"I—I *think* so. Please—help me to my feet."

The priest was unsteady, but he managed, and they walked back to Kat Socolov, who was just staring now, apparently all cried out.

"Kat—you have to come with us," Harker said as gently as possible.

She trembled a bit, then looked up at him. "They're just *children*, Gene! Little girls! What have these bastards done to our children?"

"Come on! From the sound of things, we have at least one more wounded. Hamille, thank you. Are you all right?"

"Some punctures. They will heal," the creature responded. "Tasted *terrible*, too."

Back at the old roadbed, they found Colonel N'Gana tending to his sergeant. Mogutu did not look very good. He didn't look good at all.

Socolov kept trying to get control with deep breaths and finally managed it. "The larger wounds need cover," she managed. "We don't have major bandages, or a portable surgical kit that works, so we'll have to make do with what's here."

"The skin's almost flayed in areas," N'Gana noted. "What can we use that could cover them all and allow healing without infection or bleeding?"

"Mud," she answered. "We have plenty of it. Gene, come on—you can be both bodyguard and mud carrier. We have to get a lot of it from the river, preferably just inside the waterline. We want it thick, goopy, and organic. Come on! I'll show you how!"

It probably looked awful, but they could barely see. Both the wounded men were placed in a sheltered area underneath the remains of the roadworks. If they were lucky, the night's storms wouldn't wash away the mud packs.

"You really think that's going to work?" Harker asked her.

"No, but it's all we have and it's a traditional treatment. We have no idea how much damage was done internally or how much blood was lost or whether or not those *things* were also poisonous, but if we're lucky it *can* work. It's an ancient remedy." She sighed. "Now you know why I'm along!"

"I doubt if this was anticipated, but I'm still glad you're here," he told her.

It was pitch dark, and there was the rumbling of thunder and the flash of lightning not far away.

He sat there next to her and for the first time put his arm around her and gave her a hug. "You did good, kid. From the very start."

"I brought them on us," she retorted.

"No, they were stalking us from the start, I think. We forced their hand. I think they were going to wait until dark, or maybe even until the storm, and then jump us. When you consider their single-minded homicidal maniac approach and if you saw the eyes you'd know they can probably see okay in the dark, at least in starlight or moonlight. No, I think you saved all our lives."

"But not deliberately," she replied, unwilling to grant him a point.

"That's the way it is in a war or any operation. What's intended isn't the point. The only things that count are success and the objective. At least we know one thing now that the whole Confederacy didn't know before."

"Huh? What?"

"The Titans know we're here. They know us, maybe all too well. You don't evolve like that in under a hundred years, and you sure don't see that kind of consistency in mutation. I didn't really have much time to study them, but I swear those two were twins. Identical twins. There's only one way you can get that kind of change in a short time—they were bred. Bred to be just what we saw. Genetically reengineered and, when they had what they wanted, probably cloned."

"But why? Why would they do it?"

He shrugged. "We still know nothing about them, and we may never understand all their motivations. Still, I can think of some practical reasons. Surely they know that some humans survived and still survive in tribal groups. If you wanted to keep the population down and ensure only the strongest survive, that's one good way to do it."

"But why not just wipe every survivor out? They could do it in a moment and you know it."

"True, but I don't think they want to. Why? Again, if we understood them maybe we could find a way to at least hurt them. Maybe we're good lab animals, or maybe pets. It might be as simple and cold-blooded as that. Sheer sport. Or it might be that they want a sampling of only the strongest and best for their own use. Whatever the reason, I don't know any way of asking them and getting an intelligent answer."

The rains came at that point, making it useless to keep talking. She didn't really feel like talking anymore, either. For the first time on the trip she needed something more from Harker, and she made it perfectly clear to him in the rain.

"You were right about the cloning," Kat Socolov told Harker in the morning, after they had examined the remains of the fight. "I looked at the pattern on the big toe of both of them and it's identical. So is just about everything else I could find. I also examined them as much as I could. I wish we had a medical doctor along or could get these two to an autopsy room. Neither of them have any grinders at all. All canines. And the tongues are smooth and extremely long. The whole mouth structure suggests that they can eat only meat. Ten to one they can only digest meat. They're not only bred to be killers, they *have* to kill."

He said nothing to that, but he did have a wider concern. "I wonder if anybody here is still human? That's only one variety, I suspect, but what about the others? They preyed on somebody. Were the prey bred, too? This is getting more complicated than we figured."

"Maybe. Maybe not. There's so much we just don't understand of all this." She came over close to him and said in a lower, softer voice, "Thank you for last night."

He smiled and shrugged. "Anytime."

"I don't want you to take it any way but one, though. I—I just *needed* it. It was pretty strange, really. It happened once after I heard that my father died, but that was the only other time. It's a strange reaction."

"It's a human reaction," he assured her. "It's nothing to feel guilty about. It's just a part of being human. This is greater stress than even I ever thought I'd be under, and I always thought I was a gutsy type of guy. I can even see it getting to N'Gana, and I always thought of him as an organic machine."

Again they said nothing for a bit, then she asked, "That woman Marine you talked about. Bambi something or other?"

"Yeah? What about her?"

"You ever do it with her?"

He thought that an odd question, but he answered it anyway. "No, of course not."

"She doesn't like men?"

"Oh, I think she likes men all too much. And almost anybody and anything else when off-duty. No, she's an enlisted soldier. Officers and enlisted may have respect for one another, or contempt, but they don't get personal. There's good reasons for that. Nobody can sleep their way up the chain of command, nobody can use sex to force someone else to do what they don't want to do, and, on a different level, you don't want to have a personal relationship if you can help it with anybody you might have to order into possible or probable death." He sighed. "I wish I had her here, though. She was damned good at her job."

Even though it was a part of his life, it was hard to think that he was separated from her and his old shipmates by almost three years, even though it had been only a matter of weeks to him. The realization made their isolation on Helena seem even more acute.

They walked over to check on the two wounded men. Father Chicanis was actually recovering rather well. He was in considerable pain, but nothing major had been damaged that could not be repaired. He was certainly functional. The same could not be said for Mogutu, whose abdomen had been penetrated by those barbed claws. Under normal battle conditions, he would already have undergone surgery and been put in a tank, recovering perfectly, but these weren't normal conditions. They had nothing with which to diagnose his wounds, and no physician to do anything about them anyway. All they had was some powerful painkillers and sterilizers, and precious little of those.

"It is a mercy that he remains unconscious," the priest commented. "Feeling my arm, just thinking about what he must feel with those wounds is chilling. There has to be a great deal of internal bleeding. Those poor creatures were designed for quick killing; they hadn't the strength or sheer power for a real fight. They pounce and by their ferocity and those claws and teeth they became killing machines. What a terrible life they must have had. I hope that God gives them the peace and joy they were denied here."

Colonel N'Gana was taking Mogutu's condition hard, but he was the consummate professional. "Father Chicanis here insisted on going back out to the little terrors and giving them last rites," he said, shaking his head in wonder.

"You disapprove, Colonel? You do not believe in such things?" The priest knew the answers before he asked the questions.

"They were animals. I don't risk anything to pray over dead vicious animals, no. And, frankly, I'm not certain what I believe in any more. At least, that's partially true. I don't know if there's a God, Father, and I'm not certain I'd like a God who could create a universe so full of misery. I never could quite accept *your* idea of God, anyway. It never made any sense. If such a God were wholly good and the epitome of perfection, why does everybody keep rebelling against Him? Such a God is also the father of evil." He looked down at the unconscious Mogutu. "Now, evil is something I believe in. I've seen it, heard it, smelled it, fought it. Most people haven't believed in evil for a thousand years or more. Everybody's misguided or misunderstood. You think of those *things* as victims. Perhaps, but they did not evolve, even unnaturally, from a state of grace, Father. They were designed as instruments of evil."

Father Chicanis sighed. "I am sorry you feel that way, Colonel. To me—well, the basic genes that were used to create them could have been from my own family. I do not believe that a creation of evil who has no choice can be held to a moral standard they cannot comprehend. That is the key difference between the devil and his minions and those poor creatures. The devil and his followers *chose* their path. A god of love is not a god of rigid order and discipline, a dictator creating sycophants. Worship, love, all that is of value is meaningless if it is not freely given. And if it is to be freely given, then the option not to give it, to reject it, must be present. No, Colonel. Those who *choose* evil define it. That is the key."

N'Gana shook his head sadly. "And in the meantime, in your universe, creatures of evil kill men of good and all's right with the cosmos." He paused a moment. "We must leave him to die, you know. Or kill him out of mercy lest he awaken and die in agony."

The priest looked stricken. "Colonel! We can't just abandon him! What were we just talking about? I'll not accept a choice like that!"

"Then you can stay with him if you like. We cannot bring him. I'm not sure how we're going to get across this river yet, but we must do it and do it today. We're sitting ducks here and the stakes are too high. The remains of Sparta are just over there, and beyond them the hills, and then Ephesus. Ephesus has what we are here to get, but it is also one anchor base of the Titans. The sergeant understood, as I did, that the mission was the only thing that mattered. He's a liability to that mission now, and he can be of no help to anyone. The best we can do to honor his gallantry is to complete the mission. Still, I will not leave him here to die in agony. He deserves better than that. So, either one of us stays or he is mercifully sent to his reward, whatever and wherever that is. I'd rather not spare anyone, and I can't spare the others, but the choice is yours."

The priest sighed. "I cannot morally sanction such an action, yet I understand your position. I will stay. It is probably for the best anyway, as I can't possibly swim with this arm. If he dies, I shall give him last rites and a Christian burial and then I will try and find what remains of my people to restore God's mercy to them. If he lives, we shall go together."

N'Gana shrugged. "Suit yourself. But be aware that Sergeant Mogutu was never a Christian. At best we might call him a lapsed Moslem."

"Colonel—it is the same God."

"I suppose it is at that. Very well. We'll leave what we can here for you, but that's precious little." He stood, looking down at his longtime companion, and for a moment there was a slight quiver in the lip, a stray trace of emotion in a man who considered it a weakness. He then stood erect, saluted the unconscious sergeant, and walked away toward the others.

"Come, then! We have a river to cross!" he announced.

Neither Harker nor Kat Socolov liked leaving the two behind, but there was little that could be done and, as N'Gana said, it was the mission that mattered. All of them were expendable if those codes could be broadcast.

Now they stood by the riverbank looking out and trying to guess a possible route.

"It's a young river," the anthropologist noted. "In fact, I'd say it hasn't been here for very long at all. Possibly it's another that's shifted its course, but it's clear that very little has been dug out. You can see where some trees and even bushes poke out of the water."

"Yes, but how deep is it?" N'Gana asked rhetorically. "If the tall grass was typical in height, so if we see the top fifteen centimeters of grass then we can assume the river is no more than two, maybe two and a half meters deep in that area."

"Shallower, I think," Harker said, looking out at the expanse. "Lots of mud bars, whole areas of minor silt build-up, and even some rises that are original and still above water. Our big problem, I think, won't be the depth but rather that it's so damned muddy we can't see what we're walking on."

N'Gana nodded. "Let's walk up a bit. There seems to be more of the original slope still—"

His voice trailed off, and his hand instinctively went to the gun barrel truncheon around his waist. The others made similar moves as they saw what the colonel had suddenly spotted.

"I didn't hear anything at all," Harker whispered. "Where in *hell* did they come from?"

"They're not like those others," the anthropologist

noted. "They look like kids. Kids out of some text on ancient human origins, but kids."

The two girls and a boy presented a bizarre sight. Burned a deep leathery brown by the sun, with long, stringy hair and wearing only ornaments of stone and bone, they nonetheless showed scars of a harsh and violent life. What was most striking was that their bodies bore elaborate mosaiclike tattoos that seemed designed to eventually cover them. The boy had the most, up both legs and on his stomach and back as well.

"Hello!" the boy called to them, apparently unafraid. "What Family are you from? We have been searching for someone for many days!"

The speech was oddly accented, with certain differences in tone, pronunciation, and emphasis, but it was clearly based on the Standard tongue the others all knew and understood. If anything, it was more familiar than they had expected.

"We are from different families," Socolov responded, trying to sound calm and friendly. "But we are here working for and representing a family called Karas."

All three of the natives looked astonished. "That is impossible!" the boy said at last. "*We* are of the Karas Family, and we know everyone in it!"

The anthropologist thought for a moment. Clearly "family" to them was synonymous with "tribe." Just how much did they know of their past?

"We are not of the family that stayed and survived," she told him. "We are of the ones who left the world before it was conquered."

The boy was thunderstruck. "You are from—*up there*?"

She smiled and nodded.

And then he said, in a tone of wonderment that made them all feel a true sense of what had been lost here, "We did not believe you would ever come back for us."

NINETEEN

The Desolation at Sparta

A day that was to have been spent in struggling against a river instead was spent in a long session of mutual discovery and information exchange.

Of course, the experience of the three young people—indeed, their whole view of the cosmos—was quite skewed, but the newcomers had been on Helena and discovered some of its ugly surprises. Now they discovered more, but the mere existence of these kids also meant the discovery of hope.

Father Chicanis, who had thought himself entirely alone only hours before, now tried to discover from the locals some sense of family connection, some familiar name in the genealogy. The problem, of course, was that the old family structure had broken down before the trio was born. For them, relationship to the community was far more important than relationship to parents or more distant ancestors.

Chicanis was also upset with their view of Christian theology, even though they said they had been led by a priest.

"Father Alex kept saying it was wrong to live the way we were," Littlefeet told him, "but Mother Paulista and the rest said it was the only way to make sure we survived. I dunno which of 'em was right. I don't even know if any of 'em are left alive now. If they are, they're trapped on the other side of that new river."

Harker was most startled that the trio had seemed to have no fear of them. "People do not harm other people," Spotty responded matter-of-factly. "Families must all help each other or we all die."

Father Chicanis found them fascinating. "In an existence where normal human beings are suspended in a kind of basic loop, where possessions mean nothing and there is a permanence only of companionship, the only things of value left seem to be spiritual values. It almost makes one think that, in a sense, the continent of Eden is closer to the original than one might think."

"The original Eden didn't have genetically engineered killers stalking around," Colonel N'Gana noted.

The young people were fascinated by N'Gana; they'd never seen anyone of African ancestry, which indicated that Helena's cosmopolitan nature hadn't survived. Even more astonishing to them was Hamille, of course; they couldn't keep their eyes off the alien creature, who seemed not at all interested in them.

The other offworlders, though, were surprised and fascinated by every gesture and every bit of knowledge that the young people displayed. It was somewhat startling for them to watch some of the middle-sized beetlelike insects and flying things be picked out of the air and just popped into the mouth. The women also showed a pretty fair knowledge of basic chemistry, whether preparing a dried cake from mixed stone-ground grasses and ground-up insects, or salves that could numb and perhaps do more on wounds and bites. Clearly it wasn't just the physically fit and ruthless who survived; some very smart people had created a system that worked, and had done so from scratch while trying to survive themselves. Of them all, only Kat Socolov seemed less surprised than impressed. A good anthropologist always knew the difference between tribal knowledge and superstition, and the first thing you had to do in that field was get it out of your head forever that ignorance meant stupidity.

Still, only Colonel N'Gana was willing to try the insects à la carte. He prided himself on his survival training. The cakes, however, were palatable, and filling, if not exactly delicious.

The day of mutual discovery ended with wonder on both sides, but no clear answers. The one thing that Kat Socolov couldn't help thinking was how fragile and vulnerable human beings had made themselves by being so dependent on technology. If these descendants of the survivors of conquest had known how to harvest and process and weave cotton, for example, they would have had no problems with clothing and blankets and the like, they would have had fabrics that did not dissolve in the engineered rains. But nobody really knew how to do that, or plow a field with human power, or to do any of the thousand and one things ancient humans had taken for granted.

They had sunk so far and so fast because nobody was left who knew how to do those things. Nobody had needed to do them for centuries.

Sergeant Mogutu was restless during the night, and at one point cried out in his ancient mother tongue. In the morning, he was dead.

Father Chicanis did what he could, and together that morning at the insistence of the priest and the colonel, they managed to bury him in a shallow grave.

"I'm next, I suspect," the priest said. "I don't mind, really. I will at least die on the world of my birth in a good cause and serving God."

"Don't talk like that! It is self-fulfilling!" Kat Socolov snapped.

He sighed. "Look, there's infection in the arm and it's not going to get better or stay where it is. You know it and I know it. And there's no way anybody here can do a competent amputation. We don't even have a sterile blade."

It was the two young women who came to his aid. They found and mixed a paste of some local herbs that really did seem to lower the inflammation on his arm; at least it eased the pain.

Still, looking now at the river, Chicanis said, "I can't come. You and I know I can't get across *that*. I'm going to move north by east and see if I can contact another of the Families. At least *try* to be of some use."

The young people were upset at the idea. "You don't have to do that! We will *all* go your way!" Littlefeet told him. "Look, we have a new Family here. We have a priest, guards and scouts who can take on and beat Hunters, three women to bear more children, and we can become one!"

It was Harker who shook his head and told them, "We are not here to start a family, Littlefeet. We're here to do a job. Over *there*, beyond the river, beyond the hills, is a weapon that might drive the demons out. We are here to get it and make sure it gets used. We must do this even if we all die as a result."

"But the demon *city* is over that way! I looked upon it from the high mountains and it took a part of my mind! No one can gaze upon it and not be changed for the worse! And going right there—they will capture you and you will become their slaves!"

"We have to take the risk. It's the same as the guards of a Family in your lives. They must be willing to give their lives for the greater good. You have no idea how many people are depending on us."

"He's right, Littlefeet," Kat Socolov agreed. "And we must begin today. You do not have to come. Stay with Father Chicanis, help him, and save him if you can from his wounds. The rest of us must cross the river."

Littlefeet didn't want things to go that way, but he was also torn. To stay behind was weakness; he could not bear for them to think him less willing to face the demons than they. But he didn't understand what they were trying to do, and he sure didn't want to go *that* way.

Spotty realized the situation and tried to suggest a middle ground. "Froggy can stay with the Father," she suggested. "They will be good support for each other. Littlefeet and me will go with you."

N'Gana wasn't all that sure he liked that. "Now, hold on! You said yourselves you don't know what you're getting into but it's all bad. I'm not sure I want to worry about you two when we're this close."

Littlefeet drew himself up to his full height, even though he barely came up to the colonel's neck, and said, "We have survived all our lives on this world. You have not. We know the dangers and how to stalk the tall grass and dark groves. We will be no burden!"

None of them really thought that they would after that. Still, one problem showed up almost immediately.

"You mean neither of you can swim?" Harker was amazed. That seemed such an obvious survival skill.

"Nobody knew how," Littlefeet replied. "There were tales that people could swim in the water in the old days, but there was nobody to teach us."

Time was far too limited to give them lessons, but a variation of Littlefeet's own idea of river travel wasn't all that hard, as it turned out. Very near were some good-sized pieces of wood that had been blown down in the storms long ago, and with a little work and trimming here and there they made a serviceable float. And the log did float, a bit awkwardly, with Littlefeet and Spotty clinging to it for dear life as Harker and Socolov took turns guiding and pushing it.

Much of the crossing turned out to be less swimming than navigating through river muck. This was a brand-new channel and a delta that was still forming. It was shallow in most places but had a sticky mud bottom that threatened in turns to drag them down or pull them under if they walked the bottom.

By the coming of darkness they hadn't quite made the opposite shore and were pretty well stranded on a wet, muddy bar a few meters out of the water. Their meager rations were long since exhausted; it would be a hungry and desolate night.

The storm didn't help, either; it put a huge amount of water into the river in a very short period of time and threatened to wash them off their precarious refuge. Finally, the storms passed as they always did and the sky began to clear.

They were all covered in mud, and there wasn't much that could be done about it in the dark. So, they just lay there and mostly stared up at the stars or dozed uneasily.

"The grid is easy to spot tonight," Harker commented to Kat. "Maybe it's just being out here with nothing obscuring my vision for a couple of kilometers, but it's a lot clearer."

She nodded. "I think if we can break one of the anchors, that whole thing will collapse, and with it their immediate hold on this continent. I wish I knew how to do that."

"You still think the grid's more than just a surveillance system?"

"I'm sure it is. I think it's managing the whole continent and everybody on and in it. Their precious giant flowers, maybe even the way the so-called survivors are developing."

"Huh?" He was interested.

"The more I think of those Hunters, and the more I talk to the two here, the more certain I am that the Titans are allowing the Families to survive, at least for a while, for some purpose. Maybe breeding stock for pets or guards or whatever. Hard to say. I've felt it since a few days after we arrived. Felt my own body respond to it. Talking with Spotty only confirmed it."

"You've felt it?" He knew that she'd been talking about this in some kind of nebulous terms, but this was the first time she was willing to articulate her feelings.

"Yes. You know, like most girls, I had the implant at fifteen and since then I haven't worried about pregnancy or suffered more than a very mild and almost forgettable period. But a few days ago, I could feel it being canceled out. I started to have feelings I hadn't had very strongly in a long time, and hadn't particularly wanted, and I became aware of going on a fairly strict cycle. Spotty says that her periods are bloody and one's due in a couple of days, and I'm beginning to suspect that I'm going to face the same thing. That's going to be bad enough, but after Sergeant Mogutu and Father Chicanis's arm I can handle it, I think. It's—after that. From talking to Spotty, I get the impression that for most of their cycle the women had little or no sex nor much urge to do so, and that the men didn't push it. That's unnatural in that kind of primitive setting. But every month, they had a period of time when that's all they wanted to do. Gene, that's like animals in heat."

"Well, that could have just developed along with their other oddball notions," he suggested.

"No, I don't think so. It's more specific than that. And since, as we said about the Hunters, these kinds of mutations—in this case a throwback characteristic—would be unlikely in large numbers in so short a time, it had to be deliberate. But the Families weren't ever captives of the Titans, nor did they spring from there. Conclusion: they are being kept in the mud deliberately. And *that* is the mechanism. It doesn't have to be specific. If they've identified the latent genes, they could just turn them on. It's a lot easier than engineering creatures like the Hunters, which may just be out there to keep the 'normal' population numbers under control."

"I liked it better when we thought they ignored us completely," Harker said.

"Yeah, me too, now. But I don't think they have any sense of us as individuals, let alone equals. I don't think they think that way at all. I think they're just playing games or experimenting or whatever with whoever and whatever they happen to have around. And that now includes *us*."

That thought was always on his mind. And, he now realized, it was even more on hers. If she was right, they had very little time to complete their mission before the grid introduced some compelling and inconvenient distractions.

It wasn't a big deal to make it the rest of the way once morning arrived, and all concerned were more than happy to get underway. They were hungry, thirsty, and exposed.

Kat didn't want to talk about it, but she'd slept very little overnight and had been nervously watching fuzzy egg-shaped balls of light dart back and forth in the distance, coming from and going to the very area they were headed for. Many times she worried that one would change course and notice them, all in the open on the mud bank, but, thank God, none did.

Littlefeet had had the same kind of night. He didn't wonder about the grid, which had always been there, or about the effects it might be having on him and Spotty. He did, however, worry about those fuzzy eggs speeding back and forth. Something in a corner of his mind sensed them. He could even, to some extent, link with them or with whatever was driving their craft and see a bit of what they saw and hear a bit of what they thought. Of course, none of their thoughts made any sense at all. It was just images and confusion, but it had an ugly, unclean feel to it every time. Like the anthropologist, he was very happy to get off that bar and back onto land.

Finding some squash and melons was relatively easy; there were also several pools of reasonably clear water that was useful for washing off the mud, although none of them felt they would ever get all the stuff off.

Having Littlefeet and Spotty as scouts proved very valuable, although somewhat embarrassing as well. Both of them were able to vanish and blend into the tall grasses and groves almost at will, and then reappear with barely a sound to report on what was ahead.

What was ahead now was the ruins of Sparta.

Not a century before, this had been home to perhaps half a million people. What remained were the grooves for the roads, and, here and there, the remnants of a building made of stone or brick or adobe mud, substances that the rain dissolved more slowly. There were also expanses of twisted metal and cracked concrete. It looked and felt like the ruins of a truly ancient place abandoned for thousands of years, not fewer than a hundred.

Here and there were also very regular-looking holes in the ground, rather evenly spaced along the old boulevards.

"My name is Ozymandias, king of kings," Kat muttered, looking at the barren remnants of the city. *"Look upon my works, ye Mighty, and despair."*

"Eh? What?" Colonel N'Gana asked, startled.

"Oh, just an ancient poem that stuck with me," she told him. "It was supposedly on a stone marker in the middle of the desert in an ancient empire. The punch line was that only the marker remained. Every trace of the king and his awesome works was gone. This place reminds me of that. This city, or what's left of it, and even this lonely, empty shell of a once vibrant world and civilization. How thin it all is! Our civilization, our institutions, beliefs, laws, comfortable ways of life. How *fragile*."

Harker looked around and understood her point. The colonel ignored it; it was irrelevant.

"The pattern indicates a subway system," N'Gana noted. "Of course, there wouldn't be any trains left, nor power for them or for lights down there, either, but I wonder just how much survived below?"

"The rains would run down into the tunnels and dissolve most of the stations and track bed," Kat Socolov noted. "Besides, it would be darker than pitch down there and we have nothing to create light." She sighed. "What a weird world this is! Some deep buried things from the past have a residual power supply so the looter could broadcast his warning before he died, and we have a crack at the codes, but just lighting a fire anywhere on the surface would ring alarms and bring the Titans. Crazy."

"Well, we're going to have to work out some way to light our way once we get to Ephesus," Harker noted. "And there has to be some way. Our original freebooter got down as far as he could until he was blocked by a cave-in. I wonder what he used for light? He faced the same bare-assed situation we do."

"It might be time this evening to see if our young natives have any ideas on how to light up the darkness," Kat said thoughtfully.

But they didn't. Their entire lives had been devoted to making no signs, no impact at all that would draw attention to themselves and those around them. The humidity was so high in the region that wildfires were virtually unknown, but they associated fire with lightning and local blazes and were terrified of it. There was no way to know short of finding and joining a Family and watching the process, but Kat suspected that one aspect of training from the time when these people were very small was an absolute terror of fire.

The only other possible source wasn't that useful in the end, either. There were swarms of flying insects that gave off white and yellow light as they flew, probably to attract mates or perhaps to recognize one another as friends or signal poison to enemies. The stuff did glow, and held its glow for a while, but it was so weak and the quantity was so small that it wasn't viable.

"The Dutchman's man found a way," N'Gana pointed out. "If he did, then we will find one, too."

Through the night, and the next three nights, they heard a good deal of clicking from Hunters about in this region, which also implied that one or more Families also roamed the area and thus provided prey for them, but none of them, Hunters or Family members, came near, and all eventually faded into the darkness.

There was one last river to cross as well. They could see the low rounded mountains of the coastal range ahead, just beyond it. This river was more difficult to handle, being old and deep, but Harker, using the knowledge of the two natives, was able to gather enough wood and strong vines to lash together a basic raft that, he hoped, could be steered with two poles. Not only the young natives, but also Hamille was very happy to have this, even though it would not hold all of them. At least the river at this point was no more than a kilometer wide.

"Two of us will have to swim it," Harker told them. "One of us should be up there as the captain and handle one of the poles."

"Don't put yourself out on my account," Kat told him. "I can swim *this*."

"I wasn't even considering being gallant," Harker replied. "I've handled these rafts before, although ones that were better made with stronger materials. I know how it handles. Colonel, are you up to a swim?"

"I defer to you in this," he replied. "I believe this sort of a swim would be easier than all the walking we've done."

There were some quick lessons on how to use the poles—logs chosen because they were somewhat flattened on one side—and particularly how to manage them when in the channel and it was too deep to reach bottom.

"We'll shove off in the raft first," Harker told them.

"Give us some time to get clear and some sense of how it handles, then follow. If anybody falls in, your job is to keep them from going under. If the raft comes apart in midriver, then each of you take a target of opportunity and I'll take the one that's left!"

It didn't come to that, although it was a pretty hairy operation. The raft was not really navigable; the logs slipped, opening and closing gaps that caused some considerable danger to those aboard. In the center channel, Harker used his pole alone as a makeshift rudder to allow the current to take them across without also sweeping them down to the ocean. Littlefeet looked scared to death, but he did his job, obeying Harker's commands exactly, and they made it, having drifted a good two kilometers south while crossing.

Once on the other side, the raft was quickly abandoned. Just in case they had to return this way, Harker and the two natives pulled it completely up onto the bank and then just into the thick trees beyond.

They jogged back up to try and join the two swimmers as quickly as possible and made very good time. Harker was both pleased and amazed at how effortless this had become. He felt he was in better shape now than he'd been in training all those years ago.

They reached Kat first, who was breathing very hard but feeling proud of herself. N'Gana was a hundred meters farther on, trying to bring his breathing under control. He was still breathing as hard as he'd been when he'd pulled himself onto the shore.

Harker wondered a bit at that. Neither he nor Kat was exactly a champion athlete and he'd never have the kind of bodybuilder shape N'Gana had, but the man shouldn't be breathing as hard as he was.

"I'm all right!" the colonel snapped. "It's just age catching up with me, I fear. I've walked this far. I'll make the journey."

There was nothing to do but accept his assurances, but it bothered Harker. It suddenly occurred to him, though, that if something did happen to N'Gana, then, if he hadn't forced himself into this party, Kat Socolov might well be the only one available to get Hamille into that bunker or whatever it was.

And just beyond those hills, no more than a half day's walk away, and maybe a day through, they would be there.

Then it would get *really* dangerous.

There was a reason why the energy grid was so clear in the night sky. They were close to one of its anchors, and a climb over the twelve-hundred-meter hills to the top of the pass between showed a sight that few humans had ever seen at ground level and remained whole.

Below, the remains of the Grand Highway still showed, joining other old routes that were still visible after all these years, even with large parts overgrown by jungle. Ephesus, the continental capital, had been four times the size of Sparta. There had been a spaceport out there, on the bluffs, which was still easy to recognize because of the sheer lack of anything growing there. That whole district was still possible to make out, and that was good, because that was where they had to go.

Straight ahead, though, the barren ruins of the ancient city stopped dead. They had not merely been dissolved or burned or swept away but replaced by a city of the new masters.

You could see pictures, you could see orbital shots, you could see it as a bizarre shimmering shape over a great distance, but now, this close, it was like nothing they had ever seen or even imagined.

"How would you describe that to a blind man?" N'Gana wondered.

It was a series of interlocking geometric structures, but virtually every possible shape was represented. It was a city of shimmering, twinkling light, predominantly yellow but with an odd pale green afterglow. It stretched for at least twenty kilometers, probably the entire old center city. Its beauty and symmetry, even to their eyes, was nothing short of breathtaking, but at the same time it was clearly built by and for minds so totally alien that Hamille seemed like a brother. At the very top were spires, actually trapezoids, not balanced or uniform but clearly serving the same function. Each of these protruded into the sky perhaps eight or nine hundred meters, and beams of energy ran into and out of them.

Kat Socolov shivered, though it was even hotter than usual. "It gives me the creeps," she muttered, as much to herself as to the others. "I feel like I'm looking into the minds of beings that I can never understand."

"Don't keep looking at it!" Littlefeet hissed. "If the demons sense you looking, they steal a little of your mind. They got part of mine when I saw this place from the farthest high mountains. They aren't looking now, but I think they will be!"

He was certainly serious, and none of the others quite knew how to take his comments. He *did* seem to have an abnormal sensitivity to, and fear of, the Titans, which he called the demons, but there wasn't that pull that he'd reported, at least not now.

"Littlefeet—how high up *were* you?" Harker asked, trying to reconcile the two visions.

"*Way* up. Up to the snow line."

"Above the grid?"

"Not exactly. But it was like right there. I could almost touch it. It actually went to ground not much farther up, I remember that much."

Harker nodded. "I think that's it. We don't know what those beams are, but they seem to have a lot of different uses. It's almost as if those energy strings are living things. That city looks like it was grown from some crystalline structure, maybe artificial but certainly brought here with the invasion ships. But those pulses, that glow, that sense of strangeness you get when you look at it, the shimmering effect—that's more of this energy. They live in it. They work it, mold it, like a sculptor with clay. It's entirely possible that they are always connected using it as well. If you got close enough to that kind of beam, your brain would be overwhelmed by the alien information it was carrying. If it's some kind of life, even artificial life, it might have sensed you in the stream and tried to incorporate your mind into it."

"Huh?" Littlefeet responded.

"Never mind. Let's just say that, if I'm right, we'll be okay so long as we don't get close to that stuff or intersect an energy stream. We'll have to watch it, though. Swing wide around over to the east and in to the spaceport highway. Let's give them no reason to take a close look at us."

That they could all agree upon.

The offworlders were more than impressed by the two natives, who were clearly scared out of their wits by the sight of the alien city, which they understood even less than the other members of the group, but they stuck it out.

Littlefeet was surprised at how little he was affected by the sight even this close. He couldn't understand it, but when he thought about it, he remembered that he'd had very few episodes in the daytime. It was at night, and particularly when he was tired and trying to sleep, that the visions came.

The great alien base city continued to dominate everything as they descended. It was no automated station, either. At least a dozen times they were forced to dive for cover in the bush as one or another of the fuzzy egg-shaped craft sped by overhead, either going toward the structure or leaving it. They made an odd sound, like the drone of a giant insect, as they went over; some headed out over the ocean beyond, vanishing over the horizon. The only place they didn't seem to go was straight up, but Harker and N'Gana knew full well that they'd be in orbit in a shot if they suspected what was inside that oddly shaped tumbling little second moon.

One of the craft flew almost over them, fortunately not stopping nor slowing down, but in that brief passage all of them, not just Littlefeet, could feel and sense a power and control, some kind of dominating energy that could affect them as well as the Titans.

"Discovery at any stage right now could be disastrous," N'Gana warned them. "That is surely the place where they breed and create the creatures like the Hunters and who knows what else, and there is no way we could escape if they decided to hunt us down on this coastal plain."

It was a restatement of the obvious, but it showed just how nervous even the iron colonel had become.

Although their descent was fairly rapid, the old city had been huge and spread out as well. They realized that they would not make their goal before sundown. That required an immediate decision.

"That place *shines*," the colonel noted. "There will be light to see by, but not enough to be comfortable in this strange and dangerous region. We can either push on and try and make it through the night, chancing that we'll be more vulnerable than they in doing it, or we can halt and spend the night in that thick growth down there."

"I would rather move than cower in the dark," Littlefeet told them. "I am afraid that once darkness comes, I may be drawn to them or they to me and I might betray us anyway. There is also water here but little food, and foraging would be terribly risky. I say we push on and do what you must do."

"I think so, too," Spotty agreed. "I am very tired, but I can see no rest if we wait and much risk."

Harker shrugged and looked at Kat. "I'm not going to

get a wink of sleep so long as I'm near *that* anyway," she told them. "I say let's do it and get the hell out of here."

"Agreed," N'Gana said. "We get to the jungle there and take a rest until dark. Then we move out. I keep wondering if they let the inmates out of the asylum at closing, and I'd rather not know the answer."

The destination had been programmed into the minds of N'Gana, Kat Socolov, and even Hamille; it was only the others who didn't have confidence in where they were headed. Even with that mental map, though, it wasn't easy to figure where you were and where you were going at ground level, and from the reclaiming jungle, even in daylight. In darkness, it was even harder.

They had underestimated the glow from the Titan base. Although things were distorted and shadows were menacing, there was enough light emanating from it for them to see pretty well, as much as the brightest full moon. It didn't help, though, that the place seemed to be far more active in the night than in the day; odd sounds came from it, echoing against the hills and seeming to go right through the interlopers. These were deep bass thumps and penetrating, electroniclike sounds and pulses that would stop, start, speed up, slow down, or just throb with monotonous regularity. It was impossible to know what those sounds meant, but there was a fair amount of traffic of the egg-shaped vehicles, more than in the day, and, in the semidarkness of the glowing structures, various beams of pastel-colored light played this way and that, both into space and out to sea and across and through the grid.

"You'd almost swear the bastards were nocturnals," Harker commented. "But who ever heard of tending flowers by night? They bloom by day, don't they, Littlefeet?"

"I can't say," he responded, unnerved by the noises and the lights. "You go into those groves, you go crazy. Period."

"They came out of the grove and attacked the Family," Spotty put in. "They were—wild. Like mindless monsters. Their eyes were staring, their mouths foaming, and they were screeching like the damned, which they were. Their souls were taken by the flowers, and their minds with them, leaving only bodies that were maniacs."

Harker kept trying to assemble the information into anything that might make sense. Okay, the Titans were so alien you probably could not exchange many common thoughts with them, but there were certain constants. Physics for one thing. Mathematics. There were certain constants to being in this universe. He was already hypothesizing a model that was something like an insect colony, with all of them both individuals and devoted to, perhaps even connected mentally to, one another and to central cores. The plasma manipulation was their technology, their key, and also their means of maintaining a uniform hive. They would see everything as connected, even interconnected. They would think in terms of systems. The whole would concern them; individuals would not, not even individual safety or life. They simply wouldn't consider such things. Everything would be coopted, modified, incorporated into the continental, then planetary, and eventually interstellar system. If, as Littlefeet suggested, the grid and the plasma gave them a kind of telepathic connection with everything else, then they might really not fear death or extinction. All that they did, were, discovered would be fed into the central database—an organic database that might not even have a center.

Kat had said that she felt that the grid was influencing even them, and certainly the Families, if only in a more indirect and general manner. That would fit his vision.

But how the hell could you ever talk with or reason with such a race? They could not even comprehend the idea of individual rights, of the kind of morality that humans put up as a standard. The Titans *were* the grid; that was what they did—extend it, world by world. The survivors of the worlds they took over would be the strongest, survivors in the true sense of the word. Eventually, as they were modified, studied, probed, manipulated, and whatever, they'd be co-opted into the grid, into the local system.

It wasn't all a spurt of inspiration; these subjects had been bandied about by some of the brightest minds and most powerful computers in The Confederacy. But talking to natives and seeing things this close made it much easier to figure out which of those conjectures fit the facts.

Kat understood and thought that he was on to something, although they might never really know. N'Gana had a more pragmatic reaction.

"It means that the only way we can stop them is to send them to hell," he said.

After waiting out the inevitable night storm in the cover of the jungle, they moved out and headed southeast, using the alien base as the directional benchmark, figuring that, at worst, they would wind up either on the bluffs overlooking the ocean or at the remnants of the old seaport. From that point, working back to the old spaceport and then to the fabrication bunkers would be relatively easy.

The plan was good, but the sounds and the snakelike colored beams coming from the Titan base made it difficult to think, let alone hear. Then they emerged from the jungle onto old sculpted rock strengthened with poured concrete and reinforced mixtures that had withstood everything. It oriented them, but it also meant that, from this point on, they would be exposed. And every once in a while those beams would play across the open expanse.

"Drop if one comes near," Harker told them. "Don't let it hit you or they'll know instantly that we're here. I think they'd *all* know. They don't seem to be able to depress to ground level—I make the minimum clearance at about a meter. So drop and wait. Understand?"

They all nodded.

From the ground, the usually silent snakelike Hamille said, "Just move like me. Not get touched."

The entire area seemed surreal. Different parts of the base, perhaps individual "crystals," sometimes whole areas, would pulse and change color in time to the noises. Whatever the hell they were doing in there, the base was clearly not just a base and headquarters, airport and spaceport, it was also in some way a single unified machine. Harker thought that they were making and shaping their plasma somehow in that thing, and then sending what amounted to programs along the flows.

Like a giant computer, he thought. They were components, programmers, and everything else all in one. They and their machines were one. And the surviving humans, culled to leave only the very strongest, with the Hunters taking out the weak and maintaining the line—what were *they* intended to be? Some new cog in the great unity, almost certainly. Perhaps several.

But why the hell did they grow flowers that drove people nuts?

Unless . . .

What if the Titans *were* the flowers? Or the flowers were Titan young? Or Titan young hatched or whatever inside the flowers? That was possible, and would explain a lot, including why you might be driven nuts if you stumbled among them.

Or the groves might be repositories. Temporary memory? Sorters? If they grew their bases from crystals, might they have organic parts of their great system, their great machine, other than themselves?

At least his suppositions reinforced Kat's and Littlefeet's conviction, independently arrived at, that if you could shatter just one part of this system, the rest would collapse in on itself. Divert the plasma, or the source of it, and the means of transference, and they could quite possibly die or, more unsettlingly, go mad at suddenly becoming disconnected individuals.

The terrible weapon created from Priam's Lens just had to work. It just had to.

"Down!" N'Gana shouted, and they all hit the hard rock and hugged it as tendrils of energy snaked all about them. This was about the tenth time that the tendrils had come this close, but their purpose remained unclear. Certainly whoever or whatever was running that huge base/machine over there could identify them and pick them off anytime they wanted. N'Gana was certain they weren't being hunted or toyed with; that would make the motivations and logic of the Titans almost understandable. They had probably been detected and ignored since they were not coming near the base and posed no apparent threat, but there was no doubt that whoever those energy streams touched would instantly be within the Titan mental network.

Littlefeet understood this better than most, and he was already somewhat connected. Terrible and unintelligible visions flooded his mind, and it was only by force of will that he managed to push them back enough to keep going. The others felt them, too, but never as strongly as when those tendrils came close.

It was, Kat thought, almost like someone practicing on a piano, only the keys were the receptors of the brain and they were being rapidly triggered and canceled when that energy approached. It was a bizarre sensation, or series of sensations; in a few seconds you could go from feeling pain to orgasmic delight to fear to absolute confidence to love, hate, just about the whole range. If it lasted for longer than that, it would have been impossible to take, but the tendrils always moved on, and the sensations and urges lessened, although they never totally went away.

"What the hell are they doing and why?" she almost wailed after it happened yet again.

Harker patted her arm gently. "They're broadcasting," he said simply. "And maybe they're receiving as well. Bear with it. We can't be too far from our goal now."

It had taken most of the night, some of it spent crawling over raw stone or broken concrete on their bellies and elbows, but this was true. Hamille, who seemed less affected by the broadcasts, had kept the physical markers—mountains, sea, bluffs, and the pattern of roads and ruins on the ground—in closest focus. They had swung way out, skirting the old spaceport ruins, then come back in along the main spaceport highway.

Once this had been an industrial park for high-tech products most of which were related to spaceport maintenance and spaceship repairs. The only exception was the special project of the Karas and Melcouri families. This was a large complex now almost completely obliterated above ground, but that went down, down into the very bedrock. Now, as the sun grew closer to the terminator, the light of false dawn was spreading, and the Titan base activities lessened. They reached the same spot that had been reached a few years earlier by another offworlder, one who could neither get to its still hidden treasures nor escape from the planet, but who had had the guts to get the message out.

Now they made their way down into a drainage ditch half-filled with debris, going along toward a small open pipelike tunnel ahead.

The emotional roller coaster caused by the Titan signals had subsided almost to a memory. Though they were extremely tired and bloodied on the elbows and knees from the night's crawls, they saw the end of the quest ahead.

It was dark and silent in there, but they weren't afraid, not after what they had had to walk and crawl through just to get there.

Some air circulated, probably from other old half-exposed vents and exhausts, but it was suddenly quite cool.

"Let's rest here and consider how we proceed from this point," the colonel suggested, sinking to the damp rubble that served as a floor inside the tunnel. The others did the same.

"I'd say that we have to find some way to get some light in here or we're going to have to go totally blind," Harker noted. "Hamille, can you see much in here?"

"Better than you," the Quadulan responded. "Not good enough."

"It's odd, but even in this muck in the darkness I feel better than I have since we landed and lost our stuff," Kat Socolov commented. "It's like—well, like there was some kind of constant background noise that's suddenly been cut off. Don't you all feel it?"

"I think I know what you mean," a weary Harker responded. "For some reason, we're no longer connected to the grid. They've been broadcasting constantly to us, to all of us, and now we can't receive the signals. Odd that it wouldn't penetrate this far. We can still see the opening."

"I can't hear them," Littlefeet said, amazed. "For the first time since I climbed the mountain, I can't hear them. And we are almost on top of them!"

"It couldn't be so simple, or there would be organized underground societies on the Occupied Worlds," Harker noted.

"It's not," N'Gana told him. "I suspect that this place, like several of the high-industry areas dealing in very dangerous radiation and other forms of energy manipulation, required shielding. What shielded and protected the population of Ephesus does the same now for us. The odds are that it began with the topmost floors of the buildings above that no longer exist. Dissolved, they've lined this conduit. Now the buildup of debris channels the water away, so we've got this protected area. Ironic, isn't it?"

"Well, it'll serve as an explanation until something better comes along," Harker agreed. "But it's pretty damned temporary. With no food, no uncontaminated water except this little bit in Spotty's gourd, and no light, we can't stay here long. One way or the other, we have to move."

"Light is our first, last, and only priority right now," Socolov agreed. "With it we can deal with the rest. Without it, we don't have a chance. Damn! I wonder what the Dutchman's man did for light? He couldn't possibly have been in any better shape than we are!"

"Actually," said an eerie voice just beyond in the blackness, "I turned on the lights when his presence awakened me. Shall I do the same for you?"

TWENTY

The Caves at the Gates of Oz

All tiredness vanished. Every one of the group felt their hearts jump almost out of their chests. In an instant they were on their feet and eyeing the distant oval, which was now showing some sunlight filtering in.

Littlefeet was in a combat stance, and N'Gana and Harker had reflexively pulled the gun barrel truncheons they still carried.

"Who are you?" the colonel called. "Where are you? Show yourself!"

"I'm afraid I can't do that, as I'm not really much of anywhere at all," the voice, a rather mild, almost bland man's baritone, responded. "However, I do believe I should turn on illumination. I apologize that it is only emergency lighting, but I dare not risk anything more powerful."

The tube did not illuminate, but at the far end a pale yellow glow turned on, showing an entry into a larger area beyond.

"What do you think?" Kat asked nervously.

"A trick!" N'Gana hissed. "I don't know what this is, but it's not possible!"

"We have a choice?" Gene Harker put in, considering their position. "Come on! If we've got light, let's use it."

"Ghosts! I will not go down to where the ghosts live!" Littlefeet said firmly. "Anything living I will take on, even the demons themselves, but you can not fight a ghost!"

"That's no ghost, Littlefeet!" Kat tried to calm him.

"I'm afraid that's about what I am," the voice responded. "But I will not harm you. I will not harm any of you. I cannot. I was built by your kind to serve and protect, and that is what I continue to do."

Both N'Gana and Harker started to breathe again. "You're a computer?" the colonel asked.

"I am a mentat. I was supervisor of this installation until the Fall. Please—come down, all of you. You cannot know how happy I am to see you. I began to fear that my message had not gotten out with Jastrow."

"It's okay," Harker told Littlefeet and Spotty, who still seemed more frightened of the voice than of what they'd just come through. "It's a friend. We know who it is now and it is on our side. Please—you trusted us this far, trust us now."

They made their way carefully down toward the yellow glow, and finally reached a point where the great tube had a section broken out of one side. Looking through the break, the first underground level of the old complex showed in eerie indirect light.

It was *huge*. It was also, astonishingly, pretty much intact. Robot arms and huge control cabs were all over, and sheets of various fabricated parts of some great machines were stacked up here and there.

Just below was a catwalk, intact except for one section immediately below that had been more or less dissolved. The remaining section was only a couple of meters away, though, and easy enough to reach.

"The breach in the pipe was quite recent—about five years ago," the mentat told them. "When the water rushes down the pipe, a little more goes, but it's not that serious. Only a small amount reaches here now."

One by one, they lowered themselves down onto the catwalk, each helping the next. Harker decided to be last, to ensure that Littlefeet and Spotty would go in as well. He not only didn't want them to run, he particularly didn't want them to go back up and outside and fall into the data stream of the Titans. Not now. Not after all this.

The two natives managed, although they were transfixed by the vast scene in front of them. Neither had ever even been inside a building before, and certainly neither had seen the ancient places when they were still whole.

"How are you getting power?" N'Gana asked the century-old machine. "Surely nothing is still running."

"No, the Titans absorb all our power like a sponge. It is only in the security areas with the low-level trickle charges—just a few amps, really—that any of the original stored power is still used or even exists. It is too low-level for their mechanisms to pick up. In truth, I was as surprised as anyone to get even this power. It is Titan power."

"Titan power!"

"When their installation was fully constructed and turned on, the grounded base intersected one of my old power plates. So long as I do not vary the flow and simply use what seeps in, I have been able to maintain this level and my own existence. Of course, I am mostly shut down unless someone is here, and you are only the second in almost ninety years."

"Nobody was left trapped here when they took over?" Harker asked.

"Yes, some were, but as I lost all power for a period of almost two years except trickle from batteries, this place was uninhabitable. No power, no food, and even the water turned off—well, they had to evacuate, those who could. I went dormant due to lack of power then and did not revive until Jastrow showed up a few years ago. Since then I have remained awake, in a standby setting. Unfortunately, I have been unable to do very much, since I cannot draw more power than seeps through and I dare not use it for any mechanical purposes lest they detect it and eliminate this place and me. They are capable of doing so, but do not bother unless there is some threat. I have detected several security stations and some places that were almost certainly old refuges for survivors that appear to have been subjected to sufficient energy to turn them and everything inside into molten rock. It is a delicate balancing act. I have, however, managed to recharge virtually all the security and backup power supplies over the period."

"Where to from here?" N'Gana asked.

"Down the catwalk, then use the ladders to go down to the floor. From that point, I will direct you to where the problem lay for Jastrow. I see that you have brought a Quadulan per my recommendations."

"That was *your* message? I thought it was that poor fellow's," Kat commented as they made their way along the very cold metallic catwalk.

"Oh, Jastrow sent it. It was the only way. He was quite a brave man. He had the morals of a thief and the qualities of a devil, but I provided him with the only thing he could do that he found satisfying—revenge. He wasn't afraid to die, I can tell you that, if in so doing he felt he could get the Titans. I was quite afraid that he wouldn't make it to one of the only three remaining monitoring stations with sufficient reserve power to send a message. He couldn't send it from here, obviously. The moment he did, there would have been a rather rapid and interested investigation and that would have given up the game."

They reached the old factory floor now, covered in fine dust. Harker noted that there were other prints there, those of a single barefoot individual coming and going. Although they were almost certainly those of the unfortunate Jastrow and years old, they looked as if they had been made yesterday.

"Follow the footprints," the mentat instructed. "You will come to it."

They walked across the ghostly floor, the huge machinery all around making it an eerie place. Every voice, every cough, was magnified and echoed back and forth in the place. Only the mentat's voice was devoid of any acoustical naturalness; it seemed to come from a closed and baffled chamber.

"What are these things in here?" Kat asked the computer. "What was it that was made here?"

"Caps and plates for genholes," the mentat responded. "The device works by capturing the stringlike pulses from the temporal discontinuity in the lens. It cannot, however, be truly capped or controlled. The only way to handle it is to capture a string and put it through a genhole and out somewhere else. Right now the junction caps direct it into an area of space where it can do no real harm. It is the *junction* that is the key to the operation. In relays, you can redirect it so that it emerges out of any genhole you determine. After that you have no control. You can, however, see the possibilities. If you can switch genholes at various junctions, then you can direct it to specific targets. There are countless genholes out there now, each a potential exit point. After that, though, it is wild. That is why they could not test it against anything planetary. Nobody knows what will happen. Nobody knows what the strings are, or if they are strings or energy spikes or temporal discontinuities or something else. Once you have an object generating these energy spikes by virtue of a temporal loop in which it is always trying to fall out of our universe, well, you can see we are in uncharted waters. That was why The Confederacy abandoned the idea even though it had no alternatives. Early tests were inconclusive. The trick was getting a burst *short* enough to keep from tearing apart everything."

"I don't see why it wouldn't destroy the genhole and the gates as well," Kat commented.

"It doesn't. It is drawn to a charged plate as if it was magnetized and goes through the center," the mentat explained.

"In a sense, the twisted space-time inside a genhole appears to be a natural, or compatible, environment for it."

"So what is in the security modules below?" Harker asked. "What is it that they need up there?"

"The control codes for the fourteen thousand six hundred and thirty-seven junctions established in this sector before Helena's fall," the mentat told them. "With these codes, anyone in the control center can route the string or pulse or whatever it is to any exit point under junction control. I made them all, you know, right here, and I am certain that they will work as designed. You can see why the codes and locations were kept separate, though. It is quite possible that the use of it on, say, Helena, would destroy the planet. Anything is possible. Nobody was sure what happened to the asteroids and small moons used in the early Confederacy tests, but it scared them. There was a sense that this was a weapon that would not only destroy the enemy but would also destroy what you wished to protect. The debate raged even as the Titans closed in. It was agreed that there would be a master code that no one person or family would have. Karas had part of it, Melcouri a second, and the supervising engineer, Doctor Sotoropolis, had the third. All three parts were needed before the station would even accept the coded commands. When the time came, sooner than they thought it would, Melcouri and Karas had no qualms about giving the code, but Sotoropolis balked. His wife pleaded with him to withhold his consent since all that they had in the world, their families, their lives, were here. He vacillated long enough that it was almost too late. He was trying to set up a close-in gate that would intersect Titan ships instead of hitting them after they were down, but when they came, it was too swift. He wasn't ready, and he died for it."

N'Gana stopped suddenly, causing an almost comic backup of the others. "Then what in hell's the use of getting these target codes? We don't have all three parts of the master code, right? Or is that down there, too?"

For the first time, Harker realized just exactly what had led to all this, and even what had led the Dutchman to the family survivors offworld rather than attempting it with his own crew.

"Sotoropolis gave the code to his wife," he guessed. "The old diva's had it all along. All these years she's been living with the guilt that she stopped her husband from using the weapon. It cost him his life, her adopted world most of its life, and, even now, we have no other way to deal with the Titans."

"Then why didn't she just come to your people—the Navy—with the codes?" Kat asked him. "Why all this time, all this misery?"

"Her code was meaningless without the master target code modules," he pointed out, "and they were down here and believed to be lost. She had the missing part of the master code, but no way to aim the damned weapon. The Dutchman knew where the necessary modules were and probably could have followed up his man's failure and gotten them, but he wouldn't have had the master code. Because they argued and agonized as the enemy came, the enemy won. Now they need each other to do what they couldn't so long ago."

"Why weren't the damned targets just programmed in on Hector?" N'Gana grumbled. "Damned amateurs!"

"Probably fear that the Navy would close in and stop them," Harker guessed. "Or take it over and maybe not use it where Karas and Melcouri were interested in using it. You're right—it was a tragedy of errors and misjudgments and mistakes, and there's enough blame to go around. That's all over and done. It's *past*. Enough people have agonized and suffered too long for those mistakes. No use in rehashing it. The important thing is that we may be able to give it a try at last. As the mentat said about Jastrow, if you can't survive, at least get even."

Kat wasn't so sure. "Um, Gene—if they use it here, then it might well shatter the whole damned planet. Might I point out that *we* are on said planet?"

He nodded. "And we're gonna be on it for quite a while. You know that as well as I do. I want to live, but I'd rather die and take them with me than live as one of their experimental subjects."

"But—"

"Let us not refight the arguments of ninety years!" N'Gana snapped at her. "If we can do it, it *will* be used. Never mind even thinking of revenge. We have nothing else we can do."

"At least now you can feel for what they were going through when push came to shove back then," Harker noted. "Imagine having to do it with everybody and everything you hold dear in the balance."

She sighed. "Well, maybe they won't even use it on us anyway. We're kind of a backwater now in the fight."

"They have to," Harker pointed out. "If they don't use it and knock out the Titans here on Helena, then the Titans are going to be quickly turning Hector into a molten mass. Krill and company are in a worse position than we are. It's possible we can escape and live—if you call it living. They can't even take a practice shot. The moment they get the codes they have to shoot and shoot straight at us. We'd better damned well think about that angle. Never mind what happens if it doesn't work. What if it does?"

Although much of the ancient factory seemed intact, the far end was a real mess. Here some of the structure had collapsed.

"It happened when they began to expand the base," the mentat told them. "The bedrock shifted, then cracked, and there was a general collapse like a small earthquake."

Not only was there a great deal of rubble, but just beyond was the bank of freight elevators that carried material from one level to another. The giant cages were at the bottom where they'd fallen, and because these were magnetic levitation systems, there were no cables—just deep, dark shafts.

"Jastrow actually managed to get down to the bottom level," the mentat told them. "However, the car itself has been crushed at the bottom, blocking access to the tunnels beyond. I have no sensors in the area, so I could not see or predict what was down there. I know he worked down there, using metal rods and other scavenged items to try and enlarge the hole, to get in there, but after two days he was only bloodied and scratched. He said it was impossible. That only a Pooka had a chance of getting through *that*."

"I do not like that term," Hamille croaked. "I am Quadulan."

"Very well. But it is a bit late to be offended. The question is, can you get down the shaft?"

The creature slithered over the rubble, then extended tentacles to hold on to what it could and stared down into the shaft. Finally, it pulled back.

"Get down, yes," it said. "Back up much harder."

N'Gana studied what he could see of the shaft. "I assume this Jastrow used the service ladder here, which is in this indented area?"

"Yes," the master computer responded. "It is the emergency service access and exit."

"How deep is the shaft?"

"One point two kilometers," the mentat told him.

That brought them all up short. "*How* deep?"

"One point two kilometers, give or take a few meters. Straight down. There are, of course, many other floors, but the security storage was at the very bottom for obvious reasons."

Harker whistled. "Well, that lets out dropping cables down, I'd think. Even if we had such cables. So what do we do now?"

"Hamille, with one of us for backup, goes down there and gets the damned modules," N'Gana replied. "Any volunteers?"

"I don't have the imprinted information and I don't think Kat is the best one in a technical situation," Harker noted. "The kids are getting claustrophobic even in this spaceship hangar of a building. That leaves you, Colonel."

"Colonel—I can do it," Kat said. Harker turned to her as if she'd just gone nuts, but he needn't have worried.

"No, Doctor, Mister Harker is correct. It's my job." The mercenary looked down at Hamille. "Rest first or should we just go do it?"

"Let's do it," the Quadulan croaked. "I would rather be tired than dying of thirst."

N'Gana took a deep breath, went over to the shaft, judged the distance as best he could, then jumped over to the indented platform from which the ladder descended straight down into the darkness. Hamille looked down into the pit, then slowly oozed in, the rows of tendrils now extended slightly, giving it a millipedelike appearance.

"I thought with that rotor action of yours you'd just fly down," Harker said.

"In the shaft?" Hamille responded. "I fly like spear. In there, you fly like rock. Get down fine, but the landing would be messy."

With that, it oozed further on in and vanished, and those who remained behind could hear N'Gana begin the long slow descent as well.

Harker turned to Kat. "Why in hell did you just volunteer to do something nobody sane would volunteer to do?"

She shrugged. "Haven't you noticed? He's got problems. Mogutu noticed, after we were down. He went out of his way to do things the colonel might well have done for himself, and he was constantly worrying."

"N'Gana's just hiked over a terrain under severe conditions that few others could," Harker countered.

"Yes, but I've seen his face when he didn't know it, and heard him sometimes in the night. I don't think he knew it or he wouldn't have come, but I'm pretty sure it's his heart. Back in civilization, he'd be put in stasis, they'd clone another heart from his heart cells, and he'd be better than new in months, but here—no. I think his tolerance for pain may be enormous, though."

"You think he can get back up?"

"I don't know. I hope so. I don't think he wants to die, particularly down there, but unless you take physicals every few months and follow the rules all the way, it can always happen. I think he knows it full well, too." She paused. "He must have been a hell of a soldier in his day."

"I never used to like him, and he had a reputation as a bloody butcher," Harker responded. "Now, though, I'm not at all sure."

They went over and sat on a long crate. Littlefeet and Spotty huddled together, staring at the mysterious shapes suspended all around them.

"Cold," she said, and he nodded.

It *was* cold in there, in a relative sense. Littlefeet had been colder, up on the mountain, but this was a different kind of cold. Dry, a little dead, and going right through you.

"Sorry, kids. I warned you not to come along," Kat said, sitting nearby. "It's kind of a creepy dump, isn't it?"

"Dump?" Littlefeet asked. "If you mean strange, yes, it is. As strange as anything the demons build. Was this the kind of place where our ancestors lived?"

She laughed. "No, no. It was the kind of place where they worked, or some of them did, anyway. They had their own kind of power, like the demons have, and their own machines, like the ones demons fly in. The voice is a machine. It was built, not born, and information was fed into it instead of taught like we were. With that information—using all this, and with the aid of just a very few humans—it could build great machines, great ships that could go between the stars."

It was tough explaining this to a pair who had no technological background at all. Even the word "ship" had no real meaning for them, and the only machines they knew were magical things of the enemy.

Spotty looked around, a little scared, a little awed. "Where is this—thing that speaks in a man's voice?" she asked. "Why can't we see it?"

"You *are* looking at me," the mentat responded. "I am everything you see here, and much of the rest of the complex. Oh, I have a brain, if you want to call it that, and it's in one place deep in the center of this complex of buildings, but my eyes, my voice, the things I see and hear come from every part of this place that's still connected, that still has power. I'm even in another far-off place at the same time. That's because the man who was here before you turned on the power there. The surge was enough for me to feel it and find it."

"You mean like the demons talk through their lines in the sky?" Spotty pressed, showing an intelligence than her quiet subservience had concealed.

"Yes, sort of. I don't know how they do it, and I think they probably would barely recognize how I do it, but the general idea is the same. In fact, at one level, energy is energy, whether it's my kind, the demons' kind, or things like the lines in the sky or lightning. I'm awake now because some of their energy proved convertible to what I needed. Unlike you, I do not need food or water, but without energy, electricity of some sort, I either go to sleep or even die."

"Plants get energy from the sun. Are you a plant?" Littlefeet asked. "The others called this place a 'plant.' "

"Not that kind of plant, no. But, again, the idea is the same. Flowers and trees and grass get their energy, their food, from the sun."

"Do you move? Can you walk?" Spotty asked it.

"No, I can't. I'm stuck here. Anything that comes in I can see, hear, and work with. But they must come to me, as you did. I cannot move."

"A big rock once spoke to me," Littlefeet remembered. "When I was a kid and all, I got scared and ran. I guess that was something like you, huh?"

There was a moment's silence, and then the mentat responded, "That *was* me. So you were one of the boys who came along after those creatures killed poor Jastrow. I would not have known you had you not spoken of it. Your voice has changed. In these three years you have become a man. And now you are here. . . . How . . . *coincidental*. . . ."

Both Harker and Kat Socolov sensed a slight hostility creeping into the mentat's otherwise bland tones, but it wasn't enough to start wondering about it. Not yet.

"We might as well try and get some sleep if we can," Harker suggested to them. "Until we hear from that hole over there, all we can do is worry and wait."

There was no effective light at the bottom of the shaft, but the moment N'Gana almost slipped on the rubble of the collapsed elevator car and started cursing, a sliver of pale yellow light shone through a small opening in the wall between the car and the shaft itself.

Voice-activated, he thought. *Handy*.

With even that little bit of light, he could see the remnants of Jastrow's frustration. *So close and no cigar,* the colonel thought. There were long, bent pieces of metal, indentations where things had been pounded or attempts had been made to pry open a larger hole, but it had ultimately only damaged the tools.

Jastrow must have been almost mad down here. The hole was a bit jagged, perhaps large enough for one leg. There even seemed to be some dried blood on some of the jagged edges, which meant that Jastrow may well have tried to force his large body into a very tiny hole.

Inside, there were rows and rows of storage consoles. He could clearly see the posts where human agents would sit, with robotic security controls around them. It looked so normal, as if everybody had just shut down and gone to dinner, and yet it was so unapproachable.

He felt the Quadulan ooze up next to him. The thing was furry, but it felt more like being touched by a porcupine. He rolled back to give it full access to the hole. "Think you can get in there?"

Although it was a bit larger around than the hole, it was an enormously flexible creature and very, very tough. "Piece of meat," it said.

"Piece of cake," N'Gana corrected.

"Whatever. Question is, if security is still powered on, will it take passwords from Hamille?"

"That's part of why I'm here. It's aware of us now, so we might as well get started."

The Quadulan eased up to the hole and then began pulsing its body, stretching itself out as much as it could, and then it pushed on in, oozing through like paste through a straw. It was not as easy as it looked, and Hamille was extremely slow and cautious. More than once, one of the sharp edges snagged the skin or threatened to dig deeper, and the creature had to stop, back up a bit, and try it again. Still, within a quarter of an hour, it was through.

Almost as soon as it hit the floor, a series of tight red beams struck it, and a voice that sounded very machine-like and inhuman said, "Halt and give the proper password signs or leave as you came. You are targeted by seven different lethal devices." It was designed to sound artificial so that there would be no doubt in the intruder's mind that it was dealing with a tightly programmed machine.

N'Gana felt some sharp pains in his chest that brought him up short for a minute, but he willed himself to ignore them. They had not come this far to have him blow it.

He took a deep breath, pressed his face against the hole in the wall, and said, in his best theatrical voice, "And let the heralds Zeus loves give orders about the city for the boys who are in their first youth and the gray-browed elders to take stations on the god-founded bastions that circle the city!" he intoned. "Let it be thus, high-hearted men of Troy, as I tell you! Let that word that has been spoken now be a strong one, and that which I speak at dawn to the Trojans, breakers of horses. For in good hope I pray to Zeus and the other immortals that we may drive from our place these dogs swept into destruction whom the spirits of death have carried here on their black ships!"

There was silence for a moment, and Hamille felt as tense as N'Gana. Then, just as the old colonel feared he had blown a line, the red targeting beams switched off.

"Code accepted," announced the security voice.

It was an appropriate passage from a little-known translation, with a devilish little trap in it. A part of Hector's great speech before the battle, but with some sentences left out here and there. The result fit the defenders of Helena against the Titan invaders as well as it did the defenders of Helen thousands of years ago on a far distant planet.

The Trojans, too, had lost to the invaders in their black ships just as the defenders of Helena had lost to the invaders in their shimmering white craft. The Trojans stupidly fell for a simple trick and lost it all; the defenders of Helena dithered until the invaders had already breached the inner walls and they could no longer decide. In both cases, their worlds died by the unwitting duplicity of their defenders. Ancient Troy vanished off the face of the earth for three thousand years, and existed after only in partly excavated ruins. Helena was in a century of darkness which might last as long as Troy's but for this one second chance.

It was odd, he thought, fighting the pains, that only military men knew any history in this day and age. Nobody else really cared. Nobody else had to repeat the mistakes of the past.

He leaned back into the hole. "Hamille! Do you have them?"

For a moment there was no answer. Then the croaking voice of the Quadulan came back, echoing slightly, "Yes. I see them. Old-fashion memory bubbles, but labels are clear. Need to type in code phrases to unlock case. Very hard with my tentacles. Will do it."

"Take it slow! No mistakes!"

The three phrases, one from each member of the triumvirate who created this project so long ago, were all in Greek. One was a line from a poem about Helen of Troy, the second a quotation from the Epistle of Saint Paul to the Ephesians, the third a line from Aristotle's *Nicomachean Ethics*. All had to be typed in on a Greek alphabet manual keyboard embedded in the security casing by a creature for whom the instrument was not designed.

The pains had subsided, almost vanished, but now they seemed to be starting up again as he saw in his mind's eye the serpentine alien trying hard to hit every last alpha and omega.

It could have been worse, he told himself. It could have been ancient Mandarin.

And if it worked, if Hamille got it all right, if that case popped open and the electronic code keys were in its grasp, could they make it back up? Could *he* make it back up? It was a *very* long way, and he was so very, very tired.

* * *

Time passed slowly while they could do nothing but sit and wait, hungry and thirsty, and very, very tense. With so much idle time, though, none of them could avoid talking about things most on their minds.

"What happens when and if N'Gana and Hamille come back with the keys?" Kat mused. "I mean, how the hell do we send it up to the others? Whoever does will be the same kind of target that Jastrow was."

"I will send them from the spaceport security system, which is still operational if I can shift the majority of power to it," the mentat told them. "The codes are supposed to be on standard data keys, although encrypted. I can't read them or copy them, but I can transmit the encrypted codes. If, as you say, your people have the station in standby mode, then it will receive the signals. Once it does, then targeting and shooting will be as simple as someone up there in the command and control chair willing it so."

"The moment you send, they'll blast you," Harker pointed out. "Probably send some of their creations down to make sure we're not hiding any other surprises, then they'll reduce this whole thing to lava."

"I know. I do not know how to deal with that, but I must accept it. It is difficult for me to contemplate the end of my conscious existence, but I see no other way. I have understood this ever since Jastrow filled in the blanks, as it were. You must be well away when I transmit. Out of the coastal plain, certainly. We have no way of knowing how long it will take those on Hector between getting the codes and being ready to implement them. I should like to be able to see it in action, even once. If I am to cease to exist, I should like to know that it was for a good cause."

God, I think we're building our machines too well, Kat thought, but said nothing. Instead, she asked, rather rhetorically, "And then what happens to us, I wonder? We're not going to get back to the ship. Not with those monsters in the way and the rafts surely dissolved by now."

"We survive until they come to find us and take us off," Harker said. "And you get to *really* do a field study."

She sighed. "I wonder if they'll bother to try and find us? How could they anyway? We'll just be two more savages out there on a world that, even if it's freed of the Titans, will be a pretty low priority for exploration and rebuilding, I suspect."

"Well, we have nothing else we can do but settle down and wait for them, no matter when or if they come," he noted. "Not unless we build and launch a boat that can sail out to the island. It's a possibility, if we use all natural wood and have the time—and I think we'll have the time."

"Do you really think that's possible?" she asked, genuinely interested.

"I think it's possible, yes. I know how to do it, although that's with modern tools and the like. From scratch it'll take a lot longer, but it's possible. If the grid's down and the Titans are run off, at least nobody will want to stop us, and maybe we can have a straw hut and a fire and all the rest. That's if we survive the next few days, anyway."

"It's worth a try. I'd like to try," she told him. "I keep being afraid that we've already been somewhat reprogrammed."

"Huh? What do you mean?"

"The general program for all survivors. The one they transmit constantly over the grid, and which transfers itself to us via that nightly special rain. I've been thinking about it and about us and how we changed even in so short a time. We should be dead. Instead, we've become more like Littlefeet and Spotty. Think about it. After the first couple of days, did any of us think of doing the absolutely normal thing and finding some kind of cover or shelter from that storm? No. Even though we knew that it was ruining our stuff, we started walking right out into it. That's the first directive. Be sure you can get the message. Maybe even the chemical bath. We're already part of their experiment. Everything in the world, this world, gets bathed like that. We eat it, drink it, wash in it. Even if the grid collapsed, I think it will continue, at least for a while. And yet I want that boat, Gene. I really do want to ride in that boat."

It may have been hours, it may have been a day, but suddenly there was a sound from the shaft. Slowly, an exhausted Hamille oozed out onto the rubble and collapsed, breathing very hard. They rushed over to the Quadulan expectantly. "Where's the colonel?" Kat asked.

"Did you get it?" Harker wanted to know.

"Go down and help the colonel," the alien croaked, each word a heaving breath. "He is not that far but he is in trouble."

Harker sprang to the shaft, saw the jump to the ladder, made it, and quickly started down, his old ship's reflexes giving him total confidence.

He found N'Gana mostly by the moans and gasps, perhaps seventy meters down, sitting on the platform and holding on to the ladder.

"Colonel! Can you make it? Come on! I'll help you!"

"No," N'Gana gasped. "I will make it on my own. You can't carry me up there, you can't *pull* me up, and if you follow and I fall, I'll take you with me." He fumbled for something, then handed a small box to Harker. "Take them and go back on up! I'll follow you if and when I can! *Go!* Without those, it's all meaningless!"

Gene Harker understood, and grasping the box firmly, he went back up the ladder toward the light above.

The three others waited anxiously at the top, and Kat's eyebrows went up when she saw that he was alone.

"He'll make it on willpower," he assured her. "I can tell you, a man like that's not going to check out by falling down an elevator shaft."

They looked at the box. It was a plain box of artificial wood, and it had a golden Greek cross on the top and a pure gold clasp. Harker slipped the tiny gold pin over and down, and opened the box. Inside, resting in a soft feltlike lining, each wrapped with a protective bubble seal, were the code modules.

"Oh, my God!" Kat Socolov breathed. For the first time she realized that they had not only gotten what was needed, but that it was almost certain to be used.

About fifteen minutes later, an ashen N'Gana crawled out of the shaft and tumbled down the pile of debris. They rushed to him; he was in awful shape. He was covered with perspiration, and not just his face but his whole body seemed a dull, almost dark gray. Still, after a while, he managed to sit up and look around. When he spied the box, he looked extremely satisfied.

"We did it," he sighed.

"We did nothing until we can blow the hell out of that satanic fairyland out there," Harker replied. "We have to feed these in to the mentat and get out of here."

"Go feed 'em in," N'Gana gasped. "Then we'll talk."

The women tried to make him as comfortable as they could, but it was pretty clear to them and to the others as well that Colonel N'Gana would not be going anywhere anytime soon.

The mentat directed Harker to an old, dust-covered terminal far on the other side of the great factory floor. It didn't look operational, but carefully he unwrapped each module and, one by one, he inserted them into the slot.

"I have the data. I have no idea what it means, but my counterpart on Hector certainly does. These mathematical algorithms will combine with what is already up there to give precise switching and firing instructions to any and all of the active genhole gates."

"How soon can you transmit?" Harker asked it.

"I can transmit now. I will not, however. Not without giving you a chance."

Harker walked back over to them and put the box back on the floor. "Too bad that's all made of high-tech state-of-the-art synthetics," he sighed. "Otherwise we could take the extras with us."

Kat sighed. "Yeah. Where's Father Chicanis's communion set when we really need it?"

"I will get the message out," the computer assured them. "I am not anxious to create the act nor am I looking forward to my own cessation of existence, but you must go, and quickly. Every moment now risks some sort of discovery. I want you well away from here."

N'Gana shook his head. "I think I'll just stay and keep you company," he told the mentat. "It's important that a commanding officer ensure that the mission is completed."

"It is not necessary," the mentat responded, unable to catch subtlety or monitor the physical condition of the colonel.

"Yes, it is. I'm dying anyway. Everybody knows that, even me. If I'm going to go, then I'm damned well going to go in action. The rest of you, get out of here! Now! I have an idea I want to discuss with our new friend here. One that'll let us do this in *style*."

"You're sure?" Kat asked him.

"Doc, I've never been more certain of anything. And I want it quick, since I don't know how long I'm going to be able to animate this corpse and I'm hungry and thirsty and there's nothing here for even a lousy last meal, understand?"

"Colonel—" She felt tears welling up inside her.

"Get the hell out of here, Doc. And the rest of you! Few men in my profession get to plot their own glorious demise! Besides," he added a bit more softly, "I would go absolutely insane stuck here for the next ten years or so. This is one of the dullest worlds I've ever known!"

Harker brought himself to attention and saluted. The colonel, reflexively, returned it.

"I, too, am going to remain, with Colonel's permission," Hamille croaked, still breathing hard. "I am too tired to go on, and there is nothing for me in this world. I, too, am fighter. My family, my young, are already in the next universe thanks to Titans. I would like to join them."

N'Gana looked over at the Quadulan. "I'll be glad for the company, but you might just get picked up."

"To go where? Not like human people. Very few worlds are Quadulan."

Harker leaned over and half whispered to Kat, "Let's get out of here before we all go down in a suicide pact."

She nodded. There wasn't much more to say, and she realized that the strange alien who'd done the job the humans could not had never intended a different fate.

The mentat had no comment on the other two, but did step in now. "Mister Harker, you and the two women should leave at once. The boy must stay."

They all froze. "What?" Kat asked in an acid tone. "What the *hell* do you mean by that?"

"At heart, all minds, all brains, whether artificial or naturally grown, are calculating machines," the mentat noted. "I can do some calculations better than any human. I can tell you the exact odds that the one boy who discovered Jastrow's body far away and who ran from my transmission should be the one who shows up here at this point in time. Unfortunately, you do not have time for all the zeros. You are here by choice. This boy was *sent*. There is no other explanation. And if you let him leave here, they will know that we have a weapon and where it is and they will move swiftly against us before we can move. The boy stays."

"What d'ya mean, *sent*?" Littlefeet snapped. "You

can't guess how hard it was just to stay alive to get this far! You don't know what we went through!"

"I've heard your stories while you've been here. I believe I do," the computer responded. "I am not saying that you are a conscious agent, only that you are a tool. You have all been speculating about how the Titans think, how different they are, how they could never be understood. Don't you think that, in their own way, the Titans are thinking the same about you? They can experiment with you, they can genetically alter you, they can mess with your minds, but they can only make you more like them or like their models. They don't understand you as you are. They got an ugly surprise at that transmission of Jastrow's. It wasn't supposed to be possible, nor was there supposed to be anyone left who could work it even if one or another device were accidentally left operational. I think they started a hunt to find mentally receptive humans they could use as monitors just in case another Jastrow came along. They couldn't recognize him—it would take a native human to do that. I think they've had some natives they could directly influence all along. Perhaps even the tribal leaders. The priests and nuns and the like. You were finally adopted into their network of control when you climbed the mountain. *Why* did you climb that mountain, Littlefeet?"

"Huh? I—I dunno. Oh—yeah. Some members of a Family got struck dead. Father Alex sent me. He wanted me to do a complete survey. To go as high as I could stand it."

"Yes. I doubt if he knew he was being influenced, either, but they ordered him to send one of his flock into the stream and he sent you. Later, they cut off your family, then attacked and scattered it when you were not there. But your one real love somehow gets away and gets right to you. She 'heard' you, she said. And you move south, even though you know that rivers get wider as they near the sea. You certainly know that. You thought you might be able to cross at some point but that defied your knowledge, experience, and logic. They wanted *you* to find the newcomers, and they even used a Hunter attack to delay them so that you could reach them. Not because they understand what's going on here, but because they do not. But if you go back out there, you will tell them. You will not even *know* that you'll tell them, but your mind is linked to theirs, they can read it out. They won't understand it, but they will get the record and know that technologically sophisticated humans have landed and risked all for some reason. It does not take a lot to understand that this would be a threat. They will know about me, and this place. You will tell them and you will not know that you tell them. You will tell them in your dreams and visions. That is why you cannot go, Littlefeet. That is why you must remain until the codes are broadcast."

Littlefeet shook his head in disbelief. "No, it is a lie! A dirty lie from some—*ghost*! The demons do not own my soul! I pray only to Jesus!"

"It is not your faith I am interested in," the mentat said, perhaps a bit sadly—if that were possible. "I do not have a lot of records, but I can guess that good men have been used unwittingly by evil since the dawn of humanity. You are full of coincidences, my young friend. Far too many coincidences. Deep down, you *know* it, I think, now that it's been laid out. You cannot go. Like the guards of a Family's night kraals, one must be ready to die for the many. All of this has come too far to be allowed to fail now. I have accepted that my existence must terminate for that reason."

"No!" Spotty screamed at him. *"You can't have him! I won't let you!"*

"I can manage a sufficient charge through the plates and catwalks that you will need to navigate, and I will not hesitate to use it. If Littlefeet does not remain, I will use a kind of lightning bolt and strike him dead as he tries to leave."

They all had their mouths open, but there was nothing any of them could say. Finally, Spotty said, "Well, then, if he stays, so do I. I do not want to keep going without him."

Littlefeet seemed to snap out of it. "No! That's wrong! And the ghost or whatever is right. Maybe I'm being used by them, maybe I'm not, but he can't take the chance. That's what he's saying. But *you*—there's a different duty for women and you know it. You didn't bleed this time so you probably have my kid in you! I won't let you kill it! Go with them! Be a part of this new family! It's your duty. Just like my duty, and the others' here, is to kill the demons." He grabbed her and held her and kissed her like he'd never kissed anybody before, and then he let her go and stepped away. "Now, *go*! And tell my son that his father died heroically!"

"Let's get out of here before we all get killed," Harker muttered anxiously.

Spotty stared at Littlefeet, and there were tears in her eyes, but she said nothing. There was nothing to say and no way to argue it further. Particularly if she carried his child, it *was* her duty, to him and to God, not to die. She turned, wiping away the tears, and gestured to Gene Harker and Kat Socolov to go. They started, and she followed, not looking back, although she knew that Littlefeet stood there fighting back his own tears and looking at her until she was out of sight in the far reaches of the catwalks above.

N'Gana shifted, uncomfortable that he would not be the only one to die, but resigned to the business at hand.

"You two! Come over here!" he managed, gesturing. "Mentat? You still there?"

"Yes. I just wish I was not. On the other hand, I have just seen the most logical justification for my imminent destructive actions that I could possible imagine. We must free these people."

"I don't just want to free these people," N'Gana told it and the others. "I want to go out with a bang. Most of all, I want to know if the damned thing *works*. Don't you?"

Littlefeet nodded. "Something that will kill demons? Yes!"

N'Gana looked up at the great machinery, frozen for nearly a century, and pointed.

"Well, if that thing up there in those giant mechanical pincers is what I think it is, and if there's a charge left in it, then I think we might have a shot. Mentat, what was the procedure when you made a gate? You couldn't do more than trickle-charge testing down here, but was it encoded into the Priam's Lens weapons system before it was shipped or after it was installed?"

"Why, it was encoded right here, since the security system was on the lower level," the computer replied. "The targets are addressed by code numbers."

"So, if I'm not mistaken, that's a finished plate up there, stuck where it was when the power failed. Am I right?"

"Yes."

"And it's already encoded by number in the keys, so if its number were called, then theoretically it would, if charged, be an end point for the energy strings?"

"Why, yes, I believe so."

"Can you determine the number? And can you bring it to a full charge?"

"Yes to both, I suppose. At the point of broadcast, I could shift whatever remaining power I had to the plate. It should charge it for a short period. But why?"

"Then let's send those codes with a command to target this one first," he suggested. "Let's shoot the bastards from right here if we can!"

TWENTY-ONE

The Ghost of Hector Rises

It was no easier getting out than it had been getting in, but at least in daylight the activity of the Titan base was far less and there weren't those energy tendrils to deal with.

Harker, Kat, and Spotty said almost nothing while making their getaway. There wasn't anything else to say. It was good to be able to stop at a depression filled with water and at least fill that need.

There was still traffic in and out of the base; the ships didn't stop coming and going day or night, and in place of the strings they could see what appeared to be large numbers of humans or humanlike creatures wandering, apparently aimlessly, across the expanse of the old city, never straying too far from the front of the crystalline base.

"Hunters?" Kat wondered when they reached some cover.

"Doubtful. Not that passive or that many together. Other kinds of experiments, probably. The people they use to determine what to do with the rest of us, or what they can do. Even so, I wouldn't like to meet up with any. At the very least, what they see, the Titans see, too."

The jungle area didn't provide a lot of food, but Spotty was able to round up some squashlike growths and an acidic but spongy leaf that she insisted was edible.

"Nightfall, after the storm, we should try and make the hills," Kat told them. "I don't think the mentat's going to give us a whole lot of grace time, and if anybody or anything, even by accident, wanders down that culvert, it won't wait."

Harker frowned and nodded slowly. "If I know Krill, she's had them drilled and checked and double-checked again and again up there and somebody sitting in the command chair on shifts at all times. Yes, the moment those codes come in, whoever is in that chair is going to take a few seconds to react, a few more to realize what they've got is a live system, maybe another minute or two to notify the others, and then it's shoot time. The targets will be at least one base on each continent just to collapse the grid, then the rest—before the Titans can regroup and move. If it's done right, then there could be just enough shock and confusion as those nets go down to allow for a whole series of positioning shoots before the Titans even realize where they've been hit from. By that time there could be enough impulse energy bouncing around, along with God knows what other bizarre effects from both the Lens energies and the collapse of the Titan nets, that they may be unable to get a fix on Hector. Remember, the commands to shoot will be short numerical commands sent in nanoseconds through the orbiting genholes' out-systems. Titan ships will go after those gates first, and probably be even more confused when they see only gates. Krill knows she needs a fast clean sweep. I expect her to do her job."

Spotty stared at the two of them. "They will do this—*thing* as soon as they can?" She didn't understand anything about the weapon, but the idea of throwing lightninglike spears into the hearts of demons was good enough.

"Yes, they will, dear," Kat replied.

"Then we cannot wait for nightfall. We must go now or we will not be able to make it to the top. The demons are most active at night, and they must expect something. No matter how we feel, we must go now or remain right here until it finishes."

She was right and they knew it. All those survivor's instincts and upbringing in a world of constant threat made her the expert. Both offworlders suddenly realized that they had been treating the girl like some poor native guide in a bad play. They were in *her* world now, and *she* was the expert, the natural leader, among the three of them.

"Let's get the hell out of here," Harker said, and they rose to go.

They had to move as much as possible through the overgrown sections, and they had to keep down in what appeared to be slowly increasing activity at the Titan base, so it was nearing sunset when they reached the point where the Grand Highway rose gently to reach the low pass between the hills.

Even before darkness fell, there were loud noises coming from the Titan base, and lights and energy tendrils were everywhere. Harker was nervous about climbing up in the face of it, but he saw no choice. "If that thing explodes or whatever, it's going to at least take most of this coastal plain with it. We *have* to be over the summit!"

"I don't understand why a race that sophisticated didn't pick us up when we came in," Kat commented. It had been bothering her from the first. "We can set up defenses even a cockroach can't get through."

"Not true," Harker told her. "Otherwise there would be no more cockroaches. They would have gone extinct when Earth became uninhabitable. We can set up a general roach barrier that works most of the time, but not if we're targeting individual roaches. In this case, *we're* the roaches, and I don't think they can comprehend total individualized behavior. No, they've been waiting for us to reappear all right, but what tips them off is the roach with the electronic implant. It's the only reason Jastrow got in and out, the only reason *we* got in and out."

"Yeah, but if somebody's getting nervous down there,

they might be looking for another candidate," Kat suggested nervously. All she wanted to do was get out of there.

Using the windswept trees as cover and the light reflecting from the great Titan base, they managed to get almost halfway up before the rains rumbled in, the low hills being no barrier to them.

Even knowing that the rains were more than mere rains, and noting their altered behavior, Kat and Harker couldn't help themselves. When the rains rumbled, they broke cover and went out nearer the road and sat, exposed, so that they could be fully bathed. It wasn't something they thought about or something they could fight. It was an irresistible impulse even as their minds told them it was not the thing to do.

From the Titan base below, the electronic thumping noise that they'd heard before, with a varying pace that rose and fell but still seemed to go right through them, was particularly loud and active. There was no question that their position could be detected; it probably could be detected at any time via the grid. The problem for the Titans was that they could not tell humans apart unless they had been selected and marked in the data stream. And if you weren't theirs, you were just one of the mass.

After the storm passed, there was always a feeling of wellness accompanied by lethargy; the trained guards were always able to overcome this, but most never fought it. Now, though, it was taking all the willpower of the exhausted trio to keep going, to keep from settling in, from finding a spot for the night and sleeping.

"Is it particularly strong because we're so close or because they just did something?" Kat wondered.

"It doesn't matter," Harker told her. "We have to push on if we can, we have to fight it. And if they did anything extra, or if two baths this close to the source of the programs did an extra job on us, we'll have to live with it, too. It's done. Right now we just need to run."

Nobody was up to running through that brush up the rest of the hill, but walking was something they could force themselves to do.

Something down there was more excited than usual, and the energy tendrils from the various facets on the base seemed hyperactive. They would sweep not only the plain but also up the hills as well, and it was getting difficult to dodge them.

Now, though, the trio, worn out, barely able to think, was nearing the summit of the pass. A few hundred more meters and they'd be on the other side, able to rest, as protected as they could be under the circumstances. Now they *did* find that last bit of adrenaline, and they started to move fast.

Leading, almost at the very top, Harker was struck by a flickering pastel red tendril of energy from the base.

"Gene!" Kat screamed. He was suddenly frozen in place. Then he turned and started looking straight at the base, where new sounds began to pulse, sounds like they hadn't heard before. Like electronic whistles punctuated with a twanging noise, and the tendril seemed to be pulsing in time with them.

Kat Socolov fought down panic and summoned up rage. She raced up to the zombielike Harker, hauled off, and punched him in the jaw with every bit of strength she could muster.

He went down, and the tendril broke off and seemed to flail away in midair for a moment, then began a new pattern to see if it could find him again.

By this point Kat and Spotty had dragged the unconscious Harker back into the underbrush and out of a direct line of sight with the base.

This was as far as they were going, that was clear. Whatever was going to happen, they couldn't drag the man that last measure to and over the top. They could only hope that he had been merely tagged and that the aliens had not yet received any data they could understand or use.

It was only a single plate for a genhole that would have been assembled in space out of such plates and that would have eventually been large enough to swallow a full-size spaceship, but the mentat thought it was sufficient and they weren't going to argue with such a machine.

The trick was to get up on the catwalks and pound on one end of the damned thing so that it was in position to do maximum damage. The giant crane had been frozen in place for decades and could not be powered up. However, to minimize potential damage it held the plate at just one central and balanced point. That point, effectively a ball joint, did not want to move after so long, but Littlefeet was very strong. He managed to budge the thing, much to his surprise and delight.

"The direction is now within acceptable limits," the mentat told him. "It won't strike dead center, but it will strike the main complex and it will do damage. You've done very well, my boy."

"I'd like to see it," Littlefeet told the computer a bit wistfully. "I'd really love to see it hit the demons. Nobody has ever seen demons die."

"We do not know what will happen, or even if it'll work like this, but I agree with you," the mentat told him. "Besides, perhaps there should be someone to sing the legends of Colonel N'Gana's grand last stand."

N'Gana was keeping himself going by sheer force of will. He was a dead man and he knew it, but he was *not* going to die of a heart attack just before the final blow.

Littlefeet was confused. "What do you mean, 'sing the legends'? I shall be in heaven with the others."

"I have been thinking about that," the mentat told him.

"And I have been dwelling on a people who, reduced to nothing, nonetheless retain all that is good in humanity. Duty, honor, courage . . . These are rare things that get obscured or forgotten by modern life. And love as well. I cannot really know that emotion, but the observable qualities make it a central part of all the rest that is good and perhaps holy in people."

It paused, as if listening for something in the silence, then continued.

"There is a great deal of additional activity up there. I am getting surges of power radiated into the old power grid at levels that are almost off the scale. They know something. I had hoped to give the others another few hours, but I do not think we can wait."

"Then this is it?" Littlefeet asked, nervously steeling himself.

"Yes, this is it. I do not think you have much of a chance to survive this close in, but you have twenty minutes if nothing else happens. Go! Use it!"

He stood there a moment, uncomprehending.

"Go, I said! You may barely make it out! Stay low and in the culvert! Do not look at the demon palace until *after* you hear us shoot! The shot may blind you. But, as soon as they shoot, run like the very devil!"

"But—but you said I may—"

"If you don't start now, you will die here! Go! I give you a chance, however slim, at surviving! By the time you get into that culvert it won't matter what they pick up! *Move!*"

Littlefeet started to say something to the two who remained, but N'Gana just smiled and pointed to the catwalks.

Hamille raised its bizarre head and croaked, "Get the fuck out of here, you asshole!"

Littlefeet started running.

* * *

They had been on Hector long enough now that Juanita Krill was beginning to worry that they might run short on some supplies before anything happened below. The temporal shift was always in the minds of those who planned this expedition; new air generators, water reprocessors and traps, and fresh food should be coming in by small automated shuttle on a regular basis now, but the timing to pick up the modules and get them to Hector was dicey.

Van der Voort and Takamura didn't care. They were in a kind of heaven in the place, with a whole new area of physics suddenly open to them, a whole new kind of mathematical approach to problems involving genhole communications. There were years of work here done by large teams of brilliant people and state-of-the-art artificial intelligence agents as well, work virtually forgotten in the slow lethargic collapse of The Confederacy. Years more of work would be needed to figure it all out, to document and test each and every revolutionary idea, but the potential here was mind-blowing. Nobody, but nobody, had been able to lick the temporal shifts of the genhole, but this came very close.

Equally stunning had been the recordings of the initial tests of the weapon based on the effects from Priam's Lens. Asteroids shattered, a small moon literally sliced in two . . . Incredible power, power that had terrified those who had built it. What purpose, they'd asked, to kill the Titans if at the same time you destroyed Helena and all upon it as well? There was hope, they argued. There was no other way. There *had* to be another way. It had gone on and on until the great white spacecraft of the Titans appeared in-system and the power was sucked dry and there was no way left to get down to the surface and get the codes and transmit them back up.

It must have haunted George Sotoropolis most of all. He had been the main roadblock, and he had been here, unlike the other two, to see the ships come in, to understand that he could have hit the ships before they devastated his beloved Helena if he'd just let them have his part of the code.

It was such a simple problem to solve, at least on a theoretical basis. The data stated that the bursts had to be incredibly short. No more than three bursts on a target, no more than thirty nanoseconds per burst, and you kept the damage localized, focused. And the best part was, you only had to hit the target, not necessarily dead center or in a vital area.

The computer models said it would work. They had spent several days running programs through the Control Center command and control computers and they had a ninety-seven percent certainty.

Only nobody'd had the opportunity to find out for sure. By the time they'd determined it, they had already been essentially overrun.

They also knew that Helena's installations and Titan ships and bases had to be first. They had to take them out and quickly. They had to do it right the first time, and they had to do it without any serious damage to the planet or the moon they were on would no longer be held in a planetary grip.

They had the initial targets picked and locked in using the genhole gates scattered around the system. As soon as any of the gates activated, it would be pinpointed by the Titans, but they would be harder to reach than they seemed, spitting an unknown but deadly stream.

They had the targets all mapped out, and the order. All they needed was the go codes. If it all worked, if they were still alive, still viable when it was over, and if at least one master genhole gate were still intact, then they could turn their attention to other conquered worlds. Not all, of course—there hadn't been time. But there were a lot of targets out there. Targets that, the early data suggested, against all plausibility, could be automatically hit by commands that would somehow arrive very quickly indeed.

Van der Voort had been working on how that could be so, since it defied established physics. The key, he was certain, was in the properties of whatever that string or stream or whatever it was that the holes captured and transmitted. It had to be something unlike anything they had ever seen before, something that, somehow, took its time from both ends of a wormhole simultaneously without breaking up.

Those earlier scientists had tried to determine the nature of this strange phenomenon coming from the small lens and its trapped and looped singularity. The strings were not true strings; they simply resembled them in the way they registered on instruments and the way they seemed to move. They had no measurable mass, but if they were energy, they did not register as such on any known measuring device. But they were as destructive as hell.

Quite rapidly, van der Voort had come to a conclusion that a number of long-dead project scientists had also considered, but put aside for the more immediate engineering problems.

"Not strings," he told Takamura. "Not matter at all, or energy, either."

Takamura frowned. "Not matter and not energy? No mass, no energy transfer, yet destructive. What can you mean?"

"I think they're cracks," he told her. "Cracks in the very fabric of space-time emanating from the collapse of the boltzmon. Because it is caught in a loop, the cracks heal as quickly as the thing cycles, and the forces in our own universe aid this to maintain integrity."

Takamura saw it at once. "And since the genholes create holes in our own space-time fabric, it is a natural attractor and conductor of the cracks. They don't heal inside! They're maintained! Inside, the crack expands instantly but is held inside the field! Yes! Oh, my! *That's* why it shattered planets, and could possibly destabilize stars! Nothing could withstand it until it healed over. Whatever it struck, even if it were a hair-thin sliver, would fall instantly out of space-time itself. Oh, my! I can see now why they were so afraid to use it!"

Krill had been adamant about that. "We will not hesitate again! There won't be a third chance! When we get those codes, we *shoot*! And the consequences be *damned*!"

Littlefeet thought he wasn't going to make it. The entrance was just ahead, but he'd slipped and fallen several times in the rubble. Now, though, he was determined to come out, even into the darkness lit only by an alien glow. He had been given a second life, and he was not going to forfeit it lightly.

"Colonel?" the mentat called.

"Yes?"

"You are still here?"

"I have no place else to go," he responded, chuckling.

"You were murmuring unintelligibly. I was worried."

"You needn't be. I was just seeing a lot of faces all of a sudden, as if a large crowd of men and women stood with us here. It was quite strange. I knew them all, too, and they knew me. I can still almost make them out in the gloom. Soldiers, mostly. Good people, the finest. Everyone I ever ordered to their deaths. It's almost a reunion, really. They seemed quite pleased to see me, and not at all holding a grudge. Not anymore."

"I do not—"

"Let Colonel have who he wants here!" Hamille croaked. "Bigger the crowd for the end of the contest, the better the sporting victory!"

The mentat started to say something more, then decided not to. It did not understand what they were saying or thinking, but its logical brain also understood that whatever it was was now irrelevant. If it made it easier for them, so be it.

"They're running traces on the energy leak," the mentat told them. "Hector is in the sky, a bit lower than I would like for optimum accuracy but it will do. I am transmitting the codes *now*!"

The colonel smiled and looked into the darkness.

"Send them to hell for me, Colonel," Sergeant Mogutu called from the shadows.

The colonel raised his hand unsteadily and gave the victory sign.

A tremendous surge of energy sprang for less than three seconds from a point near the cliffs just beyond the old spaceport area. Almost immediately three egg-shaped craft of the Titans raced from the complex and zeroed in on the exact spot, focusing their energy drains first, then opening fire with full blasts of energy until the entire area for half a kilometer square was turned first red, then white hot, liquid and bubbling.

Their reaction time was incredible; they were at the spot in under ten seconds and had it reduced to molten rock within a minute.

Much too late.

The command and control board suddenly lit up with hundreds of fully active targets. It so startled Takamura that she failed to act for several seconds. Then it dawned on her what she was seeing and she screamed, *"Krill!"*

Juanita Krill was awake in an instant; she walked swiftly to the board. Van der Voort was not far behind, yawning.

"Take it easy," Krill told the nearly hysterical physicist. "So far we've only received the codes in a broad beam. They still don't know that we are here. To do that we're going to have to power up our genholes and read in our optimum targets. Takamura, let me take the controls. Any of us can initiate the sequence on the bases but I'm going to have to take the initial ships manually until the command and control AI unit can get the hang of things and go automatic."

She sat in the chair and pulled the command helmet down on her head. The whole system was now within her purview, a three-dimensional model that, unlike all the other times they'd done this in modeling, now glowed with both active targets in order and potentially active gates.

She had been prepared to wait until she had at least some of both continents of Helena in view, but she found that she didn't have to. They were both there, although she'd lose one within forty minutes.

Well, she thought to herself. *All this time you've played your security games and fooled with your codes and computer systems and let others fight and die. Now the whole thing is in your lap, Krill. And the only companions you have can't help you because they don't even believe in God.*

"I'm powering up five and nine," she told them. "Here we go!"

All targets hit in turn, order of battle gamma delta epsilon, she sent to the C&C computer. *Five and nine on. As soon as they are energized, fire at will.*

Far off, more than a dozen light-years away, a signal came through the genhole to shut down the transfer and divert to a new location. Helena five and nine, in turn, *now*!

Colonel N'Gana screamed out into the darkness. "Goddamn it! *Why don't they shoot?*"

"Have patience, my old friend," responded the shade of Sergeant Mogutu. *"It won't be much longer now."*

"They are firing at the ground not far above us," the mentat told them. "I think we will miss the final show. Just a minute or two more and they will be through to here, and they will also be finished tracing the energy surges. I am sorry."

There was a sudden buzzing and then the entire ancient charged genhole plate, still on the crane above them, crackled with sudden life.

"C'mon, Krill, you beautiful bitch!" N'Gana screamed. *"SHOOT!"*

Although within seconds Krill was quite confused at having not two but three shoot orders in her sequence, something not in the plan, the important thing was that it all happened.

They shot.

The plate suspended above cracked like thin ice. The jagged rupture spread through the side of the underground complex, and up into the left side of the Titan base itself. The one shot was too much for the small plate, which was never intended to be used in any way, much less like this, and it fell and shattered on the factory floor below.

The crack continued to spread. Where it struck the Titan base, the crystals shattered like so many thin glass bulbs under pressure.

From high on the hillside, two women, mouths open in awe, forgot their unconscious charge and watched as an indescribable sliver of something shot out of the very earth and shattered a large segment of the base. It was followed by a sonic boom the likes of which not even most space pilots had felt before—a boom that deafened them, flattened some trees on the plain below, and knocked both women down.

The base itself was in serious trouble. It flickered and shimmered as popping and crackling sounds were heard inside, and the whole center structure, all twenty-plus stories of it, began to collapse in on the already ruined left section, which could no longer provide structural support.

Two more Titan craft flew out as it collapsed, but they

were unsteady, wobbling, and both crashed to the ground in front of the disintegrating base.

The towers anchoring the grid fell in as the structure imploded in dramatic slow motion. For a brief moment the grid shone brightly in the sky in spite of the glow, as if it had suddenly received more power than it ever had carried before, and then, just as suddenly, but completely, it winked out.

"They did it!" Spotty cried, still not sure she could hear after that big explosion but too excited to remain scared. *"They killed the demon city!"*

The plain was slowly dimming, going dark, as the base continued to collapse. A multitude of tiny figures were moving like excited insects all around in front of it, but from this distance it was impossible to tell who or what or how many they were.

A good dozen ships, however, had already left before the shot was taken or had managed to break out before the impending collapse; these now hovered over the area, save only the two finishing off the transmitter and the two others now turning to molten rock an area between the old spaceport and the base.

Spotty watched, and her joy was suddenly muted. "Littlefeet," she muttered, an agonized expression replacing the jubilant one.

Harker groaned in back of them, then opened his eyes and cried out, "No! I—"

He suddenly realized he was on his back and in the trees and that the two women were there and paying no attention to him whatsoever.

He tried to get up, failed the first time, then managed to sit up and feel his jaw and the back of his head. He tried to remember what had happened but it was all a confusing blur.

"Kat! Spotty!" he called.

Spotty continued to look at the spectacle, which was

now becoming harder and harder to see as most of the illumination faded, leaving only that from the surviving ships and the areas they had transformed to magma. Kat, however, turned and bent down. "You okay?" she asked him.

"What—what happened?"

"Oh, they took the shot," she told him. "The base is no longer."

He tried to get to his feet in a hurry and, with her help, he managed it. "You mean I missed the damned show? After all that?"

"You got caught in one of their beams. The only way not to have you turned into one of their spies was obvious, so I knocked you out."

"*You* knocked *me* out?"

"Well, you *were* kind of spaced-out, you know. Easy target."

He felt his jaw and then the back of his head once again. "I think you got lucky. Feels like my head hit a rock or something when I fell. Damn! Was it worth seeing? Help me to where I can at least look at the rubble!"

"C'mon, helpless! Not much to see anymore, though. And stay out of the way of those ships. They're reeling but they're not finished yet!"

But, they *were* finished, at least at Ephesus. The ships patrolled the area, back and forth, and occasionally one of them sent out a searchlight of some kind, checking on something below, but there was little more they could do. They seemed aimless, confused, unable to accept that they'd just suffered a tremendous blow and that something was definitely out there hunting *them* for a change.

Harker watched it, and something in the back of his mind understood.

"They don't have any connection with the rest of the network," he commented. "They can't consult, they can't get orders, they can't make collective decisions at the speed of light. One thing's sure—they didn't trace the shots to space. They're not going up in a hurry to take on Hector, Krill, and her gates."

She shook her head. "It didn't look like it came from there," she told him. "For some reason, sheer luck, I was staring down at it when it happened. It was like it came out of the ground. I expected a bolt from the blackness, and it came from out of the ground. Go figure."

He looked up at the night sky. "No grid. No giant continental neural net. Now it's the flowers that'll be going mad."

"Huh?"

"Nothing. I'm not even positive myself what it means, but I can tell you that they are hurt bad."

Spotty turned and looked at him. "Will they build it again? Will it come back?"

He sighed. "I don't know, Spotty. I honestly don't. I hope not. If they don't, at least we'll know that Krill reclaimed *this* system. How they do this in places where they're not orbited by a peanut moon like that I don't know, but it doesn't matter to us anymore."

Kat looked back at the now darkened scene. "Now what?" she asked.

"Now we're out of the battle and out of the war," he told her. "Now we get to go someplace where I can sleep off this pounding headache, where we can all eat and drink and relax. Maybe, when we get back to the Styx, we'll take some time and teach Spotty how to swim. She's already got an oversized flotation collar on her chest. Two of 'em. Shouldn't be too hard for somebody who walked into a demon city and walked back out leaving it a pile of rubble."

"Okay, *then* what?"

"Well, we find a really pretty place near the coast with a nice view of the ocean and no monsters under the sand and with lots of food and water and good wood, and we work up some tools. We live there and we do the best we can and see about building a boat. We defend the place and protect it. If they find us before I finish the boat, well and good, or if I finish the boat first, well, maybe we'll go find out who won the war. There's nothing but time now, and there's no hurry at all."

TWENTY-TWO

Something of Value

The shuttle craft circled the area and studied the settlement below. It was quite typical of small communities on Eden, although those on the other continent had not developed as smoothly, and those who lived there were still primarily nomadic hunter-gatherers.

Not that Eden's small villages were any wonders of technology, but the people did tend to stay put and trade a bit with their near neighbors.

Like the others they had surveyed, this one had shelters but no totally enclosed structures; rather, the "houses" were basically earthworks with roofs of woven straw held up by bamboolike poles. They had no sides, and were open to the elements.

There was a small fire pit, but it was well away from the rest of the village and only a wisp of smoke could be seen from it. These people had an inordinate fear of fire, and while they used it, particularly on Eden, they used it minimally.

At one time there appeared to have been taller earthworks as a kind of outer wall, but these had now been so dug through with access paths that they were more a boundary than a hindrance.

As with the others, the people painted their faces and bodies, sometimes with dyes but sometimes with permanent and elaborate tattoos. They wore no clothing. The women had long hair but the length did vary once it reached the shoulders; the men tended to wear shoulder-length hair and medium-full beards, but clearly hair and beards were cut and trimmed.

The newcomers had already seen how some great sea beasts could sneak in under the sand and present a nasty danger to anyone on it, yet these people seemed to have no fear of them. There weren't too many coastal communities, but the few that there were seemed to have found a way to divert the creatures or keep them well at bay. Indeed, the coastal types were mostly fishers, who used small, rough dugout canoes to spread nets woven of hairy vines native to the more junglelike interior. They used the sea creatures—"fish" was a relative term for creatures that filled the same general niche and were edible—as trade goods for dyes, fruits, vegetables, cooking oils, and the like from villages farther inland.

The cliffs seemed to be almost solid salt.

So far they had contacted a number of tribal groups on Eden—and particularly in the Great Basin region, the vast bowl-shaped area ringed by high mountains—looking for any traces of the expedition that had been sent in and had performed its duty.

The two-person shuttle craft did one more lazy circle, then the uniformed woman in the left seat said to her similarly attired male companion, "Let's put down. This is the most sophisticated-looking group we've seen on the coast yet, and the closest to the site of old Ephesus."

"You're the boss," the man responded, and hordes of young children scattered and people came from just about everywhere pointing to the sky as they descended.

"Jeez, they really make a lot of babies around here," the woman noted.

Her companion shrugged. "After dark there doesn't seem an awful lot else to do."

The shuttle gave a thump and was then on the ground.

The hatch opened, and a set of steps came out, leading to the ground on the side away from the village wall.

They expected to see everybody start running or hiding behind the battlements. Instead people, particularly the kids, rushed to them with laughing, smiling faces.

Amid childish greetings that amounted mostly to "Hello, lady! Hello, man!" there were a few older faces, mostly women but at least one man who, even through the beard, had a somewhat familiar look to the uniformed woman.

He made his way through the kids, who had to be dissuaded from climbing into the shuttle by automatically closing the hatch from the outside, and he finally got to the two of them.

"Hello," he greeted them. It was an oddly accented voice, but firm and deep and clear. "They said you would come one day, but most of us no longer believed it."

She stared hard at him. "Mister Harker? That can't be *you* behind that beard, can it?" She knew it couldn't be—he was too young for that—but he sure looked a lot like the warrant officer.

The young man laughed. "I think you want my grandfather. I'm afraid he's not here right now, but my grandmother is overseeing the salting of the morning catch. Would you like me to take you to her?"

"Your grand—" She caught herself. "Yes, please. We would like to meet her."

"We don't use long names around here," the young man explained. "It's not worth it. And, as I understand it, they never *could* decide on what family name to use, so they finally just said to heck with it and haven't used much since. Instead, when they founded this village they named it Treasure. That's all we've called ourselves since I was born. The Treasure People. I'm Curly, 'cause of my curly hair. 'Course, half the people here got curly hair, but I got the name first."

"Well, I'm Barbara, and this is Assad. We'll keep it on a first-name basis, then," the woman said.

A lot of the villagers looked very, very related; the new arrivals had to wonder just how close some of them were. Still, there was some variety, and it was clear that they had sprung from more than two people.

An older man, with deep, ancient scars carved in his skin and a body covered with faded tattoos, his hair and beard gray, but who looked of more Mediterranean ancestry than Curly did, got to his feet with the aid of a carved walking stick and came toward them. He limped from what was clearly a very old wound, but he seemed not to notice.

"Hello!" he called to them. "I am so happy to see that you arrived before I was gone to God."

"We seem to have been expected," Assad commented, smiling and relaxed. "Are you from the original expedition?"

"In a manner of speaking," he replied. "But I was born and raised here, before the Liberation. I was simply lucky enough to be there and be a part of it. I should have died, but God decided at the last minute that somebody had to tell the story of those who were there at the end. I've waited many years to tell it to somebody."

"We will certainly listen," Barbara assured him, "and people who'll follow us will interview everybody and record it for future generations. You know what I mean by that?"

"I have been told that the voice and even the image can be somehow captured and shown elsewhere, yes, but I never saw it and I got to admit it's a little wild to think on."

"Uncle, these people want to see Grandmother," Curly put in.

"Huh? Oh, all right, sure. Let's all go over. She's right over there."

They headed toward an older woman who was still in

excellent physical shape but who clearly had lived long and been through a lot. Her hair was almost white, and her skin was weathered and wrinkled, but there was a tightness to the form and she still was a handsome woman. She was giving instructions, mostly critiques, to younger women packing fish in salt loaves, when she heard them and turned.

"Hey, Kat! I thought you'd be running for the air boat!" the gray-haired man called.

She turned and smiled. "Littlefeet, one of these days you're going to grow up! I knew they'd come in their own time."

The two officers stared. Finally, Assad said, "You are not Katarina Socolov, are you?"

The old woman smiled. She didn't have all her teeth anymore, but she had more than many her age. "Yes, although it's been a *very* long time since anybody called me anything more than 'Kat,' or more often Mom or Grandma."

"But—we've been searching all over for you and the others! There are stories about you around the region, but we thought we'd never find you!"

"Well, we've been right here since six months or so after the big bang. Couldn't do much more. By then I was pregnant with this hairy bastard's father," she gestured toward Curly, "and I was scared to death as it was. Never thought I'd ever have a kid at all. We set up right here, the four of us, after Littlefeet reached us at the Styx."

"Four? There are other survivors?" Assad pressed.

"Well, not really. Depends on how you look at it, I guess. There's Gene, of course—he's Curly's grandfather, as well as a lot of others you see around here—and Father Chicanis was around for some time, but he died a year or two ago. Spent half his life trying to reestablish the true faith on Eden, only to fail miserably not only at that but even at keeping it up himself. See, those Titans, they were using *everybody* as guinea pigs. Mostly it was keeping everybody out in the wild, well, *wild*. Raw material for their experiments, we figure. They used a broadcast net and some biochemical agents to do the job in a general sense. Worked on us as much as it had on the ones born and raised here. Still around, so maybe it's inside the genes now or something. Weird stuff, too. Like extreme claustrophobia. No buildings, you see? We built a nice big straw and bamboo hut—we call 'em straw and bamboo, even though they aren't really—using designs I remembered from my anthropology studies. Real pretty thing, and sturdy. But we couldn't spend the night in it. In fact, we couldn't spend ten minutes in it before we were all climbing the walls and rushing outside. That kind of stuff. It actually gets worse as you get older, too. I don't think we could ever go down that tunnel now, and even that big factory is the stuff of nightmares. I don't know how Littlefeet and Spotty did it. More force of will than me, anyway."

"Is that why you never went back to your shuttle?" Barbara asked her.

"Oh, we did. Not right away, of course, but a couple of years later, when we managed to get real beach access and test the dugout canoes. Thing was, we couldn't get in the damned thing. That claustrophobia again, you see. And then we got to thinking, that even if we forced ourselves in, even if we took some of the organic drugs and maybe knocked ourselves out for the trip, where would we wind up? In a little room on the little moon, and then to a little enclosed shuttle, and—well, you see? We couldn't do it. Wouldn't have mattered anyway. By then—two, three years—we had a couple of kids. Couldn't leave 'em, and we couldn't really take them into that environment when we weren't sure we wouldn't go crazy. That kind of settled it."

They nodded. It was consistent with the behavior several of the survey teams had monitored, and now, coming from someone familiar with the outside universe, it made sense.

"So you stayed and you built all this," Barbara said, looking around.

"Yeah, eventually we solved the serious problems. It rains a lot in this place, so we dug out those big cisterns and lined them with a clay that proved pretty waterproof and we've never been without fresh water. About five years ago we found a kind of forest stalk that's pretty big but hollow inside, and, sealed with clay, it actually works well as a pipe. Now we got running water and a basic system for getting rid of waste. A lot of the kids are pretty clever, too. They've been coming up with stuff. We're actually building a new kind of society here. It's different, it's not evolving anything like what I grew up with, but it's a good society. You know we've never had a murder here? There's virtually no crime at all. The Hunters, poor devils, have been pretty well wiped out. When we run across a possible survivor or the result of some other sick Titan experiment, we put them out of their misery. Otherwise, there's little in the way of violence. You feel safe and secure here. There's plenty of food, the climate's good, and these kids have never really known want or fear. If somebody, even a stranger, comes, they're welcome, as you are, to anything we might have and free to help out or go along."

"Any regrets?"

"Oh, a few. I spent some time feeling really miserably sorry for myself, until I suddenly realized that I was crying over missing very superficial things when I had what was really important right here. Good kids, good friends, and a lifetime to study and see how a new society develops. One of these days, maybe, I'll record it all. If not, somebody else will come, maybe from my old school, and critique us. My old mentor led off a lecture, once, on primitive cultures and societies by cautioning against prejudgment. He said that we measure our progress by the wrong things, by whoever has the most *things* at the end of life. That people spend their lives, whether part of an interstellar civilization or hunting wild boar in the rainforests with a spear, searching for something of value. That something is different for almost every individual, and impossible to define, but you know it when you see it, you know it when you have it, and you know it if you've lost it. Most people at the end of their lives never do have it. Now look around. This is *mine*."

They let that stand, unable to think of anything to say in reply. Finally, Barbara asked, "Where is Mister Harker? You said he was the other survivor."

"Gene? Oh, yes. In one way he agrees with me on this, but for many, many years he was still missing something, and he had this maniacal drive to have it no matter how long it took and no matter how many tools he had to reinvent. Well, he's had it now for a while, and there's few days when he doesn't revel in it. I like it now and then, but it's not really a part of my satisfaction in life."

"And it is . . . ?"

She pointed out to the sea. "There he is now! You can see him just on his way in from the islands!"

They both turned, and gasped almost in unison. Still a way out, but heading in, was a sleek and sexy sailboat. A distant figure on board was just trimming the sails to let the tide carry him in the rest of the way.

"He built *that*? With what you have here?" Assad was almost speechless.

"Indeed he did. He and a lot of the others here, anyway. He did it without computers, without blueprints, although he did use designs he baked in clay, and had to fashion and perfect out of stone and salvaged bits of metal and whatever all the tools required. He also had to wait until enough kids were old enough to help him build it, too!

Now he's out there half the time with two or three grand-kids. He's too old to do it, but he swears he's going to sail it all the way to the other continent someday. I told him I knocked him cold once for turning into an idiot and I can damn well do it again!"

Barbara looked at the beach below. "I thought there were some kind of sea monsters that burrow under the sands," she noted. "Why don't they pose a danger to your men and boats?"

Kat laughed. "Oh, when I first came ashore I *panicked* at those things! I got hysterical with fear! But when you find out how to detect them before they detect you, and you have good enough spears and maybe mallets to drive them in, you wind up getting them before they get you. You know—they taste pretty damned good, if you're willing to spend enough time with enough people digging 'em out. We don't see many of 'em anymore. We think maybe either they know better than to come up here or maybe we've eaten the whole damned local population."

"Then—it's safe to go down there and meet him?"

"Oh, sure. Take a couple of the boys with you just in case, but you won't have problems."

It was a long walk along the cliffs until they came to a place where the land dipped. Into that spot somebody, maybe the four from the original expedition, had carved well-worn steps that switched back all the way down to the beach.

"We have to carve a new set every year or two. They wear away, even if you coat 'em with clay," Curly told them. "It's no big deal. It's soft, mostly salt, and if it gets too dangerous it's not that far until there's another dip almost down to beach level."

They needn't have worried about going down to a potentially dangerous beach alone. It seemed like half the kids followed them, mostly gawking, and a lot of the older ones as well.

More than once they were asked why they had sails on their bodies, and they realized that these people had never even seen folks wearing clothes. The best they could manage was, "Well, not all the places are as nice as this, and in many you need protection or you will get hurt."

They waited a bit for Gene Harker to come in. He came in fairly fast, with all sails struck, and rode the sailboat right up onto the beach. Children rushed to take thick ropes and drag it out of the water. Then the young kids who were the passengers jumped out first, and, finally, the old man.

Gene Harker also looked very good for his age, but he was white-bearded, and what hair still on his head was snow white as well. Still, he had those same unusual blue eyes that had always made him stand out to the ladies.

He did one last check and then jumped down to the sand with an *"Oomph!"* He straightened up, and only then saw the two uniformed people waiting for him. He stopped a moment, squinted, then walked forward and stared right at Barbara.

"Holy shit!" he exclaimed. "Is that *you*, Fenitucci?"

And, to the very last one, all the others on the beach suddenly shut up, turned, and said, as one, "*That's* Bambi the Destroyer?"

She turned purple at that, but could only manage, "Oh, my God!"

"But she's so—*young*," Kat noted when informed of who one of their visitors was.

"I think it's been a lot longer for us here on Helena than it was for them up there," Gene responded. He looked at the Marine. "Jeez, Fenitucci! Not enough time to age one whit but enough time to somehow pick up a direct commission? You're a lieutenant now?"

She nodded. "For service above and beyond. You'd be an admiral if you'd have made it back."

"So what the hell did you do other than be a pain in my butt for a time?"

She grinned. "You aren't the only one who can ride the keel," she noted. "Commander Park got the idea. You were on one side of the *Odysseus*, and they knew it, and I was on the other side and they didn't because they only picked up your signal and figured that every time they spotted me I was a ghost echo of your suit."

"Huh? You mean you were along all the time?"

"Sure. Only while *you* went inside and joined the club, *I* stayed outside, nice and sedated, until we rendezvoused with the Dutchman. Then I detached and went over to his ship. He never suspected a thing. The moment your little party took off, the *Hucamarea* came through the gate. He tried to activate weapons and blow the joint, but I'd had a full week to play with and interface with his systems. It was a souped-up ship, but it was still a damned tug, Orion class, a real antique. I had no problems accessing and reprogramming some key areas. The only thing I didn't figure on was how nutty he really was. I barely got off that tub before he blew it and himself and whatever crew he had to kingdom come."

Harker sighed. "So you still don't know who he was?"

"Oh, we know. I had that from his data banks early on. His name—his *real* name—was Akim Tamsheh. He was about as Dutch as Colonel N'Gana. But he had a lot in common with the old Dutchman of legend, and he apparently knew the legend from the old opera, or so the old lady told us later. In the early days of the Titan invasion, it seemed he was a tug captain on some backwater planet and then the white ships started showing up. He panicked, cut and ran, and disappeared. That was why we couldn't trace him. All his records were lost as well in that early takeover. Seems he left his wife and two kids on that world when he chickened out. You can guess the rest."

Harker sighed. "I think I see. What a shame. Still,

without his pirate crew of gutsy looters like Jastrow, we wouldn't have been able to free this world. I guess that brings up the big question. We've been here a *long* time. I don't know how long—we don't have seasons to speak of, and there's no particular reason or means of keeping time here except your basic rock sundial like that one we made over there. So I don't know how long it's been. A long time."

"Three years, four months for me, a tad over twenty-seven years for the two of you," she told him. "We've had a lot of cleanup to do, and a lot of scouting. We're still in the risky business of going behind Titan lines and laying more targeting genholes. It'll probably take until I'm older than you are before it's finished. It's not without cost, either. Word of what we're doing hasn't outpaced us yet, but it does appear that they're catching on. It's not like we can put the Priam bolts on ships like laser cannon. Turns out they aren't bolts of energy at all, they're cracks in the universe! Even so, building more control rooms and intercepting more exchanges from that thing, whatever and wherever it is out there, is giving us an edge. We've failed on a few other worlds, and we've—well, some worlds weren't as well targeted. It's going to be long and nasty, and the weapon, in the end, won't be decisive. What it *did* do was give us back Helena and a dozen other worlds so far, each one of which they developed differently, it seems, except for the flowers that we still haven't figured out yet. You kill that energy net they set up, the flowers die. Not much left to study."

"I know. So they may yet come back?"

"They could. We're gonna try like hell not to let 'em. Besides, now that we have something that does work, we have leads on other things that maybe aren't so draconian. The thing is, I'm not sure we're ever going to be able to contact them, speak to them, figure out what the hell they really think they're doing. Even if we're not winning, we've stopped losing. That's thanks to you, Harker. You and Kat, here, and the others."

Kat cleared her throat nervously. "Lieutenant—the main thing is, we don't want us, or our children and grandchildren, to be some kind of specimens here. Social research and bringing the surviving primitives back into the bosom of civilization. This is *our* world now. We have a right to develop it our way. Otherwise we'll go right back to doing to ourselves and others just what the Titans were doing to us. *Some* things we could use. Some versions of modern medicine. Some ways to restore some of the cultural heritage, at least in stories, songs, and legends. That kind of thing. But colonial administrators, social scientists, geneticists, and, God save us, missionaries—no."

Fenitucci sighed. "We'll do what we can. At least this world was a private holding. The Karas, Melcouri, and Sotoropolis families still have power and position, and can exercise a claim. If they can keep it out, they will."

"You must also carry back to the people of Colonel N'Gana, Sergeant Mogutu, and even poor Hamille the story of their bravery and dedication," Kat told her. "Many soldiers die obscure and meaningless deaths, I know, but they did not. They died for something, and they succeeded in what they set out to do. They gave their lives so we could, well, not lose. They deserve to be recognized for that."

"We'll take the oral histories down," Fenitucci promised them. "And we'll carry your own wishes to the First Families of Helena. That's all I can promise." She looked over at Curly, lounging nearby, and at several of the other young men with rippling muscles and substantial proportions in other areas. "Hell, I might even drop back for a bit when I get some time off," she told them. "Be kind of interesting to go native for a few weeks here. There are some real possibilities. Besides, it seems, thanks to you, that my reputation's already preceded me anyway."

Harker looked sheepish. "Hey, there are only so many stories I could tell . . ."

As the shadows grew long and the sun began to touch the distant mountains, the two marines headed back to their shuttle, got in, and prepared to depart. They had reports to file, contacts to make, and, as military personnel, perhaps battles left to fight.

As they lifted off, they circled the small coastal village one last time.

"Treasure," Barbara Fenitucci muttered.

"Ma'am?"

"Nothing. I was just looking at folks one step from the cavemen who live in the open and age at twice the going rate and even though it's not *my* idea of how to do it, I can't shake the idea that I've just spoken with some of the richest human beings left around. What do you think, Assad?"

The sergeant shrugged. "I think I want a gourmet meal, the finest wines, in climate-controlled splendor. And for now I'd settle for a soak in a spa bath."

Fenitucci laughed. "God!" she wondered. "I wonder what my legend's gonna be like with those people in another fifty years."

"You think they'll let them alone?"

"For a while," she replied. "But, eventually, it'll be irresistible to the powers that be to meddle. We never learn, we humans. That's why God sends plagues, pestilence, and occasional Titan invaders to kick our asses and make us think for a while. But we forget. We always forget . . . Maybe it's the way things work in the universe?"

"Huh? What do you mean, Lieutenant?"

"Maybe the Titans aren't so hard to figure out after all. Maybe individuals live to find something of value, but maybe, just maybe, the way the universe works is that the race that dies out last, and with the most worlds, wins."